The Paris Writers Circle

NORMA HOPCRAFT

The Paris Writers Circle

Published by Jaguar Publishing.

Pete J. sat one desk behind me in sixth grade and called me Norma Jaguar, which felt like a huge compliment that obviously I've never forgotten. Thanks, Pete!

ISBN #978-0-9994089-1-9

For further information, please contact the author by leaving a comment at her blog: https:// njaegerhopcraft. blogspot.com.

Also by this Author:

Why Spy?, a Tricia Maguire romantic novel of suspense

Numbers Count, a Tricia Maguire romantic novel of Suspense

Travel Stories from All Over

Dedication

This story is dedicated to my mother, Louise Clotilda Miller Jaeger, who loved yellow roses, taught me to read, wouldn't let me teach my younger sister to read, regularly read aloud to us as kids, made sure we always got to the library, and was an engaging storyteller and talented poet.

Acknowledgements

I thank poet Rainer Marie Rilke and Project Gutenberg (Gutenberg.org).

Many people critiqued this story and helped to improve it.

I thank Women Who Write in New Jersey. I attended every two weeks for a decade, probably more. This was an incubator of improvement.

After living in New Jersey for years, I got exiled to Paris! I want to thank my writers group there (you can join them via Meetup at Paris Scriptorium). Hazel Manuel, Ruth Druart and Lucas M. Peters were my beta readers of the entire novel. Other helpful critiquers in that group include Margaret Rogers, Kseniya "Kass" Novozhilova, Jim Rushing, Cris Hammond, Stephen Wendell, and Graham Elliott. All great writers.

My writers group in Barcelona read the chapters towards the end of the novel: That's a Meetup: Writers in Barcelona.

My writers group in NYC critiqued a few chapters. That's a Meetup, too: New York City Writers Critique Group.

The final two chapters were critiqued by May Lum and Ann Leander in Paris, and Patricia Cook and Tong Blackburn in New York City.

Many Indian expats in Paris helped me with my character Anjali: First was T.S. Anil, whom I met at Shakespeare & Co., across the Seine from Notre Dame. He gave very clear and concise answers to questions and suggested some refinements and plot twists that I immediately adopted!

Thanks to Priya Thapa and Marute Chavan, who met with me in Place Monge and helped me greatly.

Thanks to Viviane Tourtet in Paris who put me in touch with Gitanjali Brandon. Thank you for your insights, Gitanjali!

And thanks to Amruta Prabhu, who answered follow-up questions brilliantly two years after we first met!

Thank you to Martine Bourreau, whose house I lived in for a year in Malakoff, just south of the 14th *arrondissment*. She provided books on Indian culture and files full of newspaper clippings she'd made when she lived and worked in India. Thanks also to her darling nieces, Christelle Lamblin and Daphné Chaigne. They taught me so much about French culture.

Thanks to La Bibliothèque Historique de la Ville de Paris, where much of this was written. Its beautiful space figures prominently in the story.

Thanks to La Bibliothèque Fontenoy, where a little of this story was written.

Thanks to the Biblioteca Nacionale de Catalunya in Barcelona, built as a hospital in the 14th century. I did a ton of revision there.

Thanks to the New York Public Library's historic Jefferson Market Courthouse branch. The top floor has an excellent work table 25 feet long where I got a lot of editing done.

Thanks to https://www.vecteezy.com for the fleur-de-lis that marks the chapter endings, and to my friend, the most-artistic Donna Oehmig (donnaoehmig.com) for her consultation on the cover art. Thanks to Mark McCabe (markmcabe303.com) who helped me with the fleur-de-lis chapter endings.

Thanks to all who boosted the Kickstarter campaign I ran to pay for publishing expenses, and especially thanks to these folks, who supported me in a maximum way in publishing The Paris Writers Circle, Travel Stories from All Over, and Why Spy?: Marian Maguire, Peg Bennett, Stephanie Falktoft, Loretta Wu, Jane Rapaport, Carol Labozzetta, Lois Zorawick, Christelle Lamblin, Thierry et Marie-Odile Lamlin, Sharon Hopcraft Alongi, Jim Ahlstrom, Peling Lee, my sister Christine Jaeger, Inara Kalnins, and my darling son-in-law Tony Alongi, who was the very first to pledge to my Kickstarter campaign! Thank you all for believing in me!

I also happily name my brother Charles H. Jaeger III, Ph.D. and Adele Vessey as loyal cheerleaders! So is Lois Zorawick. I'm much indebted to her for encouragement and wise counsel.

Thank you to Higher Power, who restores me.

Chapter 1

"I'll give him the message, sir." Anjali dropped the receiver into its slot with a clatter of black plastic.

That had been Monsieur Chaigne, rich as Croesus, her boss John had said. She must let him know about this call. But first she'd check the post. What was this official-looking envelope? Internal Revenue Service? What was that? Part of the United States Department of Treasury. Okay, *trés importante*—she knew that much rudimentary French. Her eyes ran over the document. She'd better tell her boss fast.

As she stood, her stomach rumbled. It would be lunchtime soon. After a month in Paris, she had begun to crave Indian food. She had been so disappointed in the Indian restaurants she'd visited so far in her new city. Aasha had told her that they dialed back on the spices for French tastes, but that there was a great place at Metro La Chapelle, on the north side of the Tenth *arrondissement*, in the heart of Little India. They'd go there this weekend, and she couldn't wait for authentic flavors from home. Home…her mother's homemade curry…

She jumped guiltily from her *rêverie* when the intercom blared.

"Anjali, come in with my calendar, please."

Anjali fluffed up her fringe of bangs and grabbed the calendar, covered in high-grade leather and trimmed with brass. She left her desk, in a room with no window, with gray carpeting on the floor. The first time she'd seen it, it had seemed quite luxurious. Until she'd seen her boss's office.

She entered John Germaine's corner office in the Montparnasse Tower, with its view north and west of the city spread below. The Tour Eiffel, the Arc de Triomphe, the Seine, and Basilique de Sacré Cœur, all gleamed in the summer sun. She felt her feet sink into the deep pile of the beige carpet, and then she tripped over the edge of the red and blue Persian rug lain over it. As she approached his vast mahogany desk, she blinked at the light pouring in the windows. The view thrilled her—the first part of her dream had come true, she was in Paris.

In one hand, she held the calendar. With her free hand, she tugged the edge of her cotton blouse. New job, new country, new culture, new life—it was nervewracking. She'd lucked into a good position, but this man was impossible. Nice, but a bit loony.

She watched as John Germaine sat back, the leather of his huge chair creaking. He pulled at the white French cuffs of his French blue shirt. He wasn't going to like her news.

"Sir, the Internal Revenue—"

"What's on the calendar for tomorrow night?" John asked blithely.

Things had to be done in his order of events, she was learning.

Anjali checked the page for the second week of July. He refused to do this by computer. Worse, he refused to work with shared documents online. Version control between his five offices was Anjali's constant nightmare.

"You're taking your daughter to dinner, sir."

"Oh, too bad." John thought a minute. "Call Emily and tell her I can't make it. Emily won't mind. She can go out with her mother. Then book me at the Jules Verne. It's up in the Eiffel Tower, you knew that, right? Potential client."

He added, "Gotta keep my kid in private school, you know." Then he winked.

"Okay, Mr. Germaine," Anjali said reluctantly. She thought he should go out with his teen daughter. Anjali's father had done that for her.

"I know you're new, but please call me John."

"Okay, thank you."

"How's life treating you? Big change from Mumbai, isn't it?"

"I'm settling in, sir." She knew he didn't want details about her condescending aristocrat landlady, and how dire the Indian food situation was in Paris. Dire!

"Very good. By the way, how was your new writing group last night?"

Anjali wondered why he was asking, but she smiled anyway. "Fun. All kinds of writers. We may never be published, but—"

"—Oh, I can do that. My Ph.D. dissertation in economics at Yale was published, you know. Maybe next time I'll go with you."

She sincerely hoped he would not. She had a character in one of her screenplays based on John. What if he spotted it? Nah, he was too self-absorbed. But what if he wasn't?

"I've been tossing around a few ideas—want to run them by people," John continued with his total self-confidence. "Novels—my buddy told me he's writing one. Can't let him one-up me." John considered himself a Renaissance man, good at everything. Besides, how hard could it be? "Well, anything else?"

"Here's a message from Mr. Chaigne." She handed him the slip. "And the IRS sent a letter." Anjali said. "I tried to tell you—"

"What do they want?"

Anjali watched warily as John leaned even further back. It seemed there was something about being successful that made men want to lean way back in chairs. If he toppled over and became a paraplegic, she'd have to find a new job—not easy in Paris. She might have to go back to Mumbai without the second part of her dream fulfilled. To be so close and yet not see it happen would kill her.

John poised his chair on the edge of destruction and ran his thumbs up and down under the discrete paisley suspenders that strapped his broad shoulders.

"Sir, they want to talk about the company's U.S. books."

"No time. Just tell them we haven't had a chance to do our tax return yet. They'll understand."

"But—"

"—They'll understand." John waved his hand, unconcerned.

"Okay, sir, I'll tell them what you said."

Anjali turned from his desk, then rolled her eyes.

Chapter 2

On the north side of Paris, in a former warehouse converted into a soundstage, in the depths of a conference room, Carol, a Brit, sat in a brainstorming meeting. Her brain was not storming. She'd been dry of ideas lately, except for the thought that she would be sacked if she didn't speak up soon. Everyone else on the Trapèze creative staff was confidently shooting off characters, settings, and plots for films. But she had nothing.

"A Parisienne—scarf tied just so, stiletto heels, mini-skirt, tights—who wants, who'd die for, her next lover to appear tonight."

That was Amandine, Parisienne, who sat relaxed yet commanding, very *décolletée*, wearing a mini-skirt with thighs bursting forth in sheer black hose, and stilletos on her feet.

Carol looked at all the flesh that Amandine had on display, and she heard her mother quoting Coco Chanel: "Modesty—what elegance!"

Carol herself was wearing a cream silk Armani suit with a deeper cream silk blouse. Skirt fashionably short, but not cut up to her crotch. To be able to afford clothes like these ever again, she just had to come up with ideas. Ones that worked.

"A Louis Jordan type."

That was Frédéric, with bulging blue eyes and adam's apple. He was always eyeing the women.

"He's debonair," Frédéric said, "wants to keep his *péniche* afloat on the Seine. He's desperate for money—the boat is a black hole. He cheats at cards, on his income tax, he beguiles rich women and tries to dupe them for money. It all backfires. In the end, in a storm, he watches the *péniche* sink into the Seine."

Frédéric looked like a Bretagne boater himself in a horizontal blue-and-white-striped, long-sleeved tee shirt.

Carol coached herself, desperate to contribute. Come on, old girl, you just have to come up with something.

She felt her phone vibrate in the pocket of her silk jacket. She checked it as discretely as she could. It was her six-year-old texting her. "Mummy, when will you be home?"

Oh, my baby! Now she really couldn't think.

"Carol, what do you think?"

That was Gregoire, the production company's executive director. His character could be summed up in two words: tight suits.

Carol's underarms itched against the silk. She crossed and recrossed her legs and tugged her skirt down, aware of Frédéric's gaze. She knew she shouldn't, and that if she did she would feel like

7

an *escargot*, a garden-variety snail, but she couldn't help herself—she looked at Amandine. As Carol could expect of an attractive Parisienne, Amandine was staring at her triumphantly, like a diner seated before an array of *escargots* roasted in their own shells with garlic and *beurre doux*.

Damn! She shouldn't have looked. Why was she so bonkers as to do that to herself?

Gregoire crossed his arms. The room was silent. And Carol had a thought! It felt weak, it would be booed, but it was all she could think of.

"How about robbing the classics? Chaucer's Alewife, and the sleek, elegant Wife of Bath, and the Knight, all updated?" Then she remembered, there was no Alewife in Canterbury Tales. Hopefully no one had read it. "They're on a pilgrimage of some sort—in the Sahara desert!—to a remote shrine nearly covered in windblown sand?" Her imagination failed her at that point. She despised herself for ending her sentence in a question, like an American.

Again, the room was silent. People were looking at her. Carol felt so vulnerable that she couldn't help it, she looked at Amandine. Carol understood the message she saw in those eyes. *Escargot!*

Within a heartbeat of sending Carol her Parisienne deathray, Amandine was sending Gregoire an admiring look full of Bourgogne wine and roses.

"How about an older woman, Catherine Deneuve in her 40s," Amandine said, and the brainstorming swept on.

They didn't like my idea, Carol said to herself. I'm so sick of my ideas not being on target, out of step, ridiculous. They're going to sack me if I don't produce. What am I going to do?

When Gregoire decided he liked the idea of Louis Jordan on a *péniche*, with a Catherine Deneuve type for a love interest, the meeting ended, to be resumed in a week.

Carol felt as though she were staggering as she fled to her office—could anybody, especially Amandine, tell? She just had to learn not to look at that Parisienne, just like all the rest—with entirely too much self-esteem. Otherwise known as arrogance. She had to learn not to look at half the women in Paris, who cultivated a superior attitude and sent it like a deathray into other women's hearts. She packed up her handbag, texted her daughter that she was leaving, and left.

On the Metro, she thought, France is only the size of Texas, yet its people have brought great beauty into the world, in art, literature, music, film, architecture. The French who weren't born in Paris were quite lovely. It was the Parisians....

She dragged herself back to her apartment in Le Marais, the trendiest neighborhood, in the Fourth *arrondissement*. Every footstep ached with self-condemnation. You're not present for your daughter, you're not good enough at your job, your ideas have dried up, and they'll fire you soon. But I'm working so hard to provide for Louise, she countered weakly. Her inner critic said, "Humph!"

She punched in the door code and opened the massive, old wooden door to the courtyard. The palms standing in the corners in their huge stone pots looked relaxed, the red geraniums in first floor window boxes looked perky. Not at all how she felt. The scene was pretty, very French. This will all disappear if you can't come up with ideas, Carol's inner critic reminded her with satisfaction.

When she walked into the apartment, she heard Jeffrey's voice speaking quietly. They'd lived together for two years. Jeffrey was a Brit expat, too, who repaired people's computers in the offices of Orange, the telecom. And he minded Louise for hours at a time. She trusted him with Louise implicitly. She wished she could be with her little girl more herself.

Carol eased down the hall. Jeffrey and the child were sitting on the bed, leaning against the headboard, pillows and stuffed animals bolstering them, reading a picture book.

"That word is 'c-a-t,'" Louise said to Jeffrey. They looked so ideal and cozy together.

"Very good, you got it, you clever girl!" Jeffrey ruffled her hair, and they both looked up and saw Carol. Jeffrey's face darkened.

Louise scrambled off the bed, her strawberry blonde curls bouncing.

"Mummy, Jeffrey and I are reading books! A fairy tells a princess, who has a cat, and, and—you're home!"

Carol swept her into her arms and kissed her warm, sticky neck. Then she lifted her face to accept a peck on the lips from Jeffrey.

"Where've you been? She's been anxious for you," Jeffrey said.

"It's seven, not that late."

"Well, are you making dinner or am I?"

"Let's order in."

"No surprise, what you always say."

His disparagement, a long-term feature of their relationship, upset her.

"Why can't you be pleasant to me? You were home since five, you cook something."

"Your daughter kept me busy."

"Then order something in."

"Mummy, come see my book."

"Jeffrey, would you order?"

"Yeah, the usual, sure," he grumbled and pulled out his cell phone.

Later, after Louise was asleep, Carol went online and Googled "writing group in English Paris" in hopes that being with a creative group, far away from her colleagues, would get her brain storming again. She wrote down the address and the time, closed her computer, stood with a sigh, stretched her back in her Armani suit, and went to bed.

Chapter 3

The day was winding down. John Germaine made calls to all his investment buddies until seven, when most of them went home and prepared to go out to dinner. The exchange traded funds, or ETFs, that he'd invested in and encouraged his buddies to invest in had been going up steadily for months. He was replete with his success.

John descended from the 52nd floor of Montparnasse Tower to the street. He had dined at Fouquet's, Maxime's, and La Tour D'Argent many times, but tonight he decided to assume Cassandra was busy so he could feel free to buy his favorite dinner—ham and cheese rolled up in a *crêpe*, Paris street food. He ate it standing, watching people mill around the foot of the tower, figuring out what to do next. He had another *crêpe* with Nutella inside it for dessert, relishing the gooey chocolate and hazelnut spread.

He sighed. It was time to check in with Cassandra.

"I'm at Dior." Cassandra sounded bored, didn't even say hello when she answered his call.

"Is Emily with you?" John could imagine her reluctance to be in her mother's shopaholic tow.

"We won't be back until late."

"Okay, see you later, hon." He clicked off. His wife spent too much, it was just a bit frightening. Well, he'd kept up with her bills so far. As soon as he landed a new client, he'd be in good shape. Until her next shopping foray.

To forget his troubles, tonight he'd take another improvisational acting class. Acting out his screwball side would be fun. And he'd have a chance to prove once again that he did well at everything he put his hand to. Except reining in Cassandra's spending.

His long legs ate up the distance through the interconnecting tunnels of the Montparnasse Bienvenüe Metro station as he put his plan into motion. He passed a guitarist and singer emoting on Janis Joplin's "Me and Bobby McGee." John felt proud when he heard American rock played in the Paris Metro. American rock stars wailed, singing from deep in their guts. There was something so raw, so authentic about it. And the French—the whole world—knew it.

He passed through the Gare Montparnasse tunnels humming "Bobby McGee." Not many men of his stature did such things, he thought, humming in tunnels, but so what? He'd earned the right to be eccentric.

He noticed that a timeline of World War I had been painted on the walls of one of the tunnels. The French were commemorating the one hundredth anniversary of the start of that war this summer. And the seventieth anniversary of the liberation of Paris in August 1944 during World War II.

John thought, you have to take into account the cost of these wars when you try to understand the French psyche. People had to survive brutal shortages, ugly occupations, and the decimation of their families.

When he thought of how Germany had been the aggressor in three major wars against France since 1870, he had to wonder: how has the modern-day European Union survived as long as it has? France and Germany were the leaders of the EU, Germany even more so, and they were countries that had repeatedly and until rather recently been deadly enemies. It was hard to understand the change of allegiances.

John shook off gloomy thoughts of war. He would take line 13 to line 1 to line 7. Fantastic system, the Paris Metro. The school was in the Tenth *arrondissement*, near Metro stop Poissonière. Who but the French would name a Metro stop "Fishmonger's Wife"? Who but the French had a language that made "fishmonger's wife" sound elegant?

Walking to the artists' space on Rue de Paradis, he passed a man lying unconscious on the pavement along the base of a building. Dogs must have peed there many times over the centuries, John thought. That guy was going to wake up stiff and sore and smelly, if he hadn't passed out that way. With all my assets, I'll never get like that, he thought.

At 40 Rue de Paradis, he dialed in the five letters of the door code he'd been given and pushed the scarred, ancient wooden street door open. He walked down a long archway—high and wide enough that a horse-drawn carriage could drive over its cobbles—and into the central courtyard.

The building rose up on four sides around him—the Paris-requesite white stone building, six stories, which was why his black glass, fifty-nine-story office tower was such an eyesore. Here in the courtyard, the noise of city traffic was muffled. People's windows were open, and he could smell onions sautéing in butter. The sound of subdued conversations in French—the French always kept their voices down, unlike raucous Americans—reached John as he mounted the steps on the far side of the courtyard.

Through the window to the right, he could see a drama class in progress. A woman in a sleeveless, formfitting red dress and red heels held a script in one hand and emoted with the other, making large gestures. She faced a nervous young man with an immaculately trimmed dark beard and glasses.

"*Bon chance*," John muttered. He was here to make up his own lines, not work that hard memorizing someone else's.

John continued up the steps, thinking to himself: open the door of the artistic space, nod hello to the glum young Parisian sitting at the reception desk—why were so many of them glum? Run lightly down the stairs, pass the dilapidated couch, and *voilà*, as the French would say. Here was his classroom.

Georges was teaching tonight. Good! He was the silliest of the bunch and awoke the most playfulness in John.

John knew it was improbable that a man with his connections, who operated at the level of society he was privy to, would be not just interested in watching improv, but in acting in it.

But it was true. The risk-taker in him, that dealt with millions of dollars in volatile investments, also liked to take risks in front of his improv class.

Georges was directing a warm-up. The six class members listened.

"I want you to work your faces as well as your torsos, arms, and legs to sculpt yourself into a new character," Georges said. "Line up against this wall and walk yourself into a new character by the time you reach the opposite wall. Got it? Go!"

With only a moment's reflection and hesitation, John threw himself into the fun. He buckled his knees and twisted his torso to the right as far as he could. Keeping his torso there, he reached to the left with both arms, and began to walk to the opposite wall.

"Work your faces!" Georges called.

John smiled, then twisted it into too wide a smile, with teeth clenched. He didn't mind being silly, ridiculous, among these folks. He felt about four years old, but in a good way.

"Okay, that's good, now change!" Georges called.

John noticed Babette, such a big smile, teeth encased in shiny braces and yet such a better smile than Cassandra's frosty look. Babette's black hair hung down to her shoulders in tiny braids. She was laughing, walking on tiptoe, swinging her arms wide from side to side with each footstep. The whole class was acting nuts.

Then Georges joined in. John laughed out loud as Georges scooted across the floor like a Hunchback of Notre Dame rugby player protecting the ball.

"Okay, good work," Georges said. John sidled next to Babette. She smiled up at him. It felt like a privilege to be a human being around that smile.

"Now we get into some improv," Georges called into the hubbub. The actors stood still, their faces flushed with exertion and fun, as he explained the exercise. John wanted very much to excel at this, to impress people with his improv as much as he did with his investment savvy.

13

"John, you and I start," Georges said. "You go on stage with a walk, as a character of some sort, just as we did earlier, and you mime an activity—chop vegetables, talk on the phone, whatever. Then, when you've established your character and your activity, I'll come on with a walk, in character, and join you in the activity, and we'll see what happens. Ready? And go!"

The rest of the class seated themselves along the wall. John couldn't wait to try it, but at the same time, he was nervous.

John pondered his character for a second, then walked in front of the group pretty much as the man he was—he had to admit it—confidence was a good thing. He pretended to open a piano and to sit on its bench. He began playing Tchaikovsky's Concerto in B Minor, as he had when he was a piano student in high school. In his mind, he heard it playing as the popularized version, "Tonight We Love."

He banged out the chords, letting his hands go dramatically high as a concert pianist might. He crossed hands—right hand playing bass notes—even though he knew perfectly well that Tchaikovsky's score didn't call for that. He was getting anxious for Georges to come on, with Babette's and five other pairs of eyes watching him intently.

Georges approached, dragging one leg. John laughed out loud at Georges' character and wished that he would stop laughing on stage, it seemed so unprofessional.

"Sounds wonderful, Your Royal Highness," Georges said, like a demented serf. John laughed again, it was so unexpected.

"It's Tchaikovsky, he's a great composer," John said, still banging out chords.

"I'm jealous, Your Highness. You know, I'm so jealous, I want to kill him."

"Oh, don't do that. It wouldn't be nice."

"I have a knife."

"Don't do anything rash," John said. Where was this going? He was scared and excited.

"Yes. I kill him, I feel better."

"That's sick. I'm taking you to the doctor," and John led Georges to Babette. "The doctor will fix you." Where were these lines coming from? He didn't know and didn't care. Everything was happening fast.

Babette mimed giving Georges a shot.

"That's better. Let's go have something to eat, your Highness," Georges said.

John led him back to the piano, which was now a table.

"But I still want to kill Tchaikovsky!"

"Look," John said, feeling and sounding demented himself, "here's a loaf of bread on the table. Its name is Tchaikovsky. Stab it!"

Georges mimed stabbing the poor *baguette*.

"Stab it more!"

Georges's serf did as instructed.

"Good, good!" John said. "You've killed Tchaikovsky!" He allowed a pause in the action. Then, in a normal voice, he said, "Now give me the knife."

Georges paused, considered, then called, "End of scene! Great!"

At the end of class, John felt once again that, yes, he was a Renaissance man, capable of doing well at whatever he put his hand to. And a little loony, which he deemed good. Before leaving, he turned up at Babette's elbow again and relished that smile one more time.

Chapter 4

On Saturday, Anjali climbed with Aasha up a steep Montmartre hill. Basilique de Sacré Cœur loomed at the top. Anjali was feeling a bit ragged. All the men that they had stood near on the Metro, all the guys they passed in the street, all were staring at Aasha, who was shaking out her long black hair and striding as though she knew she looked great. Her hard heels rapped assurance on the cobbled street. The sound rang between the stone buildings, so close to each other in the narrow *rue*.

With each rap, Anjali felt worse. She had a big nose with a strange bump on it when viewing her in profile. Her face looked better with short hair around it, so Anjali had had it chopped off in feathered layers. She felt envious of Aasha's looks—and the confidence she enjoyed because of them. Anjali fought to let go of it. If she loved Aasha, she would be happy for her. She decided to at least be willing to be happy for her.

Just then a tall young Frenchman, with a balding head and exquisitely trimmed dark beard and mustache, approached them as he descended the hill.

"You look like an angel," he said to Aasha in passing, admiring her.

Anjali would never have anybody say that about her. She thought, I'm willing to try to be willing to be happy for Aasha. Her shoulders drooped. As usual, she was fading next to this luminous flower of the East, as a colonizing, patronizing Brit in the days of the Raj might have said.

The two young women ascended the last incline.

"Almost there," Aasha gasped.

And finally they reached the place at the top of the hill, with the steps to the *basilique* leading even further upward. They paused to look over the city.

"What's that ugly black skyscraper in the middle of the city's low, white buildings?" Aasha asked.

"That's the Montparnasse Tower, silly, where I work!" Anjali poked her in the ribs.

"It's an eyesore," Aasha said.

Anjali was silent, feeling like one herself. A group of young men near them were looking right past Anjali at Aasha.

"I love the view from this spot. You can see that Paris is a small city," Aasha said. "You can cross it by Metro in less than an hour, even though it makes eighteen stops within city limits. Nothing like Mumbai."

"It's a pearl of a city," Anjali said.

Aasha's and Anjali's parents were friends. Aasha had forged the way to Paris as a young single Indian woman, and Anjali was grateful because she didn't think her parents would have agreed if Aasha's hadn't. Aasha had preceded Anjali to Paris by one week. It was enough to put Aasha forever in the role of expert.

They lingered over the view, and then agreed without speaking that it was time to tour the *basilique*. They climbed the steps and went in the door on the left.

Signs posted around called for silence and no photography. They took a circuit around the edge of the *basilique*, stopping to look at each chapel. Then they took seats in the front half of the church.

The mosaic of Jesus above the altar captured Anjali's eyes. He was portrayed by the artist as the most important figure, with much smaller figures facing him. The folds of his robe, the fingers of his hands, the expression on his face, were portrayed by tiny pieces of colored tile. Anjali thought, the artist wrought a miracle, using hard bits to give Jesus a kingly yet compassionate face.

She pondered the mosaic and felt her spirits lift as she identified with the huge effort that had gone into making it. The artist had painstakingly chosen one piece after another until millions of pieces made a picture, telling a story that moved human hearts. As a writer, she did the same thing, choosing word after word, nearly one hundred thousand words for a novel, considerably less for a screenplay, but with the same goal—touching hearts.

The girls stood and walked to the exit. Outside, in the sun, with the city spread at their feet, they stood and gazed.

"I love this city," Anjali said.

"You'll never be the same for coming here," Aasha said. "You should be proud of yourself."

"We both should be."

"I can only stay three months," Aasha said. "Not that I want to stay longer. Lucky for you, you were born in Pondicherry. You could stay forever if you wanted to." Pondicherry was a former French colony, and its citizens automatically had French passports.

"Being born of parents from traditional, restrictive old Pondicherry ought to have some upside to it," Anjali said.

"Thank God they moved to Mumbai, don't you think? So much more progressive."

Not that Aasha was all that progressive, Anjali thought.

"But growing up in Mumbai, we were caught between two worlds," Anjali said. "Our parents let us 'hang out' with friends, but only until the sacred curfew. Remember lying that we had to go meet our study group, so we could leave and go home without looking uncool?"

"Yeah."

Aasha doesn't seem to feel the constraints the way I do, Anjali thought.

Just then a couple went by chatting in French, the girl wearing a short flippy skirt and deeply scooped blouse. There must have been a push-up bra under the blouse.

"Look at how Parisian women dress: everything so short, so much cleavage. It's so different from India," Anjali said.

"Don't you think they ought not to reveal so much, to keep a little mystique?"

"But it's so free!" Anjali had been eyeing a blouse in a boutique window that would reveal a little cleavage. If she bought it, her parents, if they visited, must never see it amongst her things, must never see it by accident on social media. What if Aasha posted a photo of her in it? No, she wouldn't buy it.

They began to stroll back down the hill to Les Abbesses Metro station.

"So tell me," Aasha, said, "what's your first impression of the French?"

"They seem reserved. And they wear so much black." It had been a shock after riotously colorful India. "How about you?"

"I think these are crazy people," Aasha said. "They are only thinking about themselves, all into themselves, thinking of nobody else. I don't know how they ever had an empire."

"Aasha!"

"I'm glad to have three months here, but I'll be glad to get back and get married." Aasha was engaged, and the wedding was scheduled. "And what about you?" she teased.

"I want the full year in Paris that my parents and Ravi's parents agreed to."

"They must be proud of their future daughter-in-law spending a year in Paris. It makes them look so progressive."

"Yes, but they're also worried that I'll get ideas and won't end up a good wife and mother."

"Whatever you do in Paris, don't lose your 'marriageability'!" Aasha teased.

"Don't go out drinking!"

"Don't go out with strange men, Anjali!"

"Stay out of clubs!"

Just then Anjali caught sight of a wonderful Montmartre staircase, lined with a black wrought-iron handrail punctuated by tall wrought-iron gas lamps, just like in the movies.

Pleased with her new home, Anjali spread her arms wide, relishing the ambience of Paris.

"I love this place!"

Chapter 5

Philippe stood up in his small office. He'd been praying. Actually, it was more like he lived in a permanent mindset of beseeching God for mercy. He stretched his back, and sighed.

He'd love to go home and have dinner with his lovely French wife, Elodie. Philippe had met many Americans who stumbled over the pronunciation of her name when he introduced her. "It's Melodie without the M," he would say. Their look of relief at understanding both the pronunciation and spelling of her name always tickled him.

Elodie would cook up something French and delicious, and at the end of the meal serve a basket of *baguette* slices with an assortment of beautiful cheeses arrayed on her mother's French country platter with roses on the border. They would converse in French and English, switching languages to whichever one had just the right word, *le mot juste*. They had developed their own private language, a Franglais all their own.

But it was writers' group tonight. He was writing short stories and needed help, he knew it. The story he had written this week in his spare time didn't meet his expectations. He'd hoped for something epic-feeling like Victor Hugo; what he'd gotten was pure Philippe.

The door buzzer rang. He flicked the switch to the intercom.

"Daddy, it's me," came Meredith's voice.

"Just a sec, honey, I'll be down." Philippe and Elodie had spoken both French and English to their children, ensuring they became bi-lingual. Philippe and Meredith, his youngest daughter, tended to speak to each other in English.

Philippe stretched, reaching for the ceiling, and then made sure that four copies of the short story were in his crumbling leather briefcase. He locked his office door and ran down the ancient wooden staircase. His shoulder bumped the wall as he descended the steps, each perched at a slightly different angle in this 500-year-old building.

Out on Rue Lanneau, he blinked in the light, still intense in Paris at six on a summer's night. Meredith stood just across the narrow *rue*.

"Hi, how's my darling girl?" His voice echoed against the ancient stone buildings pressing toward them.

"Okay, I guess." Meredith was dressed in jeans torn strategically across the fullest part of her thighs, and a T-shirt with a deep V-neck. She had a summer cold, with pink nose and upper lip. She wasn't eating right, Philippe thought.

"What did you have for dinner last night?"

"Don't start!"

Yes, it had been a ploy to find out where she'd been. He knew the answer to his next question, and his gut tensed.

"What can I help you with?"

"Well, I need a little money."

Now his gut clenched. The support group had said not to enable.

"You're twenty-two, you need to get a job."

"Bye, Dad." She turned away.

He watched her march off, his gut getting tighter with her every footstep towards a bar. When she turned the corner onto Rue Valette, his powerlessness over her alcoholism and its cascading effects overwhelmed him. He sagged against the carved wooden door. Don't seek a confrontation, and don't avoid it when it's necessary, they had said.

He found an ounce of strength to make sure the street door had shut and locked behind him. Next to the door, in an art gallery's window, the woman who ran the gallery had put three easels, each of them displaying a painting of a nude woman, legs splayed. It's difficult not to look, he thought. I can't look in *patisseries* or in wine store windows either, with this stupid sugar addiction. Where can I look?

He headed toward the Seine. He crossed it on Pont au Double, exchanging narrow, dark Rue Lanneau for the expansive view along the river. The pointy towers of Le Conciergerie caught his eye. It was the first royal palace built in Paris, converted into a prison during the French Revolution. These days it sported a mock-up of the rooms in which Marie Antoinette had awaited the guillotine. At least she had a view. In the space and light and air on the bridge, his mood lifted.

He thought it strange that Meredith had asked him for money. She knew he never carried more than five euros and no credit cards. Early in his marriage to Elodie, he had gone out to buy a parsley plant for their tiny herb garden. He'd come back with three cypress trees. They were planted at the foot of their garden. Another time he went out for a *baguette* and came home with a scooter. Elodie handled the money after that.

Philippe leaned his elbows on the parapet and stared into the Seine, coiling and recoiling around the pillars of the bridge. I have my health, he thought, and I'm thankful, but there is a glaring need: Meredith needs to stop drinking. And another one: we sure could use more money. I need to write a book of great short stories, and then a novel, unique, sweet, and petite, that hits the bestseller list and never leaves.

And that has a message, the message of…no, forget messages, just a story. Or must it have a message to make it meaningful, worthwhile? Doesn't every novel have a message, even if the message is, "Messages are meaningless?" That sort of story seemed to be the fashion, what the editors in New York City chose. Why would an author bother with the struggle to write if he felt that life was meaningless?

He straightened up and crossed the tiny island on which Notre Dame stood, Île de la Cité. He crossed the Seine again into Le Marais, his favorite neighborhood.

A small woman passed in a low-cut navy dress, bust pushed up, flaunting a big, stiff red bow at the waist. She had on navy blue high heels with white polka-dotted bows on each toe. With all these bows, she was dressed like a gift for a man to unwrap, he thought. And those are sexy shoes.

Not long later, he passed a man in a black T-shirt with big white letters:

Great

Shoes

Let's

Fuck

It's so raw, but it's so funny, Philippe thought. I understand completely.

Chapter 6

The Tour Saint-Jacques loomed above Philippe at this point. The tower had four impossibly long gargoyles at the top, leaping out from each corner, defying gravity as if the laws of nature didn't apply in Paris. Which they very well might not. He turned to walk toward Le Café Livre.

At this point in his life, he was more at home in Paris than America. He was descended from Huguenots, Protestants who fled persecution in Catholic France. His family had settled in New Jersey and passed down the French spelling and pronunciation of his first name—accent on the last syllable—to the amusement of his vicious childhood enemies. After twenty years in Paris, Philippe thought and dreamed in French more often than he did in English.

He noticed outside the *café* that, when a motorcycle went by, it was so loud it would drown out what people in the *café* were saying. In spite of it, he wanted the writers' circle to meet outside. He had been in his office all day and wanted the fresh air, or air as fresh as it ever was in Paris. The city was located in a geographic bowl. The air didn't get blown away and refreshed. Sometimes the Tour Eiffel was grayed out by pollution, much of it from all the diesel cars the French drove, and the mayor would declare that the Metro was free so people would walk less and breathe less.

The *café*'s woven wicker chairs stood in neat rows, inviting customers to sit and disarrange them. The black asphalt beneath the chairs was dimpled with circles where the chairs' feet, under the weight of diners, had pressed into the softer pavement on a hot day.

He opened the door, from which hung a sign, "*climatisée*," but he knew the air conditioning would be inadequate, as it was everywhere in Paris. He went in to talk to the bartender and could feel, in the warm, humid air, that he was correct about the French acceptance of dreadful air conditioning.

Inside, thousands of books stood neatly on hundreds of white shelves, on every wall of the *café*. Their creative presence sparked Philippe's interest. Maybe there was a take-one, leave-one policy here.

"I called earlier, for a table for four," he said in French to the man behind the bar, who had white hair and mustache and was a little slow on his feet.

"Outside or inside, monsieur," the bartender asked. He exuded bonhomie and welcome, and Philippe knew that at least this one human was in the right job. So many people came to him and complained about their work.

"I think on the street."

"As you wish," and the bartender gestured graciously toward the door.

Philippe chose a table for four under the awning, against the wall of the *café*. The plastic barriers that came down when it rained or got cold had been rolled up tight, so the air moved out here. Of course, that meant smokers would sit out here, too. Philippe, a reformed smoker, regretted that the best spots in Paris *cafés*—outdoors—were smokers' territory.

A waiter appeared in the doorway.

"Bonsoir, monsieur," he said.

"*Bonsoir.* I'll just put two tables together, if you don't mind." The waiter stepped in to help him.

"*Combien?*" the waiter asked.

"*Quatre.* Just four. We'll order dinner."

"*Oui, monsieur.*" The waiter hurried to whisk the used wine glasses off a nearby table, just vacated by a couple holding hands.

The long evening, full of light, that blessed Paris in summer because of its location so far north in the world, not that far from the Arctic Circle, was just getting started. More people arrived and took seats and tables. Philippe looked at his watch, then twitched his shoulders, trying to relax. He read the first page of his story, got out his pen, and made a change on all four copies.

"Hi, are you Philippe? I'm Carol," said a woman with a British accent. She was wearing a sleek, expensive dress.

"*Bonsoir*, Carol." He gave her the *bisous*, a kiss on both cheeks. It was the traditional French greeting between both men and women. Sometimes he didn't want to greet strange men that way, but then again, it certainly did break the ice. "We'll have another new member coming tonight."

"That's nice." Carol took a sheaf of papers out of her leather Louis Vitton handbag, almost the size of an artist's portfolio, and sat down opposite Philippe.

John strode under the awning, with a rolled up wad of his first draft in his hand. He looked around, saw Philippe's and Carol's papers on the table, and edged his way around people and chairs.

"Hello, is this the writers' group? I'm John Germaine."

His accent gave away his American origins.

Philippe nodded.

"I'm Philippe. This is Carol." John leaned down to Carol to give her the *bisous* on both cheeks. Neither of them was French, but this was just the way it was done in France. He folded his tall frame into a black and white woven-wicker seat.

Anjali stepped under the awning, saw them, and came over. As she edged around tables, knocking a chair accidentally with her knee, she was thinking how, in Mumbai, diners went to restaurants like cloisters—behind walls—with air conditioning and sealed windows, to escape the dust, the heat, the poor, and the noise and smells of the street. Here in Paris, everybody spilled out onto the sidewalk, so open.

She saw that John had indeed availed himself of her critique group. Too bad, she thought. I have to watch myself.

"Hello, sir," she said.

"Just call me John."

"Okay."

To Philippe, she said, "Hello, I'm Anjali. Just arrived from Mumbai."

"Welcome, please, sit down," Philippe said. "Let's get the waiter and order our food."

The group studied their menus, with occasional furtive glances at the others.

Philippe clutched his menu and thought, they seem like nice enough folks. But let's see how this unfolds. I wonder if anyone gets mean in their critique, which happens so often. I formed this group. I'd hate to see it get nasty. I'm responsible, in a way, if anyone rips into other members, especially if they do it perceptively and demolish the person.

I want people to feel safe, he mused, running his hand up and down the edge of the menu, to feel safe to share the truth of their experience, so they can become better artists—better truthtellers. That's what's at stake here: nothing less than the truth. The honest expression of the ugliness and beauty of the human experience.

He heard cutlery clank on china—probably a noisy American dropping his fork on his plate. The French did everything quietly.

He noticed that, like him, Anjali ordered the cheapest item, with tap water to drink. John ordered a steak with *pommes frites* and Carol ordered a salad with grilled chicken. They both asked for wine as soon as possible. The waiter left with their order.

There was a pause as people glanced at each other. Anjali was thinking, I came here for critique, but I'm terrified, too, of being slammed with criticism. I want encouragement to be a better writer, not to be *guillotined*.

John was thinking, I wonder how this writers' critique thing works? Interesting to do something new. I hope they like me. Maybe I'll get a new client.

Carol was thinking, that John is a hunk. A ring, unfortunately. You know what, I wish I were home with Louise. This group better be worth my time.

Philippe was thinking, well, here goes.

"All right," he said, "let's go around the table, do a proper introduction of ourselves, and say what we're writing and what we hope to get from this group.

"I'll start. I'm Philippe, and I love short stories. I read both the classics and the recently published ones, in English and in French. I'm writing short stories, but I can tell they lack a certain...*je ne sais quoi*. Maybe you'll know. I've gotten rejections from literary magazines, and I want that to stop. I hope this group will help me see what I'm doing wrong, help me figure out what to do about it. That's all! Not much to expect!" He laughed.

When John heard him say that, he thought that he himself would be published forthwith, unlike this guy in a cheap, ill-fitting suit.

When Carol heard him say he'd gotten rejections from magazines, she thought his honesty was commendable, especially among strangers, and among writers, who were a competitive lot. She wondered if he'd be of any use to her, however.

Anjali thought Philippe had a nice laugh.

"Okay, you're next," Philippe said to Carol.

"Hi, I'm Carol, and I work for Trapèze, a film company in the north of Paris. I'm writing a screenplay—of course. I'd like people to give me feedback on my characters and their story arcs."

What she didn't say was that she wanted their ideas, not just their feedback on her ideas.

Anjali played with the knife by her plate and thought, maybe Carol can help me break into the movie business! I might be in the right place!

The intros continued.

"Hi, I'm John Germaine, I own an investment company, and I'd like to try my hand at a novel." Now it was time to follow up on an opportunity he had spotted. "Carol, when you sell that screenplay, let me invest the windfall for you. You'll be in good hands."

Anjali put a hand up to screen her face from John and rolled her eyes. Carol saw her, and her mouth twitched up a bit.

"I guess I'm next. I'm Anjali, I work for John. I just moved to Paris from Mumbai, and I'm wondering why Parisians look so glum." Everyone laughed.

"It's better now, when there's sunlight. In winter, when they're all Vitamin D-3 deprived and don't know it, then watch out," Philippe said.

He continued as master of ceremonies. "What are you writing, Anjali?"

"A screenplay. The Big Sleep, but set in Paris instead of LA."

"Paris has its dark side," Philippe said, "like any city—like any village out in the countryside, for that matter. Well, I'd just like to say welcome to everyone, and I hope you'll bring your work regularly. So, to start—Oh, here's our food."

Each person looked at their plate as it was set before them. Philippe and Anjali had *crocque monsieur*—ham and cheese on toasted bread with a tiny bit of fresh arugula on the side. Anjali, a Hindu, avoided beef but ate other kinds of meat. John was served his steak with French fries and a small salad. It didn't occur to him that Anjali, being from India, might be offended by someone at her table eating beef. Carol had a bowl of crisp lettuce with grilled chicken and *vinaigrette* on top.

"Mmm, good." John was attacking his steak and chewing. "Cooked to perfection. Tender."

"My chicken is good, not excellent, but then, I'm fussy," Carol said.

"I like it." Anjali wanted to eat with her fingers, but she cut her sandwich with fork and knife, as one must in Paris, she'd been told. "The cheese is delicious and toasted just right."

"Good," Philippe said, concentrating on his dinner. He wished he'd had the strength to just order tea. Still expensive, however, at five euros in Paris. Maybe after a few more meetings in a neutral public place, he'd invite these people to meet in his office.

"After the plates are cleared away, I'd like to do a short exercise with you, before we read the work you brought," Philippe said.

"What's the exercise?" Carol asked, tucking a leaf of lettuce, stabbed and neatly folded French style on her *fourchette*, into her mouth. She'd been here long enough to learn that trick.

"I'm going to read a line from a poem. We each write it down and then write our own poem, using it as our first line."

"Oh, I love doing that!" Anjali said. "It's amazing, the different directions people go in!"

First they finished their meals, listening to John talk about the stock market. He told them he had a mansion in Greenwich, Connecticut, a sailboat on the Long Island Sound, and another one in Cherbourg, France. He rattled the Rolex on his wrist.

Carol thought, crikey, I've met Mr. Inventory.

Philippe thought, just what we need for people to feel safe—a braggart.

"I'd like to have you come to my apartment for one of these meetings," John said. "I'll order in for everybody."

Carol flinched—she was tired of take-away food, and of Jeffrey's complaints about it. But it was nice of John to invite them all.

Anjali thought she'd love to see how her wealthy boss lived.

The waiter took their plates and brought tiny cups of coffee for John and Carol. Anjali and Philippe poured from the *carafe d'eau*, which was free. People brought their work out and placed it face down on the two tables.

"Do we have to write poetry?" John asked.

"Anything. Whatever you like," Philippe said. "Okay, let's start. The first sentence is from a poem I wrote, inspired by Rainer Maria Rilke's Book of Hours. And a few other poets. We'll see where it takes you. I'll give you ten minutes. Here it is." He paused, then spoke slowly.

"'I walk toward you now. It is for life that my body aches.'"

The table went silent as pens scratched. John used a Mont Blanc fountain pen, Philippe noticed, while he had to be content with a blue medium-point felt-tip. They each paused, wrote, paused, scratched out, and wrote. Carol was aware of silverware clinking against china around her, civilized-sounding. John heard a man start up a scooter that had been parked on the sidewalk. The man roared off, the air reverberating.

After ten minutes, Philippe cleared his throat.

"OK, one minute to finish up. Just one thing: We want to help people write better, not discourage them so that they give up. So after each person reads, we say at least one thing we like about it. Then we say what we think didn't work. We keep it in 'I' statements: 'I think that phrase didn't fit here,' as opposed to, 'You're an idiot to write that.'

"Keep in mind Abraham Lincoln's words: 'He has a right to criticize, who has a heart to help.'

"We always conclude our critiques with one more positive thing, something else that we think works. A critique isn't well done unless it has a balance of positive and negative. If you can't think of at least two positive things to say about the text, you're not thinking hard enough.

"I call it the praise sandwich: praise, then the gentle suggestions for improvement, and praise again. Some people call it the Oreo cookie."

People were looking at him rather blankly, he thought. He'd have to model his own rules and remind everyone constantly. What was so hard about "praise sandwich?"

Yet nobody would remember. Their praise would be tepid. When it came time for the criticisms, their eyes would light up, and they'd dive in with relish.

"OK, anybody care to start?" Philippe said. He wondered if people would take risks, dig for the truth, be honest.

A long pause. Everyone was hanging back, some from fear, not wanting to possibly receive scathing criticism, some from not wanting to appear selfish and too "me first." Then Anjali raised her hand. "I'll start."

The table settled down to listen.

> "I walk toward you now. It is life
> that my body craves.
> I don't know you.
> you speak – hollow,
> you shout – shrill.
> Unmask yourself!
> Who are you really?"

John whispered, "Good," and gave his assistant a congratulatory nudge with his elbow.

"I like the way you took the first line and made it your own," Philippe said.

Anjali nodded, happy in the praise.

"I'll read." John capped his magnificent pen and placed it on the table, rather than hide it in his pocket. Then he changed his mind and put it away. Showing it off was a bit too much like Cassandra, with her luxury-brand ostentations. He flicked his paper. At the last second, before he read, he changed the first line to make it his own, too.

> "I go toward you, longing to really live.
> But to you, I'm dead
> a lynch pin in your mighty wheel
> My mettle frays
> Strengthen me,
> lest I am battered
> at the foot of your spinning gears."

The table was silent again, though diners around them chatted, and forks and knives continued to clink on china.

"I like the way you had 'wheels' and then you returned to it with 'gears,'" Carol said. Everybody was being so nice in the new group. It was so boring.

"Yeah, 'mettle' and 'metal' connote strength." Anjali flexed her bicep. "He's strong, and yet he's fraying." Am I getting a little too forward with the boss, she wondered?

"Thank you." John gave a gallant bow of his head.

"I'll read." Carol riffled her papers and cleared her throat. She heard a Paris police siren in the distance, sounding like a bagpipe that played just two notes: high-low, high-low. The French called it the *pin-pon*. She'd read that in a driver's education manual over a woman's shoulder in the Metro: "*Céder le passage à la pin-pon*," or "Yield way to the pin-pon." Carol, old dear, she thought, what are you nattering on about? Come back, wherever you are. "Yes, okay, let's see what happens."

> "I go to you with tiny steps
>   You step back just as fast
> If I could reach you, I'd be complete."

"It's haiku," Carol said. "I think it's my relationship with my art."

"What's haiku, seven-five-seven syllables?" John asked. "Aren't there rules?"

"I agree with the school that says it's whatever gets the job done," Carol answered. "This one is eight-six-nine."

"I hear so much longing in that haiku," Philippe said.

"Read yours, Philippe?" Carol asked, uncomfortable talking about longing.

"Okay. Here goes." He was silent for a few seconds. He noticed a scooter go by with a woman in white stilettos and white crash helmet clutching the man driving in front of her. Another couple ambled past with a young girl, head all-over golden curls, holding her parents' hands and peering at the street-side diners.

Meredith, my little girl. Oh, honey. You're causing me so much pain. I can't walk it out on the streets of Paris, I can't write it out, and I can't talk it out, especially with this group.

He glanced around at the writers, all intent on hearing his work. He cleared his voice, smoothed his paper, and began to read.

"I walk toward you now. It is for life
    that my body aches.
I seek you, demand you, and wait.
You build me up,
you dash me against the rocks.
Even so, I know you love me.
Yet though you slay me, still
    will I trust you."

"I think there are too many yets and buts and even so's in there," said John.

Philippe thought, John's forgotten the praise sandwich already. *Mon dieu!*

"Okay, so let's read what you all brought tonight," Philippe said.

John read the first chapter of the novel he'd started. It had a tough male protagonist named Chuck, who got into a fistfight with four equally tough bad guys within the first two double-spaced pages. Chuck, needless to say, prevailed. He left the scene with the four ruffians rolling on the ground holding their battered jaws, fists, or groins, not to mention shattered egos.

"It's entertaining for a certain type of reader," Carol said cautiously. She shifted in her wicker *café* chair. Enough of all this "make nice" rubbish. Time for someone to be incisive. "I wouldn't buy this book."

"I wouldn't either, but you'll laugh all the way to the bank, John," Anjali said.

"Good! That's what I like to do," John replied. His assistant wouldn't buy his book? What? What kind of people were these writers?

"It's not my type of reading, either." Philippe drank a bit of his free water. "Could it be a little more nuanced? Maybe there's some value that Chuck cares about other than winning fist fights?"

John dug for a quick answer. "Uh, he fights for justice."

"I don't see a fight for justice in this text," Philippe said. "I see a fistfight that's revenge for one of the bad guys calling him stupid."

"Well, he'll fight for justice in the next chapter." John took out his Mont Blanc again, proof that he was a Renaissance man who was good at everything. He'd get good even at writing novels.

31

"Your book needs to have a theme," Carol said. "I've had films produced, and I know. Your theme in this novel needs to bubble up through every word, every paragraph. Just like in a film—every word of dialog, every scene, has to explore the theme."

John twitched his neck and shoulders. He'd expected people to love it. He knew this type of story sold well. What was all this harping on theme? He wasn't writing *War and Peace*, after all. "Well, I don't know—"

"—well, it's true," Carol said, defending herself, wondering if she had come across as preachy. "Even in this genre, there are writers who stick to the theme. They sell best."

Even in this genre? John twitched his neck again. Who was she? Well, she was a professional screenwriter, true, but a bit too braggy about it. His story was different. This was a novel with a chance at being a blockbuster. Maybe her production company would buy the option to make a movie of it.

"I'm establishing the kind of man my character is in this first chapter," John said.

"Yeah, somebody who beats people up for nothing." Anjali smiled cheesily at John.

She's smiling to keep her job, John thought. This writing business brought out the beast in people, apparently. Even his brand new assistant was turning on him. The corporate board rooms he'd experienced weren't much different than this.

"I'd like to see your main character have some principle that he struggles to uphold," Philippe said.

That hurt. John loved his main character just as he was.

"And the bad guys can't be all bad," Carol said. "They aren't interesting unless you show that they have good points."

"Okay, I'll make them all good tippers," John said.

"Each one different," Anjali insisted. "Nuanced. Worthy antagonists to your worthy protagonist. What's even more interesting is when the antagonist wants something that's just as good, or good to him, but opposite to what your protagonist wants. For example, a protagonist fights against the building of a dam for ecology's sake, and his antagonist fights to build the dam because it will create jobs for the town."

John nodded to the group and motioned for their marked-up copies to come back. He would have to find some time to think about his story. Antagonists wanting good things? This fiction-writing gig was harder than he'd anticipated. He was taking more flak than he had on his Yale dissertation.

Philippe thought, John's poem was quite honest, but not his fiction. Interesting.

Anjali handed out copies of her one-page poem. She'd brought it instead of the screenplay she was working on because she was too frightened to present that. And she wrote poetry because it forced her to condense images and feelings into just a few words. "Poets say it best," she'd read somewhere.

"I had a chance to go to a poetry festival in Goa, with a lovely pool at the hotel." She laid her page flat on the table and picked up her felt-tip. Her left hand fidgeted with the top corner of the page as she read.

"Pool Man

"He works with fluid motions,
gracefully using his cleaning equipment,
working quickly.
He perspires in the tropical sun.
A bead of sweat gathers on his nose and
    plunges
into the water.
He's late for his next pool.
The water is cool and blue, but
    it belongs to someone.
Will he ever get a swim?"

The table was silent for about thirty seconds.

"It has too many words," Carol blurted out. "You don't need 'cleaning' before 'equipment.'"

Anjali flinched. To tell a poet she used too many words was like telling her she was both ugly and depraved.

"If she took out 'cleaning,'" John said, "it would become: 'He works with fluid motions, gracefully using his equipment.' Maybe it's just me, but that has sexual connotations maybe she didn't want."

Anjali studied her poem, oblivious to what he was talking about.

Carol laughed. "That would make it better. Either everything is about sex, or nothing is. Decide."

Philippe thought, I have no control over the topics that come up at a writers' circle. If the ladies in my church knew all the topics I've heard discussed, they'd fire me.

"Nice line," he said, "'the water belongs to someone.'" He was determined to follow his own critique guidelines and offer some praise. "As if people could ever own the elements of the earth."

"Earth, Wind, Water, Fire," mused Carol. "I feel a haiku coming on."

"You might want to experiment with deleting 'a' and 'an' and 'the' and 'he,' Philippe said. "Try it and see what happens. But great image of the overheated worker and the cool pool." There, he did it, a praise sandwich.

Anjali nodded and took back her pages.

Carol handed out five pages of a screenplay, working title: *Lien on Your Assets*. There were four characters and a narrator, so each person had a part, plus Carol read the narration and stage directions. It was about an actress who, when the automobiles she hawked on TV commercials were recalled for bursting into flames, became a secretary in a firm that was run by a crooked businessman.

"This is good, high-level writing," Philippe said. "But—"

"—there's always a 'but.'" Carol sighed.

"Yeah, I know. I was going to say that your protagonist obviously has a visceral, urgent need—she needs to work in order to eat. But your antagonist, that shifty businessman, doesn't seem to have an opposite need that's as acute."

"He needs to stay rich," Carol said.

"Don't forget to make your bad guy nuanced," John said. He was still smarting from the reaction to his first chapter.

"Now, John, don't be mean," Carol said lightly. She glanced at the next table, where dessert had been served. She'd love to have a beautiful French *chocolat* creation for dessert. She touched her midriff and decided against it.

Tomorrow morning she'd go to her favorite *patisserie*, where the confections looked like little jewels. One of them might be garnished with a fresh raspberry, like a giant ruby, with an emerald-green mint leaf, set off at just-so an angle. And the treats were presented like jewels, in glass cases that sparkled, with brass trim that gleamed. Best yet, their taste rarely disappointed, unlike pastries she'd had in London and New York City.

"Philippe, you're up," John said.

Philippe passed out a short story. It was full of tension and stress between an alcoholic woman, who had no clue about how ill she was and how much damage she was causing, and her boyfriend, who was ready to leave her. Philippe read it aloud with his voice tight, thinking of Meredith.

The group commented, not gently, because they had no clue the turmoil Philippe was in over his daughter's illness. Each criticism felt like a knife blade in his already tenderized heart. Everybody in the group forgot to offer so much as a word of praise.

And then the evening was over. They settled the bill and stood.

"Thanks," John said. "I guess I'll be back with revisions. *Bonne soirée.*" He dodged easily around tables and strode into the still-bright dusk. He thought, at 10:30 in the long Paris summer evening, you could still read a book if you were so inclined.

"Yes, good night, everyone." Carol grabbed her giant bag and headed out.

Philippe started toward his suburban rental near the end of the 13 line in Malakoff, just outside the Peripherique that marked the perimeter of Paris, and a mad highway if ever there was one.

"Carol, can I talk to you?" Anjali scurried after Carol, who was striding through the crowds of ambling tourists that annoyed Parisians so much.

"Sure, what's up?" Carol asked.

"You're a screenwriter—and a good one, obviously—and I wondered if you'd be willing to read a screenplay I wrote. My critique group in Mumbai loved it."

"Is it in English?" Carol asked impatiently. She didn't want to do this.

"Yes, of course." Didn't Carol know that English was one of the official languages of India? Hundreds of millions on the subcontinent didn't speak it, of course, but it was an official language—one of more than twenty—nevertheless. People didn't know much about India, it seemed. And the Frenchified version of Indian food was pathetic.

"Here's my card." Carol kept them in an inner pocket at the top of her huge handbag. "Email it to me and I'll take a look. Good night."

"Thanks!" Anjali said, hopes rising, dreams of having her movie optioned dancing before her eyes, of being able to leave her job with John. Of working full-time as a screenwriter.

Chapter 7

In spite of the late hour, and having to get up to go to work the next morning, Anjali decided to stroll just a bit in Le Marais before crossing the Seine to go home to bed. She crossed Rue de Rivoli and turned left on Rue Vieille du Temple. Not to be confused with nearby Rue du Temple, as she had been her first time in this neighborhood.

She was excited about the writers' group. They seemed like talented critiquers. And maybe she actually could critique John there, even though he was her boss, the same way she'd read that Japanese businessmen go out with their boss, they all get drunk, the workers say what they want to say, and all is forgiven the next day. She hoped John had read the same article.

She tried to calm herself and not worry. She just wanted to wander and soak up the atmosphere.

A man went by on a bicycle he'd converted into a one-man band. The bicycle had a bass drum mounted above the rear wheel, and a small electric keyboard forward of the handlebars. An amplifier for the piano stood in the front wire basket.

The man had a harmonica and a trumpet mounted on a homemade bracket. Both instruments were within easy reach of his mouth. He wore a frizzy blue wig, white harem pants, red curly-toed slippers edged with gold sequins, and no shirt. He was quite a show.

Anjali loved shows. She remembered years ago, when she was just eight or so, and she had the idea to put on a show for her parents. At that time, they lived in an apartment building in

Pondicherry, a very traditional Indian city, meaning no freedom for women and girls, among other things. Next to their apartment was an empty lot. Parents in the building had chipped in and bought a small swingset. It had two swings, a trapeze, and a slide. As Anjali moved from one bit of equipment to another, she felt inspired to develop a routine, something like the dancing interludes in Bollywood movies, which her mother adored.

Anjali developed a little routine using all the pieces of equipment. When she felt ready, she rounded up her friends and their parents to come to her show. She begged and cajoled her parents to bring their small boombox to the playground with a tape of the score of Kuch Kuch Hota Hai, one of her mother's favorite movies, already loaded.

When everyone was standing, watching, and the music playing, Anjali performed the routine she'd created. It took all of three minutes. Everyone clapped politely, and her friends jumped on the swings. The parents stood around talking.

"Appa, did you see me?" Anjali asked.

"You're quite the showman," her father said. "You have a lot of talent for that."

"She's a girl. She'll grow up to get married," her mother retorted.

Anjali felt as if she'd been slapped. Hard. "She's a girl" had sounded like a condemnation. Marriage sounded like a box, the end of her dreams, the end of living.

Now, walking on the narrow sidewalks of Le Marais, she wondered if she could break away from her parents' expectation that she marry, instilled and reinforced for more than two decades, and instead write a great movie, maybe shoot one, even a short one, while she was living in Paris for just one brief year.

The bicyclist disappeared around the corner of Rue des Rosiers. That man certainly defies people's expectations, Anjali thought. I'm not sure I want to go quite that far.

Chapter 8

Carol hurried across Rue de Rivoli and up Rue Saint Bon, a street in Le Marais that was too narrow for cars. Ahead of her, the window boxes on the stone wall of l'Église Saint-Merri flowed with pink and red clouds of trailing geraniums.

She turned right on Rue de la Verrerie and walked past closed shops and dwindling crowds in the *cafés*.

She figured the writers' circle might be just the thing, in her desperate effort to get her creative mojo back. She had missed an evening with Louise, though.

She walked past a second-hand clothing store, known as a kilo shop because a shopper's selections were weighed and sold by the kilo. She had grown up wearing second-hand clothes, so ashamed of it, so afraid that her schoolmates would find out and pick on her.

Carol remembered two children in her class at age seven or so, a brother and sister who looked ragged, dressed in worn hand-me-downs. They would stand back-to-back in the schoolyard. For some reason, Carol's schoolmates had singled these two out, and quite a few of them harassed and bullied the two relentlessly every recess. Carol had joined in once. She had run at the two, shouting names in their faces.

That night, in bed, she'd felt terrible. So terrible, she knew she had to change. She resolved to show her parents what was happening at school so they'd do something to make it stop.

The next morning, she'd snuck into the hall closet and found her parents' video camera, a great heavy thing. She stuffed it into her bookbag, which she took out on the playground at recess. The camera worked great as she filmed her classmates running at the suffering brother and sister, screaming names and swear words.

"Hey! What are you doing!" One of the playground monitors, who should have been protecting the victims, grabbed for the camera but knocked it out of her hands. It shattered on the asphalt. Bits of plastic and glass scattered everywhere.

Carol got a caning that night, and she could still feel it, here on the streets of Paris.

She had decided back then that she'd do something, somehow, to influence people to put themselves in the shoes of people like that brother and sister. I haven't done it yet, Carol thought. I'd better get cracking.

She walked on toward her apartment—thank God she could afford to live in Le Marais. Weary from the long day, she couldn't wait to get home. Her place was two flights up from a pricey *boutique* that never seemed to have her style.

Her building was on Rue Pavée; she liked that the street had been mentioned in a scene of the French Revolution in Les Miserables. She was exhausted, mostly because of guilt at being out all evening at the writers' group, trying to save her career instead of being home with Louise. It remained to be seen if this group would be the answer.

She was doing this to keep her job, to provide for her daughter. Jeffrey made a salary, too, and paid half the rent, but Carol didn't believe in relying on a man for income. She had to have her own money: you never knew what might happen.

Weariness started in her feet and worked up her body. Trapèze had been difficult all day—Gregoire had insisted that she make stupid changes to a script she had written, and she felt he was ruining the story, as usual—so she felt spent and in no mood to fend off the constant flow of Jeffrey's criticisms.

She passed a corner where the streets came together at much less than right angles. In fact, there wasn't a single right angle intersection anywhere in Paris. How could you position furniture in a room like that? Hard to imagine. She was happy with the apartment she was in. She had longed all evening to get home, and here she was, and sad to say not feeling much peace. She was just hoping that Jeffrey was asleep.

Jeffrey was such a critical bloke, she thought.

Bloke. What a useful word. Carol used slang from every level of British society. As a writer, she had an ear for great words and used them with relish, giving only a passing thought to what society-people would think of her for using them. Her attitude was, artists steal. They see an idea they like, they take it. They use every gleaming thing, like magpies lining their nests.

She let herself in her big old wooden door. Getting up the wooden circular staircase presented a new challenge. Each step had settled over the years at a different angle. The banister, polished with beeswax by the porter, was slick under her hand.

Her apartment faced La Bibliothèque Historique de la Ville de Paris, a library built in the 1550s. She anticipated looking at that hotbed of French intellectual activity from the tiny balcony off her living room. Without Jeffrey.

She opened the door to her apartment. All was quiet. Perhaps she'd have a moment to herself, to gain a respite from the day. Then she'd sneak into Louise's room and gaze for a moment.

Silently she dropped her purse among the pillows covered in fabrics from India, put her keys quietly in her bag, and bumped her knee against the coffee table, which was covered with more richly colored fabric. She opened the door to the balcony and stepped out. Footsteps and voices sounded in the Rue Pavée below, echoing against the stone walls of the *bibliothèque* opposite. She began to relax.

"Did you have a good writers' group?" Jeffrey said behind her. He stepped onto the balcony. She felt herself tense up with fear that he would start in again. Keep your poise, Carol.

"Yes, I have a feeling I'll get good ideas there," she said.

"Louise was whining for you. You really ought to be here more."

"I'd like to be, but I have to work," Carol said. That was a bit tetchy, she said to herself. Put him in a good mood. "I'm grateful that you take care of her."

"You should be," he said. "I sometimes wonder if you don't think you're a better mother than you really are."

This was the ten-thousandth in a long litany of criticisms he had leveled at her in two years. She had gently pointed out his tendency to criticize, had quietly asked him to consider her feelings, and when he had continued, had yelled at him to stop. He had just blithely kept doing it.

"Ouch!"

"Well, it's true."

"We've barely said hello and you're already tearing me down. Can't we just stand on the balcony for a minute without criticisms?"

"You're the one criticizing. I'm not the bad guy, Carol."

"Oh, for goodness sake, have mercy on my soul!" Carol brushed past him to go back into the apartment. She was tired: of his digs at her, of protesting, of how obtuse he was. She felt his fingers clamp on her wrist.

Carol had had enough. The longer she stayed with him, the lower her self-esteem—and her ability to be creative—became. And what about his influence on her daughter? Louise could hear the difference between how he talked to her and how he talked to her mother. Carol didn't want her daughter to grow up thinking that this was what she should expect from men.

Carol had been thinking about all this for months now, and it flashed through her mind in a second. She tugged her arm, but he wouldn't let go. She lifted her free hand as though to slap him. She halted the motion, staring at him. Then she worked at prying his fingers off her wrist.

"Jeffrey, you praise Louise, the little girl, to the skies, and that's nice, but you criticize me, the adult woman, up and down, day in day out. What am I going to do?"

"Think hard before you say anything else. I mind your daughter morning and evening, and many weekends, while you're working."

"I know, I appreciate it, but—"

"I'm just telling you what I see happening. Louise needed you this evening."

Carol knew that was true, and it fueled her anger. She tore at his fingers but couldn't pry them off her wrist.

"I know, but I'm having professional difficulties, and—"

"What difficulties?" Jeffrey's eyes narrowed. "If you think I'm going to carry this place alone, think again."

"You know I don't expect that. I'm going to this group because I need ideas for films that people will like."

"You'd better figure something out."

"Jeffrey, I just told you, I did figure something out. I'm going to this group."

"Now who's got the attitude?" He let go of her wrist.

"Oh, for goodness sake, Jeffrey, find something to do besides belittle me."

Carol could tell their voices were carrying outdoors, reverberating along the stone walls of the *bibliothèque* and the houses opposite it. Every neighbor could hear them. And the argument might wake Louise up. She cringed inwardly, then whirled away from him.

"Carol."

"What?"

"You know I love you."

"I know, but please—"

"—We'll discuss this later. Let's go to bed."

Carol took off her scarf, its cool silk brushing her flushed cheek. After all his snide comments, how could he truly believe she wanted to make love? Yet he did. He was lighting tea candles and putting them on the coffee table.

His lack of awareness of how he was hurting her was a nightmare that droned on and on. Yet what could she do? Louise loved him. Carol knew she couldn't forget that breaking up with Jeffrey would rob Louise of the only father figure she'd known.

"Jeffrey, please put the candles on a plate or something. When the wax drips, it gets into the fabric that I lugged all the way from India."

"You're frigid, Carol, that's the problem. You care more about fabric than sex."

"I believe in candles and romance. I just don't want to destroy the place!"

"We don't make love enough."

"Crikey!" That complaint again. "What on earth is wrong with once or twice a week?"

"You don't like me lighting candles. You don't want to make love."

"Because you constantly belittle me!"

"I do not!"

"Yes you do, Jeffrey." How could he be so oblivious? And yet he was. Just like her father.

"It's time you left."

Jeffrey's eyes narrowed. "Be careful."

"I'm sure."

Carol wasn't sure.

"Get out," she said.

"What about Louise?"

"I'll figure something out. Go. Now."

Jeffrey stared hard at her. "You can't accept the truth, that's your problem."

"Aargh!" Carol picked up an Indian pillow, its little mirrors and beads in paisley patterns gleaming in the candlelight. She whacked him as hard as she could with it.

"Ouch!"

"Go!"

42

"What about my stuff?"

Carol was desperate to be alone, to face what this break-up meant in peace. Every moment that he remained in her sight meant acute pain rather than dull pain. But she relented.

"Okay, pack a small bag. You can pick the rest up on Saturday at noon, when we're not here. Give me your key. I'll leave word with the porter to let you in."

"Carol, don't do this," Jeffrey pleaded. "Think of me, of my relationship with that darling little girl."

"This darling big girl can't tolerate your criticisms anymore. Go get your toothbrush, and leave."

"I want to look at Louise, I want to kiss her."

"Oh shit! You're making me crazy. Okay, Okay."

Jeffrey loped down the hall and Carol hurried after him.

"Don't wake her up!"

Jeffrey knelt beside Louise's bed and took one of her small hands in his big ones. He kissed it. He stroked her hair. Carol saw tears in his eyes, and she felt grief in her throat. Poor Louise, losing Jeffrey. And what am I going to do without him here to care for her? Without someone to share my bed?

Jeffrey looked up at her, big glistening lines on his cheeks, like snail trails.

"Please, Carol, reconsider," he whispered.

"You treat her the way you ought to treat me," Carol whispered back. "I've been telling you to stop. I'm sick of telling you."

Carol saw that his one moment of tenderness was over. His face hardened to its usual lines.

"Don't get your knickers in such a twist," he said.

Carol marched out of Louise's room and into the bathroom. She grabbed Jeffrey's toothbrush and shaving gear and jammed it into his travel shave kit, which was sitting on the back of the toilet. She returned to the door of Louise's room.

He was still kneeling, stroking Louise's hand. Carol went in and poked his shoulder.

"You've got to go," she whispered.

Finally he stood up, but as he did he leaned one hand on the edge of the bed, and Louise's small body rolled toward the depression he made. Her eyes opened.

"Hi, Jeffrey," she smiled.

"Honey, Jeffrey's leaving on a business trip, but I'll be here," Carol said. "You go back to sleep, okay?"

"Can I have some water?"

The water routine again. Carol wanted to curse him for waking the child. She was exhausted, and she still had to arrange a babysitter for tomorrow. No, she couldn't get it arranged this late. She would have to call in sick. Her career was sinking, there'd be no man in the house, she'd feel all that misery again, she'd have to grieve the loss of Jeffrey, she had to help Louise grieve, too. Fuck! She went and got a glass of water, and let Louise sip it. The child of course knew something was wrong.

"Jeffrey, where are you going?" She sounded plaintive.

"I'll be back, don't worry."

"You'll see him in a day or two, honey, there, lay down, off to sleep with you." Carol left the room to put the glass back in the bathroom. Please, Jeffrey, get out of there, she breathed. Please get out before I'm dead-exhausted. Please!

Carol sighed with relief when she saw him moving away from Louise's bed. As long as he was in motion, it would be easier to steer him toward the door. It was when he stood, feet separated, hands on hips, that he was impossible to budge. Go! she whispered to herself. She headed to the apartment door, opened it, stood back. Jeffrey was moving slowly, hooray, as long as he was moving, there was hope, wasn't there.

"Carol, are you sure?"

"Yes, I'm sure. Come back Saturday for your stuff."

"I need a clean shirt." He headed back down the hall, past Louise's door to their room.

"Mummy! Jeffrey!"

Carol thought she would crumble right there on the floor. She had nothing left, yet she had to give Louise something.

"Louise, I'll be right there. Jeffrey!"

He appeared with a small suitcase in one hand. Thank God, he was getting closer to the door again, a chance for relief, privacy, a moment in which to recoup some energy.

"See you, Jeffrey," Carol said, exhausted and past caring what it sounded like to him.

"That's all you have to say to me? After all I've done for you? Really, Carol—"

"Learn to stop criticizing with every breath you take. Until then, bugger off." Carol closed and locked the door. Then she remembered something. Fuck, another chance for him to get back in the apartment. She opened the door again.

"Give me your key," she called after Jeffrey, who was heading down the uneven staircase. He paused, turned, dug in a pocket and threw a key at her.

"You can't do anything right, Carol, not even breaking up."

"Shut up!" she shouted. Then she worried about Louise hearing her, and the neighbors who didn't like the British.

When she started to regret this breakup later, she would remember this comment. Proof that she was doing the right thing. She locked the apartment door again, blew the tea candles out—he never had put them on a plate—and stood in the darkened room. She was quiet, feeling the difference, the empty space that Jeffrey had left in the apartment and in her heart.

"Mummy!"

She went to comfort Louise.

Chapter 9

After the writers' group disbanded, John hit his stride as he marched toward his apartment on Boulevard Raspail, a street in the tony Sixth *arrondissement*, otherwise known as the Sixth. The sky was still light. So, when he crossed the Seine on the Pont des Artes, the thousands of padlocks that couples had locked to the chain link fence on both sides of the bridge gleamed gently in the dying light.

He and Cassandra had honeymooned in Paris, had gotten a lock engraved with their names and wedding date, and attached it in the middle of the bridge, near a post. John didn't feel like trying to find it.

As the Seine roiled below him, he thought of how a person could cross the powerful Seine in approximately two minutes' walk, but crossing the equally dangerous East River in New York City took half a day. He was reminded of the time, when he was four or five, when his father had decided to make him walk across the Brooklyn Bridge "to toughen him up." They'd left his father's Park Avenue apartment and taken the 6 train to City Hall. Then began the long walk up the interminable on-ramp. Finally they were on the bridge itself, above the restless East River. Then down the interminable off-ramp, before they were on terra firma in Brooklyn.

John had been wearing new shoes; they were causing blisters. They hurt. More and more. So he'd complained, a lot, as a little boy was likely to do.

His father didn't acknowledge his first five complaints.

Another few footsteps.

"Daddy, will you carry me?"

His father turned on him.

"You'll never be a success," his father shouted. People walking near them veered away.

John remembered how those words had hit his heart and blown an aching hole in it. It had never healed. The pain was as real today as it had been that day, high above the East River.

A *bateau mouche* emerged from under Pont des Artes and chugged with its load of tourists downstream. John watched for a while.

Then he turned away and continued home, smarting from his father's meanness. He just walked, covering ground quickly, passing Parisians, and tourists from all over the world speaking to each other in incomprehensible languages. Occasionally he passed someone who sounded American or British. The snatches of their conversations made no sense, but they distracted him from his memories.

"—quite a scene—"

"—that falafel place—"

"—just call your boss 'Your Royal Highness'—"

At that, John spun around, but it was just two Asian girls chatting and laughing.

The people came toward him and disappeared behind him. John felt good as he reflected on the lunch he'd had with Brad Harrington yesterday. Soon, very soon, he'd have this fish not just on the hook but landed in the boat. In a good way, of course. John would invest Harrington's money and take a broker's share. The sailboat in Cherbourg needed a new GPS, to keep him off the cliffs of Dover. That was one way to spend part of his commission. Cassandra's credit card was another.

Musing gently on his boats on either side of the Atlantic, and their relative strengths and weaknesses, he came to his door. The French porter greeted him. John disliked the words "porter" and "doorman." In both languages, it referred to a man in service to a door.

He bounded up the marble stairs, with slight hollows worn out by centuries of footsteps, and unlocked his apartment door.

"Honey, I'm home!" he sang out. Then he told himself to shush, people were sleeping. The fourteen-foot-tall ceilings gave a lovely sense of gracious space. The *parquet* floor, with mahogany, oak and maple creating a *chevron* pattern, was polished to a sheen. A French aristocrat used to live here, he mused, and now an American one did.

Cassandra had left lights on for him. The Baccarat crystal bases of the lamps in the living room gleamed beautifully and sent little prisms onto the walls and the maple tables they stood on. The paintings on the wall were the work of some artist Cassandra had become enamored of in New York City. A visit to Sotheby's, and Cassandra had herself some of her very own. Never mind they were moving to Paris in a month, a city with hundreds of galleries. No, Cassandra had to have those specific paintings. John still remembered the bill for insuring them and shipping them to Paris.

Well, there was more dough where that came from. He certainly was a success. In spite of his father. Filthy lucre, that was the scorecard, and John was way ahead of most men, including Philippe, in his off-the-rack suit, not tailored. That guy needed an upgrade.

He whistled softly on his way to the kitchen. He stumbled over some shopping bags. Both Dior and Chanel. Well, he'd see what these were about in the morning. He poured a half tumbler (also Baccarat) of organic milk. The French called organic food *"bio,"* pronounced "beeo." Very amusing.

He put the glass in the sink and rinsed it with a little water, as he'd learned to do in college, when suddenly he'd found that there was nobody to clean up after him. Cassandra could care less, the cook did the dishes. He walked quietly past Emily's bedroom door to his. It was closed, the signal that Cassandra was not in the mood. Oh well, that would change. At some point.

Chapter 10

Anjali passed the Tour Saint Jacques on her way home. The four elongated gargoyles at the top of the tower—like panthers leaping out from each corner—were black silhouettes against the royal blue twilight. Like John, she also walked to the Sixth, also to Boulevard Raspail, but to the opposite end of it, where she lived in a *chambre de bonne*, a maid's room, on the top floor of an aristocratic family's Paris townhouse.

Six flights up to a bedroom all of ten square meters. Enough room for a narrow bed, a sink, an electric stove with two burners, a tiny table that also served as her desk, but not a chair. No microwave, no oven, no counterspace other than her desk/table. But she did have a view of the Eiffel Tower if she put her head out the window.

She had found the flat and her job online. Her mother and father in Mumbai were terrified of her being on her own in a distant city, but she thought of it as a grand adventure. Amma and Appa had given her a year to settle down and get the screenplay thing out of her system. Then they expected her back, to marry Ravi.

She used the toilet in the water closet out on the landing. She didn't mind standing up—unlike millions in India, at least she had a toilet. She re-entered her flat to wash her hands at the kitchen sink. The towel to dry hands was in the shower. The shower's etched glass wall was what her pillow leaned against when she read in bed. The flat was tight, but it was all hers. She would write a killer screenplay here, and then another. She wanted Hollywood to know her name— not Bollywood, she had no interest.

Sitting on her bed, she indulged in her usual late-night activity— looking up a Mumbai newspaper online, curious about the news from her homeland. As she scrolled through the headlines, one jumped out at her: "More than 8,200 Women Treated for Burns in the Last Ten Years in One Bangalore Hospital."

What on earth?

She read the article thoroughly. A university team had studied police reports of "stove bursts" in which wives had died.

"It's amazing that stove bursts kill only the wife; not the mother-in-law, not the sister-in-law, and surely not the husband," the leader of the study said. Researchers believed that the police had a complicit role because they often did not investigate the site of the incident and based their enquiry on the victim's statement, made with the husband and his family around her. When researchers did investigate several cases where a cooking accident or stove burst was blamed, they found that the burning took place in the bathroom or living room, while the stove was in the kitchen.

Most of the women were in their twenties, and most had been married for less than two years.

While she read, Anjali thought, what if Ravi or his sisters did that to me? She had met all of them and couldn't picture it, but probably none of the burned women could have conceived of their marriages taking that turn, either.

She got into her pajamas and curled up in her bed, thinking.

Chapter 11

After the critique group, Philippe walked to l'Hôtel de Ville Metro stop and took the 1 train west to the Champs Elysées station, then the 13 south to his rented house in a suburb just outside the Périphérique, the frantic highway that encircled and marked the limits of Paris proper. In Roman times and the Middle Ages, walls had defined the city limits. Now they were defined by a wall of cars.

As the Metro rocked him, he reflected that he'd grown up in a suburb, in New Jersey. His parents spoke French at home, and they talked about life in their Huguenot village. Of French country life in general. The peace of it. The delicious *croissants* and *baguettes*. The cheese. The *foie gras* and the duck *confit* and the comfort of a *cassoulet* on a winter's evening.

And he'd decided young that he wanted to live in France, wherever he could find a spot. And here he was. In Paris, not a Huguenot village. But that was okay. He was married to a lovely French woman who made him *cassoulet* for winter evenings. And he had a daughter who'd started on wine and was now so addicted to alcohol, she was loosing all good judgment. She was making bad choices, ones that would haunt her entire life.

He was six stops from Malakoff, in a car with all its windows open since there was no air conditioning, of course, when he realized he'd left his jacket at the *café*. He had to retrace all the distance he'd come.

Philippe had been a wild man growing up, and he'd cussed non-stop. Now he was trying to be a different man, trying to fill a special role, but sometimes a swear word was the only satisfying response to a situation.

"*Merde*," he muttered, picturing the long ride back to retrieve his forgotten jacket. He got off at the next stop. He followed the stairs up and then back down to the other side of the tracks. He had been 10 minutes from home, but now he wouldn't be home for another hour, at the earliest. He sighed as the train approached. He hated having to go back.

He took his seat in a fog of weariness. Then he smelled something raunchy. He looked up to see a man near him on the train, a bum who smelled so bad that even the women upwind of him had their noses buried in their scarves. His blue jeans were stained almost entirely brown and were so low on his hips, they would fall off and totally reveal his filthy underwear—if he had any—if he stood up. A drip hung from the end of his nose and hovered over his huge beard, splayed over his chest. He appeared to be asleep, slumped in his seat.

As the Metro rumbled along, Philippe thought, a mother once lifted him as a baby to her lips and kissed and kissed him. Now he was a wreck. What if Meredith followed this path? A baby once kissed from head to toe becoming a shambles.

The Metro jolted into the Varenne station. Outside the train's window, a replica of Rodin's black statue of Balzac leaned perilously backward, in danger of falling. Philippe thought he'd give this fallen human near him a good look, to acknowledge his humanity. He wasn't going to give him money, however, and he wasn't going to take him home, feed him, give him a shower or fresh clothes. The man couldn't be trusted around his wife, in his home. He was hopeless. He would say a prayer for him. What a great Christian he was.

At the *café*, he picked up the jacket. Going home he missed a train by five seconds. The doors closed as he descended the Metro stairs, and the train moved inevitably out of the station—without him. The helpful sign hanging from the ceiling said the next train wasn't for ten minutes. At eleven thirty at night, when I'm exhausted, ten minutes is an eternity, he thought. The only thing that can express my disappointment is to say, "Shit!"

He thought, if people who knew I'm a Christian were to overhear me, they'd be shocked and disappointed in me. I know it. But to relieve my negative feelings with an expletive seems to be irresistible to me.

"Shit" and *"merde"* both stand for ugly, stinking stuff, he thought. But considering my troubles with Meredith and how much I've prayed for her to no avail—it stands.

Chapter 12

He plodded from the Metro to his house and unlocked the gate. The points on the ends of the wrought iron bars embedded in the concrete wall along the front gave him a feeling of security against burglars. He quietly closed the gate behind him.

Instead of going up the front steps, he followed a tiled path to the back of the house. Fourteen-foot-high walls surrounded the property in back. Within the walls, behind the house, he and Elodie had a private garden. Well, the neighbors on one side could see it out their rear windows, because their house was attached to his. But they usually had those windows shuttered, so it felt private. He loved it.

He sank onto a weathered wooden bench. In the light evening breeze, his favorite thing was happening: each leaf of the ivy clinging to the walls was trembling individually. Philippe loved it when it rained, too: drops of water would collect on the five points of each leaf and swell until they dropped in their own sweet time to earth. He sat out in the garden in all seasons except winter, when Paris was locked in a damp, bone-numbing cold.

A bird flitted by, late to his nest. What did it feel like to be a bird, outdoors year round? What did they think of a Paris winter?

He looked up at the sky, finally dark. Worse than the humid coldness in winter was the lack of light. Philippe usually got up at seven and would wait, desperate, until eight-thirty for the sun to rise. And then it was always behind thick layers of clouds. If it occasionally broke through, he would drop what he was doing and rush outside to find a place where a sunbeam actually struck the earth.

With the sun so deep in the south that it barely made it over the tops of two-story buildings, finding a sunbeam in six-story Paris to bask in was difficult. He would plant himself in a sunny spot, and people would *bousculer* him, bump him with an embedded message: you're taking up too much room, as he stood soaking in the light.

But as soon as the sunlight reached the earth, moisture would rise and clouds would form and block the sun again. A week might go by before the sun came out for another five minutes. This past winter had been a particularly bad one. He had felt shaky inside for months, he had been so desperate for light.

But now it was summer, and the sky glowed until almost eleven at night. Glorious! It was after midnight, and time to go to bed.

"Hi, Elodie!" he called as he let himself in the front door.

"Philippe!" she called back. "In the kitchen."

Their house on Chemin de Fer—literally "the narrow way of iron," in other words, Railroad Street—was a beautiful refuge. Yes, the countertop in the kitchen was too low for a standard-issue human, but the house was spacious, with cross-ventilation in summer and snug windows in winter. It would do.

Elodie shook her sudsy hands into the sink.

"Meredees is drunk again."

Philippe groaned and leaned against the refrigerator. A postcard from his eldest daughter, living in Barcelona, Spain, fell to the floor along with its magnet. He bent wearily to pick them up.

"She wouldn't 'elp me—couldn't—wiz ze dishes," Elodie continued. "When I ask' her to 'elp, she stomp out in a fit. I watch her stagger up ze stairs."

"I don't know what to do," Philippe said. "I just don't know. I guess I'll talk to her tomorrow."

"Good luck with zat," Elodie said sourly. She carefully brushed her long bangs out of her eyes with a soapy index finger that she drew across her forehead.

"We've tried everything the Tough Love people suggested." Philippe's voice was near a whisper. "I've detached. Mostly with love. I've set boundaries—you have, too. We've insisted on respect. But what happens? She came to my office today and asked for money. I didn't give in."

"Good."

"Yeah, but where did she get the money to get drunk tonight?"

"Friends?"

Neither of them wanted to think too much about what Meredith might be doing for money. Philippe thought, her friends must be sick, like I am, of the way she gives everybody the touch.

"We've tried everything except—"

"Anyway," Elodie said in a new tone of briskness, "How was it at ze group?"

"I think it has talented people," Philippe replied, glad to let the painful topic of Meredith drop. "Their feedback will help me write better. But there's this one guy, John. Makes a lot of money. I know I shouldn't compare, but I get tired of being so strapped. I can only afford to sit in a *café* once a month."

"Eet's what you signed on for," Elodie said, her hands submerged in soapy water. "Unless you resink what it is you want to be when you grow up."

"Hah! Well, I guess I'll head to bed."

"Dry zese dishes?"

"Oh, yeah. Of course."

Chapter 13

The next morning, John was up early and surprised to find his daughter Emily in the kitchen. The cook didn't come in until eleven, so they had privacy to talk.

"So, cutie, what's on your agenda?" John asked, sitting down to a *croissant* that was by some miracle simultaneously flaky and buttery.

Only the French. He sipped his coffee. "Thanks for going to the *patisserie*, by the way."

Emily, sixteen years old, wavy blond hair halfway down her back, blue eyes, was dressed in a cute, tight, pink knit shirt that showed her curves and cleavage. John knew that it had cost her all of six euros at the Sunday outdoor market on Boulevard Raspail. Thank God she wasn't following her mother's footsteps. Yet.

"Well, I have school—"

"I have a great day planned," John said enthusiastically. "I'm meeting another potential client—a Saudi prince. Oil money! Won't run dry in my lifetime. Hard to impress these Saudi princes, though. They race around Paris in Bugattis, they have high-priced whores—whoops, sorry, honey—they eat at Maxime's every night. What should I do to impress him? Huh?"

She quietly watched her father.

"What's in the shopping bags? You went with your mother?"

"I didn't buy—"

"I'm like a gentleman in Victorian times, wondering how I'll keep my women in all their ribbons, bows and finery. Did you buy something cute? I'm thinking, when I land my next client, I'll buy a GPS for the Grey Skies. I want you to come out with me this weekend. I'd like to talk—"

Emily had picked up her *croissant*, but now she threw it down on her plate.

"Hey, watch out!" John said, still in an expansive mood, leaning back in his chair. "Don't break your mother's Royal Copenhagen Flora Danica—the most expensive china in the world. Of course."

He said it to her retreating back as she marched out of the kitchen.

John threw his arms wide in surprise and leaned back on two legs of his chair.

"Emily, what did I say?" he called.

The door slammed.

"Women!" John muttered. "Must be that time of the month."

Cassandra came into the kitchen wearing a floor-length white satin *peignoir* over a floor-length white silk nightgown.

"Hi, honey!" John said. "You look great!"

"Don't start, John," Cassandra muttered as she poured a cup of coffee.

"What, you've got it, too?"

"Got what? Make sense, John." Cassandra grabbed a no-fat, no-sugar yogurt out of the refrigerator and sat down where Emily had been. She didn't bother with the flakes of *croissant* Emily had created by throwing her breakfast. The cook would take care of that.

"Never mind," John said. "What's in the shopping bags?"

"Just some stuff."

"Well, show me, I'd like to see."

"Later maybe. I'm meeting friends at the gym in a few minutes."

"Nobody talks to me around here," John said, pushing away from the table. He put his breakfast dishes in the sink. "I'm going to work so we can afford all the Gucci and Dior and Chanel you buy."

Cassandra didn't answer. In two minutes, John was out the door.

He ambled along Boulevard Raspail, passing unique little shops. Paris was a city of almost nothing but *boutiques*. Cassandra was getting into a world of trouble here.

Oh well, in spite of the credit card bill, he was looking forward to his day in the office. His pet investment, the Dow Jones-UBS Precious Metals exchange traded fund, otherwise known as an ETF, was indexed to gold and silver and had been doing brilliantly on the New York Stock Exchange. By luck, or maybe instinct, or maybe inborn talent—John smiled to himself—he had caught it at a deep low. It had grown steadily since.

The other two ETFs tracked silver bullion and had grown almost as substantially.

He had bought similar ETFs on the EuroNext and the Hang Seng markets. He had cleaned out his less risky investments to put all the money into these new ones, and had advised his clients to do the same. They had gone along with it because of his renown as an investor.

His approach was unconventional. It went against prevailing Wall Street wisdom, all that stuff about not putting too many eggs in one basket. It defied convention, it was risky. And it was brilliant. His gold and silver ETFs had increased everybody's money by twenty percent in just nine months.

He was in a good mood when he opened the door to Germaine & Co.

"Anjali, hold my calls," he said, walking into his office.

"Sir, the phones—"

"I said hold the calls."

"Sir—"

He stopped mid-stride and looked down at her, behind her desk.

"What is it, exactly, about 'No calls' that you don't understand?"

"Sir. Your top three stocks are tanking on the Hang Seng. You've had calls from Chen in Hong Kong."

"They aren't stocks, they're ETFs."

"Yes, sir."

"So the ETFs are tanking in Asia. That's different than the New York Stock Exchange or the European market. Why didn't you say so?"

"Sir, you had calls from Dieter at EuroNext also."

"It's just a correction. Get Chen in Hong Kong for me."

"Yes, sir."

Anjali was dialing as John closed the door to his office. He took his suit jacket off, draped it carefully on a hanger, and put it in the closet. He took his father's cuff links off, placed them carefully on a corner of his desk, and rolled up his sleeves. The intercom buzzed.

"Chen on line 1, sir."

John pushed the button for line 1 and put the phone to his ear.

"Chen, what's happening?"

"I'm not sure, sir, I'm hunting to find out why, but I do know that our ETFs are tanking here."

"Let me log on and look at it, and I'll call you back," John said.

"It's still falling. It's extraordinary. I think we should sell right now." Chen sounded deeply concerned.

"Give me a minute, damn it!" Suddenly John's heart was pounding. His gut began to scream that this was a bad one. He tucked the phone under his chin and fumbled with his keyboard.

What to do, what to do? He needed facts. He hit a wrong key as he typed his password because his fingers were suddenly sticky with sweat.

Why was he so slow? Hurry, man! he urged himself.

Finally he was logged in, and the charts of his three favorite metals ETFs on the Hang Seng were on his screen. Yes, it was confirmed, he could see for himself that everything was caving. He brought up his New York ETFs on his screen. The New York Stock Exchange wasn't officially open yet, but his ETFs were tanking there, too, in early morning online trading.

His holdings—and his clients'—were losing value at the rate of hundreds of thousands of dollars per minute. He had to sell while there was still some value left.

"Chen, what are you doing, still on the phone, man? Go, sell!"

"I was selling while we talked, John," Chen said quietly.

"Why didn't you call me at home earlier?"

"I did but your cell phone was off."

John didn't have a landline in the apartment—Cassandra had never gotten around to having it installed. Waiting for Paris technicians irked her: it cut into her shopping, exercise, and *café* time. John remembered that he had turned his cell off the night before in order to pay attention at the writers' group and had forgotten to turn it on again. Just for that, he would quit that blasted group.

He'd lost millions of his own and clients' money because his phone was off. An expletive launched out of his gut and flew past his lips.

John clicked off Chen's line and hit the intercom.

"Anjali, get our trading desk in La Defense on the line."

"Yes, sir."

At that moment, line 1 lit up.

"Pierre on line 1," Anjali's electronically distorted voice said.

John clicked in.

"Ze bottom falling out on the EuroNext exchange," Pierre said with his heavy French accent. "Our 'olding—"

"—Sell!"

"Yes, sir," Pierre said. "Our biggest ETF lose sees point' while I been on zuh line."

"Why? What's happened?"

"It's zat a beeg new vein of silver 'as been discover' in Canada. Close to zuh surface, easy to mine. Should be on zuh market fast."

John could not have foreseen that. He couldn't be blamed for this. But he would be.

Anjali's voice broke in on the intercom. "Sir, Dieter on line 2 from Amsterdam."

John clicked off line 1 and onto line 2.

"Yes, sell! Sell!" he shouted at Dieter. He clicked off line 2. Line 3 lit up. He punched the button.

"John, did you pay the bill? The credit card isn't working," Cassandra's relaxed, smooth voice said.

"Stop buying things, it's not a good time!" John shouted and clicked off line 3. Line 1 lit up again.

"Aw, shit! Shit!" John said. He punched the intercom button.

"Who's on line 1?" he shouted at Anjali.

"Sir, it's Mr. Chaigne."

John punched line 1 while taking a breath and exhaling his panic so his voice would be calm.

"John, what's happening to my money?"

"The market is going through a correction—"

"Correction! Shit on that! Get my money out NOW!"

"Already done, just take it easy, what goes down goes up after a while and does even better. We'll buy at the low—"

"I'm not buying, I'm suing you every which way I can! My lawyer will be in touch."

"Max, you knew those ETFs were risky before you—"

"I'll wring whatever I can out of your hide!"

The line went dead. Lines 2, 3, and 4 lit up, one after the other.

"Anjali." John poked at the intercom button. "Anjali!"

"Yes?"

"Call the New York head of office on his cell, his landline, whatever. Keep calling him until you wake him up and then put him through to me."

"Yes, sir."

John spent the rest of the day tracking his portfolio on his monitor and trying to reassure clients. He figured that his personal net worth had dropped to less than the level he'd been at when he was twenty-seven. Six clients were threatening lawsuits.

Against traditional investment wisdom, he had put all of his money into one commodity, precious metals. His instincts, honed by years of watching the ticker tapes and then the electronic screens, had told him they were going up. And they had done so beautifully, for a while. His instincts had failed to tell him when to sell. Now he was close to broke. He had no IRAs—he'd always made more than the federal maximum to be able to invest in them. He had a small 401K. He had been more interested in buying status symbols than building his nest egg. He'd always figured he'd have time and money to invest in that later.

In other words, he'd been loony.

At the end of the day, John sat in his big leather chair and tried to rally himself. You've been through downturns before, he thought. But this time was much, much worse. Keep your head, John, he thought.

He opened a drawer and poured Happy Van Winkle, the most expensive Kentucky bourbon in the world at $2,000 per bottle, into one of two Baccarat tumblers. When he had his drink poured, he capped the bottle and laid it back down carefully. The drawer slid silently, elegantly shut. The intercom buzzed.

"Sir?" It was Anjali on the intercom.

"Yes?"

"The IRS wants an appointment with you."

Chapter 14

That evening, after learning that Cassandra and Emily were out together again, John went down the elevator to the street to buy a *crêpe* and then back up to his office to eat it while looking out at his panoramic view. The *crêpe* artist had toasted a two-inch fringe of cheese that spilled out onto the hot griddle. The golden brown lacy fringe crunched just a bit and dissolved in his mouth as he bit into it. He watched a *péniche* motor slowly down the Seine and pass under the Pont Alexandre III, a riotously decorated bridge with gilt pegasuses, river gods, and cupids.

When he had savored the last of the *crêpe avec jambon et fromage*, he washed his hands, fingertips shiny with delicious grease, in his little bathroom. He dreaded what he had to do next. He sighed and sat down to do it.

John woke up his computer and opened the Excel spread sheet, the one that kept the score between him and other men, between him and his father, the one entitled "John's Worth."

The vast majority of his investment balance had nosedived. He was now worth a fraction of what he had been yesterday.

He felt nauseous. He looked out the window to get his bearings. A sleek cabin cruiser was racing downriver, the current helping to push the boat toward the sea. John felt with pain that he could no longer afford toys like that. Salesmen at the boat shows used to kowtow to him. Now it was possible that he couldn't afford even a GPS.

He turned back to his computer screen. He had to do this.

Step one. The value listed next to his ETFs' names had to be drastically reduced. John's head spun as he typed in the new figures. When he summed up the column, he was heartsick. He used to have the advantage over most men. Now he was just an ordinary schmuck.

He studied the detailed list of his and Cassandra's property and each item's monetary value. When he saw mention of the Gull, his sailboat harbored on the Long Island Sound, his father's face came to mind. His father had owned a boat, too, a fifty-foot wooden craft that Teddy Roosevelt had been aboard once, according to the ship's log.

Shame over his father's suicide, committed after the crash of 1987, perhaps after he'd made an evaluation like the one John was making now, washed over him. His father couldn't take the losses in stride. John wasn't sure he could, either.

John had put on his father's cufflinks to go down to buy the *crêpe*. Parisians, he had noticed, dress for everything. Unless they were in spiffy nightwear. They answered the ring of the postman at the street door in their *negligées*.

He tugged at his cufflinks now. They had large squares of black onyx set on larger squares of silver. A *marquis* diamond glittered in the center of each one. He wore them to remind himself to work harder so he didn't end up like his father, broke and broken.

It appeared as though his father's failure had become his own.

Through the haze of his desire to deny the truth, John could see he would have to sell the mansion in Greenwich. He would have to fire people and close offices, to downsize and live and work somewhere more affordable in Paris. He would have to sell his vintage cars—the Model T, the Bentley, the Rolls, and the motorbikes, stored in the Greenwich mansion's garage. What else? The Astin Martin Vantage in Paris.

What about the boats? No, you gotta have a boat! He couldn't sell them. Not the Gull, that won regattas on the Long Island Sound.

Not the Grey Skies, that challenged him in the English Channel. Oh, God, no, not the boats!

Next to each item of personal property, he typed what he estimated he could sell the thing for. The mansion's potential price would have to be confirmed by a real estate expert. He sent off an email to the broker who had sold him the house.

He started a new sheet, listing what he could save when he downsized to a smaller apartment. He went online to research the rents for smaller offices. He calculated what would he save when he no longer had to pay garage fees for the Aston Martin.

Let's revisit the boats idea. Maybe not two boats. Try to find a way to save the Grey Skies in Cherbourg. Sell the Gull, and that way, I'll save on fees for its berth in Greenwich, and the cost of having a crew winterize her, pull her from the water in November, store her in the boatyard, and get her ready in March for the new season.

In his mind and on his spreadsheet, he sold and sold, cut and cut. Drastically.

When he saw what he was left with, he sat, aghast. No toys, no luxuries like a big apartment in the Sixth, and he saw that he might not even be able to hang onto the Grey Skies.

How could he have risked so much on just a few ETFs? How could he have been so loony?

He leaned forward, leather of his chair creaking, and held his head in his hands. He wished he could cry, but after a few minutes he sensed that there would be no relief for his emotions tonight.

Chapter 15

John didn't tell Cassandra the day of the crash.

By seven in the evening of the second day after ground zero, he was exhausted. He knew he had to go home and tell Cassandra what had happened. He wasn't too sure how she was going to react.

He limped from his office to the apartment, a Princeton intramural rugby injury to his right knee flaring with pain.

"Bonsoir, monsieur," said the elderly porter, short, wide of girth, and hoping against hope for a tip. He had no wine to go with his dinner.

"Evening," John said, nodding in his direction to acknowledge him but not seeing the man. He dragged himself up the stairs to the apartment.

"Kids, we have a problem," John called as he opened the door.

He was met with silence.

"Hello? Where is everyone? Cassandra, I have to talk to you."

He found her in the kitchen.

"Why didn't you answer when I called?" he asked.

"I knew you'd find me," she said casually.

The cook had roasted a chicken with sprigs of rosemary and slices of lemon under the skin of the breast. The kitchen smelled wonderful. That was another thing they could save money on—lay off the cook and the housekeeper.

Cassandra sliced the chicken breast, taking one slice for her and putting three on the Royal Danica for John. A bit of *blette*—Swiss chard—and she put both plates on the kitchen table.

"Thanks, honey," John said and sat. His stomach suddenly tightened at the sight of the food. "I'm not sure I can eat."

"So what's wrong?" Cassandra cut the tiniest bite that any human possibly could. She lifted it slowly to her mouth.

"In a few words—darling—the bottom has fallen out. Most of our investments—they did so brilliantly for months—suddenly tanked on a bit of news that I couldn't have foreseen."

"What?" Cassandra's blue eyes were riveted on him.

"We're not rich anymore. I'm afraid we have to sell some things."

"What things?"

"I'd like to sell—we need to sell—the Greenwich mansion. I'm sorry, Cass, I know you love that place."

She put her knife and fork on her plate.

"I can't believe it!"

"Well, it's true. I spent hours yesterday assessing what we could do, what kind of life we'll have. I'm afraid we have to fire the cook and housekeeper, and I have to ask you to stop shopping. We simply can't afford it."

Cassandra stared.

"I'll regroup, I'll build the business again. Don't worry, we'll be on top of the world again in no time."

"Well, let's not be hasty. I'm not going to fire the help just yet."

"I need you to do it tomorrow. Pay them to the end of next week. That's 10 days' severance pay. That's the best I can do."

"Slow down, just a minute!

"Really, we have to economize. We have to make do for a while, like the rest of the world. Believe me, Cass, I don't like it any more than you do."

"I don't want to be the one making all the sacrifices!"

"I'm selling all the cars, the motorcycles, the Gull in Greenwich—"

"And if I know you, you're keeping the Grey Skies!"

"It's the one thing—"

"Of course, you get to keep your toys, but you expect me to —"

"I'm selling everything but the Grey Skies, just until I see how things work out."

"What do you need a boat for?"

"You gotta have a boat."

"Well, I gotta have my gym, my cook and my housekeeper. Lunch out. That's minimum. All my friends have that—and more."

"And we will again, Cass. Let's call it quits for the night. Come on, give your old man a hug."

Cassandra and John stood, and he gathered her into his arms. She didn't snuggle into him, she just stood there, didn't contribute.

"I'll start again. We'll be flush again soon," he said. "Just stop using the credit cards."

She pulled out of the embrace, gave him a skeptical glance, and left the room.

Chapter 16

Two days later, John returned home. He had spent the day putting all their Greenwich possessions on the market. He felt that, in losing the Greenwich house and boat, he was losing all ties to his native country. With them sold, what reason did he have to go back?

He felt like he had no home, no country. This is the expat feeling, he thought.

"Cass? Emily?" he called. He heard voices down the hall.

He found them in the master bedroom. Cass was trying on outfits from an assortment of shopping bags, each emblazoned with a famous designer's name. Emily was lying back on the gray satin duvet, propped up by pillows covered in black and white silk.

He sat in an upholstered chair near the bed, even though it was heaped with Cassandra's bras and slips.

"Kids, what is all this?" he said.

"Can't it wait, John." Cassandra sounded bored and kept posing and eyeing herself—tall, sleek, shapely—in a little black dress by Dior. It still had its tags dangling.

"No, it can't wait!" John snapped, annoyed by her condescension. "I told you to stop shopping!"

"Don't be so boring," Cassandra said. She posed in several attitudes in the mirror.

John turned to Emily. "We've hit a speed bump in our finances, honey. No worries. But for now we aren't rich."

Cassandra was finally looking at him, thinking. He stood up, and a black bra, one of eight on the chair, slipped off and fell to the floor. He walked toward her, arms open for a hug.

"Cassandra," he said, "we can get through this. I'll start again. We'll get there."

She dodged his embrace.

"How could you let this happen?" she said. Standing In her little $2,500 black dress that he had paid for, she wound up and slapped him, her slim white arm a blur.

"Cass!" Her handprint began to show pink on his face. "We have to work together. Be reasonable!"

"I'm not interested in 'starting over,'" she said, mimicking baby talk. She turned her back on him. "Unzip me."

"Where's 'please'?"

'You're deadly boring, John. Emily, unzip me."

"Aw, Mom, take it easy."

In two quick strokes, Cassandra reached behind herself from the top, then the bottom, and unzipped the dress. She stepped gracefully out of it and threw it over the chair John had been sitting on. It slipped off. John picked it up.

"This goes back to the shop tomorrow," he said. "That's for starters."

When Emily heard that, she made herself scarce, running out of the room and closing the door behind her.

John said, "And we have to move into a smaller apartment."

"I'm not going anywhere with you!" Cassandra said, grabbing one end of the dress. She pulled. John held fast.

"You have six other ones like it in there," he said, gesturing to the huge armoire.

"Yeah, but I want this one!" She stripped its price tags off and then yanked again. Stitching popped somewhere in the dress.

John let go. He was sick of her. "Fine, take it, I hope it falls off you in public." He lurched toward the door, his old rugby injury flaring up.

"Bastard! Loser!" Cassandra screamed at John as he left, slamming the door shut after him. Then she yanked the door wide open. "You're a failure! Go to hell!" she screamed and slammed the door again.

As John lurched toward Emily's room, she slammed her door shut, too. John knocked on it softly.

"Open the door, kitten, this has nothing to do with you."

Emily opened the door and stood with one hand on her hip, the other still holding the door, ready to slam it. She glared at her father. He took a step into her room.

"Honey, let's talk. Let me tell you what happened."

"Daddy, I—"

"—It was the worst day. Clients are threatening to sue me."

"Daddy, I—"

"We'll get through this. I'll keep you in private school for now. No, no, forever! Don't worry, your friends won't know--"

"Daddy, listen—"

"I'm on your side, baby, you know that."

"Daddy—"

"I promise you—"

"Daddy!"

"What, baby? I'm listening."

"No, you're not! That's the whole problem. Why don't you just leave me alone!" She pushed on John's stomach with all her tiny girl strength, trying to budge him, trying to shove him out of the room.

"Not you, too, Emily! What's this family coming to? What are we, monsters? Stop! I'm going, I'm going." John stood just outside Emily's door, looking in.

"Honey—"

"You don't listen to me. I won't listen to you," Emily said with an inescapable logic and slammed the door shut in her father's face.

John clutched his knee and grimaced with pain. He muttered to himself. "The brat! Slamming the door on her father!" He could hear his father saying, "I brought you into this world and I can take you out of it!" His fist hardened into a knot, but he knew he could no more threaten Emily than he could fly.

He limped to the living room. With all that had been spent to decorate, money gleamed from every surface. He could hear Cassandra's footsteps on the parquet floor of the hallway. She stood before him, half his size.

"Cass, let's keep our family together."

"My final answer on that is no," she said coldly. "You have to leave."

"I'm not going anywhere until I'm ready!" he roared. A hotel would just be more expense. Cassandra could go stay with one of her rich girlfriends until things got sorted out. That's all he and Cassandra had in common: things. The bigger the price tag on them, the better, in Cassandra's mind.

"Cassandra, you should be supportive of me as your husband."

"I'm not the failure here, John, you are!"

"But I can start again, we'll rebuild—"

"I don't want to. I don't want you, I just want my things, and I'll find somebody else."

Suddenly a rage exploded in John more ferocious than anything he'd ever felt. It boiled and fumed. She wanted this Baccarat cut crystal lamp more than him? He grabbed it, and little prisms jumped over the walls, ceiling, and parquet floor. He whipped its wire out of the socket.

"What did this cost, $7,000 was it?" he asked in a cool voice, revealing nothing of the anger roiling within.

"$10,000."

He lifted it above his head.

"John, don't, don't—"

He raised his arm as high as he could and, with all the force of his six foot two inch frame, he dashed the lamp onto the floor. The crystal shattered, the shade bounced off, and the lightbulb exploded.

Cassandra shrieked.

"You idiot! $10,000! It was beautiful!"

"This stuff is shit!" he screamed.

His rage ebbed swiftly. He'd spent his life working for this stuff. And now he needed to sell this stuff. It wasn't shit, it was cash. He could not afford to indulge his anger like this.

"Get out, you little bitch," he said quietly. Cassandra heard the threat in his voice and retreated. As she went down the hall, she pounded on Emily's door. "Pack up, we're leaving," she shouted.

Emily, that was another issue. John was too tired to take that one on tonight. One battle at a time, he thought.

John went to Emily's room, hugged her, and said he'd see her Saturday, to keep her cellphone on and answer when he called so he'd know where she was. She nodded, tears streaking her face, tendrils of her blonde hair stuck to her wet cheeks.

When the taxi came, John let the driver heft Cassandra's two huge, matching suitcases on wheels into the trunk, and Emily's smaller bit of luggage.

"You'll pay," Cassandra snarled as she climbed in the back.

John stooped to peer more deeply into the car, where Emily sat crying quietly.

"I love you," he whispered and closed the door. The taxi pulled away. He watched it go until it turned at Boulevard Saint Germain and disappeared.

The pain in his knee was now blinding. Suddenly he was exhausted. He staggered back up to the apartment, through the dining room to the kitchen. The cook had left a casserole on the countertop, covered with a glass lid. The kitchen smelled good. I need something to eat, he thought, then I'll go to bed. He lifted the lid and the casserole's fragrant steam, full of scents of thyme, bay leaf, rosemary, and *crème fraiche*, wafted to his nose. His stomach twisted. He leaned one hand on the counter, feeling lightheaded, and put the lid back down. He couldn't eat.

Chapter 17

After church, Philippe went to a photography group he'd discovered online. The afternoon was beautiful—a breeze, sun, and occasional relief from the sun when thick Paris clouds blew over. The leader was a blonde girl in her twenties who had everybody stand in a circle outside Temple Metro station and introduce themselves.

A young woman emerged from the Metro and joined the circle. She looked a bit like Meredith. She wore short-shorts and a white lacy tank top with a neckline so deeply scooped that a substantial portion of her bosom and her see-through lacy bra showed.

He wrested his eyes away. *Mon dieu*! Here's yet another one who didn't get the memo about modesty. And she'd probably set a trend. Young women dressed like this all over the city—what havoc.

He hoped Meredith wouldn't follow the trend. But she probably would…he had failed to instill…

"Okay, we'll go to the park first," the leader said, "and figure it out from there. Any questions?"

Philippe raised his hand. "Can anyone show me how to change the light settings on this camera?" He had looked in the handbook, but there'd been no information.

"I can help you," the half-naked young woman said sweetly.

"We'll figure it out," a tall Asian guy with the biggest camera said with a friendly grin.

"Thanks."

Everyone but Philippe had big cameras with huge lenses. He didn't care. He was here to see what these photographers took shots of so he could improve his own eye. He was also here to relax, to wind down after church, which still had an element of performance for him. How could it not? All eyes were on him for half an hour, forty minutes if he went too long. Thank God Protestants expected a sermon longer than seven minutes. Short was even more work. Next sermon: a review of verses on modesty. No, that's not the most urgent topic…

Philippe spotted an interesting architectural detail high above the street, under the eaves of a building. With his camera, he zoomed in. Oh, it's a naked woman. Ha! That sounded strange. It's a statue of a naked woman. Of course, Paris, you need one under the eaves of every building, not just this one. And on every easel in every gallery.

Well, who was he? An arbiter of art, architecture, and fashion? I'll take a picture—why'd I do that?—and let go of that train of thought.

The young woman dodged ahead of him as the group ambled to a nearby park. He tried to look somewhere else. He looked across the street, and there was a *patisserie*, full of sugar he couldn't eat. He looked back. Wow, look at that bottom move! he thought. He yanked his gaze away to look at something else.

The leader turned to them at the entrance, marked by a frilly wrought iron gate.

"It's against the law in France to photograph children not your own, so keep that in mind," she said. "There's plenty to shoot here, though."

They ambled into the park. Philippe noticed that its paths were paved the usual Parisian way, with hard-packed sand and fine gravel. A child chased a football, and each step raised a cloud of dust. If the air pollution didn't get him, Philippe mused, or the cigarette smoke from the multitude of French smokers, then the dust in the parks would. Or maybe his demise would be all the minerals in the tapwater, the *calcaire* known to cause kidney stones. Heat water in a brand new pot and watch a white rime of calcium stick to the sides. Living in Paris had some health risks.

The Asian guy stood just inside the park, peering around him, so Philippe asked him about the settings on his little look-and-shoot. The Asian guy showed him what to do, speaking in perfect French. They formed a bit of a bond as they huddled over the tiny camera and poked at its settings. Philippe could not have concentrated with that young woman's bosom in front of him, rising and falling with every breath. Thank God for Asian guys with cameras.

They paired up for a while. His name was Ji, and he was of Korean heritage, born in Paris. They strolled the dusty park paths, chatting amicably for a while, firing off shots. They turned a corner, and Ji whipped his camera to his eye and clicked. Philippe looked to find the opportunity Ji had spotted.

A three-piece rock band was setting up in a corner of the park. The tall male guitar player was wearing a schoolgirl's red plaid jumper that fell to mid-thigh, black socks to the knee, and red high-top Keds. His skinny thighs between the socks and the jumper were white and hairy. He had a white Zorro eyemask painted onto the upper half of his face, and smeary red lipstick on his lips. It was noteworthy.

Philippe had nowhere near Ji's zoom power on his little camera, so he strolled closer. The drummer played a riff, which inspired the guitar player to chime in, and his electric notes pierced the hum of people chatting in the park. The guitarist turned to look at his drummer and nodded happily.

Philippe lifted his camera, feeling guilty for singling this guy out, but how could he not? This guy expected it anyway. As he focused, the guitar player turned back to him, smiling right at him. Philippe smiled back, a little worried for the guy—where was this mode of dress going to lead? Or had already led? Or was it just part of the act?—and took a few shots. The musician never stopped moving, bobbing his head, bobbing his guitar's head. These shots would be blurry.

Ji came up next to him. "Pretty interesting, isn't it?" he said.

"Yes, but I'm having trouble capturing it," Philippe replied. He waved his little camera in the air. "But what can you expect for eighty euros?" and he laughed.

"Shame on you!" Ji said with a smile as he patted his long zoom lens. The bond they'd forged so quickly did support Ji's making that statement, Philippe thought. He laughed at himself, too, but he was also thinking, if you don't have a thousand euros for a camera and fancy lenses, you just don't.

Ji moved on as Philippe looked back at the guitar player. God loved this guy dearly, no matter what outfit he wore. Cross-dressing for a rock concert wasn't so bad. What else had this guy been up to? Same stuff I did…

The guitar player hit another crazy riff, and Philippe looked at the man's hairy white thighs. I hope this guy will be in heaven, he thought. We need people like him. It would add to the fun.

Chapter 18

He moved on and took photos of the houses surrounding the park, of black wrought-iron balconies flowing with red geraniums that cascaded against the white walls of Paris. He captured the sculpted details on the steeple of a church. He met up with Ji, who took a shot of a candy seller's stall. The huge table was spread with bins of different colored candy.

Great, I wouldn't have seen that shot, Philippe thought, snapping two from different angles himself.

After two hours, the group found an Irish pub and parked themselves under an awning. Philippe left because beer was not possible and a soda would cost too much, in both euros and calories. Diet soda was rare in Paris *cafés*. Besides, there was music blaring from the loudspeakers, and it would be hard to talk. He wasn't in the mood for small talk—he wanted to warn people that everything wasn't jolly good, let's all have another beer, that there was a war between good and evil going on, and the front lines went straight through their own hearts. But they didn't want to hear it. So he waved goodbye to the leader and Ji and headed for the Metro.

He sat in the rumbling train and prayed for Meredith. A Muslim family got on and sat across from him, the wife wrapped in scarves and encased in robes. As the train started to move again, the father kissed the bare toes of his little girl in the stroller. She waved her arms in delight. Meredith used to be like that, in my care, under my protection, Philippe thought. I kissed her toes, too.

He was three stops from home when he began to reflect on the photography group. He felt thankful for the nice day and felt a reprieve from worry about Meredith. What great people to be with, so helpful about my camera, and nice people in this Metro car, too. You know what? These are the only people I have in the whole world right now. Not Elodie, not Meredith, just these dear folks.

I bless this Muslim family in front of me, this infant girl in a stroller—were they going to smother that girl in scarves, too, just like her mother, when she got to what age? Twelve or so—but at least it was modest—a little too modest?—but I bless them and I wish a strong voice for that girl, to get through all the fabric that will bind her, and I bless everyone on this train.

The train is humming, I feel a warmth, a golden honey energy, it's enough to make everyone happy, isn't it, they're all happy, and it's enough to make this train run, it's God, he makes the trains run, he's the source. I can see sparks flying where the wheels meet the track, not the harsh pointy kind that shower down and disappear but the gentle kind, the kind that hover and linger over the steel, they shimmer and float like fairly lights, they bless the train and make it go faster. So much joyful energy around, let's use it to make this train really go…The train feels like it's flying, it's running so smooth, God is here…

Chapter 19

Before she had left Mumbai, at her parent's urging, Anjali had agreed to call them first thing every Saturday morning. For her it was nine o'clock; for them, it was three and a half hours later. She longed to hear their voices and yet dreaded what they would say. She used her laptop in her *chambre de bonne* to call with video.

"Amma, Appa, how are you?" she said. Anjali addressed them with the Tamil names for Mom and Dad, as a nod to her Pondicherry roots.

"Darling! How are you?" Her mother's voice was shrill with excitement. Her parents looked like themselves on her laptop's screen, except with huge noses. Anjali assumed that her laptop was making the most of her nose, too.

"I'm fine. I'm in my flat, a little small, but good. I love Paris."

"Oh, a little different from Mumbai?" her father's voice boomed. He didn't sound happy. He might as well have said, Don't love it too much, we expect you back.

"The Gupta's called yesterday," her mother said.

Anjali felt pursued.

"We said you would be back soon." And ready to marry their son.

"I won't be back for a year, Amma, don't mislead them. And they know that. We all agreed."

"It's too bad you didn't have your engagement finalized before you left," her mother said. "But I guess it's no problem, everything's fine." That meant she was stressed. "But you don't need a year, six months should be enough."

Anjali had been afraid they would do that—start whittling.

"I have to take this chance," Anjali said, "to see if I can do it, write the screenplay of my dreams. We said a year. You agreed before I left. Don't—"

"No worries. Everything's fine." They peered at her through the computer, all nose, wishing her home and married, she knew it.

"Well, I'm going to this great historic library to write in a little while," Anjali said. "It was built in the 1550s. It has a stone circular staircase, gilded beams, turrets, diamond-paned windows, and Wifi!"

Her parents didn't smile under their big noses.

"I loved taking you to the Taj Mahal," her father said. "Remember that trip, when you were little?" India has lots of history, too, he was saying. More history than Europe.

"Yes, Appa, it was nice. Well, I have to go. Lots of scenes to write. Then I'm meeting Aasha at the Eiffel Tower. You know what's funny? I work in the Montparnasse Tower, and Parisians say it's better to look at the city from the top of that than from the Tour Eiffel for many reasons. Because you can see the Tour Eiffel, which you can't when you're standing on it. Because the Tour Montparnasse is cheaper to get in, and the line is not as long. And the extra bonus—when you're in the Montparnasse Tower, you don't have to look at it!"

"Write down your first impressions of Paris and send them to me," her mother said. Of the two, she was the most interested in her writing.

"Okay. Well…"

"Anjali! Don't go just yet. Show us around your apartment," her mother said.

"Sure." Anjali manipulated the laptop to show them the shower, bed, sink, window.

"It's small…" Her mother sounded doubtful. "Show me the inside of your fridge!"

"Amma!"

"Go ahead, you can show me."

Anjali opened the door to the two-foot-high fridge.

"See, there's a container of *dal* I made yesterday, and rice, and some chicken *masala*, and a package of *rotis*. Nowhere near as good as you make, Amma!" It might be a reason to go home, as a matter of fact. Frozen *rotis* just stunk compared to her mother's laboriously homemade ones. Anjali didn't have time to do all that.

"What's that on the door?" Amma croaked.

Anjali was horrified at what she had mistakenly shown her mother. An opened bottle of white wine.

"Have you been drinking?" Mummie's terror was evident.

"I had a friend over, and we each had one glass."

"Was that Aasha?"

Yes, it was, but Anjali couldn't ruin things with Aasha's parents.

"No, a new friend. A girl."

"Is she Indian? From a good family? Who is she?"

"Don't worry."

"You aren't safe if you're out drinking, and neither is your friend."

"She stayed over with me. Everything's fine."

"Be very careful, Anjali."

"Yes, I will be."

"Take care of yourself," Appa said, his deep voice resonating with concern.

"Great, Appa, I will. *Ciao*, you guys!"

Her parents echoed her, and Anjali disconnected.

That night, after a whirlwind day of writing and sightseeing, including taking a selfie with the Mona Lisa in Le Louvre, Anjali sat on her bed with the table/desk pulled over to her, her dinner of hurriedly reheated *dal* and thawed-out *rotis*, and wept with homesickness.

Chapter 20

Sunday morning was Anjali's time to talk to Ravi. He was a little erratic, calling ten to twenty minutes late sometimes, or postponing their chat for tennis, football, or cricket. But he was a nice young man. Anjali usually forgave him these inconsistencies.

Today he called her computer eight minutes past the appointed time. Not too bad, she'd get to the Musée D'Orsay to meet Aasha in plenty of time. Today was the first Sunday of the month, and all the museums in Paris were free, with commensurate lines of tourists.

"How's it going?" he asked. His brown face had regular features that made him incredibly handsome. A heartthrob. He could work in Bollywood with those looks, Anjali thought.

"Well! I got lots of scenes written and revised yesterday," she said. "And you?"

"I'm going out to play tennis with a colleague," he said. "I have to leave in five minutes."

This irked her. If he hadn't been late calling, they'd have more time to talk. But she looked at his appealing face, big brown eyes, and settled down.

"How was it at work this week?" he asked.

She couldn't tell anybody in India that something big had gone wrong for her boss the previous week. She didn't want people to worry and order her home. So she focused on the least worrisome event.

"Okay. John couldn't print out a letter for himself on Friday. Who can't do that? I had to do it for him."

"Well, you lived up to the stereotype people have of Indians, that we're all tech wizards."

"Well, aren't we?" Anjali laughed, and Ravi smiled. He worked in the information technology department of a bank in Mumbai and was on his way up that particular ladder. At least her family and his family hoped.

"And your week?" she asked.

"Nothing interesting. Listen, I have to go. I just thought of something I have to take care of before I leave."

This hadn't been a very satisfying chat. But at least they had connected for a little while

"Okay, have fun."

"You, too."

"Au revoir."

"What's that? Oh, yes, you, too." He clicked off.

Anjali stared at her laptop's empty screen for a while.

Chapter 21

Carol walked into Trapèze on Monday. Trapèze meant both trapezoid and trapeze in French. She thought it was a pretty clever name for an off-beat moving pictures company that tried to take viewers on a wild trapeze ride. In better times, the name had given her inspiration to write freewheeling scenes. Today didn't feel like that kind of day. The loss of Jeffrey was rather pressing on her, indeed driving her into the ground.

After plopping her huge pocketbook in its own file drawer, she turned her fan on because the air conditioning was so pathetic, like everywhere else in France. She aimed the fan carefully at her chair. This was likely to be the only thing she had control over today.

As she stood, her eyes glanced over but failed to see the colorful framed posters of Trapèze films on her walls. Gregoire had provided them when he first hired her three years ago. Two recent additions had her name in the credits as screenwriter. Some days, when she noticed them, she felt proud. Not today. The only energy she could muster was to drag herself off to get coffee.

She had told the new babysitter to call her every half hour on her first day with Louise. The woman was a trained English nanny, in her fifties, came with references, but Carol prayed her child wouldn't be kidnapped or worse.

She stepped out of her office, built against an inner wall, its only window overlooking the corridor. It might be years before she earned an outer office with natural light. The film world, like the corporate world, was a society without grace. Everything, down to the size of one's stapler, had to be earned. She pasted her brightest smile on and walked to the kitchenette.

Gregoire, her boss, was there, lifting a *croissant* out of the *patisserie* box. The golden crescent shed buttery flakes.

"*Bonjour!* Good weekend?" he said, looking at her face carefully. His wiry brown hair had been carefully combed into place but still looked stupid, Carol thought.

Her weekend had been just a bit brutal. Carol had cried buckets over yet another failed relationship. She felt miserable without a man around. She had cried when Louise cried over Jeffrey. And then Louise was sick. Carol knew she didn't look her best.

"Yes, fine!" she chirped.

"Well, we need a rewrite of the scene I told you about in the animated film, and I want you to start a new script on that idea I gave you." It seemed to Carol that he stressed "*I* gave *you*." It was supposed to be the other way around. Panic made her sweat in her fresh silk blouse.

"I'll get my best man on it," she said with a smile she couldn't put any warmth into. She had heard an American use that expression and thought it rather clever. Gregoire didn't understand it, obviously—he was staring at her, puzzled. She grabbed a *croissant* and a cup of coffee and headed back to her office.

She sighed as she sat and let the fan blow air over her. Could she work in spite of her emotional misery? Maybe—if not today, then soon—she could use it to deepen her characters.

After the coffee and a good hour writing, she felt better, because she saw that she could still call herself a professional, someone who did the job no matter what. To reward herself for a great effort while in such great distress that her body was emitting SOS signals from every pore, she took a break.

Venturing out of her office, she passed other people in their cubicles, or inner offices, or outer offices with windows onto the parking lot. People didn't look up, they were all concentrating. She began to feel her aloneness. She felt the need for human company, adult company, somebody to talk to. These people were too busy.

She stepped down the hall to Amandine's office, peered around the doorjamb, and saw her looking relaxed with sunlight streaming in the window. Carol rapped her knuckles on the door.

"*Cherie!*" Amandine said when she saw her. "Come, sit down." When Carol was seated, she said, "You don't look well."

Carol wished she hadn't sat down.

"Well, I had a more difficult weekend than usual." True enough, considering the spot of bother with Jeffrey.

Amandine was interested.

"*Je suis désolée.* What 'appen'?"

Carol had needed to confide in someone, but the gleam in Amandine's eye reminded her suddenly that she had been a prat to come here, this was not the right set of ears. She'd forgotten the Amandine *escargot* factor.

"Oh, Louise was sick. We were tied up with that all weekend." She carefully dropped that "we." Amandine had a boyfriend and felt infinitely superior to women who didn't. Carol had felt her attitude in the year she'd worked at Trapèze before she met Jeffrey. An unattached woman was to Amandine what a floundering swimmer was to a great white shark.

Amandine smelled blood and started to circle.

"Jeffrey 'elps out, you 'ave told me." She left it at that, the unspoken question demanding an answer.

Carol had been a reporter and knew that human beings were wired to answer questions. When she had been on the beat, people had divulged the most amazing things to her as a result of her questions. Right now, she had a nearly irresistible urge to answer Amandine, to say that she had managed all weekend alone because Jeffrey was gone. She needed to not say it. If she did, Amandine might use it against her somehow.

"He helped, it was fine." Jeffrey had come to the apartment to pick up his stuff on Saturday, at the worst possible time, of course, with Louise vomiting in the bathroom, dishes piled in the sink, and dirty laundry heaped on the living room floor. Nothing was fine, and it felt like nothing would ever be fine again. She had to get out of this office.

"Well, Amandine, I just remembered a phone call I'm expecting." Amandine's eyes were narrow as she watched Carol stand and grab her mug.

"Stop back any time," she said, sounding so nice, so comforting, but deep down Carol knew she was an unrepentant jerk. Carol had just forgotten, that's all. She slouched disconsolately down the hall.

Chapter 22

Philippe and Elodie were in pajamas and robes late at night, worrying about Meredith, when the doorbell rang. They opened the front door, and Meredith spilled over the threshold. A man twenty years older than her, with a grizzle of facial hair and red, bleary eyes, followed her in. Her blouse was on backwards.

The man looked Philippe insouciantly in the eye, then left without a word. Elodie and Philippe supported Meredith up the stairs to her room. Their eyes met over their daughter's dangling head. She reeked of bourbon and vomited just inside her room. Philippe lifted her over the puddle she had made and put her on the bed. She was oblivious.

Elodie began to take off Meredith's shoes.

"No! Leave them!" Philippe said.

Elodie began to wrestle with the quilt—a red and white compass rose on a white field—to cover Meredith for the night.

"No! I'll clean up her mess. But I'll be damned if I'll help her any more."

"I'll get a bucket and some paper towels," Elodie said.

While she was gone, Philippe stared at his daughter. Vomit had caught in her long brown hair. The make-up on her eyes and lips was smeared. Where had she been tonight? What had she done? How much say did she have in what had happened to her?

Philippe couldn't help himself, he dabbed at the vomit in her hair with his handkerchief. Her helplessness took him back fifteen years.

Meredith, more than her two sisters, had loved the ocean as a young girl. The Mediterranean with its small waves was not enough for her. She wanted the Atlantic. When the family would arrive on the French coast of a summer's morning, she would stand in the shallows with the waves lapping around her legs, letting the receding water dig her feet deeper into the sand.

She would beg her daddy to take her wave jumping. He would put the yellow waterwings on her arms and blow them up until they were snug. He could still feel her little body on his right hip, her arm around his shoulder, as he taught her the timing, to catch a wave's power. When she seemed big and strong enough to get in and out of the surf on her own, he would stand near, at the ready to save her. He was still at the ready to save her.

He was crazy about her.

She was killing him.

Elodie came in the room with water and paper towels, and they cleaned the mess on the floor together. Then Elodie hurried downstairs, and Philippe stood and looked at the photographs Meredith had taped to the mirror above her white dresser. In the midst of her two sisters, laughing harder than anyone else, brown hair parted in the middle. A beautiful set of white, even teeth. Laughing so hard her eyes were slits. Beautiful. Fun. His lovely girl.

He went downstairs and found Elodie doing dishes again. By mutual, silent agreement, they stood side by side, leaning against the counter in the kitchen.

"How many times have we done this in the last couple years?" Philippe said.

"I lose count. It's 'appening more often wis Meredees, don't you sink?" Elodie asked. He had married a French girl, and she couldn't manage the "th" sound. He'd insisted on naming his daughter after his sister, even though it meant that Elodie would never be able to pronounce her own daughter's name accurately.

"We have to do something different," Philippe said. "She's gone back to drinking after every hospital stay. You know what some other parents have done."

"I don't want to do zat," Elodie said, shaking her head. She tugged at a piece of her short blonde hair. "Some of zose parents nevair see zair child again."

"We can't save her."

"We can't kick her out ze door." Elodie's voice was pleading. "Let's give 'er an ultimatum."

"We did that two weeks ago. She broke it within four hours. We have to kick her out. We help her to be a drunk—we give her a bed, we feed her when she doesn't have a job."

"How will she earn money?"

"Elodie, I don't know." Philippe's heart had been wrung for well over two years because of Meredith, and now it broke at the thought of his little girl at the mercy, day after day, night after night, of men like the one who had brought her to the door.

"I'm so scare'," Elodie said.

He pulled her to himself. As they clung to each other, he tried to think of a way to encourage both of them. Light sentences fit for a Hallmark card, like "this cloud will pass," flitted through his mind. They felt like wisps of vapor when what they both needed was solid ground to stand on.

You know what Scripture says," Philippe said. "'Be strong and of good courage.' It's the only way she'll change. It's our only chance to save her."

"She might not change."

"True, but can we live like this the rest of our lives?"

"I'm exhaust'," Elodie said.

"I'll tell her when she wakes up tomorrow."

"Oh, dear God, I 'elp you," she said.

Chapter 23

John walked into his office. He would love to keep its grandeur, in order to impress clients. But the expense was too high.

He had looked at a much smaller space that morning, a former shop in Le Marais. Its best feature was an exposed wall of ancient Paris stone. Someone had put a fixture at the bottom of it that washed the rough wall with light. A spiral staircase in the corner led down to the loo in the *cave*. Anjali would sit by the window; passersby would be able to look in on her. John would have an office behind a screen.

He tried the intercom to summon Anjali. It didn't work. He fiddled with it for five minutes and it still didn't work. He called Anjali in a loud voice, and she appeared at the door.

"Please find a technician to get the intercom fixed," he said. Then he panicked.

"But find out how much he wants first. These Paris workmen expect cash up front. What a racket! Tell me what he says. We're on a budget now, kid."

John felt terrible about having to think before hiring someone to repair something. This was not his style.

"Okay," Anjali said, making a note on a yellow pad.

"I'm making calls to drum up new business. Cross your fingers."

"Yes, sir!"

"Are you ready for the writers' group tonight?"

"Yes, but I need to print it out. Can I use—"

"Yes, yes, fine." He waved his hand dismissively. "Oh! I'll email you mine. Print it out, please."

"Thanks," she said and disappeared.

John swiveled in his chair and stared out at Paris, the city of small, narrow shops. He thought of the rough stone wall in the space he had looked at. He imagined all the French shopkeepers who had worked there for centuries before him, standing behind a counter, resting their backs against the bumpy wall, desperate for customers, for money to change hands so they could grab a part of it. It must not have been easy during the French Revolution, he thought. Or the Prussian War or World War I or during the Nazi occupation. Then again, being in business was never easy.

He sighed and picked up the phone. It weighed one hundred pounds. He opened his little black book, started at A, and flipped through each page, hunting for a name that he would feel comfortable calling. It wasn't until he was in the Ls that a name jumped out at him. Kurt Langen. He had taken him out on the Grey Skies two times so far this season, and they'd had a great time.

John dialed. A woman's voice answered.

"Put me on with Kurt, please." John could feel a little of his confidence returning. Cassandra would come panting to him by the time he was done rebuilding. Not that he would take her back.

"Who's calling?" She was poised, she was snooty, she was good at being a rich man's gatekeeper. He felt his ego deflating just a bit.

"John Germaine."

"Please hold one moment."

John held the line. And held some more. His confidence ebbed as he sensed that he was about to hear a lame excuse. Finally she came back on.

"Mr. Langen is with a client. Leave a message?" She sounded so very bored.

"No, I'll call back." John thought, I can try him again in a week. Maybe he'd relent, pick up the phone for his old bud John with the sailboat.

John went back to his black book.

Chapter 24

That night, Elodie and Philippe knelt next to their bed together and prayed fervently for Meredith to come to her senses. The next morning, they packed Meredith's suitcase while she was still sleeping it off. They called a friend from the Tough Love group, someone with years of experience supporting parents in decisions like this. They cried together.

Elodie made small waves of soapy water in the sink as they waited in the kitchen for Meredith to wake up.

When she came down at eleven, groaning and holding her head, they told her that she had to be out in one half hour. It seemed extra cruel to Philippe, to push her out when she was so hung over, but if he waited for that to end, she'd be drunk again, which was a worse state for her to be in to find a place to stay.

She made a call; a girlfriend said yes. Meredith deigned to kiss her mother goodbye at the door. Philippe muscled her suitcase into the trunk of his tiny, third-hand Peugeot, then looked back to see how Elodie was reacting. The doorway was open but empty.

He drove Meredith to her girlfriend's in the laboring car. She was silent the entire way. Philippe guessed her head hurt too much to scream at him. But when her bag was on her friend's top step, Meredith turned to him.

"You're a shit, Dad."

"It's for your own sake," he replied, the lump in his throat catching, and tears swimming in his eyes. How long was this girlfriend going to put up with Meredith? And then where would she go?

He was weary with grief by the time he parked again near his house in Malakoff.

Elodie had closed the door and was sitting in the living room, bleary-eyed.

"'ow did it go?" she asked.

"As well as can be expected. She called me a shit. Maybe I am."

"Well, I was 'oping we could try—"

"Elodie, don't second guess! This is it. She either straightens out or she lives in the gutter."

Philippe thought, you're a pastor, why can't you think of a single comforting thing to say to this grieving person?

Because no such thing exists.

"Well, I'm so tired, I have to rest a little." He creaked his bones up the stairs to the second floor, but instead of going to his own bedroom, he lumbered into Meredith's.

He and Elodie had left it neat after packing for her, but she had torn through drawers looking for more stuff and had left the room a turbulent mess of socks, tights, T-shirts, thongs, and other things that made Philippe sick to see.

He left it all where it was. He sat on her bed and looked around. A short red candle in a wine bottle caught his eye. Meredith had placed it on her dresser even though, because she was so unsteady so often, they'd told her not to burn candles in the house. It had dripped so much, only a tiny nub was left. The once-tall candle had been converted by flame into drops of red wax congealed along the side of the bottle. It looked like his heart felt—like the fires of adversity had made the blood drip out and harden, and there was nothing left to burn.

Chapter 25

Philippe walked into his church's sanctuary, a *cave*, a cellar, converted into an intimate theater. It had been carved out of Paris soil in the Sixth *arrondissement*, not far from the Seine, in the 1500s. Theater lights were attached to the arched stone ceiling and stone walls. Short rows of black seats descended in 12 ranks to the small stage.

He set up the projector for the words of the songs, and the screen on which they would be displayed. Elodie covered a small table with a white cloth and arranged a simple, royal blue runner. She set out a crusty, round loaf of bread, and opened the wine for communion.

That done, they went up two flights of pink marble steps to the theater's lobby. People began to come in and have small cups of the coffee Elodie had made, and to eat the *madeleines* and treats provided. As more people walked in, the noise from conversations increased and echoed in the lobby, which was walled and floored in pink marble. Only posters from past theater productions that hung on the walls softened the noise level.

A rather chunky woman in what Philippe guessed was her late fifties approached him and Elodie.

"Hi, I'm Naomi. Happy to be here."

Exuding "hail friend, well met." Obviously American.

"Hi, I'm Philippe, and this is my wife, Elodie."

The woman's face went blank.

"I'm sorry, what's that name again?"

"It's Melodie without the 'M'," he said.

The woman's face brightened. "What a pretty name!"

Once you get the hang of it, yes. Now it was time to ask the question every expat seemed to ask of the other.

"What brings you to Paris?"

"I'm on a writing sabbatical." Her long earrings brushed her shoulders. They were teal-and-blue peacock feathers, the ends trimmed with teal beads. Philippe wished he'd brought a pair of pliers. He'd lop them off at half their length. More age appropriate for Naomi. He didn't want to be mean like this, but he was so out of sorts. He wished her a good Sunday and turned to greet the next person.

An American millenial approached Philippe, and he could hardly stifle an inward groan. She fancied herself an intellectual, Philippe guessed, and loved to tell him what she was thinking about.

This time she wanted to offer gems about meditation.

"And I just think it's really helpful," she said. "I think I'm just really rushed, you know? But I like, just, just like to be really present, um, you know."

Please say "um" and "just" and "you know" one more time, Philippe thought. Just for me.

"And just the temptation and just the, um, awareness, just being really wonderful, you know, um, like you don't really…and like totally, just um awesome."

Philippe said, "Awesome," smiled, asked God to keep her away from him for at least two weeks, and escaped. Wow, he thought, I'm so grumpy. I'd better watch my tongue.

It was time to ring the small chime that signaled the end of coffee hour. Philippe descended to the *cave*, people followed. The musicians struck up the first song, and the service began.

As he gave his sermon, Philippe looked out, seeking faces, but they were hard to see because the theater's lights were in his eyes. He mostly saw glints of the exit signs bouncing off of people's eyewear.

He knew that somewhere in the rows of seats was a visual artist from China, in Paris on an artist's visa (who but the French?) who spoke French with such a heavy accent that he had trouble holding a conversation with her. He tended to avoid her, but not without a twinge of guilt.

Another regular was a young man who wanted to go to seminary, but who for now made a living translating between English and French for the Madagascar embassy. Philippe wanted to tell him that being a pastor was a noble calling, but it tested every assumption one ever made about God and people and life and oneself. Another parishioner was a sweet soul from New Caledonia, a former French penal colony in the South Pacific. She worked with the elderly, cooking and cleaning their homes. He wanted very much to say things that would hearten these folks for their coming week.

The air in the *cave* felt clammy, and Philippe thought of the Seine, flowing relentlessly less than two hundred meters away. Five hundred years ago, it had flowed right next to this spot on Rue de Nesle. There used to be a tower marking land's end on the corner of this street. You could see the tower in a miniaturized model of the area as it was back then if you went to the Musée Carnivalet.

The river was now sweeping along, close, held in its banks by stones like the ones lining the ceiling and walls of this *cave*. I hope it holds together, Philippe thought. Just until Meredith comes back.

Chapter 26

As soon as he said the final blessing and pronounced the final amen, and had said, "Enjoy your Sunday," the *cave* exploded in conversations. Philippe loved the energy in the room. People were deepening friendships and connecting in this city that could be so lonely, making lunch and movie dates with each other. The buzz in the air was a sign that his church was healthy, with people encouraged, challenged, and affirmed during the service. He took satisfaction in that.

He talked with a newcomer who approached him with questions about the three points he had made about Jesus in his sermon. He enjoyed these inquiries, these seekings. Wise men still seek him, including *moi même*, he thought.

He saw Madame Babineaux approaching, dressed as some older women in Paris still did, so elegantly, at the height of great taste in fashion, a mode of dress that was so out of fashion in this era of jeans and T-shirts. He groaned inwardly. She was a good soul but had no idea the effect she had on him. She was upon him before he could rush away, busy himself with someone else, and protect himself.

"Philippe, you really must stop."

His heart clutched. Oh Lord, what now? "Yes?"

"When you give your sermon, you really must stop pushing your glasses up your nose. It's so distracting. It takes away from the sermon.

"I'm praying for you," she threw in, turned on her exquisite Paris pumps and took herself off.

What about the 20 hours I put into writing the sermon this week? The way you could hear a pin drop during most of it? Why can't she ever give me a praise sandwich, one that includes the things I do right? Why were her critiques focused on things that weren't important? She just gave a lopsided and therefore shattering critique: she forgot to say the good things about him.

He remembered that she had been widowed and had lived alone for 38 years now. She had contented herself, she'd told him, but didn't really want to be alone so much, for so long. Philippe knew she had a tender heart and had born a lot of sorrow.

There! That was his balanced thinking about his parishioner.

Feeling slightly better than he had when Madame Babineaux walked away, Philippe dashed down the stone steps of the *cave* to pack up the altar and turn the church back into a theater.

Chapter 27

Anjali was determined to learn as much French as she could, in the time available to her in Paris, however much that was.

So one day, walking past a bookstore, her eye was caught by an array of used books on a stand outside the shop. Read in French, she thought. That would be a good way to learn.

She picked through the books in the box marked "Poesie." It turned out to hold a jumble of all sorts of books, including Camus and Sartre, which she'd read in college and did not enjoy at all. Why did people fuss over them? So hopeless. Of no use to her.

Her hand touched a book of poems by Rimbaud, *Une Saison en Enfer*, A Season in Hell. She'd heard of Rimbaud before. She probably should read him. She considered how his name would be pronounced in French. Well, truth to tell, it would be pronounced

"Rambo," but with the accent on the last syllable. Hmmm, that name was quite funny actually. She bought the book.

And struggled to understand it. Lots of words were new to her. She had to look up *les larmes* (tears) and *abîme* (abyss) and *méchant* (nasty, mean) and *fainéant* (lazy). *Cadavre* was easy. Needless to say, the poem seemed to be a bit unhappy. And she wasn't sure she wanted to read about dead bodies.

But Rimbaud was world famous.

She sighed and plowed on.

Chapter 28

The writers gathered at Le Café Livre two weeks after their first meeting. Outside, a family of gypsies—mother, father, and three small black-haired children under the age of five—sat on a mattress on the sidewalk and held out their hands to passersby, within two feet of people sitting and eating outdoors.

Philippe gave them a few coins. He'd heard that gypsy beggars gave a portion of their take to some sort of Mafia. This family didn't need a few coins, they needed a meal and a roof. Well, he did, too, and he didn't have enough for both. You're quite a Christian, he thought. I wish I could do loaves and fishes, but I haven't learned that one yet.

Standing under the awning, the waiter smiled upon the writers congenially and cleared away debris.

"Could I see a menu, please?" Carol asked with a sweet smile.

"*Bonjour*, Madame!" he corrected her pointedly.

Carol didn't understand, not being from Paris but from London by way of New York City, with time served in Los Angeles, and then she remembered. She had forgotten to say "*Bonjour*" first, which was the French definition of good manners.

"*Bonjour*," she answered a bit sourly. My goodness! What was the fuss about *bonjour*? Couldn't she get one break? This waiter and

Gregoire were both on her back. Louise was recalcitrant and withdrawn, in mourning over Jeffrey, Carol knew, and rightly so, he had been good to her. How could men treat the little girls with kindness and then turn on the grown women with sarcasm? And why had she chosen that sort of bloke—again?

Once she had the menu in her hand, she lingered over it. A *pavé de saumon* (why did they call it a *pavé*, wasn't that a cobblestone? Not too appetizing sounding, she critiqued the menu-writer) with lemon butter sauce, served with rice and *ratatouille*. That sounded weird— tomato sauce on the veg and lemon butter on the fish? Wasn't she in France, where the *cuisine* was always exquisite? Or she could have a *pavé de veau grand cru avec crème de morilles, purée*. Carol decided on the salmon. Whatever strength they had to swim upstream against river currents she needed tonight.

John eyed the menu and ran his free hand over his chin. He had dined in the city's finest restaurants and brasseries constantly in his two years in Paris and had enjoyed it. But tonight he felt homesick for the States. Americans, at least in New York, his hometown, were teeming with ideas, energy, and optimism. He found the French to be quite pessimistic. When he asked for assistance from any Parisian clerk, the first answer without fail was *ce n'est pas possible*.

Here in France, he'd heard, the education system was so rigid, the teachers so mean, that people emerged scared to express a single thought that the teacher might mock them for. In honor of the States, where teachers hadn't stamped out the fertile weirdness of the population, tonight he would order a hamburger. And it wasn't too expensive. He felt so stupid, that this had to be a consideration now.

When the waiter had taken their orders (Philippe and Anjali picking the cheapest item again, the *croque monsieur*, ten euros), Philippe heaved a big sigh.

"What's wrong?" John asked. "The sky cave in?" Of course, he wasn't about to tell the group about his own last two weeks.

"Well, to be honest, my wife and I kicked our twenty-two-year-old alcoholic daughter out of the house a few days ago."

Everybody in the group was silent.

"She went to live with a friend, for what that's worth. We don't really know where she is, or what's happening to her." He kept turning his knife—blade up, blade down, scoring and shredding his paper *serviette*.

"I'm so sorry," Anjali said in her crisp Indian-yet-British accent.

John thought, his daughter possibly out on the street? Now there's someone with worse problems than me. With this cataclysm in my finances, I might end up like her…will I have even a mattress like that family on the sidewalk?…and he closed the door firmly on that thought.

"Oh my God, that's awful." Carol pictured her little Louise wandering the streets.

"Well, at least I'm writing." Or weeping, he thought but didn't say.

"How can you write?" Carol said. "I'd be distraught."

"I am distraught. I write so I won't go crazy."

"You're doing the right thing," Carol said. "My parents kicked my younger brother out. It took three years, but he did straighten up."

What could happen to Meredith in three years on the streets? Philippe thought. He made a deep crease in the napkin with the knife he had been twirling. His deepest fear was that she'd be drunk and sexually assaulted in every corner of Paris. And its suburbs.

"Wow," John said. He thought of Emily. He missed her skeptical little presence. He had closed the door to her empty bedroom because he couldn't bear to look in as he went down the hall. The image of Emily on the Grey Skies, sitting on the upwind side, her hair in braids but blonde wisps flying every which way, and the sun catching them on fire, came to his mind. He wanted his little girl near him, with a weight of longing that staggered him even though he was seated.

Everyone's *plat* arrived. John looked at his meal, described on the menu as a "Genuine American Hamburger." He had come to writers' group tonight in order to distract himself from his financial and marital problems. Usually he could compartmentalize brilliantly. But today he wished he hadn't ordered the hamburger with two slices of bacon glistening with evil on it. And a mound of *pommes frites* next to it.

Everybody sat and looked at their plates, not picking up their forks and knives out of respect for Philippe. He didn't notice at first, staring at his *baguette* piled with dripping cheese and ham. He sighed again and looked up.

"Please, everybody, enjoy your dinner. I didn't mean to say anything. I'm sorry I've upset you."

"No, we're glad you told us," Carol said. She thought, the meal is quite ruined, isn't it? But there is a bright side. I can't wait to get home to Louise. My sleeping child's temple will smell so good to kiss.

Anjali picked at her *croque monsieur*. She liked a glass of wine now and then. May I never have the problems with alcohol that Philippe's daughter has, she breathed. She wondered if Carol had read her screenplay yet. And life at the little table went on.

John picked at his French fries but didn't feel much like eating them or the hamburger, nor did he think he'd feel like eating them at home later.

"Would you like to take this home with you?" he asked Anjali. Paris was an expensive place to live, he knew. To give his assistant a little boost in the form of a free hamburger would help Anjali. Or, as the French would say if somebody helped them, *"Tu m'as retiré une épine du pied,"* or, "you've pulled the thorn out of my foot." The French expression sounded so painful...

"I'm Hindu," Anjali said, "I don't eat beef."

"I'm so sorry, I forgot," John said. He hailed the waiter. "Would you please wrap this in a doggy bag?"

"Monsieur?" The waiter was puzzled.

"I want to take it home, *á la maison,"* John said. He mimed wrapping the hamburger in imaginary paper and tucking it into his pocket. The waiter was looking from one to the other of them desperately. John had just read an article in a free newspaper handed out in the Metro about the French slowly adopting the doggy bag. This man hadn't read it, apparently.

"S'il vous plait, est ce que vous voulez bien m'emballer les restes pour qu'il les prenne avec lui," Carol rattled off in her Brit-inflected French.

"Oo-là!" The waiter thought it a very strange idea, obviously.

"Moi aussi," Philippe said.

"Me, too," Anjali added.

"As you wish," the waiter said in his limited English. Most of the food he had served tonight was going home with people, instead of being enjoyed in the *ambience* of this nice *café* on the edge of Le Marais. A very strange turn of events, but that was the influence of the American culture for you. The tall, debonair man had started it, and he looked and sounded very American. *Pffffff!* The waiter exhaled through his lips in the classic French expression of frustration and trotted off with all the plates.

"Okay, let's get started," John said, taking the lead since Philippe was obviously in even worse shape tonight than he was. Each person dug their work out of a pocket or handbag. Anjali handed John the copies of his masterwork she had made for him.

With their pages in front of them, they each looked at the other, all wanting to go first but not wanting to appear selfish. Then they each decided they didn't want to go first, in case their work wasn't good enough.

"All right, you twisted my arm, I'll go first," John said.

He had revised the first chapter along the lines that they had suggested two weeks before. His protagonist, Chuck, was still investigating a shady phosphate mine in the wastes of Nevada. Chuck still had plenty of machismo and swagger, and he still relished sinking his fist into the gut of a bad guy. But the bad guy now had a hobby—*haute cuisine.* When he exhaled in a woosh of breath, with Chuck's fist lodged deep in his diaphragm, Chuck smelled garlic. The fact that he could identify it as such rather pleased Chuck, who walked away from the fistfight—leaving the bad guy rolling his corpulent body on the ground—to find his dinner.

"This is better," said Philippe. He hated it. He couldn't think of a thing to say in its favor.

"Sir, your protagonist could probably use a hobby, too, to make him a more rounded character," Anjali said.

"Lacemaking?" said John, who had trouble accepting criticism, especially from his own assistant, all of twenty-two years old.

"Men like to needlepoint," said Carol, "I know several—one or two—who do." She couldn't resist taking just a tiny dig.

John didn't notice, but Philippe did. "I think your protagonist needs more depth," Philippe said. "Something he really wants, something he needs on a gut—" maybe that was an unfortunate choice of words— "level."

"Okay, got it," John said and gathered his chapter back from the group. Geesh! He'd thought they'd love it.

"I worked on my screenplay," said Anjali, who began handing out copies. It was scary, and also thrilling, to show the group her work. How much would their critique hurt? They chose roles and read out loud, dramatizing with relish. When her ten pages of script were done, there was a pause.

The waiter stepped back to their table with four bundles wrapped in previously used plastic food shopping bags. He distributed them carefully. Anjali wanted to ask for one more plastic bag, to make sure cheesy grease wouldn't leak onto things in her handbag, but she looked at the waiter's face and thought it wouldn't work. It just wasn't done in Paris.

Nobody wanted coffee, so they got on with it.

"This is coming along nicely," Philippe said. He thought the ideas about God the characters had discussed briefly were unorthodox, which meant misleading. A shame. But he was too exhausted to think about it much more.

"I really enjoyed your script," Carol said briskly, and Anjali's face brightened. "But I think you need to differentiate each character's voice more. The actors will do a lot with that, but to get your screenplay sold, before the actors get their hands on the script, the characters have to sound different from each other on the page."

That phrase, "on the page," and the condescending way Carol said it, annoyed Anjali no end, but she nodded and took notes, eyes down. Carol was so preachy. But knowledgeable.

"And this is not a novel. You can't go on and on when you write movie dialog—or any dialog. Each character's bit should be like haiku—or shorter. That's why I write haiku, to practice getting the essence of things into just a few words. Watch Kandahar, a world-famous film. Everything's conveyed by the pictures and the expressions on people's faces. There's hardly any words."

Anjali felt there was no hope for her future in moviemaking at this point. Carol was a professional, and she was spotting all sorts of weaknesses in her writing. And being so annoying while she was at it.

John tapped the script in front of him. "This is quite good, Anjali. I'm interested in what will happen to these characters. You had me gasping with that twist you put in."

Anjali was not sure that John was qualified to say what was good or bad writing, but then again, he was a human being, and he was interested in her characters, and he had gasped. That was something to cling to.

She'd write John's reaction down and tape it to her closet door. Any encouragement at all was like rain falling on the desert and should be stored up for the long droughts.

She gathered up her papers, and Philippe handed out his.

When everyone was ready—John had his Mont Blanc pen in hand again, Philippe noticed with covetousness, because he loved good pens, and a Mont Blanc was 900 times more expensive than his current tool, a fine-point rollerball—Philippe began to read his short story aloud, rather slowly because he was exhausted with grief.

> She had been a great student, a classical pianist who could make her family's grand piano shake when she made music. She was tri-lingual: English, French, and German.
>
> And she loved a glass of wine. Or two and a half, these days going on three, more like four.
>
> "I'll put the knife down," she said to Jim, "when you leave."
>
> "Put it down, sweetie, I won't hurt you."
>
> Tamara took a step toward him and waved the knife.
>
> "Get out," she said softly.
>
> At the tone of her voice, the hairs pricked on Jim's neck.
>
> "Okay, okay. I'm backing up, see? Just be careful with that knife."
>
> He kept his eyes on her while he reached behind him for the knob of the door, his leather jacket creaking.
>
> "It's to your left," she said. "I mean, to my left, your right since you're facing away from the door."

Carol put a big red circle around that sentence. "Comedy or tragedy?" she wrote in the margin.

> "Thank you," Jim said. "Bye, babe, call me anytime," and he left.
>
> Tamara stared in horror at the shiny knife in her hand, just as Macbeth had gazed at the bloody knives

in his. She missed Jeffrey's haphazard company already. Could she have physically hurt him? No, she hoped not. But what if? She needed a drink. And to make love. The tune to Dave Western's song, "Let's Get Drunk and Screw," went through her head. She poured another glass of wine. Her cell service had been discontinued a month ago, so she couldn't call anyone in her cast of characters to keep her company. Everything in her life was awry, and she felt so alone, as if the walls were sucking the life out of her. This little bit of wine might help.

Stumbling a bit, she walked to her bedroom. Things weren't going well, she thought. The lights would be turned out in a week if she didn't come up with some money. She'd check and see if she had candles around after this drink. Rent was due in two weeks, and she had been fired last week. She thought of who could help her, and her mother's face, and then her father's, came to her. No, she wouldn't give those self-righteous prigs the satisfaction.

She sat on her bed and smoked and drank. She passed out later, a cigarette smoldering in the filthy ashtray beside her. Its filter burned and stank. Finally the fire went out.

The group was silent for a moment, thinking. John capped his formidable pen. Carol poured water from the *carafe*.

"That's as far as I got." Philippe coughed. He, at least, had taken risks and been honest in his writing. Of course church ladies would be scandalized by what he'd written. Sorry, dears, he thought. This is the way rowdy drunk people talk.

"You're so brave to write about this while you're going through it," Carol said. She hated stories about alcoholics.

"I don't know what else to do," Philippe replied. "I'm consumed with worry about her. I know I'm not supposed to, but I just can't help it. I feel that God has let me down terribly. I don't know why I'm telling you all this when I can't even admit that to my wife."

"What was it you said you did for a living?" asked John. "I don't think I heard you say."

"I'm a pastor. Of a start-up church."

The table was silent.

"Let's get back to the text." Carol jerked her papers, shoving one page quickly under all the others. She was thinking of the guy she had sex with while she was with Jeffrey.

"Number one," she said. "'I'll put down the knife when you leave' should be your first line, not that dead information about playing piano." Duh, she thought. It was so obvious. "Stupid to bury a great line like that.

"And you have a comic line in the middle of this tragic story—I mean, tragic so far."

"Oh? I didn't notice," Philippe said, smarting at the word "stupid." Was he going to have to "say something" to Carol? He fervently hoped not.

"It happens in the doorknob scene," Carol said. "'Your right and my left, no, your left and my right.' A bit of vaudeville, like 'Who's on first?' You might want to think about that."

Philippe asked her what she least wanted to be asked.

"What do you suggest?"

Carol wasn't sure what to say. Constructive critiquing was difficult.

Anjali piped in.

"It gives comic relief. Isn't that important in a tragic story? Shakespeare did it."

"Well, we aren't Shakespeare, are we," Carol said. She had read the first half of the screenplay Anjali had emailed to her. It was quite good, better than she had done at Anjali's age, she suspected.

"I kind of liked it," John said.

You would, Carol thought.

"Isn't it all about artistic freedom?" Philippe asked. "We can write from the heart. If it's funny and then tragic, that's okay, isn't it?"

"But as a Christian, don't you have lots of taboos?" John asked. He couldn't wait to get his own first chapter fixed, and some more real-life financial decisions made, so he could focus on the sex scene he envisioned for Chapter Two. Wouldn't it be great if this book sold like hotcakes! Come on, John, don't kid yourself. That's a pipedream. "You are a Christian priest, am I right? Or some other religion?"

"I follow Jesus," Philippe replied. "Not perfectly."

"But you have a daughter—you're married?"

"Oh! I'm a Protestant pastor," Philippe said. Catholic, Protestant. Thank God we aren't killing each other over those differences any more. "I admit, I do have an aversion to offending God with what I write. But I'm not convinced that that limits me as an artist. Jane Austen was terrified of offending God, and look at the stories she wrote. They'll live long after the work of people who don't care disappears."

"Maybe," Carol said. She didn't at all care.

"I also have a deathly fear of offending church ladies." Philippe laughed.

"How can you write a sex scene, then?" John asked. "Especially between unmarried people?" His protagonist was going to meet a waitress in a diner, where he'd eat after knocking the air out of the bad guy with garlic breath. They'd be exchanging intimacies in bed together within an hour. Wasn't that real life?

"I don't believe in throwing in a sex scene for the sake of titillation." Philippe poured himself another glass of water from *la carafe d'eau*. "I don't believe in being explicit. That's not art. When we write or paint or make movies, I believe we need to ask, 'What if a child found this? What example am I setting?'"

"Think of the classic movies," Anjali said, "that fade to white after the man and woman kiss." She had been a self-taught student of the classics, having so far watched eighty-six of the American Film Institute's "Best 100 American Films." She had found the list online while in Mumbai.

"I truly think that artful suggestion is more powerful," Philippe said. He wished with all his heart that American culture wasn't so saturated with explicitly violent and sexual films, books, TV shows, and video games. They went to every corner of the globe. He especially hated the ones that melded violence and sex. It made him fear for his someday granddaughters. And for Meredith.

"That's not in style today," Carol said. "You might have trouble finding a publisher."

"I know," Philippe said. He hated to think about that. Once he was invested in something, he was wired to seek "success." It felt to him that writing stories but never getting them chosen by a publisher and printed between the covers of a book would be a black failure.

But sometimes—not so much lately—he was hopeful. At least he wasn't trying to get poetry published. That was truly impossible.

"I read an interview with a writer," he said, "who believed that if you tell an excellent story, it will find its way to the right audience."

"That's a bit New Age, isn't it?" Carol said with a sly smile.

Philippe laughed. "You may be right."

Carol began handing out pages from a screenplay she was working on for Gregoire. The group chose parts and read it out loud.

"Critiques?" Philippe said, falling again into his leadership role.

John went first. Even though he faced personal calamities, he was pleased to see that he still had the ability to see holes in scripts. "I'm interested in all these characters. But something's missing. You need a catalyst event to start your character on her journey."

Carol answered. "I thought I did that for the girl when the telephone rang and her mother told her that her sister had been in an accident."

"I think you need to give the young girl more time to react," John said. "Maybe she could race around her room, distraught, trying to dress to go to the hospital but getting her blouse on backwards"— Philippe flinched, thinking of Meredith—"or maybe she could get all wound up and smash something. Maybe her wall TV."

As he said that, John relived smashing Cassandra's Baccarat lamp on his *parquet* floor.

Anjali said, "I like the man she's dating, but I'd like to see him squirm a little under life's tough hand. I think something bad has to happen to him. Maybe he gets fired and loses his apartment." Anjali looked sideways at John, who was listening intently. She didn't sense that she would be fired anytime soon, in spite of the downturn in her boss's fortunes. "Maybe his father, that he's close to, gets sick."

Carol busily wrote down all the ideas.

"Thanks, everyone," she said. "I'm sorry, I have to run, the babysitter's probably getting anxious for me to arrive." Actually, Carol thought, I'm anxious to see what the new babysitter's up to.

"Shall we do a writing exercise?" Philippe asked.

"I love those!" Anjali wiggled in her wicker *café* chair. "It's great seeing how differently everybody thinks. I vote yes."

"I can't resist," Carol said.

"Okay, I have a first line for you," Philippe continued. "Three lines, actually. Ready?"

People flipped their papers over and scribbled a bit to warm up their pens. John looked at his Mont Blanc and thought he'd better not lose it because replacing it was out of his league now.

"Here it is—from Rilke's Book of Hours:

"I circle about God, sweep far and high
on through milleniums.
Am I a bird that skims the clouds along,
or am I a wild storm, or a great song?

Anjali and Philippe thought for a few minutes, while John and Carol scratched away furiously. After ten minutes, Philippe interrupted.

"It's getting late. We can finish at home. But who would like to read what they've got?"

"I'll go," said John. He flicked his paper. He was proud of this one.

"I circled you like a falcon
a storm
a great song.
Then you disappeared
in a morning mist.
I was left
empty
a black man with no center."

"That's racist," said Carol.

John's head whipped up, and he stared at her.

"Well, look at it. Black men don't have a center?"

"The poem's personal, about me, not black men."

"The way it's written sounds racist," Carol insisted. She just couldn't back off. "And 'morning mist' is a cliché."

John wondered how he'd get revenge on her.

Philippe wondered if he was going to have to say something to Carol about her critique style. People needed to feel safe to speak the truth about themselves. The stakes were high in writers' groups. Only the truth can set people free.

"Folks, let's speak in 'I' statements," he said.

"I'll go," said Carol tartly, thinking that was a fine "I" statement, "and then I literally have to go. I'd love to hear everybody's work, but..." She cleared her throat.

"I circle like a falcon,
    hunt the wildest storm,
then dive into the tumult.

"A triumph! Seven-five-seven!" she said. "You wouldn't believe how many scratch-outs I have for those three lines." Laughing, she held up her paper: four versions, words blacked out, words inserted and crossed out again.

John unfortunately didn't see an opportunity for a snide comment.

"Well, changed my mind," Carol said, "I have to stay and see what Philippe and Anjali wrote."

Anjali said she'd read. "It's not very good, somehow I know it, but it has a great last line—just kidding:

"A young man
smiling
offers a type of happiness.
I circle him like a falcon, a storm.

"We all chose 'falcon' instead of 'bird.' Interesting," Anjali said. "I wrote this poem from the bottom up." Funny how creativity works, she thought.

"It's not very good," Carol said.

The table was silent.

"Well, I think it's dumb," she continued. "Rilke gave us great words to start with, and yours goes right down the old trap, "I wish I could get married.'" She said it in a whiney voice.

Anjali felt as though she'd been chopped into quarters, and each quarter sent to the far ends of India. Wow, that hurt.

Philippe thought, I can't speak to Carol in front of the group. But looks like it's got to be done. Definitely don't feel up to it tonight.

Anjali thought, when is Carol, the writing expert, going to read my screenplay? Should I remind her? How many pieces will she chop me into if I do?

Philippe sat forward to bring the evening to a close. "I'm last," he said. "Here goes:

> I circle her like a falcon
> crying great tears.
> When she gives the signal
> I'll return
> in spite of the storm
> to rest on her gloved hand."

He was suddenly choked up, wishing Meredith would return sane and sober. He glanced up, ashamed of the tears in his eyes, especially in front of John.

"It's okay," John muttered, sitting next to him.

Meredith is so not okay, Philippe thought, but he appreciated John's attempt to comfort him.

"Well, until next time," Philippe said, his voice under a better control.

Everyone stood and gathered their papers.

"I hope we do that writing prompt thing again," Anjali said.

Chapter 29

Carol walked to her apartment in Le Marais, anxious to relieve the babysitter. She'd give her a big tip, Carol decided—keep the masses happy. She walked on the streets, not just cobbled but cobbled Parisian style, in a scallop pattern, to make the streets more elegant, more pleasing to the eye.

The falcon haiku she'd written tonight was good, she thought. It expressed her new life *sans* Jeffrey. She was in a storm, a tumult of emotion. A couple strolled in front of her, holding hands, gazing into each other's eyes. A stab of worry ran through her: would she ever find a man who wouldn't turn out to be like Jeffrey, with his critical attitude? And Jeffrey made love like a squid. She worried about her tendency to date men like him. Unless all men were like him? No, that couldn't be true. Generalities were for idiots, weren't they.

She couldn't help but watch the couple closely, looking for the snake in their Garden of Eden. They puckered and kissed as they walked very slowly. Then they pulled their lips apart and smiled. No snakes in their garden, at least not tonight.

A Northern European breeze that had strayed from the Seine wafted down Rue Pavée and lifted the hair off her brow. As it tickled her, she thought she was quite pleased with the writers' circle. Strange that John, the least likely to be literary, had the best ideas in the whole group for her writing. She'd better not tell him. He was quite full of himself as it was. Though he'd seemed subdued tonight.

Chapter 30

Anjali walked across the Seine to Île de la Cité, using the Pont au Change. Then she crossed the Seine again to the Left Bank, noting the river's turbulent waters, and turned right on Quai des Grands Augustins.

Motorcycles blasted by at high speed. Girls on the back wearing high heels, fluttering scarves, and helmets, clung to the men who raced their machines against the taxis. The booksellers' stalls, that perched so precariously on the stone wall high above the Seine, were locked for the night.

Anjali strode out. The hard heels of her flats rang on the pavement, expressing her confidence that she could adjust successfully to her new home.

She climbed the six flights to her *chambre de bonne* nimbly. Sitting on the bed, she wrote down what John had said about her work, "interested in these characters" and "you had me gasping with that twist," on two small squares of yellow construction paper. She wrote what Carol had said about the characters having to sound different from each other, and to say less, on two more squares. She taped them to the doors of her closet, the two compliments on the left door, the two criticisms on the right, and got ready for bed.

Chapter 31

Anjali wanted to learn lots of French. But the Rimbaud poetry wasn't going that well. It taught her words like "abyss" and "hell" and *tomber*, which meant to tumble or fall. But they weren't happy words, and she didn't think that knowing the French word for "abyss" was going to be all that useful in everyday conversation.

So she had joined the Paris public library system and gone to the children's room for books, looking for easier reading than Rimbaud.

In those books, she found that she was learning the words for "fairy" and "dragon" and "spell." Not really any more useful in everyday conversation than "abyss" or "cadaver."

So she'd decided to take lessons in conversational French. This would be her only extravagance. On the bulletin board at the legendary Shakespeare & Co. bookstore, Anjali found the name of a French teacher. They'd agreed to meet at a *café* in the Latin Quarter.

Christelle was brunette, with big brown eyes and a happy smile.

"*Bonjour!*" she said as she slipped into the *café*'s woven red and gold rattan chair.

"*Bonjour!*" Anjali answered. She was finding that learning French, in which sometimes nearly half the letters in a word weren't spoken, was conducive to good writing. What to say, what not to say? That was the question every writer faced, word after word.

"Today we learn ze verb 'to have.' But first I tell you a story, to help you feel better about French pronunciation.

"When I lived in New York City, I work in an office wis, 'ow you say, a dragon lady. One day I say to my colleague, 'zat lady is such a beach' and 'e laugh at me. It's not beach, it's bitch, 'e say."

But Christelle was still saying 'beach.' She couldn't make a short i sound.

"That's the same problem I have with *peu* and *bleu*," Anjali said. To do it right, you had to smile while puckering your lips into a "u." She couldn't get it right most of the time.

"Don't you worry, dear. We begin." And they went through the conjugation of the verb *avoir*, to have.

"Now watch yourself with '*ils ont*,' 'they have,'" Christelle said. "Sometime in French you make ze liaison between words, and sometime you don't. For example, you don't say ze 't' in '*ont*' when you say, '*ils ont été*,' or 'they have been.' If you do, what you'll really say is, '*ils ont tété*,' which means 'they have nursed.'"

They both burst out laughing.

"I don't ever want to make that mistake," Anjali said.

"Oh, people will laugh, but that's all right, don't you worry."

They worked together for another forty-five minutes.

Then Anjali asked, hoping for a break from the intense concentration, "I've heard that French teachers are very hard on their students, that they kind of crush their spirit. Did that happen to you?"

Christelle's face took on a serious air as she answered.

"Once I took an English vocabulary test. To answer the questions, I used a few words I had learned the previous year. My teacher marked them wrong, but I knew they were right. When my parents went to see her about it, she said, 'I want her to only use the words that I teach.'"

"No!" Anjali said. "That's terrible."

"But true. Here's another example. In high school, we had to write lots of essays. We were given a problem to solve. We had to list three reasons why the solution might work, and three reasons why it wouldn't. In America, kids are just asked to write three ways to make it work. That's the French system. It breeds negative attitudes and pessimism."

Anjali had already been told *"ce n'est pas possible"* a few times in stores, in libraries, before people even took a moment to think. That was the standard reaction. She nodded.

Christelle said, "How do the Americans say it: it's not all gloom and doom. I tell you a joke about the French before I go.

"God created the world, and Jesus took a look at the whole thing afterward.

"'You have freezing cold in the North," he said to God. "You have jungles, heat, humidity, and mosquitoes in the South. But in the middle you have this country. It's not too hot, not too cold. It has mountains, ocean, fertile land. It's perfect.'

"'Yes, I call it France,' God said proudly.

"'Actually, it's a little too perfect.'

"'Okay. I'll invent the French!'"

They both laughed.

Anjali thought, yes, that joke expresses some truth. And a Frenchwoman told it on her own countrymen, so I'm in the clear.

Chapter 32

Carol was at her desk the next morning, incorporating the ideas the writing group had given her into the screenplay she was working on for Gregoire. She used both of John's ideas. In her screenplay, the young girl got dressed to go to the hospital, realized her blouse was on backwards, and, angry at life for putting her sister in the hospital and for getting her so upset that she couldn't properly dress herself, she pulled her hi-def TV off the wall and threw it down. On the movie screen in Carol's mind, onto which she projected all her scenes as she wrote them, the electronics exploded handsomely.

As for the young man John had mentioned—

"Carol, can you come into my office?" It was Gregoire standing in her doorway, and he looked very happy.

His tone of voice stopped her heart for a second. Carol said, "Sure." Gregoire stepped away, and she knew this wasn't going to be good. So she quickly dug in her massive Louis Vuitton handbag for her coral lipstick. A little color on her lips would give her courage.

She straggled into Gregoire's office. It looked out over the parking lot, which was not glamorous, except for his sporty BMW Z-3 parked right outside his window.

Inside, the office was beautiful. He had a cherry desk with little on it except a crystal elephant, as big as a fist, with its trunk raised. Carol had heard that when it came to statues of elephants, the trunk had to be raised for good luck. Gregoire obviously had enjoyed some.

He also had cherry bookshelves filled with published screenplays. If you needed "Little Miss Sunshine" or "Sense and Sensibiity," he had them, and he lent them carefully, keeping track of who had what.

In a glass case, with cherry shelves, he had created a shrine to himself with the awards he had received, framed in cherry if they were on paper, or, if they were glass or crystal, standing proudly where the sun could hit them. She knew there wasn't an Oscar or a Palme D'Or among them. But still, an impressive array.

"Sit down, Carol."

She sat in a barrel chair that she suspected Gregoire had chosen to be lower than his chair. And Gregoire was a tall man. A tall man in a tight suit. So now he was looking down on her, and she was looking up at him. He was framed by light from the window behind him, and she was forced to squint up at him. He liked people to be at a distinct disadvantage.

"Carol, your contributions at our brainstorm meetings haven't been of great caliber lately."

How could he expect someone to improve under this demoralizing heap of criticism, she thought. Businessmen are needlessly cruel, and because of it, people can't flourish and help them make money.

"What do you say to that, Carol?"

She thought, I think it's a good thing John gave me those ideas last night. I joined that group in the knick of time.

"I think you'll see that I'm doing better," she said, "starting today. I had some great ideas last night, and I was just incorporating them into the script when you stopped by. Ideas that will add lots of drama."

"I want to make my concern very real to you," Gregoire said, and in reaction to his tone of voice, Carol's shoulders slumped. "I'm putting you officially on probation for three months. Only Marine in Human Resources and I will know about this, I assure you."

Well, that was good, she wouldn't want her colleagues to know. But *merde*, this felt awful, to not be trusted to be doing her best, to be told that her best, which had pleased them for the last three years, was not good enough now. Though she had to admit, she had launched a few duds off her rocketpad lately, hadn't she?

"I'd like to see us move through this and come out the other side as better people and better artists."

"Yes, I agree." Her stomach twisted as she said it. She had read that it had been scientifically proven: people who had power were less compassionate, were less able to identify with the feelings of the humans in their clutches. Gregoire had just dumped a load of his ego garbage on her and expected her to function better, not worse, as a result. What bloody nonsense!

She left his office reeling. She had to talk to someone, she had to have someone on her side. No one at Trapèze, that was certain. She made herself a cup of tea in the kitchenette and closed herself in her office, with its window onto the hallway. Colleagues not on probation passed by from time to time. She looked at the screenplay she had been happily working on before Gregoire's little visit. Any pleasure she'd had in it was now gone. She typed each word of the next scene with pain-stiffened fingers.

Chapter 33

Philippe and Elodie had not heard from Meredith for days. They didn't have the girlfriend's telephone number and hadn't asked for it.

They had been advised that their letting go ought to be total, not to check up, not to ask if she needed anything.

Late on a quiet afternoon, after working on his sermon and visiting elderly parishioners, Philippe went to Meredith's bedroom to beseech God on behalf of his little girl. He passed her dresser and noticed that the red candle wax had splattered onto the white surface during one of Meredith's forbidden burnings. She must have been the one who chipped at the wax with a fingernail, marring the paint. Everything she touches turns lousy, Philippe thought. Just like me. I can't parent, I can't preach, my church isn't growing, and my short story stinks.

He heard the gate clang, then the front door open.

"'Alo," Elodie called. He heard her footsteps tap into the kitchen.

"'Alo," 'he called down the stairs and descended.

Elodie leaned against the counter, the stance she'd taken when they'd discussed Meredith a hundred times. Philippe looked at her, at the stale half a *baguette* on the table, the *carafe* of water from last night's dinner, a *cantaloup* waiting to be sliced, and felt it was impossible to go on in this strange, stale world. Life was now just too hard.

"I'm a failure," he burst out, "as a parent and as a pastor. Probably as a husband, too."

She had heard these doubts before. She poured two glasses of water at the tap and led him to the terrace. The leaves of the ivy that clambered over the railing trembled in a light breeze. A Metro train rumbled as it emerged from its tunnel and passed at the end of their street.

"*Cheri*, tell me what's bozzering."

Philippe sighed as he sat on the bench. As usual, he was seduced by her French inability to pronounce the "th" sound.

He wished he were having wine, not water. But he couldn't, so that was that.

He sat pensively for a moment.

"I envisioned a church with young Parisian families. I wanted to reach the French, the countrymen of my Huguenot great-grandparents. And what do we get but this odd bunch of expats. A Luxembourg diplomat and his wife. An Italian scientist doing his post-doc at the Sorbonne. A middle-aged artiste from New Jersey in dangly earrings and bracelets that clank during my sermon. And we're not growing."

"Philippe, ze fact is, we are growing. Jus' more slowly zan we 'oped," Elodie said. "Isn't zis really about Meredees?"

"I did this to her by being a pastor!" he said. "It's my fault." He had to keep his voice down. The neighbor on the other side of the garden wall had his windows open. "The pressure on her to always be good, to behave, that she endured as a preacher's kid. I'm sure she resented it. She needed freedom from it."

"Maybe she just addicted to alco'ol."

"No, really! You've felt pressure as a pastor's wife. People tell you, 'That sermon was too long' and expect you to tell me. They complain about the snacks before the service, the humidity in the *cave* during the service, the sermon topic. It's not easy being a pastor's wife—or daughter. I'm a lightning rod for their dissatisfactions, and my family is, too, by default."

"Remember zat book we read by Thomas Merton? Someone ask' him, 'What's ze 'ardest sing about being a monk?' And he said, 'Ozzer monks.' Ze 'ardest sing of being a Christian is ozzer Christians sometime'. It doesn't mean you aren't doing ze right sing."

"If I've been doing the right thing, then why is Meredith in so much trouble?

Elodie sighed. "Her choice?"

"Why isn't God sparing us this heartache?"

"'He will use it for good, *mon cher.*"

"With all the human suffering that God used for good in all of history, why aren't we better off?"

"Aren't we? Medicines, treatments, democracies, books, libraries, computers, jets, telephones to connect us."

"What took so long?"

"Human nature?"

"And you can't trace those accomplishments to God."

"You're so cynical today. 'e is ze source of creativity. 'e made *les etoiles, la lune.* 'e gives us our talents. You know all zis."

"What possible good can come from Meredith being a prostitute?" Philippe snapped.

Elodie sank her face into her hands. A moment later, her shoulders shook as she began to cry.

"I'm sorry, darling," Philippe said.

She lifted her face and said in a constricted voice, "You know what ze Bible tell' us. In all our distress, 'e too is distressed."

"I know," he whispered. "But right now, it doesn't feel like enough."

He pulled her toward his chest.

Chapter 34

John had found a person who managed estate sales, and the sale was today. He made coffee and wandered around the spacious apartment. The remaining Baccarat lamp was priced at $7,000. A $3,000 loss from the original price. It was all a loss, this terrible swamp of stuff. The responsibility to care for it sucked energy from him with each footstep. He owned these beautiful things, and all they did was drain the life out of him.

Cassandra's lawyer had sent a list of all the things she wanted from the apartment. John had tossed it away in a $1,000 antique brass spittoon converted into a wastebasket. Tough! He had acted fast so he could make cash before court orders and such nonsense started flowing in.

He had surprised himself when he realized that he didn't have a sentimental attachment to a single thing in his apartment, that the one thing he wanted in all this mess was Emily. Oh, yes, and the sailboat. He dialed Emily on his cell.

"Hi, cutie," he said when she answered, sounding sleepy. It was nine o'clock, time for her to be up so they could do things together.

"I'll be there to pick you up in thirty minutes," he said. "Didn't your mother tell you?"

"My alarm went off, but I fell back to sleep," she mumbled.

At least Cassandra wasn't causing trouble about seeing Emily, John thought. Although she might when he sold all this crap she treasured. Well, he needed the cash, he was not calling off the sale.

"I have a big day planned," he said. "Wear comfortable shoes." He signed off with Emily as the door buzzer rang. He pushed the button to let the estate sales team through both the street and foyer doors and waited while they climbed the flight of stairs to his apartment.

He invited the team of seven to come in, one person to keep an eye on each room, and the French estate sale guy, Henri, who had a cashbox and a phone with a credit card cube attached. John offered them coffee.

He rummaged in the fridge, to see what he might make for dinner when he got home that night. He felt like eating a hamburger. He remembered asking the cook a year ago to make them for his family one night. He had expected his burger to taste of French beef raised on French grasses springing fresh and green from French soil, soaked with French rain from French clouds. It hadn't tasted of anything.

But the cheese! That was a different story. Charles de Gaulle had lamented that he couldn't govern a country that had more than 400 kinds of cheese. John had been back across the pond to New York City several times since moving to Paris. He had tried cheeses billed as French, and then had had them in Paris, on *pain rustique*, criss-crossed with lovely X's where the crust had a chance to bake even crustier. The cheeses were better in Paris. He guessed that the hold of a ship crossing the Atlantic was not as beneficial to cheese as a *cave* in France.

He didn't see much in the fridge to tempt him or Emily. They'd dine out, even if he couldn't afford it now. He headed to Cassandra's friend's apartment, not far away in the Fifth *arrondissement*.

He had the street door code, and Emily buzzed him through the foyer door, so he started up the gray marble staircase. It was vastly wide, and a strip of green carpet went up the middle, anchored by brass bars. Cassandra wasn't going to hole up in some dingy place while she waited for her divorce. He had canceled the joint credit cards, so his paying for Cassandra to stay at the George Cinq amongst Saudi princes was not in the mix.

Emily waited for him at the top of the first flight, propping the apartment door open with her foot.

"How's my girl?" John swept her up in his arms and lifted her off her feet, Emily protesting, and the apartment door clicked shut by mistake.

"Everybody's still in bed. They're going to be mad if I ring the bell," Emily said.

"Can you just go like this?"

Emily looked down at her jogging shoes, shorts, and T-shirt.

"My cell phone is inside. And my jacket for later." Even in August, Paris could get cool at night.

"You can have my jacket. Let's go!" John was glad to see Emily was willing to leave without her phone.

"Where are we going?"

"I'm going to surprise you all day long!" John said as they trotted down the stairs and out the wrought-iron door.

They strolled down Boulevard Saint-Michel past Starbucks and the traditional Paris *cafés* that Starbucks had originally been patterned after. Strange that Starbucks had come back to Paris. And been successful. It wasn't allowed anywhere else in France, so as not to put mom and pop *cafés* out of business. The French government was not open to every market force on Planet Earth. John thought that was wise.

They turned left to walk past the bookstalls on Quai des Grands Augustins. It was way too early for the stalls to be open—they were locked up tight, perched on the stone wall above the embankment.

They crossed the Seine at Pont des Arts. The padlocks fastened to the chain link fence sparkled in the sun. John couldn't look at them. He focused on Le Louvre and its ornate architecture ahead of him instead.

They queued up outside I.M. Pei's pyramid in the courtyard of Le Louvre. John was aware that they were standing before one of the most photographed architectural sites in the world.

"I want to take a selfie of you and me and the Mona Lisa," John said. "Us and her together." Emily smiled.

"Another day I'll take you to the Branly, to see the art of Aztecs and Mayans. And the Musée des Moyens Ages with The Lady and the Unicorn tapestries."

"Okay."

She didn't sound all that enthused, but they had to go out and do something together, John thought.

When the line in front of the glass pyramid hadn't moved for ten minutes, he got restless.

"Where did all these people come from?" He had never been to Le Louvre before. Never had time.

"This is tourist season."

"Oh. I forgot. Well, let's leave this and the Moyens and Mayans for wintertime and go do the next thing. Surprise destination." In the past, he would have hailed a taxi, but they used the Metro.

They descended the stairs of Le Louvre Metro station. John reflected that the Paris underground system had no express trains. In New York City, he had to watch carefully which train he stepped into, because he could be whisked away by an express train to a stop 30 blocks or more from where he intended to be. But in Paris, every train made every stop. It was less stressful.

By accident, they ended up in the first subway car. Line 1 was automatic—there was no driver. So the front end was all glass. New York subways didn't have all this glass in front, John mused, just one little window and whoever got there first could watch the tracks. But here, the view was accessible to anyone in front. New York subways didn't have as much glass on the sides, either. More space for American advertising that way.

A train going in the opposite direction approached them from a distance, slowly, it seemed at first. John could see light spilling from the oncoming train, and people standing in the first car, getting closer, the tracks changing elevation a bit like a rollercoaster, and then whoosh! The two trains passed each other, so close! Two glowworms glissading past each in a dark tunnel. John watched as his train streamed toward the Tuileries station, which appeared as a pool of light far ahead in the black tunnel.

People had opened some of the small windows in the train, but it was still sticky and hot inside and smelled a bit too much of hot people. The French didn't seem to mind stuffy air. Most people had a sheen of sweat on their faces but didn't bother to open the window near them.

In summer in New York City, John reflected, the subway cars were crisp and cold but the platforms were insufferable because the trains dumped their air conditioner exhaust onto them. Here it was the opposite. The train was hot, but when he and Emily stepped out at the Champs Élysées Metro stop, the platform felt much cooler than the car.

They walked across Pont Alexander III admiring the life-sized gilt Pegasus atop each pillar, and the bronze gods and goddesses with gilt spears in their hands guarding the bridge. After they crossed, they descended the stairs to the Seine embankment. John looked back at the bridge.

"Look, Em! The sides are decorated like a wedding cake. Unbelievable!"

Emily took a quick glance, to please her father, John guessed, and then they walked to the Eiffel Tower. They queued again, but the line moved faster this time. To the middle level they went, and they gazed over the city. There was his fifty-nine-story Montparnasse Tower, looking like an ugly black tooth jutting up among the pearly white six-story buildings of Paris. People strolled on the Champ-de-Mars below looking as tiny as the little figures on a miniaturized train set.

Tourists kept pouring onto the observation deck. The platform was crowded, and people kept bumping John, quite deliberately, he felt, with a little message wrapped in each bump: You're taking up my space.

"Someone's going over the edge if they *bousculer* me one more time," John said.

"We should do this stuff in winter."

"You're so right. Let's go."

"What's next?"

"Surprise, *ma cherie.*"

Emily went along with grace.

Near the Eiffel Tower, but on the other side of the Seine, they clambered aboard a *bateau mouche* for a boat ride.

"Good thing we got seats," John said. Emily was being nudged on the side opposite John by a German family. As the boat moved down the Seine, each member of the family saluted—with a snap— every single person on the embankment that was watching boats go by. The father was the leader in this silliness.

"Germans are martial even when they're sightseeing," Emily whispered to John.

"Funny, honey! I hope you're having a grand day," John said.

"Yeah, sure," she replied dutifully.

"I didn't understand before how many tourists were at these sights. I've been too busy working."

"Everyone in Europe wants to come here," Emily said. "I've heard Paris is the capital of Europe."

"Well, that may be, but New York City is the capital of the world," John answered. Then what was he doing here? Hunting oil-prince money. He hadn't gotten very far.

When the boat returned to the *quai* it had started from, John was hungry.

"Let's have lunch," he said, and Emily nodded.

"Yours will be alcohol free," John said, thinking of Philippe's daughter. "You can have an Orangina."

"I'd rather have a *diabolo grenadine*," she said.

"Does that have alcohol?"

"No!"

"So be it! Let's get out of here." They took line 1 east to City Hall, better known as L'Hôtel de Ville, the big house of the village. Dozens of statues of venerable men of Paris stared down at them from their niches along the walls of City Hall. John steered Emily toward a *café* on Rue de Rivoli.

"Too noisy, too much traffic," Emily said. "Let's go into Le Marais."

"Fine idea, young lady, how did you get such a good head on your shoulders?"

She smiled, and they walked away from Rue de Rivoli on Rue Vieille du Temple. The sidewalks were crowded with people peering into the boutiques, licking gelato on cones, and generally being a pain. One person *bousculer*'d John, but he was happy to have Emily with him and didn't mind so much. They ended up picking out a *café* named La Chaise au Plafond, on Rue de Trésor. It wasn't a *rue*, it was actually an *impasse*, a dead-end, and quiet.

"Ah, you were right, this is a much better place to talk," John said. He liked Le Marais, which translated into "The Swamp," his favorite neighborhood in Paris. It was full of unabashed gay men talking *tête-à-tête* over small *café* tables, and Jewish men hurrying to business or the synagogue with black hats and white prayer shawl fringe showing under their black jackets. John thought of it as the boundary crossers living in the same neighborhood as the boundary builders.

They sat under the trees outside and looked at the menu. John was not yet as practiced at austerity as he needed to be, and he ordered an item that cost eighteen euros, even though there were less expensive choices. He picked *côte de boeuf extra rôtie, avec beurre marchand de vin*. The menu's English translation: chop of beef. Emily asked for rice *avec champignons*. When Emily's drink came—a tall glass one quarter filled with a deep pink syrup, accompanied by a bottle of lemon soda to pour in—John insisted on having a taste.

"That's good!" he said.

"Duh." She gave him a reserved smile.

"What's new with you?" John asked.

"Not much."

"Well, I joined a writing group!"

"Yeah?"

"I'm writing exactly the kind of book that I think will sell. And the group is critiquing me."

"Cool." Emily shifted in her chair and took a sip of her drink. John thought, evidently she's not too interested in my writing. Or in how much the critiques hurt.

"Tell me what's new for you. Any boys you're crazy about?"

"Stop!" She looked annoyed.

"A girl as pretty as you must have them lined up! I remember a girl in high school—" and John was in gear, motoring through topics like a Saudi prince in a Bugatti blasting through Paris.

As John talked, a frown line appeared in her forehead, and then she wiggled in her chair. She sucked her soda dry with the straw and made a loud burble at the bottom of the glass.

"Emily, you're not supposed to do that, it's not polite," John said. But it was half-hearted. He was so glad to see her, wanted so badly to connect with his daughter, needed so deeply to hold some sort of family together.

"Let's go," she said.

"We're just getting warmed up, and you want to go? Okay, we're going to Notre Dame."

"Nah, Dad, I just want to go home. I'm pretty tired." She slumped back in her chair as if to prove her point.

The fact that she called Cassandra's friend's apartment home stabbed John's heart. He leaned forward across the table. He was afraid to ask, afraid of Emily's response, but he would ask anyway.

"Listen, pumpkin, what if you were to come live with me?" He reached for Emily's hand.

"Dad—"

"I know, you don't want to hurt your Mom. But think about it. You're sixteen, you can decide for yourself where you live. I want you with me." He caressed her knuckles with his fingertips, then pulled his hand away.

Emily was silent, twisted her fingers in her lap, and looked down at them, frowning.

"In two weeks I'll take you out on the Grey Skies!" John declared. He didn't like her frown. He had to sell this idea, just like convincing a prospective client to invest with him.

"Can I bring a friend?" She looked up expectantly.

John no more wanted a friend of Emily's along than he wanted Cassandra to be there.

"Couldn't it be just us?" he wheedled. Why was Emily so withdrawn? Why did she tell him nothing? Suddenly John's heart double-clutched. Maybe this was how it had started with Philippe's daughter—closing up her life, not talking. Emily was headed for perdition, just like Meredith, John thought, and there's nothing I can do about it because I can't seem to get Emily to talk to me.

He looked at his daughter, who was staring toward the street. Hold on, John, you're exaggerating. Aren't teenagers known for their silence to parents? He wasn't sure, this was his first teenager.

Still no answer. She was looking down again, scowling, as she did when she was a little girl and wanted her own way.

"Okay, a friend." John was disappointed by Emily's reaction but decided not to press for an answer. He signaled to the waiter and paid the bill. Then he tried to tempt her into not going "home."

"I wanted to watch a movie tonight. They finally sell microwave popcorn in the food stores in Paris, we could have that and—"

Emily threw herself back in her chair, frowning.

"—Sorry, Dad, I'm not up to it this weekend."

"Honey, I wanted so much to spend the day with you."

Emily didn't answer. She just glowered at her hands.

Disappointed, aching—thinking, this is how Philippe feels— John stood up to go, and he noticed that Emily leapt to her feet. He felt worse.

When they got back to Cassandra's friend's apartment in the Fifth, the security code worked and Emily whisked through the street door.

The second security code let them pass through the foyer door, from the mosaic-tiled lobby to the stairwell, just like thousands of apartment buildings in Paris.

"Bye, Dad, thank you," she called as she raced up the marble staircase. When John knew that the apartment door had been opened to her, he closed the foyer door, then the street door, and walked away.

Chapter 35

He'd thought he would spend Saturday night with Emily. With that plan crushed, John had nothing to fill a Saturday night for the first time in many years. He used to take potential clients out to dinner at the city's best restaurants, with Cassandra dressed to dazzle and flashing her engagement rock, even tapping it on the stemware if people hadn't seemed to notice. Or he might take Cassandra and Emily out to dinner, or just Cassandra when Emily was at a friend's. What could he do with so much time this evening? If he went out to eat tonight, couples would be lurking in corners, gazing into each other's eyes. He just didn't want to see it. What was he going to do?

When he got back to his apartment, he saw that it had been stripped. He couldn't make so much as a cup of coffee. He had told the estate sale crew to keep certain kitchen things for his everyday life, like the microwave. But every item had been sold except his bed, a dresser, and one lamp—not Baccarat.

It was all too much. He went for a walk and saw a sign for the celebration of the seventieth anniversary of the liberation of Paris on a wall. He headed over to l'Hotel de Ville.

The *son et lumière* show, projected onto the *façade* of City Hall or onto screens erected in the *place* that surrounded the building, started just as he arrived. It wasn't very crowded. The French were *blasé* about the liberation of Paris, evidently. John found a place near the front, along the crowd barriers that had been erected.

Images of tanks were projected onto the screens, and the sound of their tracks rumbling boomed through loudspeakers throughout the *place*. A narrator spoke in urgent French, too fast for John to understand. A filmed re-enactment of men and women ripping cobblestones up off streets paved elegantly in scallop-shell patterns ensued. A black and white picture from the 1940s of people huddling behind a barricade of cobbles followed.

The show was long on special effects, faky drama, and glancing references to tanks and marching men. It was short on facts about the Resistance, the danger, the price people paid. It's a cheesy bit of entertainment, John thought. Cassandra would have loved skewering it with her viper tongue. He missed her brittle intelligence.

Halfway through, somebody must have disconnected a cable, because the whole show suddenly stopped. John had nothing better to do—he stayed, mostly to see how long it took the French to find the broken connection. Fifteen minutes later he thought, this would not happen in New York City. A disruption like this, so prolonged, simply wouldn't be tolerated. Six back-ups would have been put in place and tested before the show began.

Finally, at the twenty-minute mark, the show resumed. A tape of Charles de Gaulle giving his victory speech was played, with the text projected in French and English. "Paris has been liberated by the French, for the French," DeGaulle said.

What?

What about the Allied forces landing in Normandy and fighting all the way here? What about their sacrifices on the beaches, in the fields and villages? Leave it to de Gaulle to ignore that, he thought. De Gaulle had a gall, didn't he?

Just then the soundtrack changed to churchbells ringing, and young people dressed in 1940s clothing streamed onto a stage. They ran from one to the other, hugging and kissing each other in celebration. No reference to the Nazi occupation, nor to the end of the oppression, which was the reason for the joy.

This show was so empty, John thought. The producers took the story of the liberation of one of the world's great cities from one of the world's great evils during the biggest armed conflict ever known and dumbed it down into a vapid bit of entertainment. Would the U.S. do any better? Maybe Ken Burns would make a factual, heart-wrenching documentary out of it.

He left and walked down Rue de Rivoli. The streets, though teeming with people, felt empty. Everybody he passed was a stranger and therefore remote.

He was loony to think he'd find some sort of companionship on these streets. Yes, he was loony—note his investment strategy, he thought. Nobody knew how hard he worked at acting normal.

How many hours could he fill walking among these vaguely evil, or at least disinterested, people? How long could he just walk amongst these thousands of six-story white buildings looming above him with their black wrought-iron balconies? Even if the wrought-iron pattern was different on each one, somehow they all looked the same on every *rue* and *boulevard*.

As he looked up and thought of Cassandra and their dead relationship, the white buildings seemed to be collapsing, right onto his hungry heart.

Chapter 36

Anjali was out and about on Saturday morning, so she called her parents from her smartphone. She was in the First *arrondissement*, near that Gothic pile, Saint-Eustache.

Her father was a history buff and had been reading up on France ever since she'd said she wanted to live in Paris. She knew that he thought the French had folded too readily to the Germans in World War II. Anjali had read that there were lots of complicated reasons, including weak government and not enough fighting men on hand because so many potential fathers had been killed in World War I. But she tended to agree with him. He was a bit of a wise guy about it, though, and it made her laugh.

"Appa, Amma, how are you?" Anjali had to admit, she needed to hear their voices.

"Fine, *cherie*," her mother said. Whatever Anjali did, her mother, too, learned a little about it and made her contribution. "What are you doing today?"

"Well, this morning I visited a Gothic church, Saint-Eustache. Took one hundred years to build, starting in 1532."

"Oh," her father replied darkly. She knew he was thinking that Indian culture was older—much older.

"Well, the parish dates from 1223," she said, to defend her being in Paris. "Mozart held his mother's funeral there."

Her parents weren't impressed.

"Where are you now?" her mother asked.

"I'm in the neighborhood near the church." Anjali turned on the video feature and did a selfie. There was her nose again. "Isn't Paris beautiful? See all the white Paris buildings behind me, with wrought-iron balconies?"

"Looks like they painted the buildings white to match their flag," Appa said.

In spite of herself, wanting to respect her host country, which had many fine qualities, but sort of agreeing with her Appa, Anjali laughed out loud on the street. A passing Parisienne decked out in the latest style—and absolutely fabulous shoes, teal, with impossibly high heels, and teal and white polka-dotted bows on the toes—frowned at her for her public outburst.

"Listen, darling, the Gupta's called again yesterday. Ravi's twenty-third birthday is coming up, as you know." Anjali heard her mother steadily building her case, fact by fact, implication by implication.

"This is their son's future they're concerned about, as we're concerned about yours."

Anjali just listened as she strolled, distracted, through the streets. People *bousculer*'d her in annoyance that she wasn't going anywhere in particular, not keeping pace, but she hardly felt it.

Anjali had known Ravi from grade school on. He was cheerful, and interested in everything, if he wasn't too busy playing tennis. He might actually be a good match for her.

"They want to know what our intentions are." Amma means my intentions, Anjali thought.

"They have given us three months to hold the engagement party, or they will find him someone else."

Anjali was fuming. She'd suspected this might happen, but it still enraged her.

"Anjali?" her mother sounded patient but concerned.

"We all agreed on a year! What is this three months garbage!"

"I know, darling," Appa said. "But this is your chance. We can't guarantee that we could find anyone else as suitable for you—most people your age are engaged or married already."

Anjali liked Ravi. This was a grand chance to have a lover, a companion, and to create her own family. Why was she putting it at risk?

"I know," Anjali said. "Believe me, I'm thinking about it."

"Why don't you come home now, darling?" her mother wheedled. "You've had enough time in Paris, don't you think? We'll have so much fun planning the wedding."

Her father coughed. The sky was not the limit in her family.

"No, I haven't had enough chance to write and explore," Anjali said. "They gave me three months, I'll take them." She would have to write like crazy to get her screenplay into shape. She'd suggest that the writers' group meet weekly. Though that meant buying dinner out four times a month instead of two. She would have to scale back to buying a Perrier, although even that was four euros in Le Café Livre. And only drinking water was awkward, when everyone else was eating dinner.

"Darling, please don't waste this chance at happiness," Amma said. Now she sounded distressed.

"I know. But I'm happy in Paris, writing. There are all different kinds of happiness."

"Long term, darling, think long term. Think the next sixty years alone, writing, just you and your laptop."

It did sound rather bleak, compared to having happy children around her, with Ravi's handsome face smiling down at them in contentment. Or did she see a critical frown?

"Look, for now, just for today, I'm in Paris, I'm meeting Aasha in a little while, and tonight we're going to a poetry—" Anjali almost said "slam" but caught herself. Her parents wouldn't know what that was, they'd distrust it and get worried about it. And she could never say it was in the Belleville area of Paris, where Edith Piaf started her career singing on the streets. Heroine addict. Several husbands. Her father would forbid her. He'd command her to get on a plane now. So she ended her sentence with, "—festival, here in Paris."

"India has wonderful poets," her father said. Anjali sighed to herself. Yes, India had more culture than a person could explore in a lifetime, but so did the West, and she was here now.

They said goodbye, with longing on both ends of the connection.

Anjali felt the absence of their voices as she scurried into the Metro. But she relished her Paris freedom to think and do as she pleased.

Today Aasha and she were meeting at the Arc de Triomphe de l'Étoile. That Napoleon, Anjali thought. He couldn't just build an arch of triumph, it had to be triumph over the stars.

Chapter 37

When Anjali got to the Arc de Triomphe, she looked at a Metro map and realized that it was named not for the conquest of the stars but for the way that twenty streets converged at the arch, forming a star on the map. Maybe Napoleon wasn't so bad.

Anjali and Aasha met up at the foot of the arch and ascended. At the top, Anjali gazed triumphantly down one of the most famous streets in the world, Les Champs Élysées. City workers kept the trees along the avenue trimmed into box-like shapes. The French believed in gardening geometrically.

As she leaned on the parapet, Anjali said, "Ravi's parents have shortened my time in Paris from a year to just three more months." She resented these adults who couldn't let a girl have some freedom.

"No!" Aasha said, turning from the view to look at her with concern.

"Yes, I have to go back and do the engagement ceremony in three months or they'll find someone else."

"That's terrible! You just got here! You like it here. With your French Pondicherry passport, you could stay forever! What about your screenplay?"

"I don't think I can finish writing it in three months. Not while working fulltime. Definitely can't get it all critiqued by my writing group. I can only take ten pages max each time."

The two girls walked the perimeter, then descended from the top of the arch back to the street. They found a *créperie* and each girl had a *crêpe* with *fromage et jambon* and a dusting of fresh-ground pepper, no salt. Then they headed to Belleville together.

While they jostled shoulder to shoulder on line 11, they peered out at the Arts et Metiers Metro station, designed to make people feel like they were inside a copper-lined submarine. They chatted.

"How is your *fiancé*?" Anjali asked.

"We're emailing every day," Aasha said with a smile. "It's a great way to get to know him."

Anjali and Ravi were talking once a week. She ought to email him more, get to know him better. So far his few emails had been terse and uninformative.

"Any pressure from your parents?" Anjali asked.

"No. Sorry yours and Ravi's are pressuring you."

"They worry too much about what other people will think."

"Like everybody else in India!" Aasha joked.

"This three-month business is probably the result of some auntie of Ravi planting a seed of distrust in his mother's brain."

"There's always an auntie meddling in India."

Aasha was right. And anybody could appoint themselves your auntie. Once, just before she left Mumbai, Anjali had been on a bus to work. A woman sitting next to her had sized up her age, seen no ring on her finger, and said, "When are you getting married?" In India, strangers ask when you're getting married! You're accountable to everybody! No wonder Indian young people felt so free when they came to the West, where no one cared what you did.

But then again, the network of kinfolk in India who would come out to help you in the middle of the night was so reassuring. Somebody would know somebody who would know somebody who would help you. Whereas in the West, even your best friends might have other plans.

Yes, in spite of having Aasha as a friend, and having her job with John, and the writers' group, loneliness in the West could conspire with her mother's homemade *rotis* to send her home early.

Chapter 38

In Belleville, they walked up the hill until they reached the funny little bar that hosted the poetry slam every Saturday night. They stepped into the *café*—a run-down affair—said *"bonjour"* as required to the barman, and took seats close to the stage, which took up one corner. The stage was only one step higher than the rest of the *café*, but it was lit with a spotlight that set it apart.

Anjali examined the posters and bumper stickers that covered the walls of the stage's corner, forming the backdrop. "Love is the lesson, life is the school," said one. "I'm not lost, I'm exploring," said another. "I don't suffer from insanity. I enjoy every minute of it."

A poster inviting people to a Human Be-In, held in 1967 in Golden Gate Park, San Francisco, caught Anjali's eye. This place had been around that long? She peered at the dingy walls, noted the unmatched chairs, the marred tables, and thought, yes, it very well could have been.

They had arrived early. The place was quiet, and they could talk.

"A glass of wine?" Anjali knew that they would be breaking the unwritten code that Indian girls ought not to be out and drinking.

"Yes!" Aasha said. Their eyes met conspiratorially over the small table.

"Not a word to your parents," Anjali urged.

"Of course not! Same for you."

"Definitely."

"What are you hoping to get from this event?" Aasha asked, sounding skeptical as she looked around at the dubious surroundings.

"If I hear interesting lines, I'll write them down. Artists steal."

"That's okay?"

"My professor of creative writing in Mumbai said it is."

"If your professor said it's okay, it must be great," Aasha joked. "What do you do with the lines?"

"I see if they spark something creative for the screenplays I'm working on. They might take me in a new direction, or flesh out a character. Usually the lines change while I'm working with them. They become my own, so it's not really stealing." Anjali felt a bit guilty anyway. Just like the wine.

"How much time do you spend writing?" Aasha asked.

"Nearly every morning before work. Saturdays when I'm not out exploring. Sundays."

"Why do you work at it so hard?"

"Immortality. I want to live forever." Anjali was a bit embarrassed that this was her reason, but it was true.

"You want your name in the credits so people see it after you're dead." Aasha sipped her wine.

"Yes, I have an instinct for eternal life."

"But only film buffs look back at old films."

"True, but when they do, they'll see my work and think of me, the way I think of Billy Wilder or John Ford." Anjali sipped her white wine, something from the Saumur region.

"What do your parents think?"

"My parents' lives are so small. Small circle of friends and influence. I want to be part of something big. To be a successful filmmaker. To change people's lives through storytelling."

"What about personal happiness? Which is more important?"

"I'd like to have both." She didn't know just how she was going to answer this question, and she squirmed in the cast-off *café* chair.

"Your parents are happy. Why is that not good enough?"

"They'll die, their love will die, I'll die, and we'll all be forgotten. I want something of myself to live on."

The place had filled up while they talked, and a young man in black jeans and gray T-shirt stepped to the stage and got the night rolling. Even though the evening was billed as an "open mike," there was no microphone, and Anjali was glad they were seated close to the stage.

"Now, Madames et Monsieurs, we bring you, live from Paris, our poetry slam! We're here every Saturday night, so come back. I see some regulars in the audience. And to new people, *bienvenue*! Welcome!

The crowd applauded and chatted.

"So without further *adieu*—Curly, you're up!" the master of ceremonies shouted over the noise.

A bald man got up, and the crowd supported him to the stage with a round of applause. He stood with his hips thrust forward, his upper torso leaning backward, and recited his handcrafted lewd poem by heart. A lewd poem with a twist—with the recitation of the last line, the audience realized he was really talking about a doorknob.

Oh well, thought Anjali, nothing for me there. And I'm so glad my father isn't here. He'd march me to Mumbai tonight.

A woman went up, wearing strappy black heels, a flowing black knit skirt and tank top, no bra, and a small red scarf knotted around her neck. The *café* was getting warm with all the people in it. The woman took the scarf off, and the crowd immediately whistled and stamped. She smiled and vamped a strip tease. The man who had recited his lewd poem yelled "Take it all off!" The woman threw the scarf to the MC, bowed to the applause, and waved for quiet. Finally the crowd settled down to listen.

Anjali was disappointed to find that she was shocked. But she was in Paris now, she was on her own, she needed to adapt to the fact that some women acted like this sometimes.

The woman recited a poem she had written that had Anjali scribbling lines. The one that really grabbed her was, "The man dug tunnels by the town wall." She'd use that somehow, she was certain.

The woman bowed to an enthusiastic round of applause, and a young woman got up on stage. She wore her hair dyed purple and cut in a spiky boyish style, a black ring through one nostril, a short denim skirt, and red high-top Keds. She had cute legs, and no bra. The men's eyes were riveted on her as she strode around the stage, breasts bobbing under her T-shirt. Using her phone as her prompt, she read a rant she'd written about the double standard that's applied to women. The men in the audience listened intently, then forgot all about what she'd said as they applauded her cute sexiness at the end.

The quality of the poetry went downhill after that. Anjali thought to herself, some of these people might have a bit of a challenge becoming immortal.

"I think it's time for me to go home," Aasha said, as the clapping for another poetry slammer died down.

Just then the MC announced an intermission.

"I have to use the bathroom first," Anjali said.

She dashed through the crowd as the MC named the poets that were coming to the stage after the break. She was the first person down the metal spiral stairs. She was a small person, but she barely fit in the staircase. Its walls were painted with graffiti, and so was the hallway at the bottom. In front of her was a graffiti-covered door. She finished up quickly and stepped out of the water closet. A line of women waited. Her mad dash down the stairs had paid off.

The two girls stepped out into the warm night air and threaded their way between performers and members of the audience who stood smoking. They decided to walk uphill to the Pyrénées Metro station. The life of Belleville's streets swirled around them. Shops full of groceries, shoes, and clothing all teemed with Far East people.

"This is like a Chinatown," Aasha said.

"I love Belleville, it's so funky."

"Some of those readings were funky," Aasha said wryly. "I don't know how you're going to use them in a screenplay."

"For the good ones, I'll find a way," Anjali said. "Thanks for coming with me." She turned around. "Look, you can see the Eiffel Tower from here!"

It stood silhouetted against the dramatic clouds that Paris was adept at fomenting, with the evening sun below the horizon behind it.

"I love this place," Anjali sighed.

"You would. It's like a movie set."

Chapter 39

Saturday morning was Amma and Appa time, Sunday morning it was Ravi. That's if he didn't postpone it to play tennis or cricket. When he was available to talk, he dialed her, as was their custom. She sat on her bed, leaning against pillows bolstered against the shower wall.

"So, how was your week," he asked. He certainly did show an interest in her life, she had to admit.

She told him about everything except her boss's financial woes, the poetry slam, and the glass of wine. In other words, I'm not telling him most of my life.

He looked very appealing in her laptop screen in a freshly pressed white shirt. His brown skin was flawless, his jaw square and manly.

"What's up with you today?" she asked.

"Mum is making fresh *rotis* and chicken curry."

Anjali knew that his mother made the *rotis* and ground all twelve of her curry spices by hand, and that the food would be tremendous. Even purchased in the stores in La Chapelle neighborhood, the Indian spices available in Paris weren't as potent as those at home. At home? Wherever that was. She suddenly longed to eat his mother's, her mother's, cooking, something that would be possible if she returned.

She fought off the longing. She could have Italian food here in Paris, French, Chinese, Thai.

"And you?" he asked.

"I'm going to write this afternoon," she said.

"You work seven days a week?"

"I have to capitalize on my time here."

"I miss you," he said. His gaze was on something lying next to his laptop.

Did he really?

"Miss you, too," she said. But did she really?

Chapter 40

On Monday, Carol staggered into work. She was so tired. All weekend long she had worried that Gregoire would not live up to his word and keep her probation a secret. In the hallways at Trapèze, she looked in the faces of people she passed on her way to her office, but nobody gave a sign they'd heard the news.

Temporarily relieved just a bit, she settled herself down in her small office and opened the animated screenplay she was writing for Gregoire. As the story line came back to her, she was able to set aside her worries enough to work.

The film was about a flock of storks that accepted delivery of a bunch of babies from the south but can't deliver them to their parents in Paris because it was so late in the year, and the chimneys they would have used for delivery were now too hot, with fires in the fireplaces. The storks found that they had to raise these humans themselves until spring. Amusing scenes of storks gently correcting young human behavior ensue.

Carol picked up a storyboard off her desk that illustrated the first five minutes. Daphné, one of the artists, and an office sort of friend, had captured the gray zinc roofs, chimney pots, wrought-iron balconies, and rooflines of Paris well.

"Obstacles to the protagonists' goal" she wrote in her "quarry" notebook (a term she had stolen from George Elliot, who kept the facts she made up about her Middlemarch characters in one).

"Think!" she exclaimed out loud, and then slapped her hand over her mouth. Her office door was open. She hoped nobody had heard. She went back to work.

An ogre. Great obstacle! Let's make him a flying ogre, no less. Let's give him Gregoire's hair, all over his body. Gregoire won't notice. I'll tell Daphné to illustrate it that way to make her laugh.

What's next? The ogre spots the storks tossing the babies to each other, playing, and he's jealous of their family happiness. The ogre is actually a prince, born in the days of the Franks and the Gauls, the victim of a spell, and a very irritable ogre indeed. Lovely! Oh, wait! He bullies the storks! A chance to right that bullying I did when I was seven.

Carol spent two hours tapping out scenes.

At 11:15, she decided to take a coffee break and stepped tentatively into the hall outside her office. Without the screenplay to distract her, her worry settled on her again like an iron cape. Nobody must know she was on probation. Success in the film world was all she wanted—the acclaim of her colleagues in the business. She'd get an Oscar or a Palme D'Or some day, and put it where Gregoire couldn't help but see it.

Frédéric was in the kitchenette when she got there. He didn't look at her any differently, Carol thought, just with his usual randiness.

"*Bonjour*, Carol," he said. His tone of voice suggested they'd spent the night together.

She returned the greeting drily and bent over to get a paper towel from under the sink. She felt his eyes on her and looked down. Her blouse was gapping, he was getting a great view. She grabbed a paper towel and stood. Frédéric smiled broadly at her.

"A very beautiful morning, isn't it?" he said.

Yes, yes, Carol thought. He was not a good bet for a good relationship. "Indeed!"

Frédéric finished brewing his coffee, leered at her, and left. Carol brewed hers and took the long route back to her office, past Gregoire's door.

Amandine was just emerging. Carol flinched, then steeled herself to look carefully at the Parisienne for any difference in her attitude.

When she saw Carol, Amandine's eyes lit up with a look of even greater triumph and superiority than usual.

"Hello?" Carol asked, hating herself for her insecurity, for making her sentence into a question, like an American.

Amandine walked past her as if she mustn't associate with a leper for fear the problems might rub off.

Carol rushed back to her office and sat with her head in her hands. If Amandine knew, the whole office would know in five minutes. People would see her in meetings and know she was suffering and yet show no pity. If they did show pity, it would be worse.

Somehow, in spite of this humiliation in front of all her colleagues, she was still expected to produce a brilliant script. Damn

Gregoire! What an idiot! So unprofessional to tell Amandine. But he was in authority and would not be brought into account. Frustrating.

Carol closed the door to her office, reminding herself that people could still see her through her window onto the corridor. She could not be seen crying, or even wiping her eyes. Chin up! she could hear a Brit voice saying. Never, never, never give up.

Maybe she had misinterpreted Amandine's behavior. She couldn't wait until her lunch break—she was too curious. She headed back to the kitchenette, for tea this time, the British panacea for all the slings and arrows of outrageous fortune.

Martine, the assistant who helped both Gregoire and Amandine, stood by the microwave. She was a young thing wearing a short blouse that revealed her belly button jewel, and black leggings that ingratiated themselves into every inch of her crack.

Carol thought, those leggings hug her so tight I can read the label on her thong. "Hello!" she said as brightly as she could.

"Oh, hello," Martine said frostily and left on her impossibly long and shapely legs. Well, she was likely to know Carol's secret, since she handled Gregoire's paperwork. She would probably be discrete.

Daphné came in. She was statuesque and had long, wavy brown hair. It had sparkled in the sunlight the week before, when they had gone to lunch outside the office together. They had had some fun chats over the few years that Carol had been at Trapèze.

Daphné gave a start when she saw Carol. Was it a guilty start? She blushed a bit.

"I'm so sorry," she said under her breath.

"For what?" Carol had to know if this was all in her imagination or not.

"I heard that—you must know—" Daphné stammered.

"What have you heard? Please tell me." She wanted to know if the thing being whispered about her was accurate. Though she had no control over how the news would morph as people retold it to each other through a long chain.

"That you're on probation?" Daphné queried. "I'm really sorry. I think you'll pull out of it in no time at all." She grabbed her lunchbag out of the refrigerator and left.

Everyone knew at this point, Carol thought, down to the people who empty the wastebaskets. At least Daphné gave me some support.

She straggled back to her office, passing two more people in the hall.

"*Bonjour*," she said to one of them, who ordinarily would have said hello. Today he compressed his lips and did not.

Carol couldn't help quietly crying in her office, all the while listening intently for footsteps out in the hall. If someone went by, she would duck as though looking for something that had fallen on the floor under her desk. Tears spilled down her cheeks. She felt desperate to talk to somebody. But who?

She fidgeted with the question, her sorrow demanding an outlet. John's and then Philippe's faces swam into her consciousness. John was a businessman with years of experience. Philippe, as some sort of vicar, must counsel people all the time. He'd be good at it.

She had both their emails. She tapped out a note to each of them, asking them if they would meet her in the next few days to advise her on a problem at work.

Chapter 41

John poured over profit and loss statements and balance sheets generated by the accounting nerds in New York City. Anjali had printed them out. He couldn't stand all that online, shared document baloney.

The numbers were agonizing. He had decided not to declare bankruptcy because of all the ramifications of that move. His father had done it. John would not.

So, to get free of financial obligations, he had to make decisions. Faster. The company was bleeding payroll. If he were honest with himself about the situation, he would lay off everyone but Anjali. He simply had to wield an ax. Sharp. Soon. Today.

He typed what he wanted to say into a document. He revised it. He envisioned his employees' children, with big sad eyes at an empty dinner table, like a multitude of thin, ragged Oliver Twists. He hoped his employees had been good financial managers and had set something aside. He hoped they'd already started circulating their resumes.

He told the little children, "Sorry," and called the heads of office in New York, Amsterdam, and Hong Kong. Forcing himself to keep his voice firm, he tore down the temple he had built to money and fired his priests.

Thinking of Dieter in Amsterdam, who had a sick mother to take care of, and Chen in Hong Kong, who had just taken out a huge mortgage, he let the guillotine fall. He told each person to lay off their staff immediately, to send him the office rental and equipment leases, and to submit the bills they were each responsible for. To head off procrastination on their part, he said they'd have a bonus if they finished those tasks by tomorrow noon. They all asked how much. Typical. But of course they asked.

When he hung up, he thought of all the paperwork these men would be sending him and felt like he would suffocate. Then he reassured himself: Anjali would help.

Last, he called Pierre on the trading desk in La Defense on the west edge of Paris.

"You have to know when to hold 'em and when to fold 'em," John said after saying hello.

"What's zat? 'Old 'em?"

John thought, of course Pierre didn't recognize an expression from a country and western song. This was France, stupid.

"Um, I'm retreating from Moscow," John said. Pierre didn't laugh. The French didn't laugh about Napoleon. The two hundredth anniversary of him crowning himself Emperor of the French in Notre Dame was coming up, and there wasn't a word about it online or anywhere.

John explained his situation in plain language.

"Sir, maybe you 'ave anuzzer chance to build a business. I 'ope so. Sink of me."

"If I can help you find another job," John offered.

There was silence. John realized with pain that these days, using his name in this industry would probably only hurt Pierre.

"Well, if you need anything," John said.

"I call. Defeeneetly. Bye-bye."

John replaced the receiver, aching all over. His name used to open doors; now it closed them. To avoid thinking about that, he stared at a spreadsheet that diagrammed how to save money. He and Anjali would move to the shop space in Le Marais next week. He'd meet potential clients only in the top restaurants. Pay with a credit card. A few Saudi princes and he'd be rolling in dough again. It was getting a first meeting that was difficult. They'd want references. Who didn't hate him? He couldn't think of anyone.

He sat back in his huge chair, the leather creaking forlornly.

Just then Carol's email arrived, requesting a chance to talk about some issues at her job. He emailed her back.

"I can meet you tonight," he offered. Thinking about someone else's crisis would be a relief from thinking about his own.

Chapter 42

They met at seven that evening at Polidor on Rue de Monsieur le Prince in the Sixth. John picked the spot because he'd heard the food was good, not too expensive, and that it was so traditionally French, it still had a cabinet in the dining room in which regular diners of the past had kept their personal cutlery and napkin in their own drawer.

Carol arrived exactly on time, John noted. She was flushed with the sun, still bright in Paris at seven o'clock on a summer's eve. She was pretty, he mused. She took off a beige and cream scarf hanging loosely around her neck.

"What was I thinking? It's way too hot for this," she said as she threw it into her huge bag. "They have air conditioning in here, don't they?" She waved her hands around to test the air.

"What you feel is what you get for a/c," John said.

The pavement was too narrow to sit outdoors so there were no outdoor tables, Carol had noted on her way in. "Well, something cold to drink will help. Though it isn't likely I'll get an icy drink, even when I say, '*Beaucoup de glaçon, si'l vous plaît.*'"

"The French don't care about ice cold beer. Or a chilled gin and tonic on lots of rocks," John agreed. He sat back and watched Carol and her feminine movements as she combed the bangs out of her eyes with a finger. She tugged at one loopy earring. Oh, John thought. Interesting. He sat forward and smiled. He missed the presence of a woman in his life: light footsteps, cosmetics lying around the sink, perfume in the air. He wasn't having trouble imagining Carol in a romantic role. But then again, her critiques...

Carol was noticing John's broad shoulders, not rounded at all with care, concern, and inactivity. He was lean, tall, and very successful—she had looked him up on the Internet before meeting him at the first writers' circle. But to her, steeped in the world of storytelling and film making, he was a pagan. He was one of those business types that annoyed her daily at Trapèze with their nickel and dime priorities. But he might be able to advise her now. At least he'd be a safe listening ear.

She checked his ring finger. How tacky! He was meeting her with an obvious white line where his ring had been. Married and cruising! No way was she getting involved in that mess. So he was married—too bad. But good, because now she could relax and just be herself.

The waiter delivered their drinks. True to French form, only three ice cubes floated in Carol's G&T, and they were already half melted.

"*Santé*," Carol said, and they tapped glasses. Carol sipped. "Bloody hell, this G&T is warm! On a hot, humid night, too."

They asked each other about their children for a while, then switched to careers. John said nothing about his problems. She glossed over her career—investment banking in New York City, then throwing that over to return to her true love, becoming the founding member of a theater company, writing scripts for BBC Radio, then some plays produced Off Broadway, then some screenwriting in Los Angeles, then hired by Trapèze. Carol began to talk about her current dry period. Admitting to John that she'd been put on probation, after all the success she'd had, took every ounce of courage she had. She told him about Gregoire's leak to Amandine.

"Sue him," John said, "so he knows he's not dealing with a pushover."

Those words hovered between them a moment.

"I'd be afraid of being completely fired," Carol said. This wasn't going well.

"Well, that's what I would do," John said.

And then—incredibly, to Carol's ears—he asked, "How do you feel about what's happened?"

A huge sob came to her throat. She tried to quell it, to diffuse it within her, but it burst out with a will of its own.

"Oh my God, the rotten bastard!" she said. She struggled for control. No outbursts allowed among the subdued French at dinner. The couple next to them was looking at her, frowning. "He has to know Amandine doesn't keep things to herself. Just vile of him, wasn't it!"

"Yes, that is low. I'd never do that." Had he ever? He'd have to think back.

"I can't stand that my reputation has been ruined," Carol said, wiping her eyes. "I always had good ideas. I just had a small lapse." Jeffrey. His criticisms. Her lowered self-confidence. Maybe three months. Or six?

"Quit. Go solo. I've heard bits of your screenplay, you've got the talent."

"Thanks for the vote of confidence, but there's lots at stake, isn't there? I have to provide a roof for Louise."

"Yes, I know," said John, who had always felt he needed to provide not just a roof but a better roof than anyone else had, hand-cut slates rather than mass-produced shingles.

"I always dreamed of sending her to private school, too, though that drops on the priority list when one's job is at stake, doesn't it," Carol said.

John desperately wanted to keep Emily among her friends in private school. Those friends could provide contact with the right people for Emily later, and maybe for him, too, if he survived that long. Much at stake here, too.

"You had some good ideas for me at the writers' circle," said Carol, who was rallying as a result of John's calm. She put her cheerful face on again and smiled valiantly.

"Never thought of myself as a literary man," John said with satisfaction.

He was insufferable, always sucking things into his ego, Carol thought. Men!

"What are you going to do with your protagonist next?" Carol asked. Reminding him of how undeveloped his main character was might nudge John back down to earth. "Chuck is his name?" John's naming choice was a bit too similar to Chuck Norris, but oh well. It probably helped him imagine his protagonist's antics better. She'd advise him to change it later.

"Oh, I'll get him into bed with a lovely lady, of course. Gotta have lots of sex scenes. Sell, sell, sell."

"I meant, how are you going to develop him, make him more multi-dimensional?" She really didn't want to talk about sex with John, because his tall frame and robust shoulders were drawing her eyes. She could hop on his lap right now. Though that didn't seem sufficient reason to have sex with a person. Used to.

"Oh, I'll give him a hobby—sailing, like me. I have a boat in Cherbourg."

"How nice! But Chuck is in Nevada."

"Oh, yeah, well, I can fix that. Yes, I'll have the whole group out on my boat. We could have our critique on board. It's a forty-five-footer." He looked at Carol steadily.

A little braggadocio, Carol thought. But impressive! She eyed his ring finger again, to remind herself of the facts.

"We could read our work while we were on a mooring or at anchor. But even then, I'm paying attention to wind and tide and how close the other boats are. Not sure I can concentrate on reading my stuff."

Too bad not to read about more fistfights, Carol thought.

"Lovely!" she said. "That sounds great! I wonder—could I bring my daughter? I'd love for her to have that experience."

John wasn't sure at first, it felt like the whole thing was getting out of hand. But then the idea seemed okay. "I'll bring Emily. They can play. Bring lots of books. Emily loves to read." Yeah, her own books, John thought: Rimbaud and Victor Hugo in French, Jane

Austen. Not See Sally Run, or the Brit equivalent of it. She might be bugged at me.

"Grand idea! So tell me, you must love sailing: how will you work your sailboat into your story?"

"I'm not sure yet," John said.

This group is behind me in literary development, Carol thought. Here he had a singular experience that he could capture for his audience and give them the joy of it, too. But even if he didn't see his own opportunities, he might still have ideas for her that saved her job.

"No worries, it will come to you," Carol said. "I'm writing an animated screenplay at work about storks raising human babies that they can't deliver to their parents because an ogre is jealous." It sounded just a bit dumb, kind of like John's fisticuffs, but Carol knew that, by the time she was done with it, it would explore a few questions about life. It might very well illustrate the question, "Does loving your enemies change people's lives?" She thought of Gregoire and Amandine. No, she did not love her enemies. Which didn't mean she wouldn't write about the issue as if she did.

"Why is the ogre an ogre?" John asked.

"Because of an evil fairy who was envious of his mother's beauty. He's a prince really, but condemned to be irritable." Kind of like Jeffrey. And every other bloke she'd been with.

"Make the fairy jealous of the mother's wealth, instead of her beauty," John suggested. "Being jealous of beauty is so Snow-White-stepmother-ish."

Wow, this guy could bust up a *cliché*! Carol was impressed.

"Why does he bother the storks?" John asked.

"Because he's envious of their role in the cycle of life." Carol was glad to be asked these questions. They helped her to cement the logic of the story in her mind.

"Your storks will have quite a few challenges raising human babies."

"We'll have storks tossing the babies, catching them in mid-air. It's a fabulous chance for the audience to fly. First rules of Hollywood: when you have a big screen, use all of it. And when it's animated, do things humans can't do."

"You could have the storks trying to discipline the toddlers from going too near the stream. Or walking from their woodland hideaway onto a busy road."

"Let me write this down," Carol said. She fished for a notebook and a pen. She kept them in a special pocket in her portfolio so they were easy to grab. She always had at least seven pens with her: at the very least one in red, green, blue, black, and a fountain pen with turquoise ink. And a highlighter.

"Lots of opportunities for tender stork/baby interaction," John continued. "And the ogre could be envious because he never had that as a child. He was raised in cold, dark castles, and his parents were aloof, royal types. You could have—what's that called—a flashback?"

"That's very good," Carol said. "I could use that." Might as well signal her intentions just a bit. He may be seeing it on the screen in two years.

"Feel free." Am I giving too much away for nothing here? John wondered. Strange. That's not like me.

"So the ogre tries to break up the happy family," he said. "The storks try to outsmart him. Everything they try fails. Then they realize he's envious. Maybe, if they love him too, he'll stop tormenting them. And you've just illustrated 'Love your enemies,' though that's not something I'm very good at. And when they love him, the spell is broken and he becomes a handsome prince again."

She had had some of these ideas, but not bad, Carol thought. Needs refinement, some fleshing out, but not bad.

"No, not a handsome prince, a balding prince," he said.

Great, Carol thought, he just busted another *cliché*.

"And when he's no longer an ogre, he can no longer fly," John said. "It costs him to become human."

"Those are fine ideas, John," she said. He just needed to use the same part of his brain to generate ideas for his own work. She couldn't say it that way. "You might want to consider putting a few ideas like that into your story." Was that gently said enough? She hoped so.

"Yes, I'm thinking about Chuck," John mused. "The sailboat could lend a bit of the mystical to the story."

"All you need is a whale."

"Huh?"

"You need a logic to your story, a hunt, a pursuit of something that Chuck wants desperately."

"Logic?"

"Yes, a progression. Like a geometric proof. My goodness, I struggled with plane geometry in school, didn't I? My mind didn't work in logical paths, with a 'Q.E.D.' at the bottom. I felt awful. Then I realized years later, that there are all kinds of logic. One company's devices have one logic and another company's devices have another."

"Did you know there's a logic," said John, "called spherical geometry? It says that the lines of longitude that circle the globe and converge at the poles are actually parallel. Simply because they are perfectly parallel at the equator."

"That's so strange, isn't it?" Carol said. "But I'm not that interested in logical thinking. What I love is associative thinking."

"Is that anything like thinking in pictures?"

"Can be. One leads to another. It's fun."

"I've learned from you tonight," John said.

"Thanks so much, actually." Carol smiled.

"Yes, well, let's do it again."

Carol thought, I need your ideas. Too bad you're married. I have ideas for a man like you...

Chapter 43

Tuesday night, Carol trudged to meet Philippe in his office on a narrow, ancient street in the Fifth. Talking with John had felt good, but she still needed advice on what to do.

She climbed two flights, on centuries-old, warped wooden stairs, to Philippe's office and knocked. He opened the door and smiled.

"Would you like something to drink?" he said, inviting her in. "I have water, plain and *gazeux*," he said.

Carol felt tears prickle in her eyes at this small kindness. No one at work had acknowledged her existence today.

After pouring her some water, Philippe sat down behind the white laminated table that served as a desk. Carol sat in a white plastic bucket chair, a bit like George Jetson's cartoon chair. Philippe didn't play power games with the seating—their chairs were the same height. She plopped her pocketbook on her lap. It was loaded with Kleenex. Philippe had a box on his desk, she noticed.

"Hot day, wasn't it?" Philippe commented. He wondered if this meeting would be a good time to talk over critiquing styles. He looked at Carol. Obviously unhappy. Not a good time.

"Yes," Carol said and tried to settle her anxiousness.

They made a bit of small talk about Paris while Carol twisted the leather handle of her pocketbook, and then Philippe asked, "How can I help?"

Well, you could marry me for starters, couldn't you. He looked great, even though he was in another of his rumpled suits. She was especially lonesome tonight. And feeling just a tiny bit randy.

"I have a situation at my job that's very difficult. I'm looking for advice. I've read your work at the writers' circle, so I feel I've gotten to know you just a bit. And you're a vicar, you must talk to a lot of people."

"Yes, that's true. Tell me about your job."

"It sounds glamorous, screenwriter for a film company in Paris, but day to day it's very hard. Because there is so much money and prestige at stake, people are ruthless, worse than the investment bank in New York City that I worked in years ago. Ideas are gold bullion in this business, and you're only as good as the one you just delivered."

She took a sip of her *d'eau gazeux*. The bubbles felt like tiny sparks flowing down her throat.

"In spite of the pressure, I've written two screenplays in the last three years at Trapèze that were produced. Financially successful. Much more than made up their production costs. And they were successful entertainment. I couldn't help but go to a few showings of each film and sit with the crowd. They laughed in even more places than I'd written. It felt wonderful. I want that feeling again. If the business people would leave their hands off my scripts…"

"Why?"

"They come into my office with the storyboards—the concepts for each scene—and start chipping away. They say, 'If we used a French cow, right outside of Paris, instead of an American buffalo,' or 'if we used stock footage of the Eiffel Tower instead of hiring a helicopter,' etc., until the freshness and integrity are destroyed. To save a few *centimes*."

"Is that what's troubling you about work?" His sympathetic voice meant Carol had to pause to settle the ache in her throat. Then she explained the scenario.

"A friend"—she didn't say it was John—"told me to sue."

"You're a French citizen?" Philippe asked.

"No, British."

"Gregoire is French?"

"Yes."

"I wouldn't recommend a lawsuit. The justice system here is incomprehensible, even to the French. And you would not do well in a suit against a Frenchman."

"I see. I'm sure you're right."

"To confront him personally with what he's done, the injustice of it, the unprofessionalism, that makes sense to me. But ultimately, your greatest happiness and freedom will be in forgiving him."

"But he's damaged my reputation—no, ruined! There's nothing I want more than to be known as a great screenwriter and to keep the respect of my peers."

"Well, you know that people are fickle. One day they wave palm branches over you, and the next day they're screaming, 'Crucify.' To spend your life's energy winning man's empty praise...?"

This was going to require a bit of thought, Carol realized. She mashed the handle of her pocketbook again.

"I've given my life to pursuing the truth through art. To creating art in spite of the business people trying to ruin things. I do such good work. I went through a tough patch with my love interest and wham! My professional reputation is ruined."

"Do you want to tell me about this tough patch?"

"Some other time we'll talk about my disastrous love life. But I'm too tired to go into it now."

She took another sip of the sharp water and set the plastic cup down on the Formica table. Lots of white plastic in Philippe's office...

"Let's just talk about your job, then," Philippe said. "The arts— movie making—that's difficult. Why do you do it?"

"I want to tell stories that show how important values are, that affirm humanity."

"That's very worthwhile."

"Thanks." *Are you sure we can't get married? I've always wanted to be with a man who encouraged me. Can't seem to find one to save my life, can I?* By now the handles of her pocketbook felt soggy under her sweaty hands.

"What value is your current movie about?"

"Tenderness between parents and children. And how humans can't do neat things like fly, but we can love. And love your enemies, maybe, *though I don't love Gregoire right now, quite the opposite, isn't it? Speaking of the devil, what do I do about my colleagues and Gregoire?*"

"Bide your time. Do excellent work. In a week or two they will have forgotten."

"What if they don't?"

"Just do your best. You could pray and forgive him."

Well, thought Carol, *Philippe was a vicar of some sort, it was inevitable that he talk rubbish about prayer and forgiveness and whatnot.*

"Well, I'll think about it. I have to go now—babysitter."

"I understand. *Au revoir*, Carol," Philippe said.

She dashed into the bright evening.

Chapter 44

Philippe and Elodie were eating dinner in the kitchen Wednesday when the phone rang. Philippe excused himself from the table and stood to pick up the receiver, which hung near the door to the dining room. He hoped to hear Meredith's voice.

"Mr. Rouviere?" A young woman spoke on the other end of the line.

"Yes?"

"I'm the person Meredith stayed with. You dropped her off last week? I'm sorry to tell you—she was doing stuff I just couldn't tolerate, coming home late, banging around, waking me up, and vomiting all over the place. Then passing out, so I had to clean it up."

"Yes, I know," Philippe said quietly. He knew what was coming. He leaned against the doorframe of the kitchen for support.

"So I told her to leave. She did a little while ago."

Philippe felt complete dread for Meredith in the pit of his stomach, making him nauseous. Elodie was watching him, eyes huge.

"Do you know where she went?"

"No, she was furious, so I couldn't ask her. After she was gone, I saw that she took some things from my apartment, nothing really valuable, but sentimental—my ashtrays and candle holders that I brought back from India."

"I'm sorry. I'll reimburse you."

"Never mind, just if you see them again, get them back to me."

"Did somebody pick her up? Did you see them?"

"It was a man with a car. I don't know his name."

"I see." The nausea built.

"I'm sorry for all you're going through."

Philippe, the politest of men, couldn't say goodbye because his throat was so constricted with grief and dread. He tried hard to speak, then simply hung up.

"Tell me, what's happened?" Elodie asked softly. She set down her *fourchette* ever so quietly. It rested next to her small piece of *poulet*. The small green mound of *épinards* on her plate huddled miserably.

Philippe thought that his wife, and everything on her plate, looked exhausted.

"That same creep that brought her here—well, I don't know that for a fact—" Philippe sank onto a red kitchen stool with a sigh. "She got kicked out of that girl's house. I don't know where she is now."

"Oh dear God."

"My gut has one hundred fires in it."

Elodie poked her chicken, then the spinach, with distaste.

"We've got to pray even harder," she said. "Only Seigneur can help her now."

"I'm weary of prayer. I've been praying for Meredith ever since I knew you were pregnant with her. It's excruciating to have twenty years of prayer ignored."

"Not ignored, *mon cher*, just not answered yet."

"He's got to hurry up."

"I know."

By mutual, silent agreement, they left their plates where they were, straggled to the living room, and sank onto the couch. They held hands as Elodie, the only one with a speck of strength, prayed.

Chapter 45

John put on his shirt, tie, pants, and suspenders in his new bachelor pad. As he dressed in the narrow aisle between bed and closet, one elbow kept bumping the closet door, making a hollow thud. Twelve square meters. A *chambre de bonne*, twelve square meters, in the Sixth *arrondissement*, where he used to rent a hundred square meters. He had sublet the big apartment on Boulevard Raspail, and he'd downsized post-haste. He was *astucieux* with a buck, except when it came to silver ETFs.

He looked around ruefully. A twin bed, a dresser, a desk, and a closet. A two-burner hotplate, a microwave, and a sink. His books were stacked on a shelf: *Good to Great* and novels full of fisticuffs. He had no bookends. How could life have driven him to this? He couldn't bring a woman here, she'd dump him on the spot. Emily couldn't stay overnight with him. And if she ever did see this room, he'd have to ask her not to tell her mother the kind of place he was in.

At least he had a sixth-floor balcony. He stepped out on it gingerly, afraid it might collapse, and gazed over Saint-Sulpice's gargoyles. Did the gargoyles stare back at him? They were freakish combinations of animals distorted by the sculptor, and then distorted further by centuries of sculpting by rain. A bit disturbing-looking. He heard organ music from within the cathedral, a cascade of tortured bass notes. Maybe he should have been a church organist making a pittance. In the end he would have been better off.

He went back inside to dress for work and reached for his father's cufflinks. That man died thinking he was a failure, John thought. Well, he was a failure. He gave up. John slipped the left link through its buttonhole. His father had lost a mansion, four cars, a *pied à terre* on Park Avenue, and every bit of status.

On top of that he was a lousy father. John pictured mealtimes while growing up: the extravagantly furnished dining room—the sideboard, table and chairs imported from an English baronial estate. His mother sat at her end of the linen-shrouded table, then four children. And his father's place? Empty. The staff didn't even bother to set it anymore.

He was always working, never a moment's thought for his children. He hadn't come to John's Choate or Princeton or Yale graduations. John steadied himself against the dresser as he thought of Emily, who would graduate high school in just two years. He wore these links to remind himself not to be like his father.

John slipped his Rolex YachtMaster onto his wrist and looked at its multiple faces, multiple hands, exposed gears whirring and ticking, diamonds marking each hour. It had cost him 15,000 euros in a *chic boutique* on the Place Vendôme. Considering what had happened, maybe he should have spent twenty euros for a Rolex rip-off hawked by thin African immigrants at the foot of the Eiffel Tower.

He clambered down the six flights in his apartment building and dragged himself toward his office. His thoughts jumped even as his gaze jumped from wrought-iron balcony to chimney pot to zinc roof. The door to business opportunity seemed tight shut, he thought. Complaining wouldn't help. Chin up—maintain a positive attitude. That's what Americans do. He had his health. He had a sailboat—for now. He might lose it. Anjali had been a find. She was managing most of the paperwork of closing the offices, so he could be free to find new business. Striding out, he resolved to turn his business around.

On the Pont des Arts, where he crossed the Seine, he noticed how so many strands of the bridge's chain link fence had unraveled under the weight of padlocks. That was like divorce: an unraveling. He imagined the padlock he and Cassandra had attached there falling off a loose bit of fencing, plummeting into the Seine, chasing the key they had blithely thrown in years earlier on their honeymoon. He leaned his elbows on the parapet. Somebody bumped him. John just stared into the greenish waters.

Wakes from passing boats flowed to the stone embankments on either side, ricocheted off, and returned, creating restless, choppy waters.

This river running below him was the same one that Inspector Javert in Les Miserables had thrown himself into. Javert had seen that the principles that drove his life were failures and couldn't find it in himself to make a new start. John stood and fingered a cufflink. The diamond, onyx, and silver were cold beneath his fingers. His father had chased money, and money had failed him. What was success, anyway? Maybe his father's deeper failure had been not finding a new, better principle in life.

I'll find it, John said. Or I'll die searching.

Just then a police river cruiser emerged from under the bridge and bounced down the river, four men in black uniforms in a big rubber dinghy with a giant outboard motor on the back. A few bullets through the rubber hull and they'd all drown in the Seine, John mused. That would be a bit of a failure, wouldn't it. Oh well, let's get going.

He made his way across the bridge. A Parisienne—someone very stylish in a flatteringly-tied silk scarf who was obviously hurrying to work—passed him, totally absorbed in her own thoughts. In this mind's eye he compared cities. He'd walked the streets of New York City many times. It was impersonal, people didn't much look at each other. But they weren't encased in indifference. Ask a New Yorker for directions and you'd get a smile and an answer, maybe even a "Come-with-me" showing of the way. But Parisians were encased in a shell. They didn't know you existed.

New York had energy, excitement. When he was there, John felt embraced by the energy and inspired. When he wasn't immersed in it, he missed it. Paris was low energy, but it had elegance. The white buildings on every street with black wrought-iron balconies, the abundance of *cafés* with their rattan chairs, seats woven in colors that matched the awning of the *café* they belonged to, all set up in rows— it was priceless. Paris was beautiful but low-energy. New York was gritty but electric.

In fact, the electricity was getting to be almost difficult to bear. In his most recent trip back, he'd felt the energy was over-the-top, out of control, like a machine with no governor.

New York was manic. Paris was magic.

In Paris, people lingered over meals, savoring the food and the companionship. They spent time talking to each other. They didn't rush off to the next activity, like they did in New York. And it was a rare meal in Paris that wasn't excellent.

His footsteps rang out against the pavement. Why did he choose to be an expat here? Not that he any longer had the resources to move anywhere else. And where would he go? Emily was in school here and should finish here. Then he'd see. Maybe Barcelona, maybe New York, both with an ocean to sail on. That was one major thing Paris lacked.

He turned right along Quai du Louvre and then left up Rue du Pont Neuf to Rue de Rivoli and along the busy commercial avenue to Rue de Sévigné. Unlocking the shop door, he flicked the *interupteur*—what weird sort of people would use a word like *interupteur*, four syllables for "interrupt the flow of electricity," when they could use a neat word like "switch"—and the stone wall was washed with dramatic light.

The mahogany desk he had enjoyed in his office in Tour Montparnasse had been too expensive to move. And it wouldn't fit here anyway. Now he had a battered wooden desk, which he hid from passersby behind a wicker screen he'd picked up at a Paris flea market. The drawers in the desk always stuck, whether opening or shutting them. He remembered the glide of his former desk's drawers. He'd finished the whiskey stashed in the bottom. The Baccarat crystal tumblers had been sold.

I've been stripped, he said to himself as he sat in his cheap chair. The market turned against me and picked me clean. How can I ever get even a part of it back?

He scolded himself. Don't be like your father.

Picking up his black book, he mused that he had already called the most likely people and had found no gold nuggets. Now it was time to dredge for gold flakes in the silt.

"Archie, how are you?" John roared into the phone with all the *bonhomie* he could muster as soon as Archie picked up. That was the only way to talk to this guy, who came from old money, a good old boy, *astucieux* with a buck.

"John, my boy. I've heard you've had some challenges."

"Yes, a correction caught me wrong-footed, nothing that won't improve with time."

"A correction?" Archie sounded skeptical. "I heard it was more than that. People are saying it was a bit of foolish investing."

"Archie! What investing isn't a bit foolish!" John joked, thinking desperately so he could keep the conversation on a charming track. "It's all risk. But I've found something I think you should know about. A tech company with a great idea—"

"I don't do tech," Archie said.

John was silenced. Then he scrambled to save face.

"That's okay, I've got a lead on another—"

"Not today, John."

His heart sank. Archie sounded very final. Try another tack.

"Well, listen, I'll keep my eyes peeled for something that's low and going. Come out on the Grey Skies with me, we'll talk."

"That sounds good, John, keep me posted."

John put down the receiver. The lines of communication were still open, after all. But his ego smarted from Archie's evasion. He made a note in his calendar to call Archie in two weeks and wrote "no tech" under the note. He had known that. He was losing form, not checking Archie's interests before.

Man, this is killing me, John thought. It killed my father, literally.

Chapter 46

Carol walked down the hall at Trapèze remembering Philippe's advice, feeling supported by his friendship somehow. She went into Gregoire's office without knocking. This was the only way to catch him. If she asked for an appointment, his assistant with the belly button jewel would put her off forever.

Gregoire looked up from his computer. Carol closed the door.

"Carol, I can't talk right now—"

"—You told Amandine I was on probation, after you promised no one would know but you and me!" Carol said.

"I did not—"

"—Yes, you did. And you did that knowing that Amandine can't keep a single thing to herself. It's all over the office!"

"Look—"

"So unprofessional of you!"

Carol quit while she was ahead, before her voice cracked or she said too much. She turned on her Etienne Aigner heels and left.

Chapter 47

On Saturday afternoon, Louise went to a friend's for the night and Carol suddenly had too much time on her hands. Used to be she would fend off Jeffrey's criticisms while cleaning the apartment for an hour, then fall into bed to make him happy, to shut off the stream of little hurtful things he said. Of course he started up again as soon as sex was over—for that matter, he kept the criticisms going all through it. You're too fat here, too thin there. Good riddance. Terrifying that she'd chosen to be with that guy, and for as long as she had. A man who drove her bonkers. As usual.

She went to a photography exhibit at the Cartier-Bresson Foundation in the Fourteenth. The people the street photographer had captured off guard had distressingly ugly expressions on their faces, no matter which city he captured them in. She left quickly, took the Metro to Bois de Boulogne, and sat in a *café* that Daphné had raved about, on an island in a lake. That was a mistake. She felt terribly alone among the families and couples.

Drifting along the paths, she thought that she really ought to be working on her personal film's screenplay but that she'd rather be walking with a nice, uncomplicated, attractive man. After yet another jolly couple passed her, smooching, fingers twisted together, all smiles, she turned back toward the Metro.

In the train, a middle-aged couple boarded and stood rather than taking seats. They were perfectly matched, the way an aristocrat in an eighteenth century novel would have matched his horses. Both were blonde and blue-eyed, tall and slim, elegantly dressed in tans and whites. The woman pressed against the man and looked up at him with adoration, then stretched way up to kiss him seductively on the cheek. When they got off, the man grabbed the woman's hand and looked up and down the platform, as if to say, "Look what I've got."

They have a long, mostly happy history together, that's what I really envy, Carol thought. They've worked things out, unlike stupid Jeffrey and his stupid criticisms, unlike every other man I've dated. Do I start with bad basic material? Or do I influence them to be that way? Do I sabotage myself?

Another couple entered, sat, and locked lips on the bobbing train.

These two are going home to screw, then have dinner together, then screw again, and I'm going home to eat dinner alone, maybe watch a cookery show, maybe a film with popcorn, maybe work on my screenplay. In what way is my creative effort tonight going to beat what they'll be doing?

She thought about it for a minute.

There was no way. Even if she buttered the popcorn, it couldn't remotely compete with a good fuck.

Celibacy was rough, but being on one's own did have one advantage: freedom. She decided, without having to consult anybody, to watch the film while eating dinner, skip the popcorn, and work on her screenplay. The writing, the attempt to get another human being to feel along with her, would keep her company.

Chapter 48

On Saturday afternoon, after a morning spent in the library writing, Anjali walked with Aasha along the Seine embankment along with thousands of others, watching *les bateaux mouches* full of tourists go by. In the boats' wakes, the water boiled and bounced off the stone-walled embankments.

"I read that the Brigade Fluviale, the river police, pulled fifty corpses from the Seine last year," Aasha said. "About ninety people attempt suicide in the river each year."

"How many of them get rescued?"

"Roughly seventy, the article said."

"So that leaves thirty persons who turned into corpses in the river for unknown reasons," Anjali said.

"Leave it to you, the writer, to do the math and speculate," Aasha said with a smile.

A roller blader, going at breakneck speed, flashed by on the crowded embankment. If he knocked some poor kid into the Seine, the child would be one of the statistics.

Anjali raised a new topic of discussion

"My mother made me bring a book from Mumbai, and for some weird reason I'm actually reading it. I'm wondering if she ever read it? Or did she pick it out for me simply by the title?"

"What's it called?"

"Hindu Womanhood. Stories from Indian history about women immolating themselves rather than lose their *satitva*, their virtue."

Aasha didn't appear to be the slightest bit affected by what Anjali was saying.

"Everywhere in this book, there's the story of a *sati*—a perfect wife—who immolates herself, who voluntarily follows her deceased husband onto the funeral pyre."

"That's all in the past, don't worry about it now."

"No, there was a revival in the 1980s, where widows were pressured by the man's family to immolate themselves—so the family wouldn't have the burden of taking care of them."

"Those are extreme cases, don't you think?" Aasha still didn't seem perturbed.

"Don't any of these stories bother you?" Anjali asked as they walked along. A family of four, all on bicycles of different sizes, whizzed by.

"It won't happen to me. I love Sameer, his family loves me. I'm glad to be in Paris, but I'm looking forward to going back and getting married."

The stories bothered Anjali, the writer with the vivid imagination.

Chapter 49

They strolled farther, enjoying the breeze off the river. Anjali noticed some long, low boats tied up alongside the *quais*. They looked like workboats in a way, but they had lace curtains in the windows, giving them a domestic air. What's more, many of them had cars and motorboats on the roofs of the cabins. How did they get the car off the roof and on to land?

"What are those boats? They're so weird," she asked.

"Those are *péniches*, barges," Aasha said. "Some carry cargo, and some are turned into floating homes. People live on them year round, take them through the canal system that meanders through the French countryside, come back up the Seine, whatever they feel like."

"I want to talk to them," Anjali said. "I need money—I'll write an article about life on a *péniche* and get paid. Maybe. If some newspaper buys it."

"People still read newspapers?"

"Funny."

"Is this article going to help you be immortal?"

"I doubt it. If it gets into print, it will end up under somebody's cockatoo. But I learn from everything I write."

They were passing one especially beautiful *péniche*, white hull scrubbed down to the waterline, brass trim sparkling. A man sat on the spacious teak deck reading a newspaper. Anjali approached the edge of the *quai* gingerly. The man bounced slightly in his big *péniche* as the wake of a passing *bateau mouche* hit it.

Anjali stood at the end of the gangway and called to him.

"Excuse me, do you speak English?"

He looked her slowly up and down. Finally he deigned to nod.

Anjali didn't like his attitude already, but persisted.

"I'd like to interview you about life on a *péniche*. Could we schedule a time to talk?"

"What newspaper are you from?"

"I'm writing an article on speculation."

He shook his head and returned to his paper.

"Don't give up," Aasha said. "See? There's another *péniche* with a woman."

The next *péniche* had a black hull and dark red cabin. Window boxes of pink and red geraniums hung from a metal railing around a deck that sported a potted palm and teak garden furniture.

Anjali caught the woman just as she stepped off the gangway, before she disappeared among the people strolling.

"You have a lovely boat," Anjali said, trying not to let her gaze shift to the white one upstream, which obviously had more money poured into it.

"Thank you, dear," the woman said with a British accent. Her blonde hair, gray at the roots, was wild and frizzy and flopped around in the breeze off the Seine.

"It must be nice to live on a boat in the heart of Paris," Anjali said.

"Yes, quite…"

Anjali sensed the woman was ready to scurry off, so she jumped to ask her for an interview.

"What newspaper are you with?" the woman asked.

"None. I'd just like to do an article and send it to The Guardian, in London, or maybe The New York Times, places like that, see what happens," Anjali said.

An extremely long, black-hulled *péniche* labored past, obviously a working boat, though it had lace curtains on the cabin windows. In its wake, the woman's *péniche* bounced and tugged at its lines. The metal gangway of the boat rose, fell, and clanged at the wake.

"Well, I'm just off to do errands," the woman said. "*Le fromagerie, le patiserrie, le charcuterie,* and so forth."

"Oh, I didn't mean now! I'd come back when it's convenient for you. On a weekend or after five o'clock." When it was convenient for Anjali.

"Okay, let's talk," the woman replied. "It'll be fun. I'm Marjorie."

"Thanks!"

The breeze coming downriver flopped Marjorie's frizz to the opposite side of her head.

"I'll introduce you to some other *péniche* owners. Not my neighbor," Marjorie said with a smile, pointing to the white boat just upriver. "He's a bit full of himself, isn't he."

"I know." Anjali giggled. She'd lucked out. This woman was as friendly as an American.

Marjorie took her phone out of her purse, and they worked out a date.

"Thank you!" Anjali said. She was surprised when Marjorie gave her the traditional *bisous*, one on each cheek. Wow, we're officially friends, she thought. That done, Marjorie hurried off.

Anjali watched her, then turned to Aasha. "Whatever people say about that French kissing tradition, it certainly gets people better acquainted." She had gotten a whiff of the woman's breath. "Great way to gather clues. Date of last shower, how much garlic in last night's dinner, favorite cologne, how much wine at lunch. Important data."

"Too much information," Aasha said, smiling.

Chapter 50

Thursday night and time for writers' group.

Carol sweated in her apartment on a hot summer's evening as she printed out the stork versus ogre screenplay. Ten pages will have to be all—can't hog all the time. Scripts take about one minute per page to read aloud, so I'm not being too selfish. But whoops! The cut-off at ten pages is too soon for the best part to be read. I have to show the group that part. So that makes twelve and a half pages. I hope nobody notices.

The group convened at Le Café Livre. Though the solstice was weeks ago, the summer evenings in Paris were still immensely long and showed no sign of slackening. Tourists milled past, on their way to explore the narrow streets of Le Marais.

They accepted menus from the waiter, who looked as though he were prepared for anything this time, doggy bags notwithstanding.

"How are you?" John asked the table in general.

"Good," piped up Carol. She thought, No need to dredge up the pain I'm in at work. "You?"

"Yes, good."

Anjali and Philippe both murmured, "Fine, thanks."

Everyone turned back to their menus, the priority issue of the moment.

John massaged the back of his neck, which ached after hours of sitting, working the phone. He glanced across the table and noticed that Carol had wonderful blue eyes, enhanced by the blue of the long blouse she was wearing. She's rather intriguing, he thought. But can be quite cutting in her critiques. I'd better not think about her too much. What to order? A great big beefsteak would be great. No, that's far too expensive. Choose something less expensive. I'm short on money but not sure how short because I haven't wanted to examine my budget. How tight is money going to have to be? What the heck, I'm hungry tonight, tomorrow will be my lucky break. Plus, I must save face and not appear to be broke. I'll have the *bœuf bourgignon*. Only twelve euros, but not so inexpensive that I look impoverished. And a glass of cabernet sauvignon. It's only a matter of time until I have a new client. It can't take too much longer, the way I'm working the phones.

But I have a weird feeling about this search. And I'm not so sure that chasing money is the thing to do with my life anymore.

Carol read the menu, her neck aching from sitting and writing all day at Trapèze. She looked up to spot two men passing, holding hands, talking intently. They'd found somebody, obviously, she thought. I stink at picking men, maybe I should find a lady companion. Yes, that's just the ticket, two people living together with too many hormones once a month. And who takes charge during sex? I hate going to ballroom dancing classes and having to lead a dance because there aren't enough men. I stink at that too, quite frankly. Too confusing. I can't remember from one second to the next what role I'm playing. Am I male, taking a step forward? Or female, stepping back? I've crashed painfully into a few ladies in my time. No, that doesn't seem to be the answer.

She glanced at John. Handsome and healthy looking, in touch with his feelings. The indentation and paleness of the skin on his finger was not as obvious as a few weeks ago. What did that mean?

Philippe looked wrung out. Poor guy.

She turned back to the menu. Now this is a simpler problem than Philippe's. Your job is very shaky, and you ought to be careful with money and not order whatever grabs your eye. Besides, the stunning, drapey, periwinkle-blue silk artist's smock that you bought

158

on your way here cost eighty euros. You shouldn't have, part of her said. But I fancied it, another part said.

Her shoulders sagged a bit. I need stylish clothes to help me face Amandine and Gregoire. But that's the last time; I hereby resolve not to buy any more clothes for months. Get the *baguette* with *emmantal* cheese and ask for *une carafe d'eau*. It's tapwater *à la Seine*, but it's free.

Anjali gazed at the menu, her butt hurting from too many hours in her assistant's chair. The menu listed French specialties, like *saumon tartare*, raw salmon, but she longed for the strong flavors of Indian food. Looking up, she noticed a Jewish man trudging by, white prayer shawl tassels dangling below the hem of his black jacket. Le Marais had a Jewish community and several synagogues in it. Judaism. Must check it out, she thought. Women in Western countries, with their roots in the Judeo-Christian tradition, get treated with more respect than in other countries. Not that Western countries are problem-free. Hardly.

Anjali noted that in Paris she had changed. She thought, To be even thinking of looking at other religions is unusual. We Indians have such a strong sense of our own culture, we are so rooted in our own spirituality, that most of us aren't seeking, we're comfortable in the tradition we have. But that mural in Sacré Cœur, and the articles in The Hindu online about women and the families they married into, and the pressure on her to go home and be a traditional Hindu and marry—it was all adding up to some new questioning.

Anjali set her menu down. All she could afford was a decaf. "Did you bring new work tonight?" she asked Carol. She knew John was bringing a new chapter. She had printed it out for him earlier.

"A challenge to get it done, but yes," Carol said. "You?"

"Yes, but a challenge, to work full-time and get your creative writing done, like you say."

Philippe heard the chit-chat, but couldn't deal with it. His heart ached with worry over Meredith. What item on this menu could give a little comfort? *Pavé de veau grand cru, crème de morilles purée* looked good. The translation written on the menu: "veal, morel cream." This restaurant needs help with its English translations, he thought. You're getting a bit of a potbelly, Philippe. Yes, and I'm sick of *croque monsieur*. I've got to try something else. Go light on the dinner and on the wallet. How about a small salad? It doesn't appeal, but it's all you can afford in two ways. It's sad to be in Paris on such a low budget.

Aw, it's okay, it's a challenge, Philippe. You know that constraints foster creativity. Chin up.

The waiter took their order and they chatted about the news headlines. Anjali didn't know what they were talking about; she never seemed to get around to looking at world news online, only the travel essays in The Guardian and the front page news of The Hindu online.

Soon the food arrived.

"*Bon appétit*," the waiter said and departed.

"*Bon appétit*," they chorused. Philippe paused and considered closing his eyes to say grace. In France, people sat down, said, "*bon appétit*," and began. The tradition of saying grace had been replaced by a bit of encouragement to enjoy your meal. Nobody thanked God for their food. And he didn't feel like being any different from the rest of the group tonight. He didn't feel thankful, with Meredith on the streets.

He stabbed at his salad. John's dinner looks so much more delicious, he said to himself, cubes of tender meat, mushrooms, and white onions in a rich wine sauce, all bubbling in an earthenware pot. What was it like to have John's kind of money?

John took a bite, savored as he chewed, and rolled his eyes. "Best ever," he said. He grabbed a piece of *pain* from its basket and dipped it in the sauce in his bowl. "Is this allowed in France?" he asked no one in particular. "I've heard it isn't, you don't use your fingers but push your bit of bread around with your fork. But you know what, I don't really care tonight."

"Enjoy yourself," Carol said. She bit into her *baguette avec emmantal* and thought, wow, the cheese is good, the *baguette* is crusty. Good choice!

Anjali felt out of step with the others enjoying their food. She sipped her decaf only occasionally. She was nervous about her work tonight.

John looked up from his dinner to observe Anjali picking up her tiny coffee cup quickly, bringing it to her mouth in a flash, tipping the cup to sip for an instant and returning it to its saucer just as fast. She doesn't realize she did all that in two seconds, John thought. She's nervous.

Even though he tried to eat slowly, Philippe just couldn't. He was anxious, and he inhaled his salad in two minutes. The picture of

Meredith in bed with a drunken lout flashed into his mind's eye. He shoved the picture away. Meredith, don't, he wailed, and his heart and stomach contracted. He ate two more bites in spite of it, then set his fork down.

Carol asked for a doggy bag for half of her *baguette*, and the waiter didn't quiver so much as an eyelash. With her food wrapped up in her big bag and the plates cleared, she said, "I elect Anjali to start tonight."

Anjali brought out her pages and distributed them. John claimed the male lead immediately. Carol took the female supporting character.

Anjali felt bad for Philippe, who had been left out of the fun. There was only one part left. Anjali decided to make a sacrifice.

"Do you want to read the narrator and stage directions?" she asked him.

"Yes, my pleasure," Philippe said. You are so considerate, he thought. As he glanced over the pages, he thought, great, I have lots of lines to read. I'm just like any actor, counting his lines.

He began reading.

"Scene 1. A helicopter provides a panorama of the city. The camera lingers on the major monuments: Eiffel Tower, Notre Dame, Sacré Cœur, Le Louvre."

Anjali blushed at that point. A professional was reading this—Carol—and Anjali wasn't sure if overweening ego hadn't led her to write this first scene, or a fresh, new talent. Megalomania came in many forms. She would find out if she suffered from it tonight.

John read the lead character's voiceover in a somber bass: "Paris is called the city of light. (Pause) But it has shadows, too."

Philippe resumed with stage directions. "While the camera pans over the lovely townhomes of the 17th *arrondissement*, with their extra-elaborate wrought-iron balconies and zinc-roofed domes, the narration continues."

John fished for his deepest voice. "The jaded wealthy, with their European vices, get their kicks in the city's private clubs and homes. And the people who want to be wealthy are willing to do whatever it takes to associate with them."

Then Philippe chimed in with stage directions.

"Helicopter-mounted camera proceeds down the Champs Élysées toward the Arc de Triomphe. Car headlights and taillights make long streaks. The camera approaches the Arc and aims directly for the opening under the arch. Just when it looks like we'll fly through, go to black."

John waited a second, to let the word "black" reverberate. Then he read, "In between the two worlds is where I operate. I'm Dick Bogart, private eye."

Philippe took over. "Scene 2. Camera catches blooming trees in spring, blossoms bouncing in a light breeze in Luxembourg Gardens. Focus on a man in a trenchcoat walking on an April afternoon.

John read the voiceover. "I was on my way to an apartment in the upscale Sixth *arrondissement* to see Madame de Denichen, a French aristocrat who told me on the phone that she had a problem for me to solve. She wouldn't say any more, except that she heard I was discrete. There was a threat in the way she said it."

Anjali felt like death inside. What do these people think of my screenwriting? she wondered.

The reading continued. Just as he exited Jardin de Luxembourg, Dick Bogart witnessed a car accident on Boulevard de Vaurigard. The plot thickened from there.

Carol shifted her body in her chair. She was impressed with Anjali's writing. But there were some important problems. When they finished the pages, she jumped in.

"You need a film-writing software that will format your script properly," she said. "Movie Magic Screenwriter or Final Draft are the two best. They're only maybe 100 euros, last time I checked."

Anjali now knew she *had* to get paid for her *péniche* story.

Carol continued. "You're writing a hard-boiled mystery, like a Sam Spade sort of thing, right?"

Anjali nodded.

"Your naming."

Uh-oh, thought Anjali, here comes a kick in the teeth.

"What you've done is Naming 101—like, freshman level."

Anjali winced.

Philippe thought, does Carol have any idea how she's coming across? I've really got to say something.

"'Dick' is slang for 'private eye'," Carol said. "Was that intentional?"

Anjali nodded again, hurting under Carol's criticism.

"'Dick' and 'private eye' are both old-fashioned terms. Is this story set in the present?"

"Yes."

"They call themselves *détectives privées* in Paris these days. And 'Bogart' harks back to Humphrey Bogart."

"I wanted to bring all those associations to this movie," Anjali said.

"It's too obvious," Carol said. "It's heavy-handed."

There's another kick, Anjali thought. And wasn't Carol's critique just a bit heavy-handed? Naming 101? That hurt.

John said, "I'm not sure an elegant city like Paris lends itself to gritty *film noir*. Los Angeles and New York? Definitely."

"There's plenty of human rottenness here, too," Philippe said, thinking of how his daughter was in the middle of it.

"The next to last scene will be in the sewers of Paris," Anjali said. "Can't get much more gritty and *film noir* than that."

"You should read *Les Miserables*," Philippe said. "Hugo gives a history of the Paris sewers, and an incredible scene happens there, a true test of human character and strength."

Anjali wrote "Les Mis" in the margin. She'd go to Shakespeare & Company and get a copy. She pictured the English edition of Les Mis she'd seen on the shelves. The book's spine was a good six inches wide. The edition in French was eight inches wide, because French used more letters to say the same thing. Maybe she'd get an abridged version.

"I like your opening—the helicopter appearing to squeeze through the Arc de Triomphe," Carol said.

Anjali couldn't take in and enjoy Carol's praise because she was overwhelmed with her criticisms. And on top of that, all the research and writing and rewriting she was going to have to do. But she wrote it down. She'd copy the praise onto a yellow square and put it up on her wall of infamy.

"Have you ever read 'Pixar's 22 Rules of Storytelling'?" Carol asked. "Look them up online."

Anjali dutifully wrote it down, angry at Carol.

"And read David Mamet's 'Memo to the Unit,'" Carol said. "It's about dramatic writing. It's in all caps, so it feels like he's screaming, but it's great direction for any sort of storytelling. It's online, too."

Anjali scribbled another note. She had to stay open to learning and improving, no matter how much the critique-er was condescending to her.

"It basically says each scene has to focus on the protagonist's visceral, crucial desire and the obstacles to getting it," Carol said. "I'm not clear as to what Dick Bogart's visceral desire is."

"To make money in order to eat," Anjali said. It was obvious to her, why not to Carol? She was overwhelmingly annoying tonight. "To bring some sort of justice to the world."

John's attention strayed. A woman walked by, wobbling on stilettos, short skirt showing off shapely long legs. Wow, he thought. Isn't that grand? It took a little while before he could tune in to the discussion of Anjali's manuscript again.

"'Some sort of justice,'" Philippe said. "That's interesting. Does he compromise his own values to make that justice? That would be very interesting."

That intrigued Anjali, too. She wrote that idea down.

"Ask your characters why they want what they want," Carol said. "Be like a two-year-old and ask 'why' until you're deep inside the character's guts and life experience."

Carol flipped through the script. She was on a roll, like a professor of screenwriting.

"I write these questions and answers down and keep them in a document I call my quarry, like a rock quarry, so I can refer to it and mine it."

Now Anjali felt really overwhelmed. Write a whole other document besides the screenplay? But Carol kept going.

"You need to know how many years Dick has lived in Paris, where he emigrated from, what his—" she almost said hobbies, but that had been discussed before—"favorite TV shows and films are. Describe the kind of flat he lives in, the objects he has chosen to have around him in his home. A filthy toaster with a frayed cord? A huge old silver cigarette lighter from the 20s shaped like Aladdin's lamp, so big you can hardly get your hand around it? Find a list of character questions online. Fill out a complete dossier on each of your major characters."

"Okay, got it," said Anjali. She was hoping to get her papers back now and end the flow of criticism. Her ego was bruised, bashed by Carol's comments. She didn't much feel like writing ever again.

"You need a logline," Carol said.

John felt exasperated. Carol's going on and on, he thought. So know-it-all! But what was a logline? In spite of his irritation, he was intrigued.

"It's one sentence that tells what your film is about," Carol continued. "Your clearly defined, quirky protagonist and what he wants, and your antagonist, who's worthy of your protagonist, and what he wants equally badly. The logline with the most conflict and the clearest, most primal goal wins the pitch fests in Hollywood."

Anjali nodded. I wish she would stop, she thought.

"You need a scene structure, you know. Establish the character's normal life, then confront him with a call to action. Then show the character giving a flawed response to the call. Then the journey begins. These sorts of structures are all available online."

"Okay, Carol, that's great, thank you," Philippe said, sensing that Anjali was more than ready to get off the hot seat, and tapping his copy of the script on the table. He just had to talk to Carol. Privately. He dreaded her reaction almost as much as he dreaded church ladies' reactions to his stories—if he ever got published.

"Carol, you're next."

Carol noticed that Anjali looked flustered. Uh-oh, Carol thought. I've been too harsh possibly. You idiot! John's looking at you askance. Why didn't I notice sooner? Try not to be so critical, won't you? But isn't that what we're here for? To help each other?

Carol contritely handed out the twelve-and-a-half pages of her script. What if I didn't follow David Mamet's advice in any of my scenes? I have a tendency to take little off-road excursions with my characters. They are interesting to write, but not essential to the story. Are there any digressions in these pages? Will these people catch them if there are? Should I warn them to look for them? No, too embarrassing to admit I didn't follow my own advice.

They chose parts. John co-opted the male lead again. So annoying of him, Carol thought.

When parts were set, she said, "Here goes."

It took twelve minutes to read the twelve-and-a-half pages of her animated film that was ostensibly about storks, an ogre, and fairies. When it was over, the critique began immediately.

"I can picture it," Philippe said.

Carol thought, he always says something positive.

"Are there any changes you would make?" she challenged them. It had to be perfect when she presented it to Gregoire. He would change it and drive her stark raving bonkers, but at least her first version would be great.

They made suggestions, and each one improved the script.

"Great ideas!" Carol thanked them.

"In the end," Anjali suggested, "everybody will be feel so loved, that the bad fairy gives up and leaves." Then Anjali thought, I'm new at this, why do I think I can help Carol. And by the way, Carol's been so bitchy, why should I help her?

"If she leaves, she'll take her foulness somewhere else," John said. "Maybe it would be better if she dissolves in a fit of *pique*. Evaporates. Fini." He thought, Carol has pumped us a lot for ideas.

"Like Rumpelstiltskin—so mad, he stamps his feet so hard, the earth opens and swallows him up," Philippe said.

Carol wanted to say, "It's been done," but didn't want to be too harsh after the group had given her so much. "It has to be fresh and new," she murmured, to herself more than anybody, and then concentrated on jotting notes.

That done, she said, "You guys are fabulous!" She was so grateful for these good ideas, all of them in keeping with her values as a storyteller—to create something she'd want to take her daughter to see. What a relief! She had all the material she needed. Except now she had to write it, and not kill the joy of the story as she wrote.

"Good night, everyone!" she said and headed home to relieve the nanny. Everyone watched her departing back.

"Anjali, it was rough tonight, wasn't it," Philippe said.

"She's got great ideas. She just says them in ways that make me want to die, to be honest."

"I'll say something."

Chapter 51

Anjali walked home from the group reeling with the criticisms Carol had launched at her. Hopefully Philippe would talk to her and she would stop making people feel so hurt, so betrayed for taking a risk and being open in their writing. Anjali wasn't sure she could continue to go back to the group if she was going to be stabbed in the heart over and over. The quality of her projects would suffer, though. She didn't want that to happen, either.

She passed the book stalls on the Left Bank, full of books, posters, postcards but closed and locked for the night. She thought of all the reading she needed to do to improve her screenplay: Mamet, Pixar, Les Mis. That was just the start.

The reading would actually be fascinating and therefore fun. Between reading and writing and working for John, there wasn't much else to her life. She thought, I'm totally absorbed in the pursuit of writing skills. It's kind of self-absorbed, isn't it?

Anjali paused to see the Seine reflecting the late-evening grey skies. When Aasha goes back to India and gets married, she'll volunteer at a non-profit that helps rural girls get an education. What do I do to make the world better? I have no time left over after working for a living and pursuing my art. Though when—or rather if—it goes out into the world, it will benefit people. I hope. That's my goal.

On Boulevard Saint-Michel, she passed two women smoking and lingering in a doorway, dressed so skimpily, in such high heels, that Anjali figured they were prostitutes. They looked over her modest clothes a bit condescendingly, it seemed.

I wonder if I could ever help someone who actually wanted to get out of that life, Anjali thought. That would be of help to humanity. And knowing more about the seamy side of life would certainly help my writing.

No, you can't do that, she thought. What would Amma and Appa think? And Ravi. And all his aunties. And mine.

Chapter 52

John walked across the Seine the following morning. He felt bereft. The losses of fortune, family, and those he had thought of as friends had stripped him of all that used to tell him he was a success. The mirrors he had worked so hard to set up around him—the 15,000-euro Rolex, the sprawling mahogany desk, the view from Montparnasse Tower, the tall, elegant Cassandra—had toppled backward and splintered into shards. He was staring at the black void beyond the mirrors, as black as the void within him.

He stopped to gaze at the river, winding through the city, flowing away to the English Channel. He had seen on maps of the city that the Seine flowed through Paris—which was shaped in a circle, like a face—in a downward arc, resembling a frowning mouth. In winter, when the days were excruciatingly short and the sun blocked by thick clouds, Parisians had downturned mouths. In the summer, the city was glorious, bathed in light for long days, and even the glum Parisians were happier.

He used to go to Barcelona in January to get sun, to rub shoulders with the ever-hopeful, ebullient Spanish. Unfortunately, he could no longer afford to go to Spain for a fix of sunshine in winter. The river of life seemed to have taken everything from him.

His heart was sending its ache throughout his body. All he'd ever worked for was success. And just as his father had predicted years ago on the Brooklyn Bridge, he was a failure.

A pigeon nearly grazed him as it flew by, interrupting his thoughts. Rats with wings, they called them in New York City, he thought. In the French countryside, people roasted them with mushrooms, cognac, and a strip of bacon over the breast.

He fell back into his thoughts about his problems, like a tongue seeking a sore spot on the gums. What was success, anyway?

As he had been dressing for success that morning, he had decided not to put his father's cufflinks on. Instead of reminding him not to imitate his father, the links now seemed to be urging him to imitate his father's choice and stop fighting. As he had tossed them back into the box of whatnot on top of his dresser, he had contemplated throwing them into the Seine. Not happily, the way he and Cassandra had tossed the wedding padlock key, in a long, luxurious arc, but thrown down fiercely, whipped straight to the depths, in an attempt to break free of a load that was pulling him down.

He wrenched his eyes off the choppy water and moved on. He'd attack his book of contacts again, even though it felt useless.

As he walked down Rue de Rivoli, he gazed at the French striding to their jobs. The tourists were barely out of bed yet, he figured. These folks he saw on the street all had the same attitude: a reserve, an inwardness, a deep focus on their own thoughts, a somberness, maybe even glumness. John wished for the energy, the excitement of the people in New York City. He wished for the nonconformity he would see there: a man dressed hat to shoes in Irish green, and not on St. Patrick's Day. Or a woman in red and purple. With a huge gold lamé handbag dangling from royal-blue gloved hands. He longed to be someplace with people full of fertile weirdness, someplace with excitement about what one can achieve with one's life. Not this French conformity to the status quo.

Yet Paris was so elegant, so Paris. He thought, I must really be an expat. Even when I'm back in New York I long for Paris. In fact, whichever city I'm in, I'm homesick for the other one. I have no idea where home is.

When he arrived at his tiny office, Anjali was waiting outside. He unlocked the door and proceeded to his desk. He noticed for the first time that a spot on his wicker Paris-flea-market screen was unraveling. Obviously, all client meetings would have to be held at Tour d'Argent. He couldn't afford it. How was he going to pull this off?

Something would happen. He was a good guy. He would get a break.

Anjali peered around the screen.

"Sir?"

"Yes?"

"A letter in *la poste* this morning. You must set up an appointment immediately. With the IRS."

Chapter 53

Carol was ready for the Monday Trapèze brainstorm meeting. Just thinking about the storks and ogre screenplay, and the way that she was giving the film something good for adults as well as children, she was excited to present her ideas to the group. At first she was seated at the glass-topped conference table. As enthusiasm for her ideas arose in her, she got to her feet in front of her colleagues.

"These storks start out clumsy, fumbling with the babies, and they become tender, skilled parents. And warriors." As she talked she strode back and forth in front of the white board that covered one wall. She grabbed a blue marker and laid out the plot points, using John's and the writing group's ideas. She had embellished and refined them while Louise was sleeping over the weekend.

"Pierre starts out in the film fussy," and she made a quick sketch of a stork with round black Poindexter eyeglasses and a perfectly tied blue bowtie. "By the end, he has been through so much, taking care of the kids and fighting the ogre, that his bowtie is all askew and he doesn't even notice." She sketched him in his "after" state, his glasses held together by a lump of tape on the bridge, his bow-tie undone, the two ends dangling askew. Rather good drawings those, she thought. Multi-talented, aren't I?

She described the story arcs for the other main characters. Everybody in the conference room was silenced, her ideas were that good. Carol allowed herself a small smile of victory as she plunked herself back in her chair. She couldn't resist a sidelong glance at Amandine. Carol strove to make it an innocent, querying look. Amandine was inspecting her nails. Bloody hell! No satisfaction ever, Carol thought. At least I didn't get the *escargot* treatment. She looked at Gregoire.

"Pretty good, Carol, now get it down on paper for us."

All he can say is pretty good? Fantastic, wasn't that more like it?

"Okay," Gregoire said, "let's move on to Louis Jourdan on a *péniche*. Carol, any ideas?"

She had anticipated this and was ready. She would keep this job and triumph in it! Armani, design me up some cool—even if off-the-rack—outfits!

After the meeting, still carried along by creative energy, she stopped at his office door. Especially after confronting him last week about his unprofessionalism, there was no way to get to see him other than to just walk in. She closed the door behind her. Everybody knew about her probation, but they didn't have to know about this.

"What is it?" Gregoire was seated behind his desk with his chair turned so he could gaze at his Z-3 in the parking lot. He swiveled, frowning, to face her. His lukewarm praise for her ideas had obviously cooled already.

It was worth a try, however.

"My dry patch is over," Carol said. "You saw my good ideas in the meeting today. Take me off probation."

"Let's not be hasty," Gregoire said. "I know it's important to you." He was making big, round sympathetic eyes. But she knew he faking—he was enjoying keeping her squirming on the hook.

She wouldn't give him any more satisfaction as a supplicant.

"I see," she said and dashed out the door.

Effing people in power.

Chapter 54

Philippe and Elodie sat in their kitchen, eating a beef stew that Elodie had burned while reheating it. It was barely palatable, but Philippe didn't criticize—he could not have done much better. They hadn't heard from Meredith since her friend had called to say she'd kicked her out. Night after night they both lay awake, not talking, each wrapped in their own thoughts, maybe prayers.

When the phone rang, Philippe stood immediately, avoiding Elodie's gaze. He picked up the receiver. On the other end was the person he wanted most—and feared most—to hear from. He braced himself against the doorjam, needing strength.

"Hi, Dad." Meredith sounded half asleep. Probably more like half drunk, he thought.

"Hi, honey, how are you?"

"Yeah, well, okay."

"Really?"

"Look, I need money."

He heard music pulsing in the background. A bar. Or a bedroom.

"I can't," Philippe choked out.

"Yes, you can!" she said.

"I'm not supposed to enable you—" Philippe stumbled in his thoughts. He shouldn't be revealing to Meredith how weak he was at following the Tough Love strategy.

"Enable? I'm your child, you're supposed to help me."

Philippe agreed with her, and not with Tough Love, at that point. He steeled himself not to give in to his urge to meet her, hand over lots of cash so she could eat and have a roof over her head. But she would just keep drinking, remember that, Philippe. Don't give in. Don't help her to destroy herself.

"Dad? You there? How about helping?"

He forced himself to say it. "I wouldn't really be helping you if I gave you money." His voice was full of air because his breathing was so shallow, he was so tense. He felt dizzy with how awful his life had become.

"What the fuck? Are you crazy?"

He wrapped the phone cord tightly around his fingertips. They hurt.

"Honey, get sober, come home, get a job," Philippe said. "You'll have money. We'll help you."

In the background, a man's voice said, "Come here, baby." Philippe cringed.

"Then what I'm doing is all your fault!" Meredith shouted, and the line went dead.

"What did she say?" Elodie asked.

Philippe's mind went blank. He had to spare Elodie the truth, but he couldn't think of a thing to tell her. After a long pause, he managed to say, "Oh, just that she's fine."

Elodie looked down. They resumed picking at their bowls of stew. In the end they threw it all out.

That night they lay next to each other, fingers touching, but just barely.

"*Cheri*, talk to me. Don't shut me out." Elodie's voice was soaked in grief. Philippe wanted to communicate with his wife. It used to be easy.

But he was so angry with God. He couldn't admit it, not even to his own wife. He was a pastor, and he wasn't supposed to be angry with God, his creator, his redeemer, the lover of his soul. He couldn't pray. Everything inside him was askew with anger and grief. All of his high ability to function, to minister, to bless, had been destroyed. When would he ever come to some sort of peace with this situation? Never. It was too dreadful.

He didn't hear his own teeth grinding.

When the alarm went off in the morning, they both crawled off the bed, dark smudges under their eyes. They went silently to work.

Chapter 55

Before calling her parents Saturday morning from her minute *chambre de bonne*, Anjali checked the Eiffel Tower out her window. It was still there, dwarfing everything around it, and gracefully curved. What was really neat about Le Tour Eiffel was that, when you were close, you saw that the huge tower was nothing but filigree.

She called her parents over the Internet. Her mother got right down to business.

"You've had almost a month to think," Amma said, her eyes on the screen huge with concern. "Don't ruin this chance to be happy."

"I'm in Paris, I have friends, I'm writing screenplays, I am happy," Anjali said. "Who knows, Ravi might be a wife beater. He might push me into the stove to get rid of me."

"He comes from such a good family!" her father said. "Don't talk like this."

"It's true! I have something I know makes me happy, but he very well may not."

"Don't say that!" her mother wailed. "You don't know what you'll be missing. The friendship, the companionship, the hugs and kisses, the children—so much joy, the children."

"Don't blow it," her father warned.

Anjali sat on her bed, her laptop in her hands. It was so cramped in this studio. She really needed a desk with a chair, but there was no room. Madame de Denichen had insisted on a one-year lease. Anjali couldn't move until the lease was up. And received a raise. Not likely working for John.

"Your father and I didn't have a choice," her mother was saying. "We were introduced, we saw each other a few times, had a small amount of time alone, and got married. It worked out! And we're giving you a choice, not like some parents we know, and you're throwing away this perfect opportunity!"

Yes, thought Anjali, a choice but also a lot of pressure.

"I know, Amma, I'm thinking, I'm thinking," she said.

"Don't go out with any other boys there in Paris, you hear?" her mother said. "You must have a reputation beyond reproach."

"I'm just going out with Aasha, no worries, calm down."

"I can't warn you sternly enough," her father said. "You're risking marriage to this nice man from a good family. If you drag your decision out, they will think that you don't really want to marry their son. I say you have one more week to decide."

"Appa, a week?" Anjali wailed. "Before I left, you told me I had a year in Paris. I've only been here two months and now you're telling me I have a week?"

"Darling, I'm proud of you pursuing your dream, you know that," Amma said.

Anjali knew her mother had dreamed of traveling and seeing more of the world. She hadn't been given the opportunity and wanted it very badly for her daughter. But she wants me married too, Anjali thought.

"I think we can get one more month out of Ravi's family, and that's it," her mother said.

Anjali knew her mother would prevail. She had a month, not a week. She wanted to be in a relationship where she could prevail too. Was Ravi that kind of person?

But ultimately it was her duty to please her parents. And she wanted to please them. They were wise, they wanted what was best for her, they had picked Ravi after investigating many other possibilities. They must see good things in Ravi. I really must give him a great big chance. I must be crazy to even have doubts.

"Did you go to temple this week?" her father asked.

"Yes, Appa." She hadn't. But she couldn't fight them on every front.

"Who are you seeing besides Aasha?"

The constant grilling done by Indian parents, especially toward their girls, Anjali thought.

"Well, I go to the writers' group I told you about."

"Who are they? Remind me," Amma said.

"My boss John. He's writing some dumb story about a man who's always getting in fistfights."

"Hmmm," Appa said.

"And then there's Carol." Anjali was glad to tell her parents about this part of her life. Maybe it would divert attention away from questions about temple and such things. "She writes screenplays for a French movie production company! She's reading one of my screenplays! She's very critical of everybody."

"Who else?"

"A nice man named Philippe."

"Married?" her mother asked quickly.

"Yes."

"What does he do for a living?" asked Appa.

"He's the pastor of a church."

There was silence. Anjali thought, that's exactly what happened at the writers' circle when Philippe mentioned his profession. There's something about telling people you're a pastor that renders people silent. I'll use that in my screenplay.

"Well, that all sounds okay. You take very good care of yourself. We'll talk to you again next Saturday," Appa said, with no humor in his voice.

Chapter 56

That afternoon, Anjali had her interview with Marjorie on her *péniche*. She went alone. Aasha was a great friend, but so happy to be going home and getting married. She seemed to have no questions, no doubts, and Anjali didn't necessarily want to plant any in her mind. But her own was full of them, and full of unanswerable questions—can I be happy without a traditional life of marriage, home, and children? Do I have the talent to make it in the movie industry? She couldn't talk about any of it with Aasha.

A nice breeze was traveling up the Seine and the water was choppy as usual.

"Bonjour!" Marjorie greeted her from the cockpit. "Do come aboard! I've tidied up the place, so everything is shipshape."

Anjali stepped tentatively on the metal gangplank, which felt quite steady under her feet for a moment. Then it began to bob violently. Anjali hung on to its rail. A *bateau mouche* had swept by and made the river wilder than usual.

"Steady on," Marjorie called. "Don't mind the bouncing. You'll be quite fine."

The gangway calmed down. Anjali finished the walk up it, hanging onto the handrails on both sides. She stepped into the cockpit, which had a beautiful wooden deck, which glowed in a mellow way with good care, and wooden benches built in. Sitting down quickly, she looked around. Study the horizon, she thought. I've heard that's what you do when you're on the water.

Feeling a bit more secure, Anjali smiled at her host. The breeze ruffled Marjorie's stiff gray-ish blonde frizz as she sat on a cushion. Anjali examined her surroundings. The cockpit was covered by a white canvas tarp, stretched over the boom above her head and tied down at each of the four corners to handrails. It protected the cockpit from the sun but allowed people to enjoy the full effect of being on the river, with the water glinting in the sun.

"I was hoping that you could meet my husband and get your nautical questions answered," Marjorie said. "But he couldn't be here. He's the pilot and navigator. I manage the lines—you know, the ropes—and do the cooking." She laughed. "We're so traditional, it's funny."

To Anjali, what this woman was doing, living on a barge in Paris, didn't seem at all traditional. She got out her laptop and prepared to take notes.

"First let me take you on a quick tour of the cabin and below decks," Marjorie said.

So Anjali got out a pen and notebook, put her camera on its string around her neck, and followed Marjorie through a small wooden door with an etched glass panel set in it.

"This barge was built in Holland one hundred years ago," Marjorie said. "It's full of nice touches like etched glass windows and carved paneling. The hull is steel. It's actually double-hulled and has a shallow draft so we can go almost anywhere."

"Was this originally a workboat?" Anjali asked.

"Yes, we think it was used to transport vegetables to market. And maybe even cows! The draft is so shallow, we can nose in to the banks of rivers and canals. The cattle could practically step off onto the grass and start to munch!"

They paused in the main cabin, the walls wood-lined except for a row of windows that ran along the right and left sides. Starboard and port, Anjali corrected herself.

Part of the cabin was taken up by a wooden table that stood in the midst of three built-in benches on three sides. The benches were covered with cushions and pillows in a sunflower motif.

"That table can be lowered and covered with cushions to make a double bed," Marjorie said. "Every square inch of space on a boat is used at least two different ways."

A blue velvet easy chair stood opposite the banquette. "That's my husband's chair, when we aren't sitting out in the cockpit enjoying the outdoors."

"My father has a chair like that," Anjali said, missing home with a flash of pain.

"Traditional male sort of thing, I should think," Marjorie said. "Here's the galley."

Anjali assumed that meant kitchen, since Marjorie was pointing to a tiny space with a stove, an oven, a refrigerator the same size as hers, and a sink.

"This boat has more counter space and appliances than my *chambre de bonne* on top of a six-story house," Anjali said.

"Oh, I love my galley! Everything is right to hand. Don't even have to take a footstep hardly. I'm cooking all the time in here."

Marjorie then took two steps down, toward the bow, and Anjali followed her.

"Here's the first stateroom."

It was taken up entirely by a double bed, except for a narrow path to a closet. Wood shelves and cabinets were attached to the walls above the bed on three sides.

"It's very cozy," Anjali said.

"We love it," Marjorie said.

"Here's the second and third staterooms," and Marjorie opened wooden doors to two smaller bedrooms.

"And here's the head." She opened the door to a tiny bathroom.

"We take showers by pulling this plastic curtain around us," she said, pointing to the tracks for the curtain on the ceiling. "It's not a life of luxury accommodation, but once you get used to it, it's a really great life."

"What do you love so much about living on a *péniche?*" Anjali asked as they headed by mutual consent back towards the cockpit.

"First, would you fancy a glass of wine? It's a lovely white from the Saumur region, and it's been chilling."

Anjali couldn't think of anything that would make her happier than a glass of wine in the cockpit of a *péniche* on the Seine, particularly with this gracious host.

"We relax so deeply on this boat," Marjorie said, carrying their drinks to the stern. They both sat on the cushions that softened the wooden lockers that they were laid across.

"It's given us twelve years of relaxation and incredible adventure, both, exploring the canals and rivers of France. Did you know that the *patrimoine fluvial,* the interconnected river and canal patrimony, of France has more than five thousand kilometers of inland waterways? We explore the Champagne, Burgundy, and Sancere regions. We've been up and down the Loire, the Saone, the Rhone, the Rhine, the Seine, the Marne and the Doubs. We can even barge to Holland, Germany, Luxemburg, and Belgium by river if we want. And we stay from September to June in Paris."

"Sounds wonderful." Anjali prayed she'd keep talking, reveal more. Stuff that readers would latch onto. And Marjorie did.

"This boat cost 150,000 euros. For that amount of money, you couldn't touch an apartment in Paris. The only thing you could buy would be on the outskirts, beyond walking distance to the Metro line. All you'd get there would be a bed and a two-burner hotplate."

Like the room I rent from Madame de Denichen, Anjali thought.

"Here we are, tied up within walking distance of Notre Dame and the Louvre. The monthly dock fee is probably about the same as your rent for a *chambre de bonne*."

"Yes, that's fabulous. So's your location."

They paused to look around at the river, the passing boats, the strollers on the *quai*.

After the pause, Anjali asked, "What's it like cooking in your tiny space? I cook in one, too. I'm always challenged. When the cutting board is full of chopped onions and I need room to chop some carrots, where do I put the onions? They end up in a bowl on the floor, I'm afraid.

"Oh, I've gotten good at cooking in my efficient space. And even if it's a little too small at times, I remind myself: We can cruise through France! We stop at an incredibly picturesque village, and our biggest problem might be: we're out of cheese! We need more wine! The *croissant* shop is closed!

"And the people we've met. People of every nationality who are a little offbeat, willing to live this adventurous way of life. Willing to help, any time of day or night. Instant *camaraderie*, everywhere we go."

Anjali took notes just as fast as she could. Everything sounded so good. There just had to be a toad in this garden.

"What's the downside of living on a *péniche?*"

Marjorie paused and looked thoughtful. "When you go to a fabulous Paris flea market, you can't buy a thing. There's nowhere to put it. And when you need to get your hands on something that you've stowed under the banquette—" she motioned toward the cabin— "it's a Chinese puzzle to move this and move that so you can get to that other thing."

Anjali thought, there had to be more negatives. Steel hull. Cold water.

"How is it in winter?"

"Yes, and that too. We run a heater in the cabin around the clock, and wear two layers of socks. But as I said, we have Paris at our feet for the price of dockage—seven hundred euros a month. That includes utilities. You can't beat that."

Since Anjali was paying six hundred euros a month for her narrow little place under the eaves, where she had to live and work in one room and had nowhere to sit outside, yes, that did sound like a good price.

She sipped her wine and watched a *bateau mouche* glide by. A few seconds later, its wake bumped the *péniche*. She turned to look at the *quai*. Weren't those people walking by looking at her with just a touch of envy?

A couple holding hands strolled by. They looked so content, so together. Marriage was a good thing. See what marriage had done for Marjorie? She was on a fabulous adventure that she might not have done alone.

Anjali wanted to discuss the decision she had to make about Ravi with someone. She hadn't known Marjorie long. She knew enough, though, from interviewing people for other articles and screenplays she'd written, that sometimes you could have a deeper conversation with a stranger.

"Marjorie, I hope you don't mind my asking…"

"Sure, dear, ask to your heart's content."

"Well, what's your take on marriage? My parents have picked someone out for me back in Mumbai. Should I marry him?"

"All I can tell you is my experience," Marjorie said. "I was married before to a controlling bastard who hardly left me room to breathe. We ended up divorced—my decision. I just couldn't go on. Simply could not bear it. Divorce stinks in the biggest way. So stressful. I've read it knocks five years off your life. Choose very wisely."

"My parents chose Ravi from lots of potential partners. The whole family—all my aunties—searched and made suggestions. But I'm not sure. Part of me says I'm a writer. I want to write great screenplays, novels, everything. He's in banking—well, worse, he's in technology in banking. He plays tennis. All the time. My parents see something in him, but I'm not sure what that is. I do like him. Part of me says, hey, we could have kids. I'd have a family. His aunties, my aunties—a great big family. A great big traditional family."

"Are you saying 'controlling family,' my dear?"

"It seems that way. But I don't want to break my parents' hearts."

"Could you write with all that big family around?"

"I think it would be difficult. I can barely find time to do it now, working fulltime. I would work until the first baby came along. From what I hear, babies don't allow time for writing, either."

"You might have to postpone writing for a while, at least until the child got a little bigger. Maybe four or five months or so. When they take two naps a day and sleep steadily, you'll have chances to write."

"I'd like to have children. That's part of being a woman, right?"

"It's great. And then they break your heart. Over and over, as they make decisions you can foresee won't turn out well."

"How will a decision to marry Ravi turn out? I know you can't answer that."

"Does he respect your writing? Does he show an interest?"

"Some."

"Enough?"

"That's my big question, really."

"Your dreams are important, dear. Find people who support you in pursuing them."

Anjali sat, silent. Boat traffic went by as she considered just how supportive Ravi was. Marjorie's hair flopped in a breeze to the other side of her head, which brought Anjali back. "I shall have to see…"

She changed the topic. "Your second husband. Was this boating life his idea or yours?"

"I was poking around online one day, and I don't remember how it happened exactly, but I stumbled upon an ad for a *péniche* and within six months we were in France shopping for one…"

So Marjorie had precipitated the adventure, she mused. Did Ravi have this kind of adventurousness in him?

The breeze ruffled Anjali's short, layered hair. What did she want? A marriage but an untraditional lifestyle, in Paris or New York or Rome or aboard a boat? What did life hold for her? Any adventure at all? Was marriage to Ravi, an apartment in Mumbai, and children all she hoped for?

She swallowed the last big gulp of wine in her glass and thanked Marjorie. How did one put oneself in the way of Marjorie's sort of adventure? Was it destiny, and one had no control? Or did God have some sort of benevolent plan that would satisfy her longings? Or at least most of them?

"…and now we've been doing this for twelve years. I feel that I'll always love it, I'll never get tired of it."

"That's really wonderful," Anjali said, sorry to have missed Marjorie's comment but not willing to show that she had missed it by asking her to repeat herself. She sensed that the end of the interview was at hand. All things come to a close eventually.

"Thanks, Marjorie. I'd better get on. Thanks for the tour. It's a beautiful boat. Enjoy it in good health."

"If you have any questions for me, feel free to call."

"I will. I appreciate it."

Anjali stood and braced herself as the deck moved again. Was it the wine, or wind, or water?

Chapter 57

After Gregoire refused her request, Carol sat in her office fuming. With angry jabs at her keyboard, she typed a letter to him, pretending to herself that she would send it and enlighten him, but cautioning herself at the same time not to indulge herself in doing it, not ever.

"Gregoire, you're playing an ego-driven power game." Her fingers stabbed at the keys, which clacked as the words flowed. "Oh yes, you seem to be getting away with it, simply because you're in a position of authority. Be warned: somewhere along the line, this will cost you. You won't let me reclaim my well-deserved place in my colleagues' esteem. Well, do unto others as you'd want them to do to you. You've forgotten that, but as my mother used to say, 'God keeps good books.'"

She wondered where the reference to God came from. She hadn't thought about him in two decades. She typed a few more lines, then realized that the best ending was her mother's quote. She deleted all the extra stuff.

When she finished, she re-read it while sipping tea she'd gotten from the kitchenette. Daphné had come to its door but then pretended she wasn't intending to enter. Instead she had given Carol a weak smile and fled.

Damn Gregoire! What could she do to make him feel some pain himself? Carol fell into a *rêverie*. She wasn't going to send this letter, so how was she going to exact some revenge? Trying to get revenge was so risky, but wouldn't it be lovely if…if she incapacitated his beloved car? So pleasurable to imagine Gregoire's face when the motor wouldn't start. She could Google how to spike a BMW Z-3's engine. Surely somebody knew, and not only knew but posted it on the Internet. Lovely idea.

Or perhaps do some espionage, learn his address, and tell his wife he cheats. She could imagine the scene. His wife crying, confronting Gregoire. And Gregoire moving in a day later with whomever he was shagging at the time. It wouldn't affect him, except maybe to be bugged at the alimony he had to pay. No, telling the wife would hurt the wife, not Gregoire.

Carol shifted in her chair and crossed her legs the other way.

Or perhaps do some espionage to get the passcodes, break into the movie production company's files, and re-edit Trapèze's films, making them incoherent? Lovely idea, really, but assuredly there were back-ups upon back-ups stored in all kinds of places. Amandine would have copies in her desktop, for that matter.

Or perhaps pick up that crystal elephant on his desk, with its trunk raised for good luck, and hurl it through the window. With a bit of luck, it would clonk the windshield of the BMW, crack it, lovely, yes…

Carol heard footsteps approaching in the hallway, so she brought herself out of her *rêverie* fast, got her hands on her keyboard, and pretended to be screenwriting for all she was worth.

Martine passed on her beautiful long legs. She didn't glance in Carol's direction.

The reality of Carol's situation landed on her full force. After the escape that her little mini-movie of revenge had given her, the pain flooding in again was fierce.

Carol nursed her wounds for a few minutes, then encouraged herself to be professional and get on with the job. She did her best on the storks vs. ogre script. She had the ogre eat some spinach that made his Gregoire-type hair grow. Then she deleted that.

The sound of new footsteps in the hall brought Carol's eyes up to her window onto the hallway. Amandine sauntered by on knife-like heels, looking down at Carol at her desk. Carol averted her gaze fast, but not before she saw *escargot!* in Amandine's eyes.

I refuse that thought, I refuse that assessment, Carol breathed to herself in a mantra. But then the lowness of Amandine's opinion of her burst all over her, leaving slime trails she couldn't deal with. She tried to, for a while, saying reassuring things about herself to herself, but she just felt worse and worse. She thought, Amandine is well liked in the office, and I'm not. Amandine has ideas that Gregoire likes all the time, and I don't. Amandine knows a loser when she sees one, and I obviously am one.

Carol sighed. She needed a little emotional support. She dug out her phone and searched to see if she had saved Philippe's number. Yes! She called him.

"Hi," she said.

"Good to hear your voice. What's up?"

Carol thought Philippe sounded tired, strained. The poor man was dealing with so much—discontented parishioners, no doubt, and sick people. And that daughter. Maybe this was a bad idea, what?

"Well, just having a hard day." She intended to leave it at that, make a light excuse and say goodbye. But she imagined Philippe's kind personna, standing somewhere in Paris with a cell phone pressed to his ear, ready to listen, and couldn't help herself, she poured out the Amandine "incident," which possibly was all in her head.

"I feel it's all a bit crazy," she muttered at the end.

"A bit of craziness spices the soup, don't you think?" he answered. "Or maybe leavens the loaf, I might say."

Carol had no idea what significance leaven might have in Philippe's world. She wasn't about to ask.

"Carol, you're a very creative person with lots of talent. Why don't you write down several affirmations, starting with those? And try to let go of Amandine. People like that pay a price, and I think it's immediate and constant."

"I certainly hope so," Carol said primly.

"We all do fall short," Philippe said. "Just a gentle reminder about reality."

"Quite," Carol said.

They signed off. Carol looked out her doorway into the hall. Nobody walked by. In fact, nobody had stopped by for a long time, ever since Gregoire botched it with Amandine.

She walked to the kitchen, hoping to bump into someone and have a friendly chat. Two colleagues, on two occasions, dashed on instead of coming into the kitchen, as they'd apparently intended.

Carol dumped her freshly made tea down the sink. Suddenly she couldn't wait to get out of the office. She wanted desperately to do some retail therapy. It wasn't wise, her credit card was groaning.

Carol snuck out of Trapèze and went to a shop in Le Marais that specialized in linen clothing. She bought a long halter dress in raspberry, and a short blouse in melon. Even with the July sales, they cost 125 euros.

The salesgirl said, *"Bonne soirée,"* as Carol left, but she was in too bad a mood to answer. She dashed out onto the pavement and headed toward her apartment. Damn these tourists, always stopping in the middle of the narrow pavement and gawking at buildings and maps, not knowing where they were. She allowed her shopping bag to *bousculer* one very fat woman moving entirely too slowly. She deliberately stepped into the path of a tall man with wiry brown hair like Gregoire's. *"Pardon, madame,"* he said politely. Carol ignored him and stormed on.

When she got home, she apologized, half-heartedly, to the babysitter for being late. She tried on the jacket and dress she'd bought so Louise could see them.

"Maman, tu es trés belle," Louise said.

Oh dear, Carol thought, maybe I should get her back to England before she's too French. If we stay here too long, she won't fit in with her mates in England, and she'll never be accepted here as truly French. More to worry about. Great.

Carol asked Louise to set the table with forks and knives. She didn't trust her heavy, earthenware plates in Louise's hands, though *serviettes* were safe. Carol thawed a *dal* she'd made and frozen on a previous weekend, and some meatballs she'd hurriedly formed. They hunched lumpy and misshapen as they circled in the microwave.

Just so long as my writing isn't lumpy and misshapen, Carol thought.

Louise had homework and was very brave about doing it without prompting or help. While the tiny girl bent her soft hair over her assignment, Carol read more of Anjali's screenplay.

She thought it was pretty good. The premise, the character development, the mounting tension, were all there. Just the formatting needed work. That was so minor. Anjali had talent, while Carol's was being questioned at work. Her heart felt like it had a piece of paper stuck between its chambers, with "You're not good enough" in letters that blazed with fire.

In her fierce mood, she typed a response to Anjali. She was hurt, angry, and it all went into the email.

"I've read your screenplay. It's not ready for prime time. All the best in your pursuits. Carol."

She hit send and went to read Louise a story.

Chapter 58

John wanted to show Emily the sights while they still lived in Paris—who knew how long they'd be here? But Paris was teeming with tourists, making it too difficult to see sights, so John invited her over for a movie night.

They brought take-out Indian up to his little room and sat on the edge of the bed, with the table drawn up to eat.

"It's a bit different from what we used to have, right?" he said.

Emily didn't answer.

"Don't tell your mother the size of my new digs," John said. Emily glanced at him but stayed silent. They opened packets of food and John tore off a bit of *naan*.

"I haven't found an Indian restaurant here that does it right, like that place I love on West 48th Street," John said. "This food is too bland. Toned down for French tastes. But it's okay."

"I like it," Emily said.

"You would, you're my great girl. Tell me, how's school?"

"I like English—"

"You can tell me anything, Em."

"Well—"

"Just spill it out, I can handle it."

"Dad—"

"What?"

"You're doing it again!"

"Doing what?"

"Interrupting me constantly."

"What? Not me!"

"Yes, you! All the time. If I interrupted you as much as you do me, you'd never want to be with me."

"I'm sorry, Em. Tell me about school." He motioned to her to go ahead.

"School's okay." She paused and waited for John to interrupt. When he remained silent and attentive, she proceeded. "The teachers give too much homework. I love English lit the best. I have this cute teacher." Emily smiled slyly. "He's maybe only ten years older than me."

"Don't go there, Em, he's a womanizer."

"Why do you say that?"

"He's teaching in a girl's school."

"Oh, come on."

"What did he assign to read?"

"We just started *Lolita*—"

"What?"

"We're reading *Lolita*," she said with a defiant look on her face.

"Don't ever let him touch you." *Lolita!* Maybe public school in Paris would be a better place to get an education. The fees were due for the upcoming school year at Em's private school.

"Oh, don't worry—"

"How's Marine? Is she still your bf?"

With that change of topic, they talked happily for an hour. John interrupted hardly at all. At the end of the conversation, it was too late to start a movie and still get Emily back on time. So they agreed to go for a walk.

They strolled up to the Seine to take a look together. The waters swirled with currents and countercurrents.

"Em, I hate to tell you, but I may not be able to keep you in that school."

"Because of *Lolita?*"

"Because of the fee. I'll talk with your mother, but it might not be doable this year. I'm so very sorry, honey, I know you want to be with your friends."

Emily stared down into the chaotic water.

"Why did you make such bad investments?" she whispered.

"I wasn't thinking straight. I got greedy. Silver was climbing like a rocket, and I got foolish."

"And now I have to pay?"

"We're all paying."

They stared into the river for a while.

"I think about Javert in *Les Mis* whenever I cross the Seine these days," John said.

Emily looked up at him, her face tight with concern. Maybe it was for her own situation and not for him, but regardless, he was proud that she had read all of Victor Hugo's novels in the original, unabridged version. In French, Les Mis was 1,900 pages. In English, the story took a mere 1,200 pages.

"Don't worry, honey, I'm not going to do what Javert—or Grandpa—did," he said. "But Javert was forced to question his deepest values, and he couldn't stand what he saw."

Emily was distracted, staring at a group of lithe young men passing. She hadn't heard him. Maybe just as well.

When she turned her gaze back to him, John noticed with tenderness that the breeze off the Seine stirred wisps of her blonde hair.

"Honey, I had such a nice evening. I love you dearly. I want you to come live with me."

"In that chambre de bonne?"

Did he detect a sneer? Cassandra was such a bad influence.

"No, that's just temporary. I'll get a place with a bedroom for you. I mean it. Just say the word." Though he had gotten the *chambre de bonne* because he couldn't afford a two-bedroom place. Not yet, anyway, there was always hope.

"Well, I need to think," Emily said.

"Fine. Let me know. As soon as you can. I need to see more of you."

Emily nodded and stared into the restless water.

Chapter 59

Philippe hurried to the Hôpital Saint-Joseph in the Fourteenth to see Dominic, an elderly parishioner who had suffered a heart attack. Philippe was anxious. Not only about Meredith. What could she be suffering this afternoon? But also about Dominic, who had been an encouraging friend for years. Also running through his mind was the broken record of his entire adult life: what about your sermon for Sunday? And the critique group was coming up.

Dominic was ill, cranky, and sick and tired of feeling sick and tired. Philippe did his best to comfort him with the idea that some unseen but eternal purpose was being furthered by his illness and his attempt to suffer well.

Dominic whispered, "Pray for me," and fell back against his pillow, his hair, his skin, and his lips gray. Philippe thought, what eternal purpose is being served by this illness, or by the craziness Meredith is in? I'm not sure I believe in God bringing good out of evil anymore. The evil is too evil.

He walked south toward Malakoff and home. Like the rest of Paris, the Fourteenth was a residential *arrondissement*, with apartment buildings that had shops at street level. He passed a pharmacy, a *café*, a *boutique*, a *chocolatier*, a *patisserie*. Then the same line-up of shops repeated itself. There were more pharmacies and *patisseries* per capita in France than any other nation. The French visited their two chemical treatment centers—wine shops made the third—as an antidote to reading entirely too much Sartre and Camus. Paris held no charm for him today. It was an endless string of the same things.

When a supremely self-assured man passed him on the sidewalk, walking with a swagger, looking down at everyone around him, Philippe found himself wondering if he'd been with a prostitute the night before—with Meredith. Give it up! he wanted to shout, to shake the man, all men, and make them stop creating the awful business. It was the willingness to do anything in order to meet one's needs, that was the problem. For both men and women, he conceded. You can survive without sex! he wanted to shout to Paris, the city of lovers. Water, air, sleep, food, work. Friends. Those were the real necessities.

Exhausted with these obsessive inner wranglings, he climbed the steps to his own front door. Elodie was still at her job as a librarian, so he had the house to himself. He felt he barely had the strength to turn the tap to make some tea. The kettle whistled finally. With a mug of chamomile in one hand, he hauled himself up the stairs to Meredith's room. He set the mug on the damaged surface of the dresser and sat on the bed.

He burst into loud prayer immediately.

"God, why? Why have you not answered my years of prayers for Meredith?"

He was silent for a moment, listening, arguing with God.

"And don't you dare tell me about her 'free will'! You're all-powerful, you created the universe, you could change her mind if you put your own mind to it! Oh please, dear God, HELP! We're falling apart. We can't do this, down here."

He slipped to his knees beside the bed, dropped his face into his hands, and wished he had the energy to cry.

Chapter 60

Anjali was in her favorite place to work on Saturdays, La Bibliothèque Historique de la Ville de Paris. It was built in 1550. In the main reading room, the ceiling was supported by beams hewn and gilded by human hands nearly five hundred years ago. Anjali looked up. Above her, staring back at her, was a cherub's face painted on a beam by an anonymous artist who, though no one would ever know his name, took pains to give the cherub's face beautiful contours and a lively expression.

This library was part of a huge *patrimoine architectural* in France, Anjali thought, of castles—almost every village had one—and cathedrals, churches, libraries, and town halls that, on her computer screen, were incredibly beautiful, incredibly old, and undoubtedly expensive to maintain.

She looked around. The library was full of Sorbonne students, as it had been for more than four and a half centuries. All of them had highlighting markers beside them. But a few had as many as six lined up, each a different color. They were underlining the texts they were studying in pink, blue, yellow, green, orange, and purple. The pages looked like rainbows by the time they were done.

Anjali turned her attention back to her laptop. Writing was difficult. So she checked her email, feeling disconnected, thinking that, instead of being in a library trying to write some entertainment, maybe she should be at a homeless shelter, volunteering, doing something real for people.

Carol's email arrived, and she knew instantly it was a rejection. It's your own fault, she scolded herself. You have to believe totally in your work. If you don't believe in it, whoever reads it will be able to tell, and they'll reject you as fast as they can.

She read the message. Not ready for prime time. Devastating. She felt like someone had clobbered her with one of the gilded beams.

She stared out the window at the library's *jardin* for a while, then summoned the strength to write an email to her mother. Anjali forced herself to make it cheerful-sounding. That done, she turned back to her manuscript. She resolved to dig deeper within herself, to really rake up the blood and guts, and then to bleed them onto the page, as Hemingway had said. Maybe he'd said it while he lived in Paris. She bent her head and persevered.

Chapter 61

Later that day, Anjali had another French lesson with Christelle.

"*Cherie!* I had a marvelous week. *Et tu?*" she said as she floated onto a red and gold woven *café* chair. She was dressed in the latest fashion: harem pants, stiletto heels, and a vapor of a white blouse. Anjali felt quite staid next to her in flats and a skirt just below the knee.

"Today, we talk about ze imperative. Not ze *aperatif*, mind you! Leettle joke. *En français*, we take the *vous* form of the verb, like ziz: *allez*, and we say it with emphasis: 'Go!' and *écoutez!*, which means "Listen!"

She rattled on a bit, and Anjali was thinking. How can you take seriously a language that ends its commands with a "z"? A silent z, no less. Where was the oomph in a command like that? She could only think of Peter Sellers in The Pink Panther, bumbling around as Inspector Clouseau.

"Now we talk about our families," Christelle was saying. "We have a nice word in common with *anglais*, 'cousin,' spelled the same way, but we say it 'coo-ZAHN' with the *nasale* at the end."

Anjali tried to say it, and it came at "cwi-ZINE," a word she'd learned the week before.

"Ooh-la! That's a kitchen, not a cousin!"

"Oop-la," Anjali said. She'd heard parents in France use that word when their small children stumbled.

"Really," Christelle said, "in between our lessons, if there's anything you don't remember from last week, you could giggle it."

Anjali was stumped for a second.

"Oh, you mean Google it!"

Christelle blushed, just as embarrassed as Anjali had been.

The lesson moved on, and as Anjali became too tired to concentrate any more, Christelle ended it with a joke.

"How can you make money?"

Anjali shook her head. She didn't know.

"Buy a Frenchman in France, take him Belgium, and sell him for what he thinks he's worth."

Christelle laughed heartily at her own joke.

Anjali had noted the supreme self-esteem, what some might call arrogance, of the Parisians. The gap between what they thought of themselves and the reality—people inordinately devoted to paperwork, and very eager to buy a *baguette* on the way home to dinner—really did invite humor, she thought. If Christelle can laugh at her own countrymen, I can, too.

The French who came from other parts of France were quite lovely. It wasn't them, it was the Parisians...

Chapter 62

Carol wore the periwinkle smock to work. She looked good in it, with her heels and pencil black skirt. Nothing like a Parisian *boutique* to set a girl to rights, or almost, Carol thought.

She dropped her pocketbook in her file drawer, got coffee, and sat down for her first hour of writing.

She didn't gain momentum at first, but she persevered, and suddenly she felt a surge of energy. The storks and the ogre began flying off the page, so to speak. She had conflict in every line, with subterfuge, plots, and counterplots. This was her best work ever. Her fingers flew.

After an hour and twenty minutes, she looked at the clock in her computer. Wow! That was great! Not as great as you-know-what, but good fun. She stood, stretched a bit, and went for more coffee.

Gregoire was in the kitchenette, in a tight suit. Carol hated him and his perfectly groomed beard and mustache, and the wiry brown hair combed and sprayed into submission. How satisfying it was that the ogre would have Gregoire's hair gone wild, all over his body. Maybe I should put back in the scene where it grows when he eats spinach...She said hello and pressed her lips into a smile.

"Please come to my office when you're done here," Gregoire said in a certain tone. She'd heard it before in her career.

Suddenly she felt naked. Her smock was not enough. She would have to put on lipstick for backbone, but it wouldn't be enough. Her ideas were not enough, either. She wasn't enough.

She dumped her coffee down the sink and tossed the Styrofoam cup. Why did he order these poisonous cups? Didn't he know that they never decomposed? Why couldn't he be kinder to the environment? Would he be the slightest bit kind to her?

With lipstick on, she went to Gregoire's office and knocked. When the door was closed and she was seated, he stood, came around his desk and loomed over her, his back to the bright window and the Z-3 parked outside it. Carol blinked up at him, trying to see his face.

"France is famous for being a place where management can't fire anyone," he said.

She just stared at him, her heart pounding.

"But it's not always true. I'm firing you. For having a bad attitude."

He was having trouble not smiling, she could see. What a jerk. It had to have been calling him unprofessional that caused this. Damn. Philippe's advice had backfired. But it certainly had been essential that she confront Gregoire on that.

Well, she wasn't going to leave with things unsaid.

"You are unprofessional."

"Carol, you'd better—"

"—Telling Amandine was unjust. It was worse than unjust, it was downright rotten."

A wave of anger swept over her. She wanted to cause him pain, like he had caused her. She ought not do something that he would take her to court over. She considered her options: spike the car or the movies or his marriage. No, those wouldn't do. She ought not to do this, but she was just so angry and in so much pain.

"God, you're a bloody bastard!" She grabbed the crystal elephant off his desk.

"Hey!" he shouted.

With the power to do damage in her hand, her anger became rage. She hated him, his smugness, his abuse of power. She hefted the elephant. Something in his glassed-in bookcase, in his altar to himself, gleamed. One of his statues. Or maybe it was one of those annoying brass plaques. Damn him! She would go out in a way that he would remember. She drew her arm back—her father had taught her to play cricket—and with a delicious sense of anarchy, she hurled the elephant.

The glass case exploded. Statues toppled. Glass flew everywhere. One shard pricked her cheek. She rubbed the spot, and her fingertips were red.

"I'll have you arrested!" Gregoire shouted.

That sobered Carol up a bit. But she had a little more to say before she stormed off stage in a memorable exit.

"You don't deserve to be president of this company, or any company! For a man who works with creative people, you're not supportive of the creative process. You're way too stingy with praise for the things that are good. And—and—your suits are too tight!"

Carol charged out of his office. She went back to her office, grabbed her Paris calendar off the wall, scrabbled through the drawers for personal items, like her box of organic lavender tea from Provence, a favorite red pen, and a nail file, threw them all in her pocketbook, and headed to the front door.

All she could think of was Louise and the rent on her apartment in Le Marais, due in two weeks.

She said "Hi" to Daphné as she passed her in the hall for the last time. Moving without seeing, like a sleepwalker, she stumbled to the Metro.

Chapter 63

John sat in his office in Le Marais. Outside, footsteps echoed off the narrow street. A siren, a *pin-pon*, sang on Rue Rivoli. Rather than tackle what was in front of him, he stared at the beautiful stone wall, washed in light, and reflected on the French news program he'd watched in his *chambre de bonne* the night before.

François Hollande had made a speech on Les Champs Élysées. John had lived in France long enough to begin considering him as his President, too. And to think of him, the way the French did, as indecisive and too easily influenced. From the expression on Hollande's face, it appeared as though he was always asking the world, "What should I do?" Like most politicians, he'd do what the people with the most money said to do. So the French had nicknamed him Flanby, a brand of packaged flan. When you open the container, turn it over and dump the flan onto a plate, it shakes. It comes with caramel on top.

John tore his attention off French politics and looked at his latest business balance sheet. Anjali had printed it out for him. And his personal one, which he had somehow managed to print out himself. He had deducted what the IRS might say he owed and had set aside money for the lawsuits sure to come from former clients. He stared at his new bottom line. He was just a hair above broke.

He couldn't maintain illusions of keeping anything he had worked so hard to acquire. Not even the Grey Skies? He would emerge from this with his father's cufflinks, if he were lucky.

As he sat on his small, uncomfortable chair, and leaned his elbows on the scarred desk, the foundations of his world were stripped bare. What had he spent his life's energy on? Why had he believed so deeply in making money and acquiring things? The rotten ruins of his life gaped open, shards of mirrors laying around, exposed to the sky, worthless to build on. It had all been in vain.

When his father had caught sight of it, he had given up. John wanted a better ending to his story. He had tried to make it happen,

calling and calling for new business. He was a pariah in the investment world. He no longer knew what to do.

Chapter 64

Philippe sat in his office above the gallery, his reference books on shelves around him, his computer running. The table that functioned as his desk took up most of the room.

He was so angry right now, it was impossible to write the sermon he had to give on Sunday.

Philippe saw that he had expected his service to God to give him an insider's advantage, a chip he could cash in to get a special dispensation when life got tough. He had made investments of good works, and he wanted them to add up to a tool that prodded God into wielding his power on Philippe's behalf, NOW, before anything more happened to Meredith.

He had started out doing good solely for love of God, but somewhere that had morphed into doing good to win points, and he hadn't noticed the change in the busyness of his life.

He saw it, but he couldn't apologize for it. Not while Meredith was out there at risk of disease, abuse, and death, and God wasn't helping.

Oh, this sermon! Based on what Elodie had said she experienced during her three pregnancies, it seemed to him that writing one every week was akin to being nine-months pregnant fifty-two times a year. And in his anger with God, it was worse. What could he tell his congregation?

I'll tell them I'm angry with God, so they know it's okay when their turn comes. I'll tell them it's not a *quid pro quo* arrangement with God, my good outweighing the bad, that's not how it works. But, with all I've done for people, for God, I sure do wish that was the way it worked.

He sighed. He found his short story in his computer and poured his anguish into it.

Chapter 65

Thursday night, John strode to Le Café Livre. He noted another difference between New York and Paris. Here there were great black asphalt pimples in the sidewalks that could launch a person ten feet if he weren't watching his step. Cobbles were missing from the streets, leaving big holes. In New York, city officials would make sure bright yellow caution tape tied to barriers was put up around each and every hole. U.S. cities were paranoid about people purposefully stepping in a hole and suing—because so many people did. That's the means

Americans used to make their American dream come true. Not in France. Nobody thought about suing. You walked at your own risk. You exercised *prudence*. If you fell, you went off to a very reasonably priced doctor and went home and poured yourself a glass of wine.

John approached the array of black and white woven *café* chairs at Le Café Livre and was greeted by the group with gratifying warmth. Even Anjali, who had worked with him all day, smiled and wiggled her fingers in greeting.

They were seated in their favorite spot outdoors. Their usual waiter passed, mouth downturned. Too soon for Parisian winter sourness, John thought. Maybe an argument with the chef? An unexpected request for a doggy bag?

Before sitting down, John peered through the door to the *café*. It was crowded, and a buzz of conversation poured out the door. Nobody was paying the slightest attention to the books standing shoulder to shoulder on the shelves around them. Books as mood-enhancing décor.

Not his book! His was going to be different, better. It would be on nightstands around the world, and it would be read! And enjoyed, dammit! It better be after all this revision to just the first chapter.

They ordered *un café* each. They were meeting half an hour later than previously, at Philippe's request, so they could eat homemade food and save money. John still had trouble with austerity, however, so he had bought a take-out falafel from one of the popular Jewish places in Le Marais.

An espresso or a decaf was obligatory in order to claim a seat. But since each of them had bought one tiny cup, approximately a thimble-full, for five euros each, they got to sit the rest of the night with no nudges or hints from the staff.

"How are people doing?" asked Philippe. His gut was churning with worry, and the bitter coffee made the maelstrom in his stomach worse.

John sipped from his cup and winced at the sour taste.

"The French stink at making coffee," he said. "They've perfected pastries, the things that go best with coffee, but you have to take your pastry to Italy to get an excellent cuppa joe to go with it."

Well, that's the least of my problems, he thought. How am I doing? First I have to create some kind of life, even if it's an impoverished one, and a reason to live it. Emily. But she will be in college soon—how will I pay for it? She'll leave. I need something that will stay with me no matter what. He looked at Carol, with her hair in a cute messy bun on top of her head. Pretty as ever, lovely blue eyes, but she seemed subdued.

Carol was the only one who answered Philippe's question.

"Oh, fine," she said. She had no intention of revealing she'd lost her job. She'd had chicken for dinner, and it was wrestling with her digestive system.

Anjali decided to risk asking Philippe what she really wanted to know.

"Have you heard from Meredith?"

"No," said Philippe. A direct lie, he mused. But I can't tell them she's selling herself, I simply cannot. And I certainly can't say that I'm stomping with anger at God.

Anjali rubbed her eyes, tired from staring at a computer all day, and looked around at the writers' circle. John, dressed nattily, as ever, Carol also looking sleek, probably ready to pounce on my work again but not a bad sort, really. Philippe, rumpled as always, dark rings under his eyes, looking compassionate and spent. She thought to herself, I've gotten to know these people a bit, I like this group, I think I can be honest with them. I need to talk to somebody besides Aasha—so happily engaged—about my life. I hope this goes well, especially with my boss here. But I need to talk. She chimed in.

"I have to decide within a month whether to go back to India and marry someone or stay and keep writing screenplays."

John was startled by her forthrightness. Then he thought, brave. Tough decision. He'd been with his assistant all day and had no idea this was on her mind. The mysteries of the human soul.

"If I can help you in any way as you weigh your options," Philippe said.

"That's a big decision, and I have to tell you something that might affect you. It's an apology really," Carol said. "I was a little hard on your screenplay. It's quite good, and you should never give up." That wasn't all I should have said, she thought, but it's enough for now.

Anjali answered, "Well, that's nice of you. But is writing screenplays going to make me happy?"

Good question, Carol reflected. I have two relatively successful films out with Gregoire's company, and two previous successes. They haven't made me much happier. Maybe I should tell Anjali that. Nah! I've already stomped on her dream enough, let her figure out what to do.

"I can say this much," Carol said, surprising herself. "The initial thrill of having my work purchased was intense. I'll never forget it. For five days I was ecstatic. I felt I had justified my existence. Then I finally came back to earth. And they changed half the script, doing things to it that drove me bonkers. Seeing my name in the credits was terrific, but the final product was so far from what I'd envisioned, I was disappointed with the film. To be honest, I'm questioning my own relationship with the film industry. It can be fun, when the ideas are popping, and it can be very tough."

"Like any industry," John said.

"Like being a pastor." Philippe's stomach twisted again. "I still haven't written my sermon, and I only have two days left. I don't know what I'm going to say." Wow, I'll bet none of my colleagues ever admitted anything like that to anyone other than their wives. This group is growing on me.

"I learned a good tool." Anjali pulled a notebook she'd bought at the Louvre, with a print of a Botticelli fresco on the cover, out of her bag. "When you're stuck, do fifteen minutes of freewriting. Actually, do it any day. Freewrite about your project and give yourself permission to let anything emerge."

"I'll use that," Carol said. "I'm starting a new screenplay."

"How's the one with the ogre going?" John asked.

"We'll see what happens." Carol dropped her eyes to her pages. She hated not to finish, it had the makings of a huge hit. But Gregoire owned that idea. That was the end of that, wasn't it? She turned her attention to Anjali. "Keep working on that script you gave me. And on The Big Sleep in Paris. They both have rather a lot of potential." There, that made up for my bitchy email.

Even with Carol's praise, Anjali didn't feel any confidence in her writing returning.

"Philippe, what do you think?" Anjali asked. "Will I be happier married than writing screenplays?"

"Hopefully, you can do both," interjected Carol. Though I've never found a man who graciously goes along with me pursuing both. Doesn't mean it doesn't exist. Somewhere.

"I guess I'm duty bound to tell you," Philippe said, "by virtue of my profession, that the real happiness of man is something you guys may never have heard of, because we live in such a secular age. The Westminster catechism says our best happiness—the chief aim of man—is to glorify God and enjoy him forever. But I'm not living it out very well at just this moment, so don't mind me."

"Glorify God?" Carol asked. What a foreign idea. She seemed to think that the chief aim of man—or at least woman—was shopping.

And for this particular woman, writing.

John wished Philippe wouldn't talk about God. But then he was startled: how strange if what Philippe said were really true. What a profoundly different principle to live by.

Philippe changed the subject. "Time is rushing onward. Let's get started, shall we?" he said.

After the usual polite hesitations among the group, John went first.

"I've rewritten the first chapter," he announced.

Carol groaned inwardly with the agony of having to read about Chuck and his propensity for fisticuffs yet again.

John read aloud from his opus while they followed on their photocopies.

"Chapter One. Out his motel window, the summer sun was a flaming soccer ball, low in the sky and ready to score a goal."

Carol sighed.

"Chuck dashed water on his face from his room's corner sink. He was desperate to sleep but couldn't because the mattress of his bed was laid on wires that creaked when he moved. He dressed and went out."

Carol wondered how long it would take for Chuck to find someone to brawl with.

"His Ford Thunderbird"—nice choice of car, Carol thought—"started up and purred smoothly as he cruised a side street off The Strip. He watched for Jake Malloy's current hangout, looking for a knot of men in shiny suits who would signal the presence of their boss. Chuck needed to talk to Jake."

Here comes the fistfight, Carol said to herself, four against one, and Chuck would prevail with nothing more than scraped knuckles. It took John just three paragraphs to set it in motion. Sigh.

"He spotted the knot of men. He drove three blocks to find an open parking space."

Nice touch of realism, Carol thought.

"As Chuck walked back to where he'd seen Jake's entourage, he passed a casino and noticed its marquee. Brenda's name dazzled him, written in black letters against a glowing white background. A strand of light bulbs surrounded the marquee. All the lights flashed in sequence, and her name appeared and disappeared as the white background turned on and off. She obviously hadn't disappeared from his heart because he was rooted to the spot, staring at her name, longing for her."

Ah, thought Carol, a twist. Not your usual action novel. It's got a babe in it, an actress babe. Now that's different. Sigh.

"Chuck strode through the casino, dodging chubby women from Peoria in mint green jogging suits, zipped up against the chill of the air conditioning. He went to the stage, climbed the steps, and ducked behind a curtain. Nobody tried to stop him."

Hah! thought Carol, not likely in a casino full of money and security guards. She'd mention it to John. Gently. Male egos, after all.

He looked good in a French blue shirt, sleeves turned up to reveal muscular forearms.

> "He found his way to the dressing rooms.
> "'Hey!'
> "Chuck turned and saw a guy in a security uniform coming toward him, and a dressing room door with a star on it.
> "'She's expecting me,' he said to the guard and slipped through the door. Brenda sat in a cream-colored satin *peignoir*, applying makeup. She looked at Chuck in the mirror. The door opened behind him, and the security guy poked his head in.
> "'Everything okay, Miss Starr?'"

Oops, thought Carol, John's naming is off again. He has Brenda Starr of the comics on his brain.

> "'He can stay.' Brenda's voice was deep, luscious.
> The door closed, and they were alone."

John read on. The fistfight didn't come until the end of the chapter, after Chuck left Brenda. They did not have sex, but there was plenty of sexual *frisson* between them—the authorial promise of something more.

"I developed my protagonist, just like you guys said to do," John said proudly when he finished reading.

You gave him an old flame to bump into, thought Carol. That's not exactly all that "character development" meant.

"Relying on fistfights in order to have some conflict in this story is lazy writing," Carol said.

John looked up, shocked.

"And I think the scene with Brenda is sexist," Carol said.

John was silenced. So far at these meetings, she had called him racist, lazy, and sexist?

"She's half dressed, of course," Carol continued, "and she has a sexy, low voice, of course. *Clichés.* What about Chuck being attracted to somebody like a librarian?" She could see the glasses coming off and the hair being loosed. Oops, another *cliché.* "I mean a schoolteacher." Schoolmarms and cowboys. Nope, *cliché aussi*. Why were there nothing but *clichés* for women's roles? "I mean something new and different. An astronaut, for heaven's sake." She eyed his ring finger. White skin gone. She turned quickly back to the pages in her hand.

John was watching Carol closely, thinking she looked great but packed a painful punch.

Philippe thought, there's no avoiding it. I'm going to have to talk to her. But first, John's text.

"You're still missing something essential," Philippe said. "It has to appear in the first chapter and in every scene: what the protagonist wants, what's driving him crazy to get."

I'm "missing something essential"? John thought. This text is great. Everybody's jumping on me tonight, even Philippe.

"Well, he wants Brenda," John said, nettled.

An author defending his work could be a bit like a bear defending a cub, Carol thought. Except that was a *cliché*.

"But he basically stumbled upon her," Philippe said. "Why is he searching for Jake Malloy? What is his deep motive for doing that? We need to have a sense of that, starting in the first chapter."

"And the other thing that needs to be in the first chapter is the theme," Anjali said gently. After all, he was her boss. "In movies, it's stated in the first five minutes or so, usually by a secondary character so that it isn't quite so obvious as the main character stating it." Uh-oh, was she getting pedantic like Carol?

"Theme?" John said. He remembered they had mentioned this before.

"In the case of your story, it could be something like, 'Justice comes in surprising forms.' Philippe was glad to think about John's novel and not Meredith, for a change. "I'm assuming that Chuck wants some sort of justice against Jake Malloy."

"Yeah, that works, that's what he wants," John said eagerly. He thought, that solves both problems, the theme and the want.

"You could have Brenda say it." Anjali was nervous about reading her own piece in a few minutes and was bored already with John's story.

"Yeah, Chuck left her in the lurch a year ago, and now he wants to make things right somehow, even if they can't be together," John said. "Looks like I have a rewrite in my future."

Nobody had mentioned the first sentence, Carol thought, and she wasn't going to. It was ludicrous imagery, the sun a flaming soccer ball about to score a goal, but then again, he wasn't attempting to write anything remotely literary, that endured through the ages. Give it a pass. An appropriate thought for a soccer ball, especially one flaming like the sun.

Anjali went next. She had labored to format her screenplay just as she had seen it done in the published screenplay for *Sense and Sensibility*, which she had taken out of a Paris library. That she'd have to format her script again when she got paid for her *péniche* article (would she ever finish it?) and bought screenwriting software was no small obstacle.

She passed out the photocopies of her ten pages. She had changed "Dick Bogart" to "Dan Price." "Dan" because it was manly, short, and strong, "Price" because there would be a price to pay for the justice he sought.

John would think that's great naming, Carol thought as she glanced over the script.

"Don't you think Dan Prince is a great name, John?" she couldn't help asking.

John grunted. Was she serious?

Anjali flushed. Carol thinks it's dumb, doesn't she? And just what sort of great naming is "Ogre?" If she shreds me tonight, I'm never coming back.

They picked parts. John claimed the role of Dan Price. He would, thought Carol, who grabbed the role of Madame de Denichen. She would, thought John. Philippe read the narration, and Anjali listened, attuned for hesitations or stumbles as they read her words.

INT. - DAY – STAIRWELL OF GLAMOROUS
APARTMENT BUILDING

DAN climbs a staircase wrapped around an elevator shaft to the de Denichen apartment.

DAN knocks on beautiful, carved wooden door, painted white with brass knocker and knob.
MADAME DE DENICHEN, 45, with short dark

hair styled in a gamin cut, framing lovely cheekbones, dressed in off-the-rack yet high-end casual clothes, opens the door.

DAN (Voiceover)
I suspected I'd get frosty treatment, and I did.

MADAME DE DENICHEN
Yes?

DAN
I'm Dan Price.

MADAME DE DENICHEN doesn't deign to acknowledge him but turns her back on him as she swings the door open.

INT. – DAY – The DE DENICHEN apartment.

DAN steps into a luxurious apartment with twelve-foot-high ceilings, candelabras on the mantel, luxurious fabrics on the sofa and the armchairs that face it. The drapes on the two tall French doors that lead to two wrought iron balconies are silk, tied back by huge tassels that cost 50 euros apiece.

MADAME DE DENICHEN
(closing the door)
My son has a bright future ahead of him. The Senate.
The President's Conseil des Ministres. Higher.

DAN
Yes, ma'am.

MADAME DE DENICHEN
It was so unfortunate.

DAN
Tell me what happened.

MADAME DE DENICHEN
My son is married to a girl from a prominent family.
Two weeks ago, he was at a party, drank, then drove
an aide—female—home, except he ran off the road.
She's blackmailing us, saying they had sex before they
left, she'll spill all if we don't pay. We want you to get
your hands on every bit of evidence she has and bring
it to us. We also want you to gather evidence of her
debauched character. If she goes public, we'll go
public and discredit her.

Not a bad scene, thought Philippe. Anjali might do well as a
screenwriter. He would tell her so that she had more information for
her decision.

Carol twisted in her seat. A little too much like that scandal with
Ted Kennedy at Chappaquiddick. All Anjali needed to add was a
bridge. But damn, her work was pretty good...

Anjali wrung the script in her hand. Oh God, I hope they like it.
I hope I hear some positive feedback, something I can post on my
wall and feel encouraged.

They continued.

DAN
I need a 500-euro retainer to start.

MADAME DE DENICHEN
I'll get it for you.

MADAME DE DENICHEN leaves the room while
DAN fingers the expensive fringe on the decorative
pillows on the sofa. MADAME DE DENICHEN
comes back a moment later with a stack of cash.

DAN
I'll need everybody's names and addresses.

MADAME DE DENICHEN

(leans against the door again, looks him in the eye,
with her bosom thrust forward because the knob is at
the small of her back.)
Hurry, Mr. Price.

DAN
I understand, Madame. I'll get to work.

EXT. – DAY – RUE DE MONSIEUR LE PRINCE

DAN leaves with a self-satisfied air, buttoning his suit jacket, and walks toward the door of a traditional French restaurant, Polidor.

DAN (voiceover)
I suspected that the girl who was injured wasn't all
that bad a sort. I felt dirty taking money to find dirt
on her. But I hadn't eaten in 19-and-three-quarters
hours, and my rent was due.

The group was quiet for a moment, thinking, and then the critique began.

Carol said, "I'd like to see you give both characters in this scene a telling quirk—a mannerism."

"Yeah, like fidgeting with the rock on her ring finger," John said, remembering Cassandra and the ways she brought attention to her engagement ring. That purchase should have warned me, John thought. "Maybe she holds her hand at a distance and admires it, maybe she taps it on the mantel in impatience."

"Speaking of impatience, any words you can cut in the dialog would speed the scene up," Carol said. "Less time spent on talking heads."

Anjali wanted to scream. You're driving me crazy! There isn't an extra word anywhere in that scene. I'm positive! Shut up!

John said, "Dan needs to meet a buddy, his favorite waiter in the restaurant, somebody soon, to state the theme."

Carol critiqued the critiques. John sometimes learns fast, she thought, especially when other people's work was on the table. His suggestions for mannerisms were spot on, too. She regarded him with a sidelong glance.

John felt her glance but didn't meet it. Time to be different than Dan Price and keep things slow for a bit.

Carol sipped her water and thought, That's all the help I'm giving tonight. Anjali is competition, isn't she.

The group handed Anjali's pages back to her, and Philippe handed out his. Nobody made money writing short stories anymore, he knew. This was pure catharsis. He began to read.

Tamara tottered in the blinding sun. She'd lost her sunglasses, and even if she hadn't, they wouldn't have helped with the way she felt today. She simply must switch from red to white wine. Fewer headaches. She wiped her streaming eyes, her tissue coming away with half the makeup she had applied to the shadows under her eyes that morning.

She'd been in five shops today already. She spotted another help wanted sign. Burger King. She must be desperate. She lurched as the door swung in more easily than she expected. A man behind the register watched her. She walked toward him as steadily as possible.

"I'd like to apply for the job in the window," she said. It was so cool in here, out of the sun.

The manager looked her up and down as she approached the counter—miniskirt, high heels, blouse down to here, make-up smeared.

"That job was filled this morning," he said. "Sorry." He went through a door back into the kitchen.

Her stomach rumbled when she smelled a hamburger being prepared for the tall young man on line ahead of her.

"Can I buy you a something to eat?" he said.

Tamara felt something uncomfortable deep in her instincts, but she had overridden those warnings many times before, so she did again. She also felt her bellybutton touching her spine.

"You're such a pretty girl, please let me buy you lunch," he said. "What would you like?"

As they ate, he told her how attractive he thought she was.

"That manager was an idiot to turn you down. A girl as beautiful as you could work for me. I hire girls to go out and have dinner with men who are traveling and need someone to talk to. You'd go out on beautiful *péniches* on the Seine, or go to fabulous restaurants. There's always plenty to drink, good food, you just talk to them and entertain them."

Something seemed off to Tamara, but she was desperate.

"I couldn't get past that point," Philippe said.

The group could guess why. None of them wanted to add to his pain by making a single comment.

"It's good writing," Carol said. She hated stories about prostitutes and drunkenness all that skanky scumminess. But she looked at John and Anjali, trying to convey a warning to go light on Philippe. They both met her eyes.

"I'm hooked," John said. Uh-oh, why did he use that word? "I mean, this is a really interesting character." I'd better shut up and leave it at that, he thought.

"Anjali?" That's all Philippe could squeeze out of his constricted throat. They are being kind to me. I hate being pitied. I hate Meredith for what she's doing. Will this nightmare I live in never end?

"Well done," Anjali said.

The group handed back his story with "Great writing" and "Nicely done" written in the margins. Carol handed out her copies.

John glanced at the first page and said, "Where's my favorite ogre?"

"I started a new screenplay," Carol said. "I wanted to see what you guys thought of it." Actually, she needed their ideas to make this excellent, sell it, and keep a roof over Louise's head. "We'll get back to those fun birds, I hope," John said.

"Oh, I guess," Carol replied. She didn't want the group reading the parts—people were always so slow, leaving big pauses in which they hadn't glanced ahead and seen that it was their turn to read. She hated that stupidity. Flow was important. "I'll read it. Here goes my contribution for tonight:"

INT.   NAOMI'S   STUDIO   APARTMENT –
MORNING

Alarm goes off.   NAOMI, 50s, sits bolt upright, climbs out of bed to make coffee.
Her old-fashioned clamshell phone jingles. She reads text message: "It's over.   You make peanuts, you don't have anything saved. You have nothing to offer this relationship. Box up my stuff and the ring and send them to me."

NAOMI gasps. She goes to the kitchenette, grabs a paper towel and starts to wipe her eyes, then halts, rips it in half, starts to wipe, then rips it in half again, tucks the unused pieces into the paper towel tube, and finally wipes her eyes. She sits on her bed.
Another text bings into her phone. "Insure the box."

NAOMI
What an incredible, irredeemable jerk.

NAOMI flops backward on her bed, arms spread wide.

Good so far, thought Anjali. But I see extra words, and I will point them out one by one and see how she likes it.
John was not intrigued by the script, but by its author, who spun these webs out of thin air. He cleared his throat and glanced at Carol, who was intent on her pages.
She continued to read the entire script (selfish of her, Anjali thought, I would have liked to read a part):

INT. CLIFTON DINER – DAY

NAOMI, dressed in inexpensive, ill-fitting clothes, and PHOEBE, mid-50s, attractive, in a long, artsy

caftan, sit in a booth.   PHOEBE eats heartily,
NAOMI stabs at her food.

NAOMI
He texted -- TEXTED -- to break up. After being
engaged for eight months!

PHOEBE
Coward.

In a mantra, NAOMI ticks items off her fingers.

NAOMI
I've been dumped. I work at a dinky suburban
weekly, the bottom of journalism. I've never been
promoted. I don't own a house or have kids. I hate
to say it, but—maybe he was right to dump me.

PHOEBE
He's an idiot. You're a great catch. You'll be fine.

NAOMI
I'll agree with you someday, but I don't feel like it
today.

PHOEBE
(with compassion)
Take some time to grieve.
(pause, then says briskly)
That guy deserves about five minutes.

NAOMI pushes her plate away.

NAOMI
He's right. I am a failure.

PHOEBE
(sharply)
Don't say that!

(Gently)
Aw, honey, success might look different than you
think.

NAOMI
The first time he held out his hand to me, and I took
it, it felt so good, so right.

PHOEBE
Yeah, men. They're a mixed bag.

NAOMI
(with a sly smile)
One time he said he thought his bottom was his best
feature.
(reflectively)
You know, I think it was.

PHOEBE
Any man who thinks his best feature is his butt
you've got to avoid, my dear.

NAOMI
(sighs)
Absolutely.

Anjali couldn't wait. She had to say it.

"I don't think anyone under the stress that Naomi is under
would say 'What an incredible, irredeemable jerk.' She might say one
or the other, but not both. Too many words." There! I said it. But
don't be an idiot and offend this professional screenwriter who might
give you a hand up in the business. Darn! I shouldn't have said it!

"I like that bit with the smaller and smaller piece of paper
towel," John said. Actually, he thought it was the only redeeming
feature of this bland chick flick. Egads! When did I get so bitchy?

"Thanks," Carol said. She didn't tell them she had been given
that bit of action by the teacher in a screenwriting class she'd taken.
Crikey, this screenplay had been in a drawer for three years already.

"I like Phoebe so much!" Anjali said. "I hope you give her lots of scenes." Maybe that will patch over my first comment. What a little chicken you are, Anjali.

"An old-fashioned cell phone, uses one-quarter of a paper towel to wipe her eyes—you've shown this character's circumstances," Philippe said. He had a clamshell phone, too.

"And 'success might look different than you think.' That's the theme?" asked John.

Carol nodded with a wry smile. It appeared that her own life's struggle to be a success was being reflected in her art.

"I see what you've been saying about theme," John said, "stated early on by a secondary character."

"The whole rest of my film questions that theme," Carol answered. "Or it should."

"You could blow it wide open by juxtaposing a successful character," John said. Wow, I really have good ideas, he thought.

"That's Phoebe," Carol replied. "At least, she seems successful. For now."

"I think that soon," John said, "you should take us out on the town of Clifton and show us its downtown, its people."

"You'll see next time," Carol answered. Really, John had good instincts for other people's stories.

"And don't neglect the ogre," John said. "I like him, in a weird way." I want to see the ogre on the screen after investing my time and creative energy in him, he thought. Next time I brainstorm with Carol, I'm asking for my name in the credits. And a share in the profits.

"And what's with 'men are a mixed bag?'" he asked. "We're simple, straight-forward creatures."

Not the kind I end up with, thought Carol. "Oh, well, what's a film conversation between women without an aspersion cast on men?" She smiled at John.

He regarded her silently. What issues were boiling below her surface?

"I like your theme of success," Philippe said. "I struggle with that question, too."

John had been curious about him for weeks now and leapt at the chance to know more. "How do you define it?" he asked.

"I'm a pastor. That says everything you need to know about my pay. I'll never swim go on safari or hike in the Himalayas and buy big experiences, the way some people define success. My bucket list has to be very short.

"Success for me, for years, was defined as my congregation growing. Then I learned that that wasn't it. On a good day, when I look at my life the way I believe God looks at it, I can define success as walking hand in hand with God, trusting him no matter what—in life, death, whatever. But lately I'm not even doing that, to be honest."

Carol had been feeling like a failure, having been fired, and she could identify with Philippe. Her markers for success—smart new clothes for her and Louise—were denied her now, if she were going to use her savings wisely. What was going to take their place?

"I've long held 'success in Hollywood' as my goal,' Anjali said.

"But how do you define that, precisely?" Philippe challenged her. Three quarters of being a pastor was challenging the assumptions of his parishioners, which he thought maybe the writers' circle was.

"I don't know. Maybe several screenplays produced," Anjali said. "Enough to live on so I can write more and don't have to be an assistant." Whoops! She glanced at John, who winked.

"'Live' as in Beverly Hills?" Philippe asked. "The bar you're aiming for could easily keep sliding."

"I could live simply," Anjali said. Though deep down she envisioned palms in tubs by her glamorous front door. People to water them for her.

"What if, from a bigger perspective, that wasn't success? What if, instead of having two hours' influence over an audience who forgets your movie within ten minutes of leaving, no matter how much magic you created, success was different?" You've said too much, Philippe thought. You're upset over Meredith, don't upset this young woman.

John touched his substitute cufflinks and thought, he has a lot to say about success, when he screwed up his daughter so bad. John paused. That might be harsh: kids do what they want to do, like Emily continuing to live with Cassandra. Wow, I'm getting bitchy. Next thing I'll be buying a feather boa.

Anjali considered the question. She had thought that writing screenplays was a chance to invest in an audience. But that was a concept, not a personal relationship. Maybe success had a bit more of a human touch.

Chapter 66

"Well, I've challenged you on that score quite enough for one day," Philippe said. The other diners had left, only a couple sharing a beer remained under the awning.

"Shall we do a writing prompt?" he asked. "It's late."

"Yes!" Anjali said.

"Okay, here it is. Ready? It's a line from one of my poems. I hope you don't mind. 'Let me not be closed to you, for where I am closed, there I am untrue.'"

Pens scratched and dotted various i's. Philippe's sadness and worry over Meredith descended on him, crushing his heart against his ribs. Now he wished he hadn't suggested the writing prompt. He wished the evening were over. He was deep in the valley of the shadow of death, exhausted.

After six minutes he said, "Please, let's stop, we can finish on our own later." The group heard the fatigue in his voice and put their pens down.

"Okay, who wants to read?" he asked.

To get Philippe home more quickly, Carol interrupted the usual polite hanging back that the group did and said, "I'll go.

"Let me not be closed to you,
for where I am closed, there
I am not true
I open the door of my heart
to face the blackness within.
The drunk, the homeless
look like what I feel."

When that last sentence had emerged, she'd been startled. Where did that come from? Rather terrifying, indeed. And 'blackness within,' a bit of a *cliché*, dear, isn't it? Did I just read this personal stuff aloud to this group? I guess I trust them.

"I'll go," said Anjali.

> "Let me not be closed
> not like this temple, shut fast
> forbidding me to pray.
> I stand before the temple wall.
> My toes dig tunnels.
>   When I pray, it is with
> my whole being."

She liked the way she'd found a home for that line she'd heard at the poetry slam. And she'd changed it, made it her own, so it wasn't stealing.

John thought, I'm a bit jealous she came up with that vivid line—digging tunnels with toes. That resonates. I'd do exactly that to get Emily to live with me.

"It's disjointed," Carol said.

Philippe thought, ouch, on behalf of Anjali. He said, "Here's my attempt." He rustled his copy, grabbed his glass of water, sipped it quickly, and began to read in a low, tight voice.

> "I must tell you, but you know it,
> that my question runs through my body
> like molten lava down hills
> planted with priceless trees:
>   Why do you not answer?"

The group paused again, out of respect for his pain.

"Love it," murmured Carol. It was a strong bit of poetry.

"Thanks," said Philippe, thinking, if all I'm going to get out of this situation with Meredith is a poem, it will be nowhere near enough.

217

Chapter 67

As Carol gathered her huge Louis Vuitton bag and said good night, the rest of the group hung back by silent, mutual agreement. Carol hurried off to relieve her babysitter, and the three who remained exchanged glances. Anjali spoke first.

"I know she has years of experience writing and giving critique. But…"

"But she's so condescending about it," John said. "That makes her harsh comments even harder to take."

"If she doesn't stop bodyslamming me to the ground, I don't think I can continue here," Anjali said.

Philippe felt awful. He should have pulled Carol aside sooner. He should have done more to spare these writers her morale-crushing, accusatory style. People seemed to have borne up so far, but inevitably they'd shy away from the barrage of artillery shells that Carol kept firing into their camps. Fear of her critique would sooner or later cause them to go into hiding from writing the truth.

He had failed.

As he had in so many things.

Chapter 68

Anjali walked home across the Pont Royal. Its streetlights clicked on, and below, the Seine's turbulent waters grabbed the light from the streetlamps and played. A *bateau mouche* plied the waters under the bridge, and she could hear the pre-recorded spiel echoing against the stone embankments. "Notre Dame took two centuries to build…"

Yes, but it was built. It was still standing. It was a success, by any measure.

What was her measure? Instead of hiding at such a distance from people, alone writing screenplays that might never get produced, she ought to get involved with humans, help out in some way.

As she walked down Boulevard Saint Michel towards her tiny, sixth-floor maid's room, she passed a *brasserie*. Outside of it stood a thin girl in very high heels, very short tube skirt, tube top, and with hair in a messy bun. The girl was vomiting against the wall of the *brasserie*, heaving great, wretched bursts. Anjali paused, kept her distance. There was a distance around the girl, too, a force field of human dignity despite the wracking heaves that her body was subjecting her to. What could Anjali really do for a person like this?

The girl's nausea seemed to have subsided. She looked furtively over her shoulder and caught sight of Anjali. She turned away from the puddle she had made and leaned her back against the stone building, looking exhausted.

"Are you OK?" Anjali asked. This poor girl might be just like Philippe's daughter. There seemed to be a softness about her. Perhaps she wasn't totally hardened to the streets.

The girl didn't answer, she just leaned with her eyes closed. A tiny purse on a long gold chain hung from one bony shoulder.

"What's your name?" Anjali said.

"Pearl."

Just then a red-faced man came out of the *brasserie*, wearing a suit that strained at its buttons and seams. He walked up to Pearl and grabbed her arm.

"Come back to the party, kid," he demanded.

"She's sick," Anjali said, scared to death he'd punch her for interfering, wondering what she was doing getting involved in this dark scene. What would Amma and Appa say? Yeah, and Ravi? And his aunties?

"Who are you?" the man demanded, his pig eyes encased deep in fleshiness.

"I'm her friend. Come on, Pearl, let's go home."

"Wha'?" Pearl said.

"Home. Come on." Anjali chose to ignore the man. Maybe he'd just go away. She took Pearl's other arm.

"I'll tell Gaspard, and you'll see, you'll pay," the man said to Pearl, and tossed her arm away.

At the name "Gaspard," Pearl shivered. She glanced with big eyes over her shoulder, down Boulevard Saint Michel. Anjali looked too and saw a few couples strolling, not an angry pimp marching towards them.

"Come on, let's go," she said and tugged at Pearl's arm. Am I really doing this? Isn't writing screenplays enough service to humanity? Do I have to get entangled like this?

"Say goodbye to your face," the man said and walked back into the *brasserie*.

Pearl gasped with fear, but took a few steps forward with Anjali steering her.

Anjali was terrified, too. Oh my God, what have I gotten into? Gaspard could come around the corner any second. She figured the best thing to do was to get off the street as fast as possible.

She hustled Pearl toward her tiny flat. Where could this girl sleep? On the narrow passage between bed and closet? In her bed? With her? What if she had lice? Madame de Denichen would throw them both out.

"Come on, Pearl, we'll figure this out," Anjali said. She decided to hail a taxi rather than risk meeting Gaspard on the street. As they settled into a cab, Anjali thought, you're five minutes into this project and you're over budget already. She said a prayer, she wasn't sure who to, exactly. Then she remembered the face of Jesus she had seen, the one portrayed in the mosaic at Sacré Cœur. Maybe he'd help with this mess she was in.

Chapter 69

At Madame de Denichen's, Anjali hustled Pearl through the street door into the foyer, then quickly into the stairwell. Shoes in hand, they climbed five flights. Anjali was nervous, trying to dodge Madame's prying eyes and sharp voice. At the door to her attic, she fumbled with the keys. Up the last flight they crept.

"The W.C. is here." Anjali showed her the stand-up Turkish toilet, tucked in a little closet under the eaves, then opened the door to her flat. Pearl tumbled in and fell onto the bed.

"You could take a shower," Anjali suggested.

Pearl looked at her with dull eyes, then shook her head.

"No need," she whispered.

"I'd really like you to take a shower." The girl's face was streaked with makeup, there was a trail of drool on her tube top, her knees were brown with dirt picked up who knew where.

"No," Pearl whispered.

"Actually, I insist. To stay here you must take a shower. Here, I'll get it started for you." Anjali adjusted the temperature, then stood over Pearl until she got up and shuffled to step under the nozzle. "You can take your clothes off in there. Leave them on the floor. I'll get pajamas for you."

Anjali's Amma had packed two of everything in India, so she laid an extra towel and a pink and white polka-dotted cotton nightie on the bed. She slipped into the navy and white one. Even with a surprise guest and all that meant, she had a priority to attend to. She wrote the praise she had received from the group on one yellow square, criticisms and suggestions on another, and taped them to the closet doors next to the others.

Pearl was in the shower a long time. Anjali worried that Madame would come up to protest. Finally the water shut off and the door opened a crack. Pearl peered out.

Anjali handed her the towel.

"I'm going to do my dishes," Anjali said. "You dry off, and here's a nightgown."

As Pearl stepped out onto the mat, Anjali went to the sink and clattered the dishes. It was getting late, she had to be at work in the morning. What was she going to do with Pearl while she was gone?

Anjali heard the bed creak, and Pearl was sitting on it, dressed, her hair a wild tangle. Anjali handed her a brush.

"I'll get you a glass of ginger ale," Anjali said. "It will help to settle your stomach." And wash that nasty taste of vomit away, she thought.

"If you have a rubber band, I'd like to braid my hair," Pearl said.

That was her longest sentence of the night, Anjali thought. She's feeling better.

Anjali went back to washing dishes, and when they were done turned to study her new flatmate. Pearl was all sharp angles—elbows, knees, collarbones jutting out. She doesn't get enough to eat, Anjali thought, as Pearl placidly braided her long brown hair.

What have I done? Anjali thought. Well, I'll try to help humanity. And it will give me something to write about.

"Are you hungry?" she asked.

Pearl shook her head no.

"Look, I need some sleep. I have to go to work tomorrow. You can stay here all day, but please be quiet so my landlady doesn't hear you. You can read," and Anjali swept her hand toward the shelf of books in English she'd brought from India and that was gradually growing with each trip to the Shakespeare & Company bookstore. A guilty pleasure, to buy books on her budget.

"Do you like to read?"

Pearl nodded.

"There's eggs in the fridge, and I'll bring up some fresh bread before I go. I hope you don't mind, but you won't be able to leave because you don't have a key to the street door, and I don't have an extra. But look at it this way, you're safe here."

Pearl was just watching her, her eyes big. She's still terrified of me, Anjali thought.

"Well, I have to go to bed now," she said. Her window was open. There might be one or two mosquitoes in the night, but up here, under the zinc roof, it had to be open in summer. Nobody in France, including rich Madame de Denichen, had ever heard of putting screens on windows.

Pearl stood up, and Anjali reached past her to turn down the coverlet. "You sleep on the inside so I can get out of bed in the morning," Anjali said.

Pearl must have relaxed quickly because she was slumbering in five minutes. It took Anjali three hours to fall asleep. Her mind was spinning with questions about what to do next. How could Pearl come and go without Madame knowing? Impossible. And what if Pearl stole everything she owned while she was gone? Well, you won't miss much except the books. And your earrings from India. They are replaceable, you could find them in shops all over Paris. Except you can't afford them on your Paris budget.

And her mind whirled for the next two hours.

Chapter 70

John sat in his office in Le Marais. Before him were the contracts to hire a realtor for the Greenwich mansion, and to engage two brokers, one for each boat. Anjali had printed them out, and after he signed them, she would scan them and email them back. Thank goodness he still had Anjali to help him. And she didn't seem to hold back in her critiques of his novel, either. Amazing girl.

He ached as he signed the realtor's contract. His dominion was getting smaller fast. He signed the broker's contract for the Gull, languishing in a boatyard on the Long Island Sound.

He took up the Grey Skies contract, saw what the French broker recommended asking for her: 78,000 euros. John had put that much or more just into improvements, upkeep, winter storage, and marina space in Cherbourg. That was on top of the purchase price of 89,000 euros two years ago. Boats truly were holes in the water into which a man poured money.

He set the Grey Skies contract aside. You gotta have a boat, John thought.

Chapter 71

Carol worked in a library she loved, La Bibliothèque Fornay, in a castle built between 1475 and 1519, located near the Seine in her beloved Fourth *arrondissement*. It was one of more than 70 libraries in Paris. The ceiling had beams hewn by hand six hundred years ago. Stone that had been carved in the Middle Ages formed the balustrade between the balcony and the room below. During breaks she could explore the stacks of books on art and fashion, the library's specialty, by using a stone circular staircase. So lovely to look up and see it spiraling, like the inside of a nautilus' shell, ever smaller as it got farther away.

Nautilus shell. It reminded her of one she'd had as a teenager that had fit so comfortably into her hand. Just like Gregoire's small crystal elephant had. She re-lived picking it up, reaching way back for more leverage for her throw, and watching it smash into his glass-encased altar to himself. That had felt damned good. Childish, yes. She'd never do anything like it again. She could have been blinded by flying glass, Gregoire, too. He hadn't sued. The French rarely did. It was a cool country.

She wasn't going to fight Gregoire for her job, though she knew people who had fought for their jobs in France and had been reinstated. Who wanted to work for a boss that didn't want them? Who wanted to work for creepy, hairy Gregoire anyway?

The art students around her hefted cocktail-table books (known as *grand formats*) of artists' work to the big tables. They wrote notes in composition books or in laptops, peering dutifully back and forth, from text to notes.

Carol just typed. All these words and ideas were coming out of her body, not other people's texts like the students writing notes. This screenplay with Naomi and Phoebe was going so well, somebody would buy it. As a screenwriter with successful films already produced, she would be paid handsomely. If she invested it wisely—maybe she'd invest it with John—she could keep going, focused on writing screenplays without having a job.

Carol thought about Louise's father, a Frenchman living in Marseille. They had not married, so alimony was impossible, but what about child support? She made a note on a pad beside her to find a French family lawyer—maybe the writers' circle knew of one—and kept banging the keys.

Chapter 72

Elodie was still at work, so Philippe was home alone in the late afternoon. He had read a Psalm that morning and prayed for Meredith's deliverance, but she hadn't called, she hadn't repented, and Philippe was now choking with worry for her. He went up to her bedroom and stood in the doorway.

All he could see was the bed. Beds, Meredith in so many beds, so many men, or should he call them boys, since they weren't man enough to keep it in their pants? Meredith! Why doesn't God answer my prayers and help her! Philippe remembered the first line of his poem that the circle had used Thursday night as a prompt. I will be open with him, Philippe thought, for where I am closed I am false.

"God, I've served you for twenty five years. Save my girl, my precious little Meredith!"

He listened. As the Desert Fathers, or Teresa of Avila, or some ancient saint once said, the heavens are sometimes as brass.

"God, at this point, yes! You owe me! I'm calling in all markers!"

And he was silent again. He listened to the empty house, hoping. But still no phone call, no doorbell, no prodigal Meredith to return to his care and protection.

And then his disappointment with God, whom he loved and had devoted his life to but with whom he was more angry than he'd ever been with anybody in his life, boiled up. The anger in him, at God who was omnipotent but didn't bring Meredith home, burst out of him with searing heat.

"I have been praying for this child since the moment I knew Elodie was pregnant with her, and things are so much worse than ever. What's wrong with you? Why don't you do something?"

He looked up at the ceiling, through the ceiling, into the throne room of God. "Prayer after prayer, years' worth of prayers for Meredith, and you have ignored them while I visited sick old people in dumpy hospitals, and took Elodie's soup to them in their smelly little flats, and sometimes, when their aides weren't around, I even wiped their bottoms.

"I've listened to parishioners who ruined their lives in spite of wise counsel I gave them. And I was patient, most of the time, because I loved you. I've modeled Jesus to the very best of my ability. For years!

"Years of divinity school, student debt so I could be a pastor, years of traipsing to dozens of churches asking for financial support so I could go to pagan Paris, the place that used to be the center of Christianity. I wanted to serve God, serve God, I've served you well, with my utmost—"

And then his anger became rage. Where was Meredith?

"God damn you, God!" he screamed at the ceiling.

The room was ringing with the screech of his voice. He couldn't believe what he'd just done. God was the creator of the universe. He deserved the utmost respect.

"I'm sorry." He pictured Meredith, vulnerable, abused. "But I mean it! I really mean it, you old fool!"

He was appalled at what he was saying.

"I'm sorry. I've taken God's name in vain. But oh my God, why don't you help? You're all-powerful, do something, damn it!"

Philippe fell on the bed and cried into the pillow. He had disappointed himself and God. He was powerless to help Meredith, and powerless to convince God to help Meredith. He had devoted his life, and this was the thanks he got. Worse, he had behaved in a way not worthy of his calling...he must never tell his parishioners...he must repent...he'd do that later, right now he was too upset...oh dear God, I'm too acquainted with grief, please spare me, spare us all...

Elodie came home later and found him on Meredith's bed. She didn't take his shoes off for fear of waking him. She covered him with Meredith's red and white compass quilt.

Chapter 73

Pearl seemed happy enough in the *chambre de bonne*, Anjali thought, high above the threatening streets, but eventually she'd have to get out for some sun. Anjali had given her a pair of jeans, which were a little too long, so Pearl walked on the hems. They'll be ruined, Anjali thought. Oh well. She had bought a packet of underwear, a sports bra, and two "I love Paris" T-shirts for Pearl. Anjali's expense spreadsheet was screaming.

"Let's get some fresh air," Anjali said. Pearl looked wary.

"You look so different from the night I met you, I don't think you have to worry. Wear your hair loose, it's the perfect disguise."

Pearl still didn't say much, even though they'd been in this tiny space together for days now.

Anjali dug a pair of flipflops from the closet.

"Here, carry these. As we go down the stairs, you step silently in bare feet at the same time I do in shoes. We have to avoid Madame."

They snuck out onto the street.

Anjali turned in the opposite direction from Boulevard Saint Michel. They strolled along, Pearl watching the street carefully from behind a curtain of dark hair, kinky from being braided wet.

"Do you have family anywhere?" Anjali asked. "Mine is in Mumbai."

"Yes, I have family. They're just outside Paris."

"Are they good to you?"

"Yes." Tears sprang into Pearl's eyes. "I admire them both."

"Why don't you go back to them? Not that you have to leave today, don't worry, but eventually?"

"I'm too ashamed."

Anjali didn't know what to do with that one. They entered Jardin de Luxembourg—Gaspard probably didn't frequent this place full of couples and families—and they promenaded with other strollers.

Pearl volunteered something for the first time in their relationship.

"I would have to give up drinking to go home," she said. "I don't know if I can. I really like it."

"But you end up vomiting?"

"Yeah, it's so stupid. I'm trying to figure out a way to not do that. It's drinking beer with whiskey shots that does that. I'll start drinking only bourbon, I think."

"When did you start drinking?"

"Oh, when I was about 15. I did it to rebel, but soon I was drinking—like—more than other people, I guess. Like I said, I don't know if I can give it up. I'm hungry, can we go to the store?"

They ended up in the Franprix closest to the flat. Oh, my budget, Anjali thought. I could barely feed myself, how's this going to work? They picked out chicken thighs, salad greens, rice, and a box of microwave popcorn.

At the check-out counter, Pearl dug in her jeans pocket. "I have some money." Then she blushed.

Anjali could guess where it came from, but it helped, and she was not going to quibble about the source. "Thanks," she said simply.

They were in the de Denichen's foyer ready to climb six flights when Madame opened the door to her apartment. Behind her Anjali could see fine draperies, thick carpet, a beautiful armoire, armchairs upholstered in soft colors, fresh flowers.

"*Bonjour*, Anjali," Madame said. As usual, she spoke condescendingly.

"*Bonjour*, Madame." This woman was such an experience, she was in Anjali's screenplay, unbeknownst to her, of course.

"Who is your friend?" She eyed Pearl suspiciously.

"Let me introduce you." That formality completed, Anjali added, "We're just having dinner together."

"I see, well, that's fine," she said and stepped back into her apartment and closed the door.

That woman had seven senses and eyes all over her head, Anjali thought.

She heard Pearl giggle for the first time as they stepped into the stairwell.

Chapter 74

Carol and John met, at Carol's request, at the Starbucks at Metro Odéon. She wanted a decaf, and the best in Paris was available only at Starbucks. The alternative was that bitter, over-priced stuff they served in *cafés*. Although she was free to meet at any time, Carol had suggested an evening so John wouldn't know she didn't have a job.

He looked fantastic in his business suit. Carol eyed him surreptitiously. He was a Gentlemen's Quarterly hunk, all right. And rich to boot. Rich, handsome men were not a good bet, she thought. They knew they could have anyone, and generally did. Besides, he was almost certainly married. Though the mark where his ring had been had faded. But that didn't mean anything, maybe he decided not to wear his ring anymore. So he could flirt and have something on the side. Like me? No, that would be true misery. You're right, but WOW! For as long as it lasted…

"So, Carol, how've you been?" John asked. He wondered if Philippe had talked to Carol yet. How much was this session with her going to hurt?

"Oh, good, good." Carol was staring at his broad chest, still a bit stuck in her daydream. "How's your novel coming along?" She didn't really want to hear about it, but it was a conversation starter.

"I kind of lost interest in Chuck," John said.

Yes, that was the problem we were telling you about, Carol thought.

"Did you ever do that character profile that we mentioned—" that I mentioned, Carol thought, but let's get the group's weight behind this—"that would be helpful to give him depth and liveliness?"

"Haven't had time." Closing the old business and trolling for new business was killing him.

"Listen, let's do it now," Carol said. "I have my laptop with me, and Starbucks has Wifi, unlike most Paris *cafés*. Let's ask and answer character development questions. We'll brainstorm. Two heads are better than one, as they say."

"Yes, okay, thanks." John leaned forward to put his elbows on the tiny table. He really did want to write a bestseller. Sad to say, right now it looked like his only chance to make some money. He was well aware that it was a long, long shot. But just in case, he would write it into the divorce settlement: all proceeds from the sale of monster hits go to John alone.

Carol Googled "character development questions," checked out two links, and picked the one she thought offered the most complete set of questions. Now, to delve into John's psyche and get the answers. This should be interesting.

"Okay, here goes: Number 1: Name. Chuck Norris."

"No, not Chuck Norris, Chuck—." In truth, that was how he imagined this character, exactly like the movie star. But he couldn't rip him off that blatantly, could he? No. Everyone would laugh at him. The way Carol was laughing at him. She was attractive, plenty of breast action, a waist—always a nice feature—trim legs under that Armani suit. Pricey clothes. But not blatant about it, as Cassandra had been. A screenwriter, so creative. Creative in bed?

"No, his name is Chuck Morris." Oops, that was embarrassing. Think, man! "I mean, Chuck Price, because he extracts a price from every bad guy. That's his name."

"Okay," said Carol, typing. So now our group has a Dan Price and a Chuck Price. Sigh.

"Let me read you the first couple of questions so you can start thinking about them:

"Name: We got that.

"Age:

"Height:

"Eye color:

"Physical appearance:

"Job:

"More than anything in the world, my protagonist wants:

"But he/she is afraid of:

"And his/her greatest weakness is."

"We have to answer all those?" John asked.

"There's forty more questions. 'What are his defining mannerisms, pet peeves, hobbies.'" That had certainly been mentioned before.

John rubbed his hands together. "Okay, let's get started." He was always up for a challenge. Especially in bed. Carol looked as though she offered that. Well, back to Chuck Norris, I mean Morris, I mean Price.

They brainstormed on Chuck for a while, then Carol said, "My turn," and they brainstormed on her screenplay. When they were tired and stopped, they both felt excited about their writing projects again.

"Wow, that's fun," said John. "You're good at it." When you aren't really bitchy, he thought.

"You are, too," Carol said. Otherwise she wouldn't be here. "You had great ideas for me. Thank you."

"We should do this regularly." If she were going to ease up on the condescending, shattering comments, there were other things he'd like to do regularly with her. He poured a drink from the *carafe* on the table. Steady, he thought. Sex could easily ruin this creative writing dynamic.

"I'd love that," Carol said. I'd love to do a lot of things with this man. She fingered her sweating glass of water. The only thing harder for me than being in a relationship is not being in one. But an affair could jeopardize this creative collaboration we've got. She sat forward, feeling John's eyes intent on her body. But she had to write and sell and great movie. Business before pleasure, that was a good principle, wasn't it?

"Listen, one more question before we quit for the day," Carol said. "I need a lawyer to pursue the father of my daughter for child support. Know of anybody?"

"Yes, the lawyer handling my divorce is a family law specialist. He's French but speaks perfect English."

"Oh!" Cautiously, she said, "So you're getting divorced?" There was more possibility here than she had imagined. What was that you just said to yourself moments ago about a business-focused, platonic relationship? Yeah, they're nice, but what about sex?

"Yes, unfortunately. She's trying to soak me, but he's good, he's helping me dodge her ploys."

"Oh, I'm sorry to hear about your divorce." She thought, Crikey, you're available. So am I. Pick me, pick me!

"I haven't thought about a new relationship," John said. Well, only every night when I climb into bed alone. Or see a woman's hips swaying as she walks down the street.

"I broke up with someone recently, too," Carol said. If it were up to her, she'd be with John. Wait, it was up to the woman, wasn't it? Yes, it was!

Carol's and John's eyes met and held. They each knew they had a green light from the other.

"We work well together," John said.

"Yes."

"I'd be concerned to ruin a good collaboration," John said.

At that point, Carol made a choice between having a romantic relationship with John and writing to support herself and her daughter.

"Me, too," Carol said. Damn! I would have liked to take a risk on it. But would it be worth ruining our fabulous brainstorming? No. So be it. Ugh. For now.

Chapter 75

Philippe sat in his office, surrounded by white plastic because of his shelves and table, and began to feel that he needed to be amongst people instead of laboring alone. Historic surroundings made of wood and stone would also be nice. He decided to work on his sermon not in his office above the gallery on Rue Lanneau but at La Bibliothèque Historique de la Ville de Paris in Le Marais.

He felt relieved. He could postpone the moment when he found he had nothing good to say about God until he got to the library.

As he crossed the Seine, he reflected on his responsibility as the man who'd called the writing group together, as perhaps pastor to the group, to foster an environment of safety in which people could write the truth. If he could just get Carol to critique in a less personal way. It was a matter of approach. And word choice. That's all, he would tell her. If only she would not launch into him when he said it and rip him apart, her fangs dripping his blood...

He snapped out of that particular *rêverie* when he stepped off of Pont Marie, which crossed from Ile St. Louis to Le Marais. He headed toward *la bibliothèque*, passing *boutiques*. He paused to glance at a window display of colorful silk scarves. He knew he was procrastinating.

If and when he talked to Carol, she might attack back with words that would cause him pain for a long time. Till he died, most likely. He still smarted from Madame Babineaux's comment about the way he pushed his glasses up his nose and distracted her from the sermon. He had a lot of those wounds, all over him, from the church ladies, from life itself. Oh Lord, he supposed they meant well, but honestly, they were rough. He'd tried to toughen up, to become inured to it. He never had mastered that one.

Well, he mused, he had a sermon to write and there was nothing he wanted less to do. Maybe he'd read the magazines and newspapers at the library.

He turned onto Rue Pavée and saw a slim, blonde woman bustling ahead of him on the sidewalk, headed in the direction of *la bibliothèque*. He was quite sure it was Carol. What was she doing in Le Marais on a weekday?

If he could catch up with her, he could have a "walk and talk" with her and maybe convince her to be more considerate at the writers' group. And he could postpone writing his sermon. That would be an excellent morning's work, he thought.

She turned in at *la bibliothèqu,e* and he ran to catch her before she got inside the library. He hurried through the massive, ancient gate of *la bibliothèque* and saw her across the courtyard, near the library's door.

"Carol!" he called.

She turned, recognized him, waved, and stepped toward him.

He walked across the huge cobblestones of the courtyard to her carefully, lest he twist an ankle on the lumpy 15th century paving. She was dressed in a skirt and well-cut long jacket of the same fabric. She sported a colorful silk scarf, tied at her throat just so. That's what Paris did for people, he thought—it gives them flair.

They exchanged the *bisous*. Carol smells of the most wonderful perfume, Philippe thought. I wish I knew what it was. I would buy some for Elodie.

Philippe is out of breath and his cheek is sticky, Carol thought. I wish I were married to a great man like him rather than slogging out every moment alone.

"You're working here today?" Philippe asked.

Carol blushed. "Trapèze allows me to work from home one day a week," she lied. "But I didn't want to be home alone."

"Yes, I've got this sermon to write and I'm desperate not to do it, especially not alone in my office." Well, this was his chance. He'd better take it. "Say, do you have time for a quick walk? A stroll might get our creative juices flowing."

"Okay."

So they crossed the cobbles gingerly and went out the gate, turning right on Rue Pavée.

"Let's check out Place des Vosges," Philippe said.

"Fine with me. For a little while. I do have to work."

At the corner of Rue Pavée and Rue des Francs Bourgeois, they turned right. The centuries-old stone walls of *la bibliothèque* loomed on the right and those of the Musée Carnivalet on the left. Their footsteps rang with those of a hundred other people on the street. The sound reverberated against the two walls, back and forth, creating quite a din that was topped by several scooters motoring by. The noise bounced around and then headed skyward, Philippe supposed, floating toward the clashing, torn, grey clouds above. A typical Paris sky. There was something about the landscape around the city that created dramatic clouds. But the French wouldn't call the clouds dramatic because for them, "dramatic" meant a tragic ending. They called the clouds romantic.

He hoped his talk with Carol wouldn't have a tragic ending. He didn't want to lose her from the circle. She brought interesting projects to the group, ones that sparked animated discussion. She had lots of experience making stories more compelling. He'd followed her suggestion to read PIXAR's rules of storytelling. That had been a great idea. The circle needed her. But he also didn't want people to end up trashed at every meeting. And then not telling the truth in their writing, out of fear.

The sidewalk along Rue des Francs Bourgeois was so narrow that Philippe had to walk in the street. Another scooter dodged past.

"How's your screenplay coming along?" Philippe thought, I could make small talk the entire time and never get down to the crux of the matter.

"Working on several, actually. Cross-pollination, you know."

Philippe wondered how his story about Tamara / Meredith and her self-destruction could possibly cross-pollinate into what he'd say to Madame Babineaux in his sermon on Sunday. Well, it did, actually. We all need to be saved from ourselves, he could say... *voilà!* Cross-pollination via Carol's idea.. Marvelous! But back to the matter at hand.

"I wondered, Carol, is the writers' group helping you?"

"Yes! Quite. Why do you ask?"

"You've been a writer a long time. I suppose you've been in many critique groups?"

"Yes." What is he nattering on about, Carol thought.

"Do you find that some people critique more—what would I call it—more harshly than others?"

"Of course! Some people go quite ballistic." Carol thought, not me though.

Philippe thought, exactly the problem. "How does that affect you?"

"Well, I feel that I quite want to hide. Maybe go away and never come back. What are you driving at?"

He paused. "I'm eager for the group to be a place where people can write truthfully, and not be judged personally so that they begin to hide the truth."

"Quite." Wait, is he talking about me?

"I'm eager for critiques to be given in 'I' statements, you know, like, 'This text comes across to me as racist,' rather than, 'You're a racist.'"

He is talking about me, Carol thought. Bloody hell!

"I think that that way, people feel safe to express the truth about their experience."

Philippe examined Carol's face. A bit flushed. She's upset, he thought.

"Well, I've taken tons of much tougher critique than that in my career," Carol said.

"I'm sure. It must be difficult in the movie business. I've heard they're always changing your words."

"It hurts like hell. But I'm an artist. I never give up." No matter how much I've wanted to at times, she thought.

"Perseverance is key." I need to not give up praying for Meredith, Philippe thought.

They crossed Rue de Turenne side by side. When they reached the sidewalk opposite, Carol stopped and put her hands on her hips, elbows akimbo.

"You know, it's all a load of B.S. anyway," she said.

"What is?" He thought, not what I've been talking to you about. It most certainly is not B.S.

"All this writing and making up stories. That's what liars do—make it up. The stories we work on at writers' circle are just the product of our imaginations. So what difference does it make, all this critiquing of lies—and doing it ever so gently, as you insist?"

"Fiction is the lie that tells the truth," Philippe said. He'd read it somewhere. "In fact, fiction is the best way to tell the truth. When we write a story that's honest about the experience we're drawing from, the story becomes a jewel box, and inside is a gem."

They turned and walked a bit farther. They were now at Place des Vosges. Philippe wondered if Carol would walk around in the park with him or stomp off and never come back. Or if she'd come back to the circle and just do the same things until he had to tell her to leave. That would be sad.

As they crossed to the park entrance, Carol thought that it was so unfair to be singled out. But she had to concede that Philippe had done it rather more gracefully than she could have, in his shoes. Still...

They now stood before a low green metal gate. These gates guarded every park in Paris. They didn't keep rats out, or pigeons, or small biting dogs. But there they were, blocking the way, and you had to push through to get into the park. It seemed like a waste of metal and effort.

"Shall we go see if the lindens are still blooming?" Philippe asked. He was relieved when Carol went through the gate with him.

They started out on the sand-and-fine-gravel path. Carol scuffed the path with the toe of her shoe. A little cloud of dust floated upward. She felt angry with Philippe, but she needed him, as a sounding board for her life and for her writing. She was careful with her tone of voice, that she not leak anger on him.

"You know, John's poetry is honest, but his fiction isn't. When Chuck slugs it out with four bad guys and walks away unharmed— ridiculous!" She gave him a sidelong glance with a hint of a smile in it. "Maybe you should have a 'walk and talk' with him too."

"You're right, his fiction isn't honest. Neither is anybody writing a story that glamorizes violence, robbery, or sex with no commitment." He turned to her. He pushed his glasses up his nose, he was so impassioned about his topic. "What about the horror of taking a human life, or the years in prison when you're caught stealing, or the guilt, remorse, shame when two people who had been one heart and one flesh in a sacred intimacy now pull apart, shredding their souls, wounding themselves deeply? It's a lie to make it glamorous." He'd had enough experience in his younger days with unethical sex to know the truth about that, he thought.

He looked up. The French penchant for trimming trees into geometric shapes was evident here. The lindens that ringed the park had been clipped into submission. He sniffed. Their scent was gone till next spring.

He thought his little walk and talk with Carol might have gone well. Maybe he should nudge John a little harder on his fisticuff stories, too. Well, he'd done enough writer-nudging for one day.

"Let's spend a minute window shopping in the galleries under the arcade," he said. "Maybe I'll get some inspiration for my sermon." Not likely if they display naked ladies.

Carol went with him, hurt, smarting, but willing to give what he'd said a bit of thought.

Chapter 76

Anjali came home one night after work and Pearl was gone.

Her ten square meters suddenly felt empty. Dinner would be too solitary.

She peeled off her office clothes and climbed into jeans and a T-shirt. All of a sudden she was overcome with suspicion. Had Pearl taken anything? Anjali checked the drawer where she kept her favorite earrings. She had never counted them, but they all appeared to be there.

You shouldn't have suspected your friend, she thought. But she came off the street, of course I suspect her.

Anjali went for a walk, keeping an eye out for Pearl. A circuit through Jardin de Luxembourg helped calm her a little. When she was hungry, she went to Rue Saint André des Artes, a narrow street near the Seine lined with small eateries. Once again, she had a cheese *crêpe*. As usual, the cook spilled some cheese out of the *crêpe* directly onto the hot griddle, making a lacy edging. The toasted cheese melted in her mouth.

She went to Shakespeare & Company just as the bells of Notre Dame celebrated six in the evening with five minutes of melodic clamor. She stepped inside the bookstore, with its series of small rooms lined floor to ceiling with books. Individuals stood with books open in their hands, blocking the narrow passageways. A sign painted on the riser of a step between rooms said, "Live for Humanity."

Anjali thought ruefully that she had tried to. When she was writing her screenplays or taking care of Pearl, that's what she was trying to do. She guessed that Pearl had returned to the streets. She caught sight of a title on the spine of a book: The Freedom of Man.

What was freedom?

Take herself for instance, under pressure from her family to marry, maybe getting only a few months of freedom in Paris, most likely to return and take up the responsibilities and limitations of a wife and mother in India. And look at Pearl, here in the West, free to do whatever she wanted and yet a slave to alcohol.

Anjali had written down thoughts and impressions while living with Pearl. They were safely stored in her laptop in a document named "Dal" in a folder named "Recipes." Not likely to be found. Now that Pearl was gone, she could move the document to her "Screenplays" folder, where it could be mined for ideas. Anjali could feel a screenplay about a lost girl brewing. She was excited about this new idea.

But that wasn't the main reason to help Pearl, Anjali urged herself. Trying to help a fellow human being, that was the real motivation. At least I hope so.

And I hope she went back to her parents, Anjali thought. As for me, I'm not really ready to do that. Maybe I've sprouted the wings that everyone was so afraid of.

Chapter 77

Anjali took another French lesson. Christelle's fee wasn't too high, and in spite of the money she had spent on Pearl, Anjali felt she just had to invest in learning French.

"Today we study the shapes," Christelle said as she floated onto the *café* chair. She was in harem pants again, a different print than last time: black and white geometric shapes, to go with her lesson perhaps.

"Square is '*carré*,' which you see on the maps of Paris for the squares and small parks, and triangle is '*triangle!*' So easy, that one, *la même chose*. And circle is '*cercle*.'"

Anjali studied Christelle's pronunciation. For "*cercle*" she had said "sairk" with just a hint of an "l" on the end.

"I'm going to my writers' *cirque* next week," Anjali said. As she was saying "seerk," she knew she was making a mistake but couldn't stop herself.

"Ooh-la!" Christelle said. "You're going to your writers' circus next week?"

Anjali blushed at Christelle's laughter. Being in a new culture, learning a new language, was causing her to make some dumb mistakes. As long as I don't make one with Ravi.

"Well, it is a bit of a circus sometimes."

Chapter 78

Saturday morning, Anjali talked with her Amma and Appa. Just saying "good morning," they sounded excited, and she knew that something was up.

"Ravi's parents told us yesterday that his company is sending him to the U.S. for six months of training," her mother said. "They want you to get married so you can go together."

Live in the U.S? For six months? Now that was something to think about.

"That's interesting," Anjali said cautiously. Ravi hadn't mentioned that this was in the works. Maybe it came as a surprise to him as well. This news certainly changes the tennis match for me. So to speak.

"Oh, darling, we'll have so much fun planning the wedding!" her mother said. Appa was stoically silent.

Chapter 79

Philippe trudged into Saint-Séverin, near his office in the Fifth. He hadn't told even Elodie what he had said to God. A pastor for twenty-five years taking God's name in vain *to God's face*. He sighed as he lowered himself onto one of the stiff wooden chairs lined up to face the altar.

Inside the Gothic pile, where the columns soared skyward and clerestory windows let in light reminiscent of heaven, he was chilly even on a warm summer day. Philippe noted that the stone columns, erected in the early thirteenth century, were pitted, gouged, and scarred at their bases from all their years of being in proximity to people.

Even though these columns and arched ceilings were made of stone, what if they gave way? They'd held for eight hundred years, but they had to fall sometime. Why not right now? To punish him. To put him out of his misery over Meredith.

A tourist snapped pictures of the plain, modern altar. Philippe loved the contrast between the medieval and the contemporary.

He looked high above him at the far-away ceiling where the gray stone arches intersected. A brown stone rosette sat at each intersection. Those would be the first to fall.

But he didn't feel an earthquake rumbling through the stone floor. He didn't see cracks forming in the ceiling. No earthquake, no cracks, no rosettes and stone ceiling tumbling to earth in a cloud of dust. No, God wasn't sending the roof down on his head today.

"I'm sorry," he said. That would be the last time he'd say it. God had forgiven him, it was time to forgive himself.

If only God would save Meredith. What was taking so long? Would she ever break free? Would she be scarred for life? Oh dear God, what are you doing?

Philippe shifted his body, and his feet scuffed the stone floor where so many generations of French people had stood. When it came to God and his mysteries, it was humbling for Philippe to admit that, for all his years of reading his Bible, studying at seminary, thinking about God all the time, serving as best he could, he was just like everybody else. Everybody bit the apple. Nobody was any better, not the church ladies, and nobody was any worse, not Meredith.

And not him. He was like everybody else, just another bozo on the bus.

Chapter 80

Anjali hadn't talked with Ravi last weekend, after her parents broke the news that he'd be going to the U.S. for six months. He'd had a tennis date at their usual talking time. The third time in five weeks. Just a bit of a pain, to be less important than a tennis date. She hadn't written to him about the training opportunity, either—she wanted to talk with him by Internet, to share the excitement with him, to see his smile on the screen. Almost like being face to face.

She waited for his call Sunday morning. When he was ten minutes late, as usual, she dialed him. He sat in front of the computer with his white shirt unbuttoned and his brown chest glowing. His parents certainly didn't know he was exposing his body like this.

"Bonjour!" she chirped. Really, the idea of living in the U.S. for six months was quite the shot in the arm. She could subscribe to Netflix, which didn't operate in France, and have access to their huge storehouse of classic American movies through the mail. Was that any reason to marry Ravi, though?

"How was tennis last week?"

Anjali saw that he had to think a minute. There was so much tennis in his life.

"Oh, yeah! Good. My boss."

"Who won?"

"We both played well. He won one, and me the other."

"Good and noble of you both. And where is this wonderful boss sending you in the U.S.?"

Ravi's handsome face went blank. He stared into his computer screen, which was not at all the same as looking into her eyes. Technology was so disjointed. He blinked and looked away. Then a flash of recognition crossed his face.

"Oh yeah! Uh. Washington State."

She sat in silence a moment, stunned. He's lying. His parents are lying to my parents. The whole six months' training in the U.S. is a pressure ploy. Her dreams of seeing the U.S. tumbled.

With the new strength in her that had formed as a result of uprooting herself and creating a new life in a strange culture thousands of miles from home, she would not let it pass with silence, which she might have done in the past.

"How could you and your parents lie to us?"

"You're breaking up," Ravi said.

"You heard me."

"What?"

"Liar!" she roared.

He had the nerve to act affronted.

"Hey!" he said in a warning tone.

"How dare you lie!"

His eyes shifted off the screen, then back to the camera on his laptop. He softened his tone. "We were worried," he said. "I just want you here with me."

It was a nice sentiment, but Anjali distrusted that too now.

"You tried to trick me."

"Look, don't get so high and mighty. You've had your time in Paris. You should come back now and settle down."

"We all agreed on a year, and I'm sticking to it!" After this lie, she might have leverage to stay longer. But she had to get past this lie to salvage the relationship. Ravi was doing well financially. Maybe he would support her as she wrote screenplays fulltime.

"Writing is all alone, into your computer," Ravi said. "It's selfish."

That derailed her. Was it? She'd been wondering herself. Parked in front of a laptop, making up characters and problems and scenes. What was it for?

She remembered a fiction teacher in university saying, "Stories are the only way to tell the truth." Was telling the truth selfish? And are my stories actually full of world-class truth? Probably not. But can I entertain people? Life is hard. I love knowing I have a good book at home to read before bed, or a great movie to look forward to watching on Saturday night. That's the gift I want to give to the world. To do so requires that I sit alone in front of a laptop. It might look selfish, but it isn't.

"You're selfish for saying that! You just want to derail me."

He looked annoyed. Anjali knew she was saying the all-wrong things if she wanted to keep this relationship going.

But he didn't believe in what she was doing, he didn't believe in her dream. No, that couldn't be true. She'd try to convince him of its rightness. "I want to bring some fun, the pleasure of compelling stories to the world. That's not selfish."

"But you're not here with me." He was frowning into his computer, his eyes not looking into hers, not really, not at this crucial moment in their relationship.

"I need this time in Paris to prove to myself that…"

"Just what, exactly?"

Good question. And he'd asked in an irritated voice.

"That I have the necessary talent and persistence. I'm learning by being critiqued by excellent writers. They help me to improve my work."

"There are excellent writers in English in Mumbai."

True. "But Paris is a fantastic place to be a writer. The French respect artists and writers so much. It's really exceptional. I've never felt that in Mumbai. The French ask me about my project. And really listen. And make suggestions. In Mumbai, I tell people I'm a writer and they stifle a yawn. It feels good to be a writer here."

"It would feel good to be here with me, too."

"Ravi, do you believe in me, in my dream?"

"Well, of course! I need you. Pursue your dream with me here in Mumbai."

"I probably will."

"Probably?" He sounded surprised. She hadn't meant to air her doubts. Now it was all going to explode, unless she thought fast.

"Unless the Seine overflows its banks and washes me to the sea on my way to work one morning." Did that do the trick? Yes! His face settled back into a relaxed expression.

"Come home."

He said it sweetly. Maybe that lie about the U.S. was out of love.

"I'll be back." Soon enough. At least I think so.

"Well listen, darling, I love talking with you, but I have to go. To be continued," Ravi said.

Another argument would be awful. "Bye, Ravi! Talk to you next Sunday!" I'll sound hopeful and positive until I figure out what to do.

His image disappeared from her screen. The smile she'd put on her face, to be reconciliatory through the computer, now felt stupid to her, sitting in her room alone.

Chapter 81

After the phone call, Anjali strolled along Quai Saint Michel to settle herself. She didn't have to make a decision today, so she walked and slowly relaxed. The sun's light on the towers and flying buttresses of Notre Dame caught her eye. How much French paperwork would be necessary to make a film inside that cathedral? She'd skip that step. She'd find the most rabbit-warren part of it and shoot there, among the mysterious winding hallways. Not realistic. Some security guard would find her and her crew. But a pleasant daydream. Maybe some other Gothic church...

She doodled along, past the stalls owned by book and postcard sellers. She had once asked one of them if he had a copy of Madame Bovary in English. A look of annoyance had crossed his face.

She was wearing a shorter skirt than she'd ever tried before—just above her knees. It flipped up a bit in the breeze, and a man gave her brown legs an appreciative glance. As the hard heels of her flats rang out on the pavement along the *quai*, she thought of Ravi and his parents and their lie. It was not the right foundation for a relationship. And if they were capable of that, of lying not only to her but to her parents, what else were they capable of? The article about "stove bursts" came to mind.

She turned to walk down Boulevard Saint Michel. At a *café* near the fountain, she saw Pearl, sitting with yet another corpulent man. She appeared sober, but she had a small glass filled with an amber liquid. Anjali walked up to their table, anxious to connect with this skinny little girl who had lived for weeks in her ten square meters. She wanted to protect her, bring her back to hearth and home.

"Pearl."

She looked up, saw Anjali, and flinched.

"Come home with me."

Pearl paused.

Maybe she's thinking of the walks we had, Anjali thought, the fun of sneaking up and down the stairs past Madame de Denichen. Come on, Pearl, we're friends.

Then Pearl reached a skinny arm for the shot glass and shook her head. "It's too late for that. No."

Anjali thought of all the evil that could happen to Pearl on the streets. Untold abuse, psychic scars, horrors beyond Anjali's experience and ken. To be spared, all Pearl had to do was give up alcohol and come with her. Obviously she wasn't ready, and in spite of the abuse she was enduring, she might never be. In that case, Anjali thought, she'd be washed away in a flood more powerful than the Seine, a flood of the raw sewage of life.

Anjali's heart broke as she turned with heavy steps and left Pearl to her dangerous preferences.

Chapter 82

John took Emily out to dinner at a *café* in the Sixth. He was going to pop the question again tonight and he was scared.

Being somewhat into austerity—if he really were, he'd cook at home, but the kitchen was so small, not an inch of counterspace, he just couldn't face it—John ordered *crocque monsieur*. Emily asked for mushroom risotto.

When the food arrived, they each picked at it, both feeling on edge. John had listened to her complete sentences—complete paragraphs, even—for weeks now and felt he had proved he had changed.

"I didn't interrupt you once tonight, did I?" he asked with a twinkle in his eye.

"No, you're doing pretty good."

"Honey, would you come live with me?" He had to have her yes in his life, because everywhere else he was failing.

She scowled. "I'm afraid of something."

"What? Tell me!"

"I'm afraid you want me so you can get back at Mom."

Well, it had crossed his mind, hadn't it? Be honest, this is too important. Where I am closed, I am false.

"Don't hate me, Em. The thought occurred to me, I can't deny it."

She flopped back in her chair, exasperated.

"But that's not the real reason I want you with me."

"Yes?" She looked up at him, all eyes.

"Your dad has just gone through a big failure in life—business, marriage, family. I would feel like I had a new chance at success if you came to live with me."

She sat quietly with that statement for a few minutes, and John let her be. Finally, he said, "Well, what do you think?"

"No."

"Why not?" His desperation was obvious even to him.

"You don't want me just for me."

"I do!"

"No, you don't. I need to go now, I have stuff to do."

They had Emily's risotto wrapped up. This particular waiter put it in an impromptu doggy bag, a big white plastic *fromage blanc* container, with plastic wrap stretched over the top, held in place by a blue rubber band. Why didn't they read the memo on "doggy bags" and get some real containers, John wondered. He paid and walked Emily home. He was near tears with feelings of failure as he said goodbye. Her small body slipped past as the heavy, ancient street door closed.

Chapter 83

John took the Metro to the Basilique de Saint-Denis, the first Gothic cathedral ever, to think.

Emily had questioned his motives. What are my motives? Think, man! He sat in a chair facing the altar, under the vaulted ceiling. He had said he wanted her to live with him so he'd have some sort of success. What was wrong with that? It was true. Why was that not good enough? Think!

So he would feel successful. Okay, that's a selfish motivation. What's not a selfish motivation?

Emily wanted to be loved just for her. That should have been my motive. That and success? No, that's mixing the selfish back in.

And he had made it about his feelings of failure. What a bastard, no wonder she'd said no.

What an *astucieuse* girl! He felt so proud of her. And now this wonderful kid wouldn't live with him. You are a failure—he could hear his father's voice.

John stood and walked around the basilica, nearly one thousand years old, built around the ruins of a chapel built five hundred years before that. French legend had it that St. Denis had been beheaded on Montmartre—the mountain of martyrs—picked up his head and walked here. Unlike St. Denis, John had never been a praying man, but he thought of the millions of prayers that had gone up through these vaulted stone ceilings over the last millennium. Prayers for babies who were sick, husbands who were drunk, jobs, food, the next meal.

He paid to enter the crypt and see the tomb of Marie Antoinette. He hoped he'd stop being foolish, as she had been—in different ways, of course. But still foolish. He'd better start living and working smarter so he wouldn't come to an equally disastrous end. Like his father.

Chapter 84

One Saturday, Anjali felt compelled to go Cimetière du Père Lachaise, named after Louis XIV's confessor. What kinds of things did Father Lachaise hear, she wondered. Wicked barbs exchanged between the courtesans at Versailles? Barbs, beddings, and betrayals. What great fodder for a screenplay.

She entered the huge gate on Boulevard Ménilmontant and checked the giant map of gravesites of notable people. Then she started up the hill into the cemetery and turned right on the narrow, cobbled Avenue du Puits. It felt like the right place to be, not at *la bibliothèque*, clacking the keys of her laptop.

The little stone tombs, with their small doors and windows, gave her the feeling of being in a miniature village. Except in this village, the residents didn't talk to each other, ever, and not because of a grudge. Holding grudges was for the living. One of the crypts had its door open. There was a simple altar inside, and drawers set in the wall with knobs, like kitchen drawers, probably holding the remains of people. She didn't feel like checking.

She passed a big stone building in the middle of the grounds. Lights on inside revealed half a dozen people working at desks. The living keeping track of the dead.

A girl her age was walking toward her, with long blonde hair framing her beautiful face. The girl met Anjali's eyes, and instead of looking away as Anjali expected, she held Anjali's gaze as she walked triumphantly toward her, so sure of herself and her good looks compared to Anjali's. After she passed, haughty—must be a Parisienne—Anjali fingered the bump on her nose and thought to herself, hey, you mean girl, you'll look like everybody else someday when you rot in one of these drawers.

Wow, pretty mean of me, she thought. Well, she was mean! That look of superiority, of triumph over me. Oh, Anjali, let it go.

She refused to give the girl any more of her energy. She became absorbed in the hunt for Jim Morrison's grave. She had listened to The Doors in Mumbai, growing up, and had dreamt of visiting his famous tomb.

But she couldn't find the exact spot. A tour group was approaching her, so she waited for them to pass and lead her to the grave. She found that it was set off the paved path and behind a bigger tomb—she wouldn't have found it without help. Anjali noted the crowd-control barriers set up around the grave, with padlocks, like those on the Pont des Artes, starting to be added to the uprights of the barriers. One had the engraved inscription, "Sam & Kelly, together in Paris."

People must have climbed past the barriers, because on his tombstone stood bouquets of fresh red roses and a small pot of live lavender. Someone had placed two white ceramic cherubs facing a photo of Morrison, which was propped up on top. He had been incredibly appealing, and utterly dangerous, at age 27.

"Does anyone have a cigarette?" a young woman with a pierced nose asked in an American accent. Maybe she had always dreamt of smoking a cigarette in Morrison's memory at his grave. Well, Anjali couldn't help her with that.

But it was incredible to have her own dream come true. Here she was. Dreams could become reality, but only if you worked toward them.

The tour group milled around, making jokes and laughing, ruining the *ambience*. Anjali left and paced deeper into the cemetery. Huge crows cawed in the trees. They were the perfect bird for this God-forsaken place, Anjali thought. As she meandered and read the French family names on the graves, she mused over the last few weeks. Pearl was digging her own grave with alcohol and prostitution. Anjali knew that she herself would die someday. What was she going to do to live, really live? Hollywood? Or Ravi and Bollywood, if she could find a chance to write while she was a wife and mother? If Ravi and his parents and his aunties wouldn't pressure her to stop?

He had lied because he wanted her near him, he had said. Yet he was usually late to their scheduled phone conversations, and he cancelled them often for tennis.

A car approached, and Anjali moved slowly aside, resenting its presence and its tires' noisy clatter on the cobbles in the hushed cemetery. People walked past, holding cameras, clicking off shots.

A monstrous black crow swooped from one tall oak to another, cawing. The sound was ominous, like death, like the enormity of the mistake she might make with her life. What was she going to do?

She prayed for guidance thinking of the mosaic of Jesus she had seen at Sacré Cœur, and she consulted her heart.

Chapter 85

Carol sat in La Bibliothèque Historique de le Ville de Paris and wrote a cover note to yet another industry buddy. He had the power to champion her script about Naomi and Phoebe within the film company he worked for. She was desperate, yet not a whiff of it must enter this note. She pasted a cheerful smile on her face and hoped the chemistry of the smile on her lips would sink deep into the words of this email.

She had a year's living expenses saved up. She had a shot at being a successful independent screenwriter. She was going for it.

She clicked send. This 1550s building had Wifi, but it was slow, with one hundred other people using it. She knew there were one hundred people because each seat was numbered.

Before you could sit down, you had to register and be given a card with a number on it. In Paris, you sat in your assigned seat and nowhere else.

When her email program said "Sent!" and returned her to her inbox, she saw that another old industry buddy had replied to one of her queries.

"Sorry, Carol, we're not looking at new properties right now."

A terse note. An excuse. Or maybe the buddy was too busy to read her script. Or maybe the problem was simply that email was a form that made everyone sound terse. But this guy couldn't have read her script, not even the first page, he had replied so fast.

Carol had been most hopeful of him buying her screenplay because he was part of the biggest film production company of anyone she knew. She sighed and felt the discouragement.

Well, she could sit like this forever, or keep going. Never, never, never give up, she thought. Thank God for Winston Churchill.

Chapter 86

John stared at the figures on spreadsheets Anjali had printed out. He had to cut, cut, cut. The Grey Skies had to go.

John rubbed his knee, which had started to ache this morning. This is killing me, he thought. I love being on a boat, on the water, more than anything else. Except Em, of course.

He decided to fight for the Grey Skies a little longer. He picked up the phone and his little black book.

An hour later he stood, and his knee stabbed with the sharp pain of disappointment. Everyone he'd called had danced around the obvious point of his call—to invest with him. No deals closed. How was he going to keep his sailboat?

Well, the least he could do was share it with his friends, while he still had the chance. He sat down and sent an email to the writers' circle: "I'm inviting you to come out on my sailboat, the Grey Skies. It's docked in Cherbourg. Please bring a friend and your lunch. We'll go out to dinner."

He clicked send.

Chapter 87

Pearl was standing two doors down from Madame de Denichen's when Anjali arrived home after work.

"Can we talk?" she said.

"Let's sneak upstairs," Anjali answered, wondering if she had enough food on hand for two. She would have to make it enough.

She heated up a pot of *dal*—lentils with garlic, onion, red pepper, and the cumin and curry powder that she'd bought in Little India at La Chapelle Metro stop. Even if she didn't take the time to roast and grind the twelve spices that made up the curry by hand, as her mother did, it was still Indian comfort food. She placed two pieces of frozen *roti* on top of the lid to warm. When the girls were seated at the little table, side by side on the bed since there was no chair, Anjali broke off a small piece of the *roti* and used it to pick up some *dal* from the central bowl.

"This is how we do it in India," she said. She looked around her *chambre de bonne*. She most certainly was not in India now. Even with the spices purchased in Little India, the food wasn't the same as at home.

They ate for a while. Pearl practically sucked up her food, Anjali noticed. She warmed up another *roti*, laid it on Pearl's plate, and motioned to the *dal*.

"Thanks," was all Pearl said.

Anjali felt that it was the right time to set a boundary.

"You can't just come and go forever," she said.

"I'm going to Alcoholics Anonymous tonight."

"Oh! Fantastic! Can I ask—what changed your mind?"

Anjali regretted asking. Maybe Pearl was too fragile to explain.

"I used your laptop one time, when you were at work. I read a newspaper story you had bookmarked, about men in India pushing their wives into the cooking fires. I was afraid of something like that happening to me. I was in danger every time—" she broke off, blushed.

Looking at my bookmarked pages? Anjali thought. That's getting pretty personal. But I'm glad it changed her mind. A round of applause for The Hindu, online edition.

Chapter 88

Carol worked in La Bibliothèque Historique all day every day now, because she could plug in her laptop at any worktable, whereas at the Fornay, only two small tables had sockets, and those tables of course were always occupied. La Bibliothèque Historique also had a lobby with six chairs. People were free to eat their lunch there, a nice feature when it rained. Or in winter, which was going to arrive too soon. Carol dreaded November, when in Paris it felt as though someone had their hand on the dimmer switch and turned the light down fast. It just got darker and darker, until one was crazy for light, wasn't one?

But now it was summer, and on clear days she sat in the garden around the corner from the library, off of Rue de Francs Bourgeois.

There she had struck up a relationship with a pigeon that had a club foot. When no other pigeons were near, she would feed him scraps.

That morning, another email saying no to her work had arrived. She looked up at the library's ancient beams, gilded in green, gold, and gray, and wondered if the artists who had gilded them had ever suffered rejection as an artist.

She was banging her head against these ancient Parisian stone walls, she thought. What was she doing? Why?

She packed up her laptop quietly. She worked here in order to be around people, but the young man next to her studying architectural drawings on his laptop screen had sniffed every thirty seconds for the last hour. She couldn't take it, or the rejections, anymore. She headed out and wandered the streets.

She passed the Pompidou Centre, its plumbing and air ducts outside the building and painted in bright colors. Such a modern eyesore among the elegant white Paris buildings.

She kept wandering until she felt that she'd like to sit down. It seemed to her that the *café* owners had conspired with the city government to keep park benches away. A person had to either sit at a *café* and pay, or sit on the pavement.

But here was Saint-Merri. What was living in Paris for but the occasional visit to a Gothic church?

Inside, the vaulted ceiling of the side aisle was breathtakingly high. But then she moved to the center of the church and the ceiling was much higher. How glorious, she thought.

She sat in one of the chairs fastened to its neighbors so they wouldn't get hodgepodge. These cathedrals didn't used to have chairs, she mused. People used to do backbreaking work all week and then stand on the freezing cold stone floors for the whole service and listen to everything in Latin, a language foreign to them. What a tough breed people were back then.

She sighed as she lowered her backpack, weighed down with her laptop, onto the chair next to her. She thought, I was thinking about money as I banged out every word of the Naomi and Phoebe script. Even though I gave it a happy ending—that in the end Naomi sees herself as a success because she helped an elderly woman in her hour of need—nobody's buying it. Evidently it has no legs.

I can't help needing money—not immediately, but soon. As a motive for writing, however, it's not helpful.

She was distracted momentarily by the sight of a young man stepping up behind a carved wooden wall. She could just see the top of his dark head. What was he doing? Oh, well, none of her business.

What was her business? To think about what Philippe had said about her critiques. It seemed that he thought the way she was going about it was shattering to people. She remembered the crystal elephant hitting Gregoire's glass cabinet and shards of glass flying everywhere.

That certainly was a shattering critique of Gregoire, she thought. I certainly do want to create sparks. But not shards. I need to be more careful. But then again, why should I try to change? What's my motive?

She sat still and waited for an answer. A thought came to her. Do unto others as you'd have them do to you. She thought, I prefer balanced critiques, that mention what I did right, myself. So be it.

What had Philippe said about motive? That her chief aim, the aim of all mankind, ought to be to glorify God and enjoy him forever.

She wasn't there yet.

She remembered sitting in a theater while a film she'd written was playing. She loved to hear the audience laugh. She'd just loved her audience, wanted to take them away from their troubles for two hours, wanted to put some magic in their lives.

Maybe if she wrote out of love for the people who would be in her audience, out of love for stories and the magic and pleasure they gave people, it would make her writing a gift to people, to affirm humane values, rather than something that she used to try to extract money from them.

She jumped with a huge start as the church began resounding with Bach's Toccata and Fugue in D Minor. In the pauses that Bach wrote between sections of the piece, she counted that the sound reverberated among the stone columns, ceilings, and floors for a full five seconds.

Maybe the music was a sign from God that he approved her ideas. That thought was uncomfortable, and she shifted her butt.

The young man's head behind the carved wooden wall was swaying with the music. Ah, he was the organist. Such a young one in such an old church, Carol mused. How many organists had worked here in succession over hundreds of years, a few dozen generations' worth? She felt the time, the ages, the weight of history in Paris.

She listened to the brilliant sound as it bounced around the stone cathedral and rushed to embrace her. I'll put some Bach on my laptop and listen with earbuds in the library. Then I won't hear people sniff.

And maybe I could start trying to write out of love for human beings. That was my first impulse—love of values and affirming humanity. Time to do that again.

Chapter 89

Philippe walked to his office in the Fifth and felt lighter somehow. In his anguish over swearing at God, he had decided he needed help. He had called a pastor friend, who helped him to concede that God loved Meredith even more than he did. And loved him no matter what he said or did.

So this morning, in his time with God, with a cup of coffee steaming beside him, Philippe had consciously wrapped her up in the woolly blanket of his love and put her in God's loving hands. When worry about her came back to his mind, he'd just do that again. It was all he could do for her. It was all he could do.

At the door to the stairs to his office, he looked in the window of the gallery on the ground floor. Three new paintings of naked women stood on easels. Wasn't there another topic to paint anywhere in Paris? He'd better not ask. Next there would be naked men with body parts at acute angles.

He climbed the uneven stairs to his second-floor office, opened the windows onto Rue Lanneau, ancient, narrow, and echoing with footsteps and voices. He booted up his computer. This morning he was going to do his creative writing for an hour. After committing Meredith to God, his mind was now more free to concentrate on the next right thing.

Today, instead of writing in order to record his anguish, he would pray that he let go to be the artist he was uniquely wired to be, to do it in the vast mystery of *soli deo gloria*. And to touch human hearts.

And to maybe make some money. He sighed as the selfish got mixed back in.

Chapter 90

John sat in the former *boutique* space with the exposed ancient stone wall washed with light. How he was going to pay rent, even here, he didn't know.

He took his mind off his financial worries and put it on Em. He pictured her, so pixie-like, doing ballet in a little pink tutu. That had been in New York City, where he and Cassandra had enrolled her in ballet lessons and private school.

When he'd decided to move to Paris, she'd been heartbroken about moving so far from her friends. Now she was in a top-rated international school with diplomats' daughters from all over the world. What a great experience for her. He just had to find a way to keep her there, to not break her heart again.

But his purpose right now was a little different. He wanted to convince her to come live with him. His eyes glanced over the stone wall. Just like it, his life had been bumpy lately. Maybe love would smooth out the rough places, for her and for him.

He grabbed a piece of copier paper from the machine next to Anjali's desk. With his Mont Blanc pen, he wrote down bits and pieces from Anjali's, Philippe's and Carol's poems that had resonated with him. He found himself saying a quick prayer for love and truth to prevail as he shaped this material.

Then he tapped the space key on his keyboard, his monitor lit up, and he began to write.

Chapter 91

When he was done writing and revising and slaving over his words, John called Emily and invited her out for dinner.

They sat under the awning at Le Café Livre, across from Tour Saint Jacques, eating outdoors. Even in September, the Paris evening was impossibly long and bright.

"Did you know we're as far north here as the northern tip of Newfoundland?" John asked. "Ever seen Paris on a globe? We're not that far from the Arctic Circle. Great Britain and Northern Europe would be a frozen waste except for the Gulf Stream. A gift straight from the New World to the Old."

"Cool." Tonight Emily was eating with relish. She was wearing a pink "I Love Paris" T-shirt with red rhinestones forming the Eiffel Tower.

When they finished eating, John took a piece of paper out of his wallet and unfolded it several times.

"Em, I took what you said last time to heart. And here's my answer. It's a poem I wrote for you." Emily sat back, looking surprised.

"Ready?" John asked. Emily nodded.

"Okay, listen." He was more nervous than he had been asking his first girl for a date.

"Let me not be closed to you,
     for where I am closed, there
 I am not true.
 I tell you, 'I love you.'
 Simple.
 I would go to the temple wall
     and tango through tunnels
 on my toes for you.

"If you say no,
 then the inebriated, the broken
     on the street
 will look like what I feel inside.

When I walk toward you,
it is with my whole heart."

John folded the poem back up. He held it in his hand, wishing
and hoping. In the distance, he heard the *pin-pon* of a Paris siren.
Sirens happened so much less often in Paris than in New York City.

"Can I have that?" Emily said.

When he handed over the paper, she unfolded it and read it
again.

"Dad? My answer is yes."

John grasped her tiny hand and squeezed gently.

"I don't know where I'll put you yet, but I'll come up with
something. Soon."

Emily smiled at him.

"I love you, you little woodsprite," he said.

Chapter 92

Carol plunked away at the new screenplay. This one felt
different. Words floated off the page, it seemed to her, though the
writers' circle would confirm that impression for her. She thought so
warmly of John, Philippe, and Anjali. She felt so much respect for
these people who had opened up and revealed themselves through
their writing, through their conversations at the writers' circle.

As she clacked at her keyboard, she looked around La
Bibliothèque Historique. People in their early twenties—students—
were lined up on both sides of the long tables, staring intently into
books and laptop screens. The girl beside her sneezed.

Carol sighed inwardly. She needed to be out writing, not just
working in her apartment alone all day. She needed people. But they
kept sniffing and sneezing, or the phones laying on the table next to
them would bing with incoming messages and startle her out of her

dream-like writing state. She really had to download more music and find her earbuds.

Such was life. The good with the bad, she mused. Like being single. Once again she had no partner, she was on her own life. But it was peaceful. She'd seen a T-shirt on a girl in Le Marais recently:

no
boyfriend
no
problems

None except the need to be at the library, among sneezing people, in order to not feel too alone while writing.

She felt different from the French students hard at work around her. They were preparing themselves for the jobs they hoped to land in banking, finance, government.

She was there for a different purpose entirely. She was writing as creatively as she could so she wouldn't have to get a job in banking, finance, or government. So she was quietly, subversively, working at cross-purposes to them. She was a stranger in a strange land, an older freelancer among duty-bound kids, a Brit among the French, an English writer amongst French students.

She thought of the writers' circle, where she felt among like-minded people, working individually on unique projects but sharing the common experience of art-making, of trying to tell a compelling story, of being Anglophones in a French environment, of being from someplace else but making their way in Paris.

She felt remorse that she might have caused unnecessary pain with her critiques. She loved the group. And individually, she liked each one so much. Anjali, on fire to write movies. John, so handsome, rich, and gifted at critiquing other people's stories, but not his own. Philippe, so human, trying to set a good example. And writing about stupid alcoholics and such. Well, she liked him anyway.

She loved that lot, actually.

She couldn't wait for the next meeting.

Chapter 93

Anjali had told Aasha just a little about Pearl. She had to say something, because now she wasn't as available as before to go out with Aasha and do things.

As Anjali stirred a new batch of *dal*, she wondered why she hadn't said anything to the group about having Pearl stay with her. For one thing, she didn't want to make Philippe feel bad, that here was a girl getting help while his daughter was treated like trash on the streets of Paris. She stirred again, and the aroma of curry spices and the extra cumin she'd added wafted up.

And the other reason: she didn't want to tell them and fall into the trap of being proud of the fact that she was helping a streetwalker to escape that life. It was a weird reverse hubris. She didn't want them to think she was making herself look altruistic and selfless. Even at her best, it seemed, she had a selfish motive.

She turned the heat off under the finished *dal* and set the pot's lid ajar so the fragrant, steamy comfort food could cool. She thought of Aasha, who had decided to leave Paris and go back to India a month before she had to. Anjali tried to understand her going back early but couldn't.

Anjali and Aasha had made a plan to meet at Le Louvre before Aasha left for India. Anjali got ready; Pearl left for an AA meeting. The two young women had gotten extremely skilled at evading Madame de Denichen. They were enjoying putting one over on the formidable aristocrat.

Anjali ruffled her hands over her blouses in the drawer, looking for one to wear with jeans. She picked one out, donned it, grabbed her *sac*, and headed toward the door.

As she passed the closet and opened the door to her flat, the collection of praise and critiques from the writers' group that she'd written down acknowledged her passing.

The little yellow pieces of paper taped to the white surface lifted up, fluttered, and fell back into place.

Chapter 94

She met Aasha on Rue de Rivoli, and they walked toward Le Louvre. As they strolled, a detail about Paris jumped out at Anjali. She had never noticed until now that almost every street had a metal stanchion every two meters to prevent cars from parking two wheels on the sidewalk. She saw the same on the next block, and the next and the next, and down every side street they passed.

The French have sunk their *patrimoine* of steel into the asphalt, Anjali thought. Why not just put up one "no parking" sign per block and tow disobedient cars to the outskirts? The French could build dozens of bridges, nuclear power plants, warships—she hoped they wouldn't, though they did have a huge weapons industry—with all this metal. Why do they sink it into the streets?

Aasha interrupted her musings. "Let's see the Mona Lisa one last time," she said. At the height of tourist season, it would take an hour locked into a press of people to work their way to the front of the ropes that cordoned off *la petite peinture*. But Anjali went along with it. She wondered what places she would be sure to see before she left Paris. She thought of her *bibliothèque* with the gilded beams. Yes, there.

In Le Louvre, they walked past Italian masters to get to the room with La Jaconde, as the French called the Mona Lisa. The corridors and rooms were crowded. People *bousculer*'d them constantly.

Anjali wanted to ask, Are you sure you want to go back and get married, and maybe never travel anywhere again?

What she said was, "How can you be so sure it will work out for you in India?" That wasn't worded much better, she conceded, but this was what she needed to know.

Aasha flipped her long dark hair and laughed.

"It's what I've always wanted, and Sameer is so nice to me. And his parents and aunties, too."

"They've never lied to you?"

"No! Whyever would they?" Anjali hadn't told her about her Ravi's lie. She didn't want to put a cloud on Aasha's happiness.

"Is Sameer late to your calls? Does he postpone them?"

"No, never! We're good together. You're so negative!"

The next day, Aasha boarded a plane and went home. Wherever home is, thought Anjali. She longed for it, but now that she was in a strange environment, with valuable steel sunk into the streets and gloomy people all in black, home didn't seem to exist for her anymore.

Saturday morning, she would tell her parents her decision. Whatever that would be.

Chapter 95

Saturday morning at nine o'clock, while Pearl was at an AA meeting, Anjali slowly dialed her Amma and Appa on her computer. When they saw her face in video, they too became very serious.

Anjali told them about Ravi's parents' lie and his complicity in it. She didn't repeat what he'd said about wanting her by his side. Instead, she told them how late he was to their Internet chat dates, how she rarely heard from him by email, how he canceled many of their chats to play tennis or cricket or do other things.

"I know this is very hard for you, but I will not be marrying Ravi," she said. "Please try to understand."

"What! Why?" Her mother's voice was full of shock.

"I just told you why!"

"None of that is so important," her mother said. "Not important enough to do this to us. How will we ever explain to all your aunties? What will they think?"

"Anjali, what will I say to Ravi's father?" her father asked. "This is awful."

"Your aunties will never stop asking us if you're married yet," her mother said. "They will ask every time we see them. We should not have let you go to Paris. It's ruined everything."

"I'm so sorry for what you have to face from everybody," Anjali said. "Believe me, I thought about the consequences for you a lot while I was making my decision. But all those people have their own lives to live the way they want, and so do I."

"You'll face the aunties and their pressure, too, when you come home."

How could she tell them she wasn't coming home, not for a long time? Maybe only for a visit.

"Appa, isn't it true that you just want me to be happy?"

"Yes, that's what we want."

"Well, I am happy in Paris, working and writing. I love my writers' group. And I've joined an Indian culture Meetup group. I've made new friends." Untraditional Indian women friends—not married, making an independent life in Paris, seeing where life took them.

"Anjali, this won't make you happy like marriage and children," her mother said. Anjali could see her wipe her eyes with a corner of her peacock-blue *sari*.

"But maybe it will," she insisted. "I want to try it."

"This is not good," her father said.

"It's not traditional, I agree. But it is good. I'll be fine."

"Well, I don't know how we're going to tell his parents." Their faces were downcast on the screen.

"I'll talk to Ravi when I have a chance." If he ever stops playing tennis.

"My dear, this is very sad news," her mother said.

"You'll see. It will work out. I'll be happy."

"Don't lose your marriageability," her mother warned. She shook her finger in the screen.

"Okay, Amma."

"Your mother's right, listen to her," her father said.

"Okay, I agree with you, I'll be traditional in some things. Please don't worry so much."

They finally hung up, their expressions sorrowful.

Anjali sighed. They faced so much pressure from relatives, neighbors, friends, anybody in Mumbai who considered themselves an "auntie." A jumbojet full of people would appoint themselves to that role. She didn't envy her parents one bit. She almost had gone ahead with marrying Ravi, considering the plight she'd be throwing them into. The way they'd lose face in front of Ravi's parents. It was sad.

But the sky was cloudless outside her little attic window, a rare occurrence in Paris. A soft breeze brought a fly in. Anjali began to feel her spirits brighten as he buzzed merrily around her *chambre de bonne*. Maybe she'd go to that boutique and buy that blouse and be just a little *décolletée* today. With Aasha gone, Amma and Appa would never see it by mistake in a photograph on social media.

She felt she was betraying them.

She felt lonelier.

She felt freer.

Chapter 96

Anjali thought Pearl needed an outing. So she invited her to do what she was hankering to do: go back to the 20th *arrondissement*—to Belleville to be exact—to the poetry slam, to be even more exact.

Pearl had said yes, and had gone to her meeting early in the day to be free Saturday evening.

The hill up Rue de Belleville to the poetry slam *café* was full of slow, two-way traffic on the street, and strolling pedestrians on the sidewalk. Anjali was accustomed to walking purposefully, either to her job or to write at the library or a *café*. This ambling was annoying. Then she made an effort to use the time to look in the shops. "Try to be someone on whom nothing is lost," the writer Henry James had said.

Lots of Asian people milled in the shoe shops, *boutiques*, barbershops, and *alimentaires*, where crates of strange Chinese vegetables, like cucumbers covered in spines, spilled out onto the street.

Anjali imagined Edith Piaf as a young Sparrow, here in Belleville, belting out La Marseillaise for coins to live on. She probably stood somewhere along this very thoroughfare.

This jostling crowd—do they know the lyrics the Sparrow sang? Anjali wondered. When people all over the globe watched a French athlete who'd won gold at the Olympics, and heard the French national anthem played, did they have any idea how violent the lyrics were?

> Do you hear the roaring
>   of these fierce soldiers?
> They come right to our arms
> To slit the throats of our sons,
>   our friends!
> Let us march! Let us march!
> May impure blood water our fields!

The music sounded jolly. Probably based on a drinking ditty, as so many anthems were. But the lyrics were full of bloodlust. Well, it had been the national anthem since 1795. The violence was a bit grandfathered in at this point, she thought.

When they arrived inside the *café*, Pearl looked around eagerly at the dark blue walls, and the stage area with its backdrop of posters and bumper stickers. They had made a point of arriving early, to sit up front. They claimed seats at a big table. Anjali ordered Perrier instead of white wine, to help Pearl out.

When they had their drinks—a *diabolo grenadine* for Pearl, Anjali was relieved to see—they began to chat, since chatting while walking on the crowded Belleville sidewalks had been impossible.

"Do you speak French?" Anjali asked Pearl.

"*Mais oui*. I've lived here all my life."

"But when you speak English, you sound totally American."

"My father's American, my mother's French. So I speak both languages sounding like a native. Or so natives tell me."

"What good luck for you!"

Just then a group of three guys loomed over them.

"Can we share this table? Do you mind?" one of the young men asked in English.

"*Mais oui*," Anjali answered, trying to see if she could convince the newcomer that she spoke French. She moved her handbag from a chair onto the gritty floor between her feet. You couldn't be too street smart in Paris.

"How are you two young ladies tonight," said the blond-haired man among them. He appeared quite the dashing young blade, loaded with extra charm. He spoke in English. Either he hadn't fallen for her ploy, or he couldn't speak French, so Anjali switched gears.

"I'm fine, how are you?" Oh, if my parents saw me now, being friendly with a stranger in a bar, she thought. Especially a bar—and a stranger—that look like this.

"I'm Lee, from Pittsburgh," he said and offered his hand.

Anjali and Pearl each shook it in turn.

"So you're into poetry?" Lee said. He's directing his comments more to me than Pearl, Anjali thought. She seems quite detached, subdued, her eyes down on the table. What if she knows him from her days as a—. Oh well. What does this guy want? To talk about literature?

"Yes, I write poetry and movies," she said. "The poetry writing helps me, because in a movie, the images and the text should work together like poetry." He was looking at her intently. Was he listening intently? "And you?"

"Can't write. But I like a good poetry slam, and I heard this was a good one."

"It can be good. Mixed bag, usually."

"Where are you from?"

"Mumbai," she said.

"So you're Hindu, aren't you?"

"Yes?" A bit of a question crept into her answer. Why was he asking that?

"If you're from India, then you must know the meaning of life."

Was he serious?

"Tell us the meaning of life," he said, gesturing between himself and his two friends, who were watching her with interest. "Tell us in Hindi."

Anjali wondered if she were being mocked.

"I'm afraid not," she said, crossing her arms and locking eyes with Pearl, who looked up that instant.

"What's wrong? Hey, did I offend you? Sorry," Lee said and turned back to his friends.

Pearl smiled at her. "You okay?" she whispered.

"I can't believe what he just said. What an idiot." She hoped he'd overhear.

"Maybe you can use it in one of the movies you're writing."

"People think Indians know the meaning of life? What a stereotype! How can they think that with all the problems we have in India?"

"People believe weird things," Pearl said.

Chapter 97

Anjali didn't capture any great lines—there were none. The performers enjoyed having the spotlight on them but didn't deliver anything worth stealing—and then making into her own, of course. But Pearl had perked up a bit and laughed at some of the baudy poems. They left at the intermission.

To go home, they caught the Metro in the center of Belleville. A couple got on the train with them. The man sat on a pull-down seat, and the young woman, in short shorts that revealed the cheeks of her buttocks, straddled him front on, a leg to either side of him. They kissed passionately.

Anjali knew she shouldn't stare, but all the way to the Chatelet stop, where she would switch trains, she couldn't help stealing glances at them and thinking how she and Ravi would not be doing this—though in India one would never do this in front of people. There was no written law against it, but if public amorous behavior offended a policeman, he would arrest people, even married people, for so much as a peck on the cheek. She and Ravi would never do this in private, she amended her thought.

She realized she might never find a person to do this with. As the train shook her and rattled along, she thought, I may and I may not, and not knowing is one of the hardest feelings I've ever known.

Chapter 98

On a Saturday, Carol was free to work in the library because Louise had a playdate with a British couple's daughter. French children didn't do playdates. They hung out with their parents.

Carol passed through the huge wooden doors into the *bibliothèque*'s courtyard. The cobbles were particularly historic and therefore bumpier here. She had to watch her feet or wrench an ankle.

She entered the outer lobby where she'd eat her brought-from-home lunch during the winter, when it was too cold and raw to eat in the *jardin* around the corner. Then she opened the inner door to the bigger inner lobby and saw Anjali getting her assigned seat from the woman behind the desk.

"Hi there!" Carol said as Anjali turned toward her, clutching the white laminated slip with her seat number on it. In France, by George, you jolly well sat in your assigned seat or the proctor would make a fuss.

"Hello!" Anjali said. She was delighted to see Carol. A fellow screenwriter! Maybe they could collaborate! This writing business meant so much time spent alone.

Carol paused. Seeing the eagerness in Anjali's face, she thought, maybe I should have let her find her seat without letting her know I'm here. She'll expect me to critique her work extra, not just at the circle. I don't have time, I have to make some money! No, there's that stupid motive again. Bollocks!

They stood just outside the glass doors to the reading room. Carol peered through to see the gilded beams hovering above young French heads bent over their books and laptops, conforming their minds to their textbooks and their teachers' expectations. They all need a year in London, she thought, among the Goths.

"I'm so glad to see you! I love this library," Anjali said.

"Nice to see you, too," Carol cooed. "Yes, it's rather a brilliant place, isn't it?"

"Are you working on a screenplay?"

That was a bit of an industrial-spy-type question, Carol thought. "Oh, a bit here and there. And you?"

"Yes!"

"Lovely! Will we see it at the next writers' circle?" That was a hint, dear.

"I'll let it steep a bit more than that," Anjali said. She thought, how nice to see Carol. What is all this frosty British reserve about?

So, Carol thought, her shoulders aching under the weight of her laptop and notebooks, she knows the steeping trick. How much do I want to teach her? We're competitors for the few slots of films that actually get produced in this world. She thought of Philippe and what he'd probably say about selfishness. I'm quite the bitch not to be more helpful, aren't I?

"Let's see if we can sit together. Or we can at least email or text each other with some ideas on each other's work today. Want to?" Carol said.

Anjali felt her heart grow warm with all the fuzziness of a stuffed Paddington bear. One with a Union Jack sewn on its pocket. For all that the British had done wrong in India, here was a Brit poised to help her.

"Fabulous!"

Chapter 99

The writers' circle had agreed not to have a critique session onboard John's sailboat but to postpone it because spouses and children and friends would be along. Besides, neither Philippe nor Carol had solved the problem of finding a stapler, and it wouldn't be easy in a sea breeze to hang on to loose pages.

Saturday morning, John dressed hurriedly, rented a car, and picked Emily up. Cufflinks were not an issue while dressing this morning, he thought. He was in a pink polo shirt, khaki shorts, and deck shoes—no socks, like the preppie he was at heart.

On the way to the parking lot in Bois de Boulogne where he'd meet everyone and lead the parade, he offered Emily a *pain au chocolat* he had picked up at his favorite *patisserie* the night before.

"When can I move in with you, Dad?" Emily said, licking a bit of custard that had squeezed out from between the flaky layers. A morsel of chocolate perched on her lip, and she nudged it into her mouth with a finger.

"I don't know where I'd put you just yet. I'm working on it with all my might," he answered.

"Mom is driving me crazy, worse than ever. All she does is shop and get her nails done."

She was not running up credit cards that he had any responsibility for, John noted with satisfaction.

"She has an addiction," he said. "I'll get you out of there as soon as I can."

They arrived at the pre-agreed meeting spot. John climbed out of his car and scanned the skies. Cloudy in Paris, as usual. On the coast he would probably find a whole different weather pattern, as usual.

Anjali and the friend she'd said she'd bring arrived a few minutes later, emerging from a nearby Metro station. Emily climbed out of the little rented Opal to greet them with John.

In her introduction, Anjali didn't go into how she'd first met the quiet young woman accompanying her.

"Sir, this is Pearl."

"Please, it's John, today and every day," he said to both girls.

John gave both of them the *bisous*, the traditional French greeting. He couldn't help thinking that the tradition of a kiss on each cheek was nice. You got to smell women's perfume. In summer, though, it was a tradition that would be better experienced among people other than certain French, who in hot weather developed pungent body odors and were quite unconcerned, even sportive, about it. Americans, he thought wryly, on the other hand believe that the human body should never smell of anything but shower gel, topped off by a favorite cologne.

But these two young ladies smelled dainty.

Carol and a little girl emerged from the Metro. Carol was no longer in an Armani suit but cropped black yoga pants and a long knit top. Svelte, thought John.

"Hi, everyone, this is Louise. Darling, say hello."

Louise was a tiny-boned girl with her mother's blue eyes and a set of strawberry blonde curls. She mumbled a hello.

What a cutie, John thought. He knelt beside her.

"Hi, did you bring some books?"

"I've got a backpack full of them," Carol answered for her.

"Good! Now we're just waiting for Philippe and his wife," John said.

At the name "Philippe," Pearl startled, then relaxed again.

"Where's your car?" asked Carol. She was expecting a luxurious ride to Cherbourg with John, in a Mercedez or BMW. Or something better. Bentley? Rolls?

John realized he had made a public relations mistake, renting a cheap car. Yet even the Opal had been scary expensive.

He gestured to the car, with paint beginning to peel on its hood. It had been the cheapest one Anjali could find for him online.

When John gestured to a beat-up heap of a car, Carol felt rooted to the earth. She was stunned. So, she thought, another surprise from John. He's not married. Maybe he's not rich anymore? Or is he ridiculously frugal? What other first impressions are going to crumble? Maybe he's not really tall and handsome? She recovered herself and smiled.

"Looks rather reliable, doesn't it," she said.

Just then a beat-up silver Peugeot pulled up next to John's car. Pearl was staring with wide eyes as Philippe and Elodie emerged from the car, both of them staring hungrily back at her.

"Meredith!" her mother cried joyfully and rushed to hug her girl.

Philippe leaned his hip against the car for support. A confusion of feelings raced through him: relief to see her looking in her right mind, anger over the wrenching several weeks—no, years—they'd been through, worry whether she would finally be long-term sober and could really be brought home.

He walked up to the hugging mother and daughter and threw his arms around them both.

Chapter 100

Anjali shouldered her backpack. She was happy to see Pearl reunited with her parents, but she was offended that Pearl had never told her her real name. Pearl must have been her street name. Anjali had read about that years ago and just remembered it now.

John shuffled his feet on the pavement. He was happy for Philippe but eager for them all to get on the road. The day was fast evaporating in the giving and receiving of *bisous* and hugs.

"Carol, why don't you and Louise come with me." He looked at Anjali's friend, still buried deep in a familial hug. "Anjali, you want to come with us, too?"

So they sorted themselves out and got on the road. Meredith climbed penitently into the back of the Peugeot.

"We're so glad to see you," Philippe said, praying for wisdom for driving safely and for talking with his daughter.

"I'm glad to see you, too."

"We're going sailing now, but are we going home together tonight? Are you free of alcohol?" Philippe asked.

"I'm doing ninety meetings in ninety days in AA."

Philippe felt exasperated. What about today? He carefully filtered any annoyance out of his voice.

"And today?"

"I was going to ask John if we could come back early enough for an eight o'clock meeting. I forgot to ask him before we left."

So she hadn't been totally responsible, but then again, it had been a shock to everyone to meet like that.

"We'll find a way to get you back by eight," he said.

"Thanks."

He looked at her in his rearview mirror. Her face was downcast.

"You get to see me dash around a boat today, weighing anchor and belaying the mains'l," he joked, and he watched her. She smiled faintly, then returned to her pensiveness.

She's returned to us sadder but wiser, I hope, Philippe thought.

"Mom and Dad, I have a sponsor, I'm going through the Twelve Steps," she said. "I'll be doing amends eventually. I'm sorry, very sorry."

Philippe saw her face crumple. She was crying in the back seat, and he didn't know what to say. His own emotions were roiling, mostly feeling anger at her stupid behavior. The tension all over his body made it hard to think, to sense what she needed him to say. Well, there couldn't be anything wrong with the basics.

"I love you," he said.

"I'm pregnant."

Chapter 101

At the marina in Cherbourg, John threaded the Opal between rows of car abandoned by sailors eager to get onto their boats. He parked, and Philippe parked nearby. They all emerged from the cars, and they all shouldered backpacks stuffed with windbreakers and lunch. The small troupe of writers and their significant others followed John and looked around them, soaking up the details of boats, masts, ropes, water, sky. They walked along pier after pier with sailboats and motorboats bobbing in their slips.

A man sitting on a canvas chair, in the spacious cockpit of his motor-yacht, hailed John and tipped his glass of champagne to him. He's celebrating the ultimate success, thought John—ownership of a boat. And I'm about to lose mine. He sniffed the salt air as if it were his last breath on earth.

The whole crew followed John to the floating dock where the Grey Skies had been waiting patiently for them.

On the bulkhead, the last bit of solid land, at the top of the gangplank that led to the floating dock, John looked out over the harbor. Boats were tied up—a dizzying number of boats. Thousands. He was glad the boats were in their berths and not out in the Channel, where he would soon be. The fewer the boats out there, the better it was for him. But it meant he was taking a risk, going out when others chose to stay snug in their slips. Here he was again, taking a risk. Being just a bit loony. He hoped it didn't turn out like his venture in silver had.

A healthy breeze was blowing, even in the protected harbor. A few sloppy skippers had failed to tie down their halyards—the metal lines for hauling up the sails that ran to the tops of the masts. Out of the thousands of boats in Cherbourg harbor, a few hundred had steel halyards that slapped in the wind against steel masts, making a chiming noise.

He felt the ebullience that arose in him whenever he was near boats, near fellow sailors. Life opened up to him in a marina. He could sail around the world. He could say goodbye to all his troubles and harness the wind to take him to exotic ports of call. He would some day.

He descended the gangplank to the floating dock, that liminal space between land and sea. The writers' circle and their family members trudged down it, too. John strode along the bobbing dock to the Grey Skies' berth. His boat bobbed and tugged at its various spring lines, which kept it centered in its slip instead of bashing against the pilings.

"How big is your boat?" Philippe asked, knowing that John would love to tell him.

"It's forty-five feet long," John said to his crew. "It has a jib—well, two jibs," he said modestly, "—and a mainsail, all self-furling. One mast, so it's a sloop." He ignored the bigger ketch with two masts tied up next to him, and instead opened the clasp of the lifelines. They began to step across the gap between dock and sloop.

It's a lovely boat, thought Carol as she stepped aboard. It's the opposite of that Opal. What is going on here? The deck rose and fell gently under her feet, disorienting her, and she grabbed for the teak handrail attached to the cabin's roof. The wind rearranged her hair. She stepped down into the cockpit and dug in her pocket for a hair tie. She quickly gathered her hair into a messy bun, and then Louise's curls, too.

Through his feet and legs, Philippe felt the boat tug at its spring lines, as if it anticipated its freedom and the sail they were about to take. This was quite the pleasure craft, he thought, euro signs spinning before his eyes. I'd better enjoy this today, because I'll never own anything like this. And I'd better be a good sailor, so he'll invite us out again.

John unlocked the cabin and clambered down its steps. Dozens of tasks stood between him and departure. Having all these neophytes on board meant so much responsibility and work for him. As he clicked the GPS, the anemometer, and the depth finder on, he fervently hoped nobody would be seasick.

"Okay, crew!" he said as he climbed up the steps and into the cockpit. "We have good weather, so let's take advantage." He took the binnacle cover off of the compass. He had already memorized the coordinates of his course.

He was all over the boat, showing people how to handle the ropes—"they're called lines on a boat," he told them—when he gave the order to cast off. He took the strings off the halyards that kept them from clanking against the mast in harbor, and started the motor.

"Okay, ready?" he shouted to Philippe in the bow.

"Aye aye, skipper," Philippe shouted back.

Carol was on the stern, Anjali and Meredith on the starboard and port spring lines, respectively. Emily was reading to Louise in the cabin, keeping out of the way. Elodie was sitting in the cockpit, praying for survival.

John whispered "Good luck" to himself as a gust of wind slapped his face. He gave the order to cast off to the people handling the lines. He put the motor into gentle reverse, and the boat backed slowly out of the slip. At just the right moment, before crashing into the stern of the boat docked opposite him, John pushed the engine's stick shift from reverse to forward and turned the boat's wheel. The Grey Skies headed toward the mouth of the harbor.

As they moved into more open water, the wind picked up and the water got choppier. Carol's sitzbones dug into the fiberglass seat of the cockpit with every lurch of the boat. She wasn't comfortable but having fun anyway. John is looking quite dashing, she thought. And he's quite the skipper, isn't he? He rents awful cars but he commands a wonderful boat. What would it be like to sail with him? To spend the night anchored in a little bay, as she'd heard people talk about at Trapèze. She hoped John invited everyone out again. If Gregoire and Amandine could see her now. Maybe she'd take a selfie and text it to them. She gave it some thought. Maybe not.

"We'll be putting the sails up outside the harbor," John said. "Everybody must be on the lookout at all times for other boats. The English Channel is just about the busiest shipping lane in the world."

Even as John was saying it, they bobbed past the jetty that marked the mouth of the harbor.

Philippe felt the wind tug his hair with new vigor. He spotted a ferry approaching them, white and sleek and formidable. And another, smaller one, coming from the other direction. He hoped John knew what he was doing.

The wind was now a stiff roar in everyone's ears. The boat shifted under them with more energy as it bounced on the even choppier waters. John shouted that it was time for the fun to begin. As a few powerboats zipped around them, and three tankers moved majestically near the horizon, he asked Philippe to handle the mainsail.

Philippe pulled on the mainsheet with all his might, determined to prove himself a worthy crew member for the future. The sail, as it emerged from its housing in the mast and progressed toward the stern in its track along the boom, rattled and flapped as the wind flowed over both sides of it equally.

As soon as the mainsail was unfurled and fastened, John spun the wheel to point the bow away from the wind. The sail suddenly billowed out as it filled with air, and the boat heeled steeply. Driven by instinct, people scrambled to the upwind side. Emily and Louise switched to the upwind banquette inside the cabin. John turned the motor off, and in the ensuing quiet—except for the noise of the wind—they all could hear the delightful sound of water running along the hull. John unfurled only one jib, the smaller one, and sheeted it in. The boat sliced through the water, rising and falling on the swells. Bits of foam from the whitecaps flecked their faces.

"Great sailing weather," John shouted, smiling.

People nodded, hung on, and hoped they wouldn't get seasick.

Chapter 102

What is the point of sailing? Carol wondered, her sitzbones now sore from rolling against the fiberglass bench with every swell. They had tacked to starboard, tacked to port, and were no closer to the mouth of the harbor, which she kept her eye on with hope.

I'd like to say something to the group, make some crack about sailing. But in light of what Philippe said about my critique style, I'd better not. And I don't want to offend John. Though I do feel a bit smothered. Sigh.

But I can do a little critiquing quietly, to myself. John looks so good at the helm, so much better than Philippe—even Philippe's casual khakis don't fit quite right, just like his suits. I'm very glad to count John as a friend and fellow brainstormer. He certainly is bonkers about boats, isn't he? He looks rather good with the wind in his hair…Philippe, however, I bet he doesn't know what the hell he's doing on a boat. I'm scared, the wind feels so powerful out here, I wish we'd go back.

Carol smiled at John, thinking that if she acted totally in love with sailing, maybe he'd stop working so hard to convince them that it was great and go back to the harbor.

Carol looks content enough, thought John, as the wind and sun burned his cheeks. But I wish she'd get into it more, look eager when it's time to tack. Well, anyway, let's race that other boat on the same tack as us. It's a bit loony, John, to race boats with no starting line, no course marked out by buoys, and no finish line. But it's fun.

John looked at his assistant.

Anjali was thinking that the wind was blowing her already straight hair straighter. She was thrilled with the unlimited volume of fresh sea air, of sun, and of the sound of water rushing along the boat's hull. This would never have happened to me if I'd stayed in Mumbai, she thought. She took stock of her life in Paris. John has been a good boss, though I wish he'd learn how to print things out for himself. He can't manage printers, but he has no problems managing this piece of technology, this bit of fiberglass hull that displaces water, and these bits of fabric that harness wind. As long as people have been doing it for thousands of years, John can do it.

Anjali smiled at John, and then at Philippe, sitting between her and John on the banquette.

Philippe smiled back and turned to enjoy the expanse of sky, clouds, and sea behind him. When he turned back, he was facing the blank white sail. He peered under it to look for boats. John shouldn't rely on us greenhorns quite so heavily, he thought. Then he thought, Here I am, critiquing him instead of being grateful for a fabulous day on the water.

Chapter 103

They headed back into the harbor and the boat's slip in order to eat lunch and get a break from the wind and choppy sea.

With the dock lines adjusted and holding the boat well in place, John relaxed for the first time that day. He accepted the *baguette avec jambon et fromage* he had packed that morning, that Emily now handed him. She disappeared back into the cabin to be with Louise.

"Thank you, John, that was great!" Philippe said. The others echoed him, a bit more faintly.

"You see, we could have had a critique session here in the harbor, turns out it's quiet enough," John said.

"Maybe we could do this again and bring our work next time," Carol said, fishing for an invitation. She liked being in the harbor a lot, with the water lapping gently at the hull. Maybe, if he invited them back, she could convince him to stay in the berth, where they were bobbing gently. Very soothing and enjoyable, wasn't it.

John frowned. Inwardly, he debated what to say, how much to reveal. He looked at each face, the faces of this group that he'd gotten to know so much better than he knew most people, and in such a short amount of time.

"Fact is, I'll be selling this boat," he said.

"Oh, that's too bad," Philippe replied, disappointed that this was his last time out.

"I've hit some financial difficulties." John said. How sad it felt to him that this was now his reality. "But I can't imagine life without a boat."

Carol thought, well that's too bad, rich and tall and handsome all in one package was too much to ask. And you're not asking, you're just brainstorm buddies.

"You know, sir," Anjali said, "I know you're looking for another place to live in Paris. I met someone recently who lives on a *péniche*. I called her to ask her something for an article I'm writing about it, and she told me she's selling it."

A *péniche* is a barge, John thought, it isn't nimble, it can't race other sailboats on the English Channel, it can't sail around the world. But then he thought, I could live on it in Paris, if it had enough staterooms that Emily could live there, too. In summer I could explore the French countryside on France's *patrimoine fluvial*, five thousand kilometers of canals and rivers that wind past classic little villages, and I'd be on the water. Maybe all of that and with Emily, too.

"How many staterooms does it have?" he asked.

"Three."

He felt a tug of excitement. One for him, Emily, and an office—or for Louise. No, don't go there, he thought. But a *péniche* might be an answer.

"I have big news about my life, too," Anjali said.

As they munched on their *baguettes* with *poulet* and *thon* and *bœuf*, they nodded their heads for her to go ahead.

"I told my parents I'm not going home to marry Ravi."

"You broke free, didn't you," Carol said, licking some *mayonnaise* off her finger.

"I broke free, I suppose, but it will be hard for them. It means they'll be pressured constantly, by every member of the family and every acquaintance, asking if I'm married yet. I feel terrible about that."

Carol thought, how very sad that in India, people are so into each other's business.

Anjali said, "Everybody is into everybody else's lives in India, but when you need help, the support network is incredible. Have a car breakdown at two in the morning, and somebody knows somebody who knows somebody who will come out and rescue you. I miss that feeling of security."

Carol debated within herself whether she should be as open as others were being today, and thought, it's interesting how I know that these guys, these fellow workers in the art of writing, will still love me.

"I'm in the process of recovering from being fired from Trapèze."

John thought, Oh no, she's in financial difficulty, too?

Anjali thought, I guess she can't help me get a job there.

Philippe thought, You just never know what's going on with people. "What are you going to do?" he asked.

"I'm working on several screenplays—and haiku—they cross-pollinate each other. I have a track record of successful films. All I have to do is sell one and I'm good for several years." Or more. If she found a good agent.

"Interesting," Philippe said. "Well, you know our good news, we've been reunited with our beloved daughter." He smiled at Meredith, sitting opposite him. Everyone was being open and honest today. But he wasn't mentioning her pregnancy because he hadn't processed the news yet himself. And I just can't tell them about swearing at God, he thought, I just can't. Maybe I'm letting down the group by being the least open. Where I am closed, I am not true. Wow. Maybe someday, in my writing. But for today, all I can do is hint at it.

"I hammered on heaven, not very politely. And God answered." At least it seemed as though their prayers had been answered. He had to wait and see if Meredith stayed sober. If she didn't, how could he kick out a pregnant daughter? Not possible.

The group sat and munched their *baguettes*, felt the breeze caress their skin, smelled the salt air, felt the boat bob under them. They made a plan to meet in Le Café Livre in two weeks. No one person dominated the discussion. And they talked. People listened to each other and said witty things and commented. As the afternoon passed, they talked of being expats, of writing, of life, and of Paris, and of an expat writing life in Paris.

Chapter 104

John stood on the deck of the Grey Skies while Emily stood on the dock waiting for him to finish his boat chores. The other members of the writers group had already left.

John felt the deck of his sailboat move beneath his feet. He looked longingly at the binnacle standing just before the wheel, both now hidden under canvas covers the same color as the hull. He looked at the sleek metal boom, its matte finish spotless. Its track for unfurling the mainsail had worked perfectly on today's sail. As usual, he thought with pride.

He had maintained the Grey Skies so well, pouring thousands of euros into her—while he had the euros, he thought ruefully. She was in fantastic shape and would command a good sum when he sold her.

If he sold her.

How could he possibly part with her?

He ran his hand over a teak handrail. He had sanded it and oiled it annually. He'd labored over the Grey Skies every spring, sanding the teak trim, adjusting things, tightening screws, waxing every square inch of her hull. Throughout the sailing season, he'd scraped his knuckles and bled onto every inch of her, too.

Starting every year on November 1, when his insurance policy ended his boating season, he started to anticipate working in his boat. That had been the only thing that got him through the gloomy Paris winters. If he sold this boat, how would he survive this coming winter without the spring maintenance work and the summer sailing to look forward to?

How could he sell the Grey Skies?

He stole a glance toward Emily. He'd asked her to come live with him. She'd said yes. He couldn't afford to pay the rent on a two-bedroom apartment in Paris. Or outside of Paris, for that matter. Or to buy one. He could just about afford a *péniche*, to pay the light fee to tie it up along the Seine somewhere in Paris, and to enroll Emily in a French public high school.

But he didn't want that.

He wanted to keep his boat.

His hand tightened on the teak handrail. The Grey Skies was his last symbol of success. Not many men could afford a boat, much less a 45-foot boat. And then maintain it. The Grey Skies had been a mirror in which he had been able to see himself as a success.

Besides which, he absolutely loved her shape, her responsiveness to the wind. He loved knowing that she was seaworthy—he could sail her around the world if he wanted to.

He still could. It wasn't too late. Provision by charging it all on a credit card and just leave…the adventure that awaited him…

He stole another look at Emily, who was staring down into the water beside the dock.

His eyes turned to the mast and drifted higher and higher, to the anemometer spinning at the very top in the freshening evening breeze.

He spun through his arithmetic. Keeping it didn't add up. But what did that matter? Did taking it and leaving Emily really matter?

What would Philippe do in this situation? Something he'd said at a recent writers group meeting resonated with John. "What do you value most?" he'd said.

His gaze returned to Emily, so small and vulnerable in her pink windbreaker. His father had valued his status more than his family, and look at the pain that still caused. If John just sailed away and abandoned Emily, how would that affect her? Or maybe he should take her with him? Then he'd be setting the example of living off of credit cards, like her mother. And they'd get revoked at some point, probably after a typhoon in the South Pacific when he would need repairs the most.

He let go of the handrail. Craving the feel of the smooth teak again, he ran his hand along its surface. He was shocked at how close he'd come to hurting Emily by choosing to sail away.

He turned, heartsick, from the handrail. Slowly he fumbled his keys out of his pocket and locked the cabin door. He felt sore in every muscle as he stepped off of the Grey Skies and onto the dock. He looked at his beautiful boat from bow to stern, his gaze caressing each line of her hull. He whispered, "Thank you."

He walked to Emily and put his hand on her shoulder. Her windbreaker felt damp with evening dew.

"Ready, honey? Let's drop off the keys at the broker's office.

Chapter 105

A few weeks later, Philippe gathered what he needed to leave for the day as he buzzed around the house in Malakoff, looking for things. His footsteps rang happily on the wooden floor. I'm glad I repented of swearing, he thought. It truly is ugly language, and often it seems to aggravate the anger I'm feeling instead of dissipating it.

He grabbed sunglasses, writing notebook, and a map of Paris in order to find an elderly parishioner's apartment later. Housebound, the poor dear. She needed to be visited every week. Dominic, too, home from the hospital but still sick and tired of heart disease and feeling ill. What people go through, dear Lord, he thought.

Help us all.

He saw a hair tie of Meredith's lying on the sofa. It shouldn't be left like that. But she was at work, and going to a meeting tonight, and going to church on Sunday. Not his church, but church. Be slow to complain about a stray hair tie, he thought.

He zipped up his crumbling-leather briefcase and headed out the front door. He turned on the top step to lock the door behind him and felt in his pants pockets for his keys. They weren't there, and they weren't in the briefcase either. He hadn't seen the keys anywhere in the house while getting ready. He was late for yet another appointment with yet another ailing parishioner. It was so annoying, there was always some stupid little thing going wrong, even when he was trying to do some good.

"Shit!" he said. It felt satisfying. And then he cringed. Obviously, changing his propensity to swear wasn't going to be easy. A lifelong struggle. Like writing, like pastoring, like staying out of *patisseries* and wine shops, like so many other things.

He went into the house to search.

Chapter 106

Later, Philippe hurried from the Metro in Malakoff to his house on Chemin de Fer. The sun was setting noticeably earlier every night, and the evenings were closing down quickly. As he walked along Boulevard Charles de Gaulle, the lady of one of the houses opened a window, reached for the metal shutters folded neatly to each side, and unfolded them with a clatter so that they covered the opening. Then he heard the glass window shut with a thud. She was closing out the little light left to her.

As Philippe strode, he reviewed the talks that he and Elodie had had with Meredith about the baby, and what they felt they could do to help her. She would have to take most of the responsibility, but they would assist with childcare while she finished college and went to work.

He had told her he was pro-life across the board: abortion, the death penalty, and euthanasia were, in his opinion, all man taking on the role of God to end a human life.

Philippe passed through the section of the public path that was lined with bushes—he'd heard from neighbors who gardened that they were Mexican orange bushes—with softly fragrant white flowers. He had an idea for a children's book and wanted to work on it that evening. Getting a picture book published was even harder than getting an adult work of fiction published, he had heard. But he'd work on the story anyway. Someday in the not too distant future he'd read it to his fatherless grandchild, the little sweetheart perched in his lap. He couldn't wait. This was the good God was bringing from Meredith's tragic choices.

He climbed the steps and opened the front door of the house. It was dinnertime. Elodie had told him she would make *bœuf bourguignon*. The rich stew simmered and filled the house with delicious smells of burgundy wine, mushrooms, and pearly white onions.

Elodie was in heels, wearing a skirt, blouse, and frilly apron. Only a Frenchwoman would cook in heels, Philippe thought with tenderness.

"*Cherie*," he said and kissed both of her cheeks, and then her lips, lingering there.

"*Mon cher*," she replied, breaking away from his embrace and reaching for the breadbasket. She began to slice a *baguette*. "Would you call Meredeez to the table?"

He walked to the bottom of the stairs a contented man. When Meredith didn't answer two calls, he climbed up, a little annoyed. Why did the kids always have their bedroom doors closed at dinner time?

There was no answer to his knocks, so he opened her door. She was laying on her side, sleeping. No wonder she hadn't heard.

He shook her shoulder gently and called her name. She still didn't answer.

He turned to the white dresser and clicked on the small lamp opposite the melted red candle stuck in a wine bottle. She didn't move, so he flicked the *interrupteur* on the wall to turn on the overhead light.

Returning to her, he noticed that her jeans seemed darker around her thighs. He smelled a coppery smell.

"Elodie!" he shouted.

He ran to the bedroom door and shouted his wife's name again. She came running up the stairs quickly, stirred by the urgency in his voice.

"Quick! Call an ambulance!" she said as soon as she had checked Meredith. *"Vite! Vite!"*

Chapter 107

A week later. Philippe dragged himself up the stairs. His sweet grandchild was gone. Meredith herself had barely survived her abortion. She was still in the hospital. Thank God she was still alive, he thought. But oh my God, I needed that child, that sign of you bringing good out of evil. Now what do I do?

He entered Meredith's bedroom, his eyes drawn to the quilt on the bed. The red compass rose on its white field had a huge brown blotch in the middle of it. Ruined. The child's life destroyed. Everything Meredith touched was still going bad.

He felt a wave of anger because of the loss of his grandchild. That stupid little slut. He caught himself. She's your daughter, Philippe, choose your words more wisely, he thought to himself. But look at the choices she's made.

His eye landed on her bookshelves, where she still had some favorite picture books from her childhood standing along the bottom shelf. He felt intense longing for that grandchild that he'd hoped to read his own work to. Perhaps a girl with curls held back by a *barrette*. He would take her walking beside the Seine, or teach a boy to how to play *le football*.

He could not endure Meredith's foolishness. Sorrow and rage dragged his shoulders down even further. There was only one thing to do with this ruined, ugly quilt. He had a powerful urge to damage, to destroy. He looked around for a tool to help him. The stupid red candle was no help.

He yanked open the top drawer of her dresser, looking for a way to do damage, to release his anger at yet another disappointment with Meredith.

He found a pair of sewing scissors, with blades ending in sharp points.

He grabbed them, opened them, turned to the bed, and stabbed. He dug at the quilt, the points digging deep, the edges of the scissors cutting his own skin. He stabbed and stabbed. This quilt was junk, and despite all the love he and Elodie had poured into her, Meredith had treated her life like junk, and that of her unborn child. He stabbed, bled, and wept, and chopped that red and brown compass rose into rags.

Chapter 108

On an October evening, the night having closed in by five in the afternoon, Elodie, Philippe, and Meredith sat at the dining room table, just lingering with each other, the anger spent but the anguish still palpable between them. Meredith was stronger, but still wan. Philippe took another small corner of Roquefort and spread the pungent cheese on a slice of crusty *baguette*. As he bit in, the cool, tangy cheese clung to his palette. Oh Lord, he thought, even in the midst of death we are in the midst of life. Or was it the other way around?

"You know, I wasn't called to the ministry," Meredith said.

While Philippe cleared his mouth, Elodie spoke for him.

"We never expected that of you."

"But just by being a preacher's kid, people expected me to be more angelic. To be morally perfect, actually, just like people expected you to be. I couldn't do it."

Philippe sat, made of marble. Let her speak, he thought. Let's have it, the blame, shifting responsibility for what she did to me. All the things humans do. Let your daughter be a human.

"Do you remember Madame Lamblin?" Meredith asked.

Philippe did. Always wore a hat with a jaunty feather. So French. She was just about the sweetest saint he'd ever met.

"She saw me flirting outside a movie known for its graphic sex. She told me to be careful. It was so annoying! No, it was worse than annoying. To be watched, to be noticed. All that noticing! People expected me to behave better, to believe better, to profess better, to set an example. They overlooked the fact that I was just another kid."

Philippe met her gaze and nodded. He was sorry. He knew being a Christian sometimes felt like living in a fishbowl, with everybody watching, looking for an excuse not to follow Jesus just because a Christian dropped some *baguette* crumbs down his chest or said "shit!" when he couldn't find his keys. Just because he wasn't perfect, and, by extension, neither was the church. Yet Philippe felt that Christians did have a God-given responsibility to strive toward perfection in their attitudes and actions. We all fail so miserably, Philippe thought. It's only by God's grace that we survive moment to moment.

"I have to take responsibility for what I did—" and Meredith's shoulders crumpled as she turned away from her parents, toward the wall. "It was the alcohol—"

Philippe and Elodie waited. He could hear that outside, at the end of Chemin de Fer, across Boulevard Charles de Gaulle, the Metro train was diving into its tunnel on its way underground to the heart of Paris.

Meredith turned back to them, her eyes big with tears.

"But I had to rebel, I had to rebel against defining myself by other people's expectations. I had no sense of freedom. I was sick of the *faux*-moral *façade* I had to wear, just to survive. I didn't know what I believed. And you couldn't tell what I was going through."

No, he hadn't known. Her unhappiness had escaped his notice. He was sorry he had failed her. But here she was, just like everybody else, expecting him to be perfect. He was trying, for love of Jesus— he meant that not as a swear word.

He stayed silent. What could he do differently in the future? Refuse to accept people's answers of "I'm fine"? Ask more probing questions? Dig deeper? Listen better? Be attentive longer as people complained, rather than interrupt with encouragement? What exactly had he done wrong? Teenagers don't accept their parents trying to know them better. Why couldn't Meredith have gone to Madame Lamblin or one of the other mature women for advice? Madame Lamblin had been right to caution Meredith outside that movie theater.

Oh Lord, what a muddle we're in. Help us all!

Chapter 109

Carol approached the *péniche*, ankles wobbling on the cobbles of the embankment. She and John had sold a script they'd written together. He'd sold his sailboat, pooled the proceeds with his half of the sale of the script, had invested part of it—conservatively, he'd told her—and bought the *péniche* with the rest. The writers' group had held a party onboard the *péniche* to celebrate their two members' success. Was she correct in her impression that Philippe and Anjali were just a little bit envious? In their shoes, she would be.

John and Philippe were becoming close friends. John had mentioned reading the Gospels and asking Philippe questions. He was changing. She'd seen him become less worried about being a failure. "God loves me no matter what," John said on a day when they'd received their umpteenth rejection, the day before their script sold. And he'd given up his fisticuff novels for stories with characters who could do more than punch and shoot. The better to write great screenplays, which was fine with her.

Carol's shoes—the ones with special soles, the only kind John would allow to come in contact with his decks—caught on the cobbled surface of the *quai*. As she steadied herself with the gangway's handrail, she thought of Gregoire and how he hadn't sued her. Was that a mercy from God or just a coincidence? Then she thought with happiness about another good thing unfolding without her being there to spur it on.

Daphné, her spy at Trapèze, had told her that the stork film with the bullying ogre was in production and that Gregoire had hardly changed a word of her script. Daphné didn't know if Carol's name would be in the film credits as screenwriter. Carol could sue and waste years in the French courts trying to get her name on the movie. And he could countersue for endangering his life with flying glass.

Maybe her name on it wasn't the most important thing. Maybe a child would see the movie, identify with the beleaguered storks, choose not to bully the brother-and-sister victims within his or her sphere of influence. The pen was mightier than the sword. At least, she fervently hoped so.

A breeze wafted down the Seine and tossed Carol's hair. She tucked it behind her ears, watched a *bateau mouche* go by, and savored the moment.

Emily emerged from the cabin. She unlocked her bike from the railing on the deck and walked it down the gangway. She was on her way to school. A French public high school.

Just then, in a brief moment of October sun, when the dramatic gray and white Paris clouds parted raggedly for a moment, the Seine sparkled, coiling and eddying and tempting onlookers to jump in and take a swim.

"*Bonjour*, Em!" Carol said.

"*Bonjour*." Emily smiled at Carol. "How's Louise?"

"Fine! I just dropped her at school."

"She'll be over later?" Emily asked.

"Yes, we'll see you after school."

"Great," Emily said. She pedaled away, her backpack huge on her little body.

Carol's heart lifted as John stepped out of the cabin with two steaming mugs of coffee. The breeze up the Seine ruffled his hair so appealingly, and tugged at Carol's, too.

She walked up the gangway and stepped onto the deck, which shifted under her feet as the *péniche* tugged at its lines.

"What are we working on today?" he said, setting the mugs on a small teak table in the boat's cockpit. Carol mused that John was working his way through bankruptcy and IRS snafus. He was diligent about it. Another plus to his credit.

The mugs steamed into the October air. Two pastries, which the girl at the *patisserie* had wrapped cleverly in white wax paper folded like a pyramid, sat waiting for them on a small plate.

John went every morning for *un croissant*. He'd recounted to Carol that when he asked for *une croissant*, getting the gender of the noun wrong, the woman behind the counter wouldn't sell him one. "*Un croissant*," she had said icily.

"Only the French," John had said. "Sometimes I miss the States, where the customer is king." No person working behind the counter in a bakery in New York would dream of correcting a customer's grammar.

As for Carol, she would have *pain avec raisins*. The *patisserie* closest to John's *péniche* made the best she'd found anywhere in Paris. The flaky pastry wound around a cream filling chock full of raisins. She was gaining weight under this regimen. But, like other things on this boat, it kept her coming back morning after morning.

"No worries, we'll have lots of ideas," Carol said.

Chapter 110

Anjali referred to the script she'd written, the paper damp and wrinkly in a late October Paris mist. Then she hoisted the portable camera to her eye again. Her arms ached with the weight. She thought, thank God that, as a film student, I don't have to rent the camera and sound equipment, or my budget would be aching, too.

"Make sure you keep the umbrella over the camera," she told the production assistant, a fellow student, at her elbow.

They were in a far corner of Cimetière du Père Lachaise, trying to get away with not having a permit to film a short. The tombs were creepy, the skies dark, the oak trees bare and mournful. A crow cawed high in the trees. She checked the camera's settings. Yes! She'd captured the tormented sound. She'd make sure it got into her story.

They were moving through her script as quickly as possible, hoping that a groundskeeper didn't go by on the cobbled street that wove through this somber village of tombs. If he did come by and ended their shoot, they'd just have to creep back the next day, but the light would inevitably be different. Then again, Anjali thought, at the end of October the light is gray every day in Paris.

The two actors were cooperating with her fast pace, hoping for more roles in her next production. The break-up scene was going well. Anjali had used everything she'd learned from her Ravi romance in this script. But the weather was against her—the mist was thickening toward rain. For now, the actors' hair was capped by a halo of tiny droplets. Great for mood. But their clothes would be soaked through and turn dark, and that would look weird on film.

"Action," Anjali said. She realized she had mumbled it, she was so absorbed in operating the camera. "Action," she said clearly, and the cast sprang to life.

She had a new day job, assistant to Mr. Chaigne, rich as Croesus, unlike John, who had disbanded his office. Mr. Chaigne knew how to print out for himself. But Anjali looked for every opportunity to do it for him, to make herself indispensible. Then she hurried home to write shorts, using the formatting program she'd bought with the sale of the *péniche* article. On weekends she filmed the shorts.

She was free to write. She was lonely. *C'est la vie.*

Her parents had given her the money for the film course. They were arriving for a visit next week. They'd probably complain about pressure from the Mumbai aunties for her to marry. But she'd show them her collection of short films, all posted online.

And she'd hide the blouse that was a little *décolleté*, maybe behind the six-inch-wide bulk of the English unabridged edition of *Les Mis*

.

Chapter 111

Philippe stood looking out the French doors to the terrace and *jardin*. It was raining cats and dogs. *Il pleut des cords*, the French would say: it's raining ropes. The five-pointed leaves of the ivy on the garden walls were besieged by wind and rain. Drops didn't take their time gathering and dangling on the points of each leaf—instead, they were whipped away into the maelstrom as soon as they landed.

The tall, dark, skinny cypress trees at the end of the garden bowed deeply in a gust of wind. It was the worst storm in a long time in Paris.

Meredith was upstairs, resting. He was thankful she had been spared. Elodie was taking the gift of an unexpected day off from the library to clean out a closet.

John had sent Emily off the *péniche* to stay in one of Philippe's spare bedrooms. School was canceled because of the storm, and Emily was laying on the bed, poking at her phone. Having the three women upstairs, under his roof while the tempest raged outside, eased his heart.

He could imagine the Seine in this storm. The tourist attraction would now be a writhing pit of serpents, all biting at the stone banks. He could picture John on his *péniche*, watching nervously as the lines tugged against the river's flow, wondering how much longer they'd hold. He called John's cell.

"How are you?"

"Okay." He sounded exhausted. "I have a working engine and bow thrusters, unlike many *péniches* tied up along the Seine. So if the lines break, I think I can keep her under control."

"Please come here and stay with us."

"No, I want to stick with the ship."

Silently, to himself, Philippe critiqued John. He was loony. But what could he do except relinquish people to doing things their own way.

"Okay, let me know how you make out."

"If I get through this, I'll have everybody on board for dinner soon."

"That would be great, John. Be careful."

Philippe clicked the phone off. With so many bridges crossing the Seine, John would be in extreme danger if his lines snapped. The river might force him onto the stone supports of one of the bridges. Philippe decided to pray for him.

And for other urgent matters. For good to come out of evil. For the truth to prevail.

He sat at his worktable, just inside the glass doors to *le jardin*. He opened Rilke and found the passage he was thinking of.

"Voice of the storm, Song
that the wild wind sings…"

He gaze returned to *le jardin*. A gust pummeled the glass doors with a burst of rain and shook them as if in a tantrum.

Philippe took a deep breath and steadied himself. He wrote.

> I call to you, Awesome One, from
> my truest depths.
> My words ascend on the wind.

Through the glass doors, he saw the three tall, narrow cypress trees he'd bought instead of a parsley plant years earlier bend in half and whip upright, repeatedly. They were ghostly, writhing dancers at the foot of the garden, half hidden by veils of rain.

> The trees groan and the cobbled avenues
> run with rain,
> the waters of the Seine tumble away.
> You are the one they flee, but I move
> toward you.

> And the fierce wind and dancing trees
> and my wild heart and you, Awesome,
> are a great chord, singing.